TROLL-TAKEN

Katherine stood in the doorway stunned, senses reeling, unable to move, to think, to act. She had been so convinced that the people who had entered her apartment and stolen her baby had been homeless drifters that she had never considered any other option. What she was seeing now changed everything.

The chamber that lay beyond the circular doorway had never served as a coal bin nor any other place of storage. It was unique, unlike anything Katherine had ever seen, as was the person, the *thing* slumbering on the low couch on the far side of the room.

Katherine's mind was a jumble of conflicting thoughts. The creature on the couch was . . . was what? She couldn't tell if it was animal, or human, or some monstrous combination of both. What was this thing, and what was it doing in the basement of her building? Had it been responsible for stealing her child?

Acknowledgments

Troll-Taken might never have seen the light of day without the assistance, support and interest of numerous friends, family members and associates. First and foremost is Bill Fawcett, stalwart friend and trusted mentor who helped bring *Troll-Taken* into the world.

Secondly, my long-suffering family: Lydia, Daniel, Max, Myles, and, of course, Tom.

Finally, Investigator Reggie Greetham, Lake Geneva, Wisconsin, Police, and E. J. Shumak, Delavan, Wisconsin, Police (inactive). Dr. Walter C. Vogel, Beloit, Wisconsin, and the Hematology Department of Lakeland Hospital, Elkhorn, Wisconsin. All were most helpful in filling in the blanks, which were considerable. Any mistakes or literary license are of course to be laid solely on my doorstep.

I would also like to thank Joe Peabody D.V.M. and Debbie Thomas for being there for me when it counted.

One final note: *Troll-Taken* was completed one month before the Chicago River breached and entered the freight tunnels that lie beneath the city of Chicago. Until that moment in time, I had not known or even guessed at their existence.

TROLL-TAKEN

ROSE ESTES

ACE BOOKS, NEW YORK

This book is an Ace original edition,
and has never been previously published.

TROLL-TAKEN

An Ace Book / published by arrangement with
the author

PRINTING HISTORY
Ace edition /September 1993

ISBN: 0-441-82414-5

Ace Books are published by The Berkley Publishing Group,
200 Madison Avenue, New York, NY 10016.
The name "ACE" and the "A" logo
are trademarks belonging to Charter Communications, Inc.

PRINTED IN THE UNITED STATES OF AMERICA

10 9 8 7 6 5 4 3 2 1

ONE

It was like a bad dream, a nightmare from which she could not waken. She was aware of her body in some strange sense, of being asleep in the large overstuffed chair in the living room. The television still droned in the background, a late-night talk show. She could almost see herself; it was like one of those stories about people near death who floated above their bodies, peacefully observing.

But this was more frightening. In the stories, people reported a sense of great calm and peace. Katherine felt only fear, a sense of something terrible about to happen. She tried to waken, tried to move, to open her eyes, but it was impossible; she felt drugged, trapped in a foggy, muzzy cocoon that held her in a soft but relentless grip. She was bound by invisible fetters that held her as firmly as steel chains.

The ominous feeling grew. She struggled to waken, to break the implacable hold, knowing in some primitive part of her brain that something terrible was about to happen. She was in danger; she knew that with certainty. She fought to open her eyes, sensing the nearness of the danger now, the sense of something or someone. It, no . . . THEY were approaching, coming near. She could feel their presence. She froze. She was no longer alone. There was a heavy silence filled with the weight of their being. The old oak floorboards in the foyer creaked. Waves of fear and rage rippled through her unresponsive body as the intruders passed behind her chair.

1

It was then that the smell struck her, filling her nostrils with the scent of their bodies. It was strangely elusive, almost indescribable. Dampness. Mold. Old things hidden away in the darkness. Images came to her, darkness and small, enclosed spaces and the feeling of fear. Suddenly, inexplicably terrified, her mind backed away from the thought.

She whimpered in her sleep and struggled to reach the surface of consciousness, feeling smothered. It was terrifying beyond measure. And then, suddenly, it was gone, the terror replaced by a deep calm that flooded through her body, soothing her, driving away the fear as easily as shadows are banished by the rising sun. She was enveloped by a feeling of warmth, a feeling that everything would be all right. It comforted her, soothed her, bathed her in its healing embrace. She sighed deeply and surrendered herself up to sleep.

She wakened. Instantly alert. All of her senses screaming in alarm. Her heart pounded in her chest, her pulse pounded in her temples. She straightened in the chair, feeling the stiffness in her muscles. In front of her, the wide-screen television was playing an old war movie. She recognized a scene and realized with shock that the movie was more than half over. How much time had passed? She shook her head in an attempt to clear it of the cloudiness that still fogged her senses. She felt as though she had just wakened after taking a too-strong sleeping pill.

Beyond the television, the room lit only by the flickering light of the screen loomed blackly. She stared intently into the darkness, the familiar contours of the chairs and couches casting ominous shadows. There was no movement, but a strange smell seemed to hang in the air. And then she remembered the dream and the feeling of helplessness that had accompanied it.

Cameron! The thought of her infant daughter brought Katherine to her feet, all fear for herself banished by her fear for the baby. What if it hadn't been a dream? She hurried through the hall toward the nursery.

She threw open the door to the baby's room. A soft pink light bathed the nursery. Mickey and Minnie danced hand in hand atop the base of the lamp, reassuring smiles painted on their faces. Katherine's heartbeat slowed and she smiled, chastising herself for her flight of imagination. She shook her head at the thought that anyone could get into the building with its excellent security measures. Her door was securely locked. No one could have walked through the apartment, passed behind her as she sat in the chair, and stolen the baby from the nursery.

Still, there was a niggling remnant of concern, no doubt a legacy of the sheer strength of the nightmare. She tiptoed over to the baby's crib, intending to straighten the soft fluffy blanket over the tiny figure, who had, as usual, bunched herself into the farthest corner.

Katherine's hand reached out, her eyes recording her movements like a documentary camera. Her fingers were long and slender, the nails shaped but short and unmanicured. Her head was aching, her fingers trembling now as they threw the blanket aside to discover what her heart had known all along. The crib was empty. The baby was gone.

TWO

❧

Katherine dropped the blanket, her fingers numb and unfeeling. Her eyes searched the crib and the area around it, even though she knew it was ridiculous. Cameron was only four months old, barely capable of inching her way into the corner of the crib, much less getting herself out of it. But hope and fear are seldom rational and so she searched the room as though she might somehow have mislaid the child.

Cameron was nowhere in the room. Wild with a rising fear, Katherine turned to the door. The phone, she had to call the police, call for help, get them to come right away! Then, even as her hand closed round the knob, something stopped her; there was something that reached out to her, something that needed to be noticed. Slowly, Katherine became aware of an intangible wisp of thought that tugged at her memory, cried out for recognition, a subtle memory that begged to be retrieved. She lifted her head and turned back to the room as though scenting the air and then, finally, it came to her with all the impact of a blow to the abdomen. The dream! The smell! That smell of dankness, of mold, of things in the night. The scent in her dream that had brought on the terror. It was here. In the room with her. It was real.

Dream and reality collided. Fingers pressed against her temples, Katherine sank into the rocking chair and forced herself to catch her breath. She had to get hold of herself, separate what was real from what was imagined. Her heartbeat slowed, her breathing became less ragged. Everything in her cried out for action,

4

demanded that she run to the phone and get help, but she pushed the thought back, forcing herself to look at the room, to see what there was to be seen.

She stared at the empty crib, the flattened blanket with its gay pattern of fat bunnies and kittens an accusation that struck pain into her heart. "No, Katherine, no!" she admonished herself. "Hysteria won't do anything but make matters worse. Think!"

She dragged her eyes away from the crib and studied the room. Nothing was out of place, everything seemed normal. Except for the smell. It was no dream. It was real. Elusive yet real, it hung on the air tantalizingly familiar, like something she had known from a long time ago. As she pondered the scent, trying to identify it, her gaze settled on a small clump of dirt on the pink shag carpet beneath the crib.

She had neglected the rest of the apartment in recent weeks, but the baby's room was always immaculate, the carpet vacuumed daily, and there was no way that such a bit of dirt could have accumulated without being noticed. She reached for it and carefully lifted it up intact. It was slightly damp, gray-black in color and . . . She lifted it to her nose and was instantly flooded with memories.

She was seven. She had been sent to live on her uncle's farm outside of Madison, Wisconsin, "to fatten her up and put some color in her cheeks," the doctor had said. She now knew that they had been worried for her health after a long winter struggling with strep throat and pneumonia. Whatever the reason, it had been a glorious experience, even the time she had ventured too close to a litter of newborn piglets and had been chased by the snorting sow across the farmyard and onto the top of an old-fashioned wringer washer where she had perched all afternoon until she was rescued.

One of the more vivid memories from that summer was the making of jelly, the Concord grapes heavy and purply black, staining her fingers and her tongue as she gathered them from the vine, competing with the clouds of hovering bees for the sweetness that dewed their fat sides. The steamy vapor that rose from the kettles and filled the hot kitchen was redolent with the heady aroma of the grapes. Katherine had been amazed that the steam was white rather than purple, and she had wished that they could capture the delicious scent and bottle it as well as the vivid jelly that they poured into the sterilized jars.

It had been like looking through stained glass, peering into the depths of those translucent jars. Even after, years after she had left the country far behind her, a jar of grape jelly could bring that magic summer back with the touch of purple sweetness on her tongue. And the smell. After they had finished with the last of the jars, washed and cooled them and wiped their lids and glowing sides with a soft cotton cloth, she and her aunt had placed the jars in the partitioned cardboard boxes and carried them down to the fruit cellar.

The fruit cellar had been reached by a heavy wood door, angled against the boulder base of the house. They had descended six concrete steps and then opened another door that rasped against the ground and immediately they were surrounded by the smell of earth, damp, dark earth that never saw light of day.

Had it not been for her aunt's protective bulk, Katherine would have bolted, for there was something frightening about the small room. It contained a bountiful harvest of the farm's produce, mounds of potatoes sacked in stiff burlap and carefully stacked to avoid bruises, carrots, turnips and parsnips layered in boxes of white sand, barrels of pungent sauerkraut, ropes of fat white onions, and long braids of garlic hanging from nails.

The walls themselves were lined from floor to ceiling with shelves and these were filled with sparkling jars of green beans, crimson tomatoes, golden squash, magenta beets, pickles, apple-sauce, cinnamon pear butter, and raspberry jelly, each jar neatly labeled as to date and content.

A single, swinging bulb illuminated the confined space as Katherine helped her aunt add their jars to the others that would re-emerge throughout the fall, the long, cold winter, and the rainy spring before the sun returned again. She had been anxious to leave the cellar and had made excuses to avoid entering it from then on. Her aunt, a clear-eyed, no-nonsense type of woman fixed her with a look one day when Katherine stammered out a weak reason why she could not fetch a sack of onions, and though she had seemed ready to rap out a rebuke, she had merely muttered something about not liking spiders much herself and had sent Katherine's cousin, who rewarded her with a good-natured pinch.

That was the smell that rose from the tiny clump of dirt in her fingers; she would never forget it. Even as she remembered and identified it, the lump warmed under her fingers and disintegrated, falling to the carpet and losing itself in the thick shag.

Katherine stared down at the last tiny fragment of earth which toppled off the whorl of her fingertip. Well, she had identified the smell, found a bit of dirt, now gone, and nothing else. What would she tell the police? What would they think? Did it matter? Cameron was gone. They had to help.

She left the nursery and passed through the dark hallway and into the cluttered living room, the floor awash in unread *Tribunes*, plates encrusted with the remains of uneaten meals, discarded clothes, lying where they had fallen, seeing it as the police would see it through suspicious eyes. They would talk to her neighbors, her doctor, and learn of Rod's sudden heart attack, his death just one brief week before Cameron's birth. They would learn of her deep depression, the fact that she hadn't stepped foot outside the apartment since she and the baby had returned home from the hospital. They would suspect her. They would think she had killed Cameron.

Had she? Had she somehow in the fog of black grief and misery that had enveloped her since Rod's death killed the one remaining thing she cared about so that she might sever her last link with the painful business of life? Her head ached. A sharp pain strobed through her head like lightning behind her eyes, and a wave of nausea rose into her throat.

No! She could never have harmed Cameron. Never. She reached out for the phone, lifted it and heard nothing but dead air, no comforting drone of the dial tone. Had it been turned off? Had she paid the bill? She had not opened the drifts of mail that slid through the door and piled up against it. Then, with a flood of relief, she remembered that she had turned the phone off so that it would not waken Cameron.

Her fingers struggled with the tiny button. At last it slid into the correct position and she poked out the numbers of the emergency code. Then, even as the dispatcher's voice answered, she hung up the phone, the receiver clattering against the base. The smell was here as well, in this room, and there on the floor behind her chair was another tiny clump of dirt.

She had not imagined it, it was real. She touched the dirt to reassure herself that it was there. The smell of dampness and mold assaulted her nostrils, the smell she knew would be there. She rose swiftly and strode to the door, noticing with a grim nod that the mountain of mail which had risen against the door like a snowdrift had been pushed to one side, the black and white marble tiles visible through the spread of envelopes as they marked the path the opening door had taken.

And there, faint, but there all the same, she saw a footprint. It was large, the heel a dusty circle on the black tile, the ball of the foot and the widespread toes imprinting the back of a large, square white envelope. And here too was the smell of darkness.

She wrenched the door open and hurried out into the hall, anxious now to follow whatever trail had been left by the kidnappers. There was no time to call the police; valuable moments had been lost. How long had she been asleep? How long had it been since they had taken her daughter? Judging from the movie, she had been asleep for at least an hour, maybe longer.

Reaching the head of the stairs, Katherine glanced up at the long window placed so dramatically at the head of the long staircase that wound its way up from the foyer four flights below. It was stained glass, one of the many in the house, but this one had always been her favorite. It featured a stern but victorious St. George astride an enormous white war horse rearing above a slain dragon. St. George's pike and sword were crimson with the dragon's blood. Katherine's sympathies had always been with the dragon. Only the edges of the window were clear, enabling her to see the sky beyond. She judged the time to be somewhere between two and four in the morning. As yet, there was no light in the east, only the lights of the city reflecting in rose tones on sky and water.

The smell was here in the hallway too, diffused, but now that her nose knew what it was looking for, it had picked up the scent. Briefly, she wondered if she were imagining it. Perhaps she really was losing her mind. As she turned the corner of the staircase, gripping the ornately carved newel post, she could not help but see herself as others, the police, might see her. Her child was gone, vanished in the middle of the night in a securely locked building. Instead of calling the police, she was following a smell that she remembered from childhood. Where was the logic in that? But still, she continued on, afraid that if she stopped now, she would never see her daughter again.

Their apartment occupied the entire length and width of the top floor. She hurtled down the wide, broad steps two and three at a time as she descended to the third-floor landing. There was nothing to be seen in either direction and she hurried on, knowing instinctively that whoever had taken her child would not be found hiding in another apartment. They would seek lower ground to escape.

Her mind was clearer than it had been in weeks. The main entrance, that was where they would go. But how could they have gained access? The heavy plate-glass doors were always locked and watched over by a doorman/security guard. During the late night hours it was not uncommon for him to nod off in the chair behind his console, but he had never failed to waken at the first sound of a key in the lock. Nor could one pass him leaving the building without being seen. The other means of exit were just as daunting. She mulled over the possibilities as she raced down the next flight of stairs. There was a side exit where deliveries were made and the garbage was collected. But that door was the realm of Mr. Kramer, the ancient overseer of the building who tended to its myriad needs. He was a scrupulous caretaker, loving the monstrous old behemoth of a building as one might love and humor a cranky and demanding child. Mr. Kramer would never forget to lock the door which was doubly guarded by a heavy ornamental steel screen. The building was almost a fortress. She felt a flicker of hope. Somehow, someone had managed to gain access to the building. Now, they were trapped inside. She would find them and get her child back. There was no other way; she would make them see that.

She reached the second floor and as she scanned the dark mahogany doors, the second door from the left, the apartment at the head of the stairs as they descended to the first floor, she saw that the door was open a crack. But even as she stopped her hurried flight, startled, the door closed with a soft click.

All of Katherine's earlier fears returned in a rush. That apartment . . . it faced the street. It would be possible to drop from the window ledge to the sidewalk below without serious harm. For a moment, she could not remember who lived there; then it came to her. Mrs. Orlowski, a tiny round dumpling of a woman who spoke with a heavy European accent and was never without an improbably large black leather purse.

She knew little about the woman. She had paid cash for the purchase of her apartment, cash which had emerged from that same voluminous purse, a not inconsiderable amount of money in wrinkled but accurately counted bundles of small bills. She attended the biannual tenants' meetings, always bringing a platter of buttery cookies that Katherine could literally feel adding pounds to her hips and coating her arteries with cholesterol. But she was pleasant and made few demands upon Mr. Kramer's services beyond plying him with fresh roasted coffee and cinnamon buns. Mr. Kramer did not seem to mind and Katherine suspected that he enjoyed the attention.

It seemed entirely unlikely that Mrs. Orlowski could have anything to do with Cameron's disappearance, but Katherine was not about to take that chance. She approached the door and knocked firmly. There was no answer. Katherine knocked again, more loudly this time and placed her eye against the peephole. There was nothing to be seen but darkness and no response to her knock. She knocked again and then pounded against the heavy door, somehow certain that someone stood on the other side.

She could not remain here, pounding on a door that would not open. She could either return to her own apartment and try to find her set of master keys or she could go down to the basement and waken Mr. Kramer. He would help her. She quickly decided in favor of Mr. Kramer. At least she would not be alone.

The first floor held only two apartments and the large marble tiled foyer, faced by the glass wall which separated it from the entryway, the doorman and his console, and the broad marble staircase fronting the main entrance onto Sheridan Road.

The foyer was empty, but here she could see quite clearly the imprint of dusty footprints, bare feet. This gave her a moment of sudden concern, for it was late September and the nights had been exceptionally chilly. What sort of person would be walking around barefoot? A desperate person. Perhaps one of the many homeless people who roamed the city in increasing numbers in recent years.

She studied the footprints carefully, noting with mounting dismay that there appeared to be more than one set of prints, several of them smaller than the first pair. A chill of fear struck her as she stared down at the prints. A glance told her that the doorman was sleeping in his chair, his chin resting on his chest, a trickle of dried spittle crusted at the corner of his mouth. A circus could have paraded past and he would not have heard or seen a thing.

Katherine rapped on the glass door. The doorman did not stir. Angry and frantic with need for haste, she pulled the heavy door open and shook the man. His head lolled slackly. She could see the whites of his eyes beneath half-closed lids; his mouth hung open and the line of drool had reached his flabby double chin. The thought came to her that he had been drugged. There was no sense in trying to waken him. Nearly wild with frustration, she flung the man away from her and his heavy body settled facedown against the keyboard of his console. Even then, with the force of the rude impact, he did not waken.

Katherine snatched the phone from the desk and quickly dialed the emergency number. Once again the dispatcher's voice responded. Quickly, before she could change her mind, no longer caring what the police might think, she blurted out her name and address and the fact that the baby was missing. Without stopping to answer any of the woman's questions, she whispered, "Please hurry," and then hung up.

She should wait for the police to arrive; she knew that. But as she paced back and forth, in the entryway, the too-big plaid robe flapping around her ankles, she knew that she could not wait any longer. Every second that she stood here doing nothing, they, the faceless, nameless *they* could be leaving the building, escaping forever with her child.

It was every mother's nightmare, dreamed late at night when one was alone with secret terrors, those that were never voiced and seemed foolish in the light of day—the baby stolen. But this was no silly nightmare. It was real. She could not just stand here doing nothing. She knew what she had to do, she had to follow the footprints herself. She would leave the foyer door open so the police could follow as well.

Even as she decided, Katherine felt the fear rise up inside her. Her fear of basements and other dark, damp places, like the subway stations and the underground corridors that ran beneath Lake Shore Drive which allowed access to the lakefront and beaches had provided Rod with the ammunition of years of good-natured teasing. It was a genuine phobia, inconvenient and disconcerting. She forced herself to ride the subway when necessary and she could traverse the dark tunnels to the beach so long as she kept her eyes on the sunlight ahead, but basements were beyond her resolve.

She grabbed the phone again and dialed Mr. Kramer's number. Why hadn't she thought of it sooner? Mr. Kramer's apartment was in the basement; he could find and stop them if they were still in the building. He would not let anyone steal the baby.

Her fingers shook as the phone rang over and over with no answer. She told herself that he was an old man, slightly deaf, hard to waken. She ignored the inner voice that asked her why she would send such an old man to do her battles. There was no answer. Katherine crushed the phone down, knowing that she must go herself, afraid of what she would find, but knowing that there was no other way.

THREE

Katherine propped the heavy inner door open so that the police could follow and then turned her attention to the footprints in the foyer. They were smudged and harder to see here on the tiles, but there was no doubt that they led both to and from the basement door. The door was located directly beneath the staircase. It was a plain wood door, ordinary in every way. There was nothing about it that cried danger or rang bells of alarm, yet in Katherine's mind it was the doorway to a realm of nightmarish fears. She could not have put a name to what it was that frightened her about such places; it was just an intense uneasiness, a faceless dread that set her flesh crawling and icy terror inching up her spine. Now she was about to enter such a place and confront her deepest fears.

In all the years she had lived in the building, she had never entered the basement. Rod had teased her, but gently, knowing the depth of her terror. For a moment, she hesitated, considered waiting for the police to arrive, but then angrily shut the thought out. How could she let something so trivial as a childhood fear prevent her from doing everything within her power to get her child back?

Her anger, anger at herself and her own cowardice, gave her the strength, the impetus, to seize the doorknob and yank the door open. After all her anxiety and indecision, there was nothing remarkable to be seen. A long wooden staircase descended into the concrete- and boulder-wall basement, two sturdy wooden railings bracketing it on either side.

The stairs themselves were covered with a thin layer of fine dust and grit which crunched under Katherine's determined steps. How unusual, the thought came unbidden, that Mr. Kramer would allow anything within his baliwick to be less than pristine, for he was a meticulous caretaker. He considered the condition of the building to be a reflection upon himself and he would not be found wanting. But had it not been for the dust, there would have been no clues, no path to follow. Katherine was grateful for the chink in Mr. Kramer's perfection.

Her resolve nearly deserted her at the bottom of the steps, for there was no sign of footsteps on the pale concrete which stretched away into the dark distance. She clutched her robe tightly at her chest and took a deep breath to calm her fragmented nerves. Lights, there had to be light somewhere. She looked around quickly and spotted a large black metal box fixed to the wall. Opening it she was faced with numerous switches, none of which were labeled. One after the other, she began to flip switches and was gratified to see lights appear like pale gold stars in the night sky. Unfortunately, the bulbs were very dim, no more than 20 watts each, which did little to dispel the heavy gloom that saturated the basement.

There were, Katherine knew, windows all along the perimeter of the building and powerful vapor arc lights on the Drive, no glimmer of which seemed to penetrate beyond the cloudy green wire-reinforced panes.

She edged away from the steps, wondering which direction to take, wondering where Cameron and her abductors might be in that vast darkness. Once again, she felt the foolishness of her actions. In the dark and unprotected, following someone desperate enough to steal a child, was surely the height of stupidity. In movies and novels, she had always been annoyed by the heroine advancing into obvious danger. Yet, here she was doing precisely that herself. Even if by some chance she did find the kidnappers, what would she do? All she could do was try to reason with them, and how reasonable could they be to commit such an act in the first place?

She stopped for a moment and tilted her head to one side, listening for the sound of sirens, hoping the police were on their way. There was the distant sound of water coursing through pipes; the soft susurration of tires on pavement, discernible even within the depths of the building; the creak of old wood adjusting, settling under the weight above; and a peculiar soft whoosh somewhere off to her left. There was nothing else.

She opened her mouth to call out for Mr. Kramer, but then thought better of it. Would the abductors feel threatened at the thought of another person? Certainly. But whether or not that would be a good thing, she did not know. What if it panicked them, made them do something foolish? Like hurt Cameron. She could not take the chance.

The thought of Cameron's danger was more than she could bear, and without thinking, she hurried forward, advancing into the darkness. She crept from one pool of vapid light to the next, her heart pounding in her ribs so loudly that she feared she might not hear anything if there was a sound to be heard. As she paused beneath one of the lights, a bulb protected by a dusty wire grid, she realized belatedly that she could be seen clearly if anyone was watching, and by keeping to the lights, she destroyed her own ability to see in the dark.

Abandoning the light was one of the hardest things she had ever done. It was like drowning and failing to grasp at a life preserver as it floated past. She stood still and silent, looking away from the lights, waiting for her eyes to adjust.

A red bicycle appeared, swam out of the shadows, solidified, took shape leaning against a brick pillar. It had fat balloon tires and a heavy frame. A large basket was attached to the rusty chrome handlebars. She remembered it from the early years of her marriage and it was like unexpectedly seeing an old and dear friend in an unfamiliar place. It filled her with warmth and the courage to continue on.

Wood storage bins, each with a padlock on its heavy door, flanked her on the left, names of the tenants affixed to each. The mesh tops rose unbroken to the low ceiling. It seemed unlikely that anyone could scale the wire—it was not heavy enough to support the weight of an adult without bending and marking the path taken—but she peered into each bin, just in case. Lamps, their shades askew, taped boxes, some stacked neatly, others jumbled into piles, more bicycles lean and sleek and painted in bright trendy colors, cans of paint, cleaning supplies, suitcases, skis, boating equipment, mounds of books and magazines.

Katherine's heart jumped and a bolt of excitement shot through her. She gripped the mesh and peered intently into the shadows of a cubicle. There! Perched atop a mountain of boxes was a child, its hand dangling over the edge. She opened her mouth to speak, scarcely daring to hope, when her questing eyes traced the outlines of the figure and she realized with plummeting emotions that it was a doll, a Cabbage Patch doll, leaning against the mesh that divided its bin from the next, eyes open and vacant, pouty mouth fixed forever in a permanent perky smirk. The disappointment was like a physical blow, a visceral pain that was almost more than she could bear.

She leaned her forehead against the mesh, felt it press into her flesh and concentrated on the feeling, welcomed the hard, sharply defined edges that shut out, if only temporarily, the sickness that was churning in her guts.

She closed her eyes and whispered a prayer to the God of her youth, when all things were still both possible and probable and prayers carried the weight of unreasoning, blind faith, praying that Cameron was unharmed and that she would find her in time.

In time for what? That was really the question. Who had taken Cameron was important, as well as how, but their intention, what they meant to do with her, that was the biggest question of all and the one that worried her the most.

The light at the foot of the stairs was far behind her now. She did not realize she had come so far from the safety that it represented. She looked back at the tiny pool of white light and then turned to face the darkness once more.

The sound of water running through overhead pipes was louder now as was the intermittent whoosh that she could not identify. Objects loomed up out of the gloom like strangers passing on foggy streets, half-seen, passively acknowledged, and then gone.

She might have given up, returned to the safety of the entryway with its bright lights and the sleeping doorman, already fading into the memory of a distant country visited once and then recalled in conversation . . . "Remember when . . ." had it not been for the scent, stronger now in the still, close atmosphere than it had been in the bright, open areas above. Coupled with the darkness, which was the vision she had attached to the scent, its impact was far greater than it had been on its own. Her fear was nearly crippling and she was amazed at the strength of her own tenacity.

Slowly, she became aware of another sensation, which she tried to identify as she crept from one brick pillar to the next, hugging the rough contours before leaving its shelter as she braved the space between. A chill ran down her back as she stopped cold. She was no longer alone. She was certain of it. The air was filled with the presence of another.

Her mouth was dry, her lips wooden. No words emerged, only a croak. She wet her lips and tried again. "Hello," she whispered. "Please answer, I know you're there."

There was no response. Twisting the robe in her hands, she leaned into the darkness. "Please," she implored. "Give me back my daughter. I'll give you whatever you want, money, food, a place to stay. Just give me back my baby."

There was no answer, no words, but listening intently, Katherine heard a movement, a scuttling sound, a rapid movement just beyond the range of her vision. They were there, she was not wrong! Anger, fear, fury, and the desire for revenge gave her speed and courage she did not know she possessed. She raced after the elusive sound, passing through a narrow, doorless opening, glimpsing thick concrete walls on either side of her, and passing into another area, another room with far fewer lights, a deeper, heavier, more oppressive type of darkness passed in on all sides. All this she sensed as she ran, following the elusive sound and the scent which seemed stronger than it had at any time since she first noticed it.

She entered an area of nearly total darkness. There were no lights to be seen anywhere and her fears returned, cluttering inside her head like swarming bats. She fought off the desire to turn and run, forced herself to remain still, silent, listening for any hint of Cameron or her kidnappers.

There was a distant sound, no more than a whisper really, like a length of cloth dragged across the rough floor, but it was something and she grasped it, turning in the direction it had come, toward the rear of the building, she thought, toward the lake.

It was terrifying, moving without being able to see where she was going. She had a sudden, terrifying sense of what it would be like to be blind. She kept imagining pits opening beneath her feet, plunging her hundreds of feet to her death, even as she realized how ridiculous such thoughts were. Even so, she moved slowly, sliding one foot before her and following with the other, hands outstetched to ward off, or at least warn her of, approaching obstacles. It was a harrowing journey.

She progressed in this manner for what seemed to be a very long time. There were no sounds other than her own hesitant, sliding steps and the peculiar, intermittent whooshing noise which seemed louder than before. Without warning, her fingers struck a cold, rough surface, a wall, a concrete wall, and she followed it to the right. The darkness seemed to lift almost imperceptibly, not growing lighter so much as appearing to become less dark.

A long rectangular opening appeared, an opaque grayness that contained hints of rosiness, like the steely edge of dawn with the first tinge of sunlight curling around the edges, more a feeling, an anticipation, than truly seen.

Katherine moved into this space with gratitude, filling her lungs with air as though she could breathe easier and better in the light than in the darkness. She was in a room, smaller than the others, what appeared to be a corner room, and quick reasoning gave her the location, the northeast corner of the building, the edge that nearly touched the lakefront barrier itself. The back wall, that which paralleled the lake to the north, was constructed of immense fieldstone boulders, native to the area and used by early builders in the foundations of buildings, bound together by cement. Katherine knew that these outer walls were more than two feet thick. The easternmost wall, which ran alongside the building and led to the street was of the same material. The two remaining walls that comprised the boundaries of the room were of plain, unfinished concrete.

The light came from the source of the strange whooshing sound she had heard since first entering the basement. It was a monstrously huge contraption, rusted steel and a veritable maze of rising, twisting metal tubes which snaked across the low ceiling. A dull rosy glow filled its interior, the heart of the behemoth, the whooshing sound easily imagined as the breathing of an enormous slumbering beast. But it was a gentle beast, no more than the furnace of the building, already sending up its first warm breaths of the season to take the bite out of the chill autumn air.

The warm breath of the furnace allowed her to quickly trace the remainder of the room, her eyes searching impatiently for what she hoped, yet feared, she would find. But there was nothing, no sign of anyone, no hint, other than the smell, that anyone had been there. Her eyes darted over the room, cataloguing what she saw: an ancient, massive wood workbench, its battered, oil-soaked surface easily four inches thick; tools neatly arranged, hung from pegs on the wall behind it. Water heaters, old and new, a history of the industry from the enormous wood-fired boiler hunched in the corner to the newest white fiberglass, energy-efficient model, barely a fourth the size of its primitive ancestor lined one of the concrete inner walls.

The room was immaculate and contained little else other than a

variety of power tools and heavy cleaning equipment, each
occupying its own neatly allocated space. Beyond the furnace,
there was another short stairway, descending. Katherine could see
the top of a doorway, nothing more. To her right, there was a
second door, leading, she thought, to the narrow service gangway
that led to the street. This, she could see from where she stood,
was secured by a heavy chain and padlock. It was but a matter of
steps to this door and she tugged on the padlock, which was indeed
fastened and gave no sign of having been opened recently.

That meant that whomever she had followed, and there was no
doubt in her mind that they had entered this room, must still be in
it. Her head was tight with tension, it was hard to breathe in the
room which suddenly seemed too warm for comfort and short on
air. She was afraid, more afraid than she had ever been in her life.
The folly of her actions struck her hard. What would she do when
she came face to face with Cameron's kidnappers?

She felt terribly vulnerable, aware of how easily she could be
struck down, killed. Her fear gave her strength, and moving to the
rack of tools, she took down what appeared to be the wisest choice
as a weapon. It was heavier than she had expected, easily two feet
long, constructed of solid steel and ending in a pincer that could be
widened or narrowed by means of an adjustable ratchet. It felt
quite solid and reassuring. She held it with both hands, braced it
across her chest, ready to swing at the first sign of danger.

Tiptoeing forward, she peered behind the giant water boiler and
felt slightly foolish to discover nothing more dangerous than a
fragile daddy-longlegs which scurried to safety at her approach.
Two more steps put her in a position to look down the row of the
remaining water heaters. Nothing. Growing more and more
alarmed that she had somehow made a mistake, somehow lost
the kidnappers, even as she dreaded finding them, she abandoned
her earlier caution and circled around each one of the discarded
machines, growing more and more fearful and frantic as it became
obvious that she was the only person in the room.

Nearly in tears now, Katherine stood in the center of the room
wondering where they had gone. Had they somehow circled
behind her? She didn't think it was possible; surely she would
have seen or heard them had they tried to leave. But where else
was there to look?

Her eyes fell on the staircase, the stone steps that descended,
down out of her line of vision. The abductors were there; they had
to be, there was nowhere else to look. Gripping the metal shank of

the heavy tool so hard that her fingers ached, Katherine crept forward, knowing, praying, that they were there, praying for strength.

Raising the tool to shoulder height, she sprang forward to the head of the stairs, her lips bared in a snarl full of hatred and anger, ready to hurt, to maim, to kill, to do whatever was necessary to rescue her child.

There was no one there. The staircase was empty. But the damp smell of fresh earth curled up toward her, and she followed, all her senses concentrated on a door that stood slightly ajar at the bottom of the stairs.

When the hand clasped her shoulder, the unexpected terror that jolted through her was so intense she thought her heart would stop.

FOUR

So complete was Katherine's terror that she was momentarily stricken by a failure of her senses; it was as though the fear had shorted out all other bodily functions. When they resumed, perhaps no more than a heartbeat later, multiple sensations poured in. She felt the hand on her shoulder, conscious of the heavy weight of it, aware of the heat that flowed from it. She turned slowly, feeling the gritty concrete beneath the soles of her feet, trying to swallow the hard lump that had settled in her throat.

Katherine stood 5′ 10″, relatively tall for a woman, but she was dwarfed by the figure that stood before her. Large, massively built, dark, male: those were the immediate impressions that assaulted her heightened senses. The hand, large and capable-looking with long, well-shaped fingers, still gripped her shoulder and shook her gently.

Words beat at her ears, but numbed by the shock of the unexpected encounter, she could make no sense of them. She raised her eyes and saw a stranger, not Mr. Kramer with his circlet of white hair rimming his shiny dome, blue eyes peering at her from behind his thick bifocals, but a stranger.

She felt her knees buckle and the strange face—dark eyes, heavy brows, high cheekbones, a strong jaw—blurred and then began to whirl in a sickening manner. When the air cleared around her, she found that she was sitting on the concrete steps, the strange man crouching before her, his hands against her shoulders, supporting her weight easily.

She raised her head and struggled to free herself from his grip. He was speaking earnestly, and as suddenly as though someone had tripped a switch, his words came clear. ". . . you all right? Put your head down and breathe slowly." He seemed genuinely concerned for her welfare; he did not act like an intruder or kidnapper. Who was he? Where had he come from, and where was Mr. Kramer?

She batted at his hands, the powerfully muscled arms deeply tanned and covered with a dense thatch of fine, dark hairs. As though sensing her distress at his touch, the man released her and settled back, crouching, balanced easily on his heels, regarding her thoughtfully.

"Who are you, where is Mr. Kramer?" she demanded.

"I'm Stone, Mrs. Sinclair, the new super. Mr. Kramer had a stroke and died nearly five weeks ago." His eyes, gray green with flecks of silver, studied her carefully as though he were uncertain how she would react to his words.

"Dead?" The air seemed to become thicker, harder to breathe, and once again Katherine felt herself go lightheaded. Mr. Kramer dead? How could that be? She felt the stab of pain, the realization that she would never see his slow smile again, nor become impatient at the length of time it took him to formulate answers to even the simplest questions. It was almost too much to comprehend. She stared at this man, this . . . this Stone, wondering who he was and how he came to be there.

"I was a friend," he said as though understanding the questions that were going through her mind. "Stan asked me to take over. I promised him that I would. Now, is something the matter? Can I do something for you?"

His words were ordinary enough, even logical considering the circumstances, but there was something wrong, an ominous undertone, almost a sexual current that underlay his words and crackled in the air between them. She found herself drawn toward him, fixing on the tone of his words like a bird hypnotized by the steely glint in the snake's eye. She jerked back, shook herself mentally as she attempted to regain control of herself. She stood abruptly, ignoring the wave of dizziness that came over her, and turned toward the door.

It was just an ordinary door—the door to Mr. Kramer's and now Stone's apartment. But her eyes were drawn to a second door that stood directly opposite Stone's apartment. It was crudely made—built of planks shiny with the gloss of great age. A gauzy web stretched from the rough stonework above, swathed the upper left corner of the planks and drifted down across the face of the old wood, gathering in a thick clump along the edges where the wood frame met the concrete. It was obvious that the door, or whatever it was, had not been opened for a long, long time. But she had seen it open no more than a moment before.

"Mrs. Sinclair?" Stone said gently, his voice ending in a question. "Would you like to go back upstairs now?"

"Where does that door go?" She turned on him violently. "Open it!"

Stone pulled away from her, his dark eyes stared at her impassively. "That door, if that's what it is, has never been open, so far as I know. Why would you want me to open it?"

"Where does it go?" she demanded, answering his question with one of her own. "Where is my daughter?" She felt her hands ball into fists. He stared at her without reply. She wanted to strike him. Instead, she turned and hurled herself at the webbed wood, knowing that it must be some kind of trick, phony cobwebs, the kind you sprayed out of a can at Halloween. Her fingers tugged and pried at the smooth planks, her nails blunted against the impenetrable grain. The wood did not give beneath her blows and the webs clung stickily to her fingers, obviously real.

The tears came now, despite her resolve, pouring forth, a mixture of fury, frustration, fear, and confusion. What was happening and why? Why would someone steal her child? How could it have happened? What was she to do? Never had she felt so alone and so helpless.

She felt his hands upon her shoulders again, pulling her gently away from the door. "No!" she cried, wrenching herself out of his grasp, turning to face him, face streaked with tears, eyes reddened and glaring. "Don't touch me!" She hissed the words as she backed up and felt for the stairs, never taking her eyes from his face. "I know you had something to do with it! I know they went through that door and took my daughter with them. You'll never convince me otherwise. I saw it open! I smelled them!"

"Let me take you back upstairs," Stone said quietly. "I think you should lie down." His voice was not unkind.

Katherine held her hand out, palm outward, fingers extended, the nails ragged and filthy from clawing at the door. "Stay away. You're part of it, I know you are. I'm going to get the police and bring them back here! You can't have my daughter!"

Reaching the head of the stairs, she gathered her robe in her hand and, turning her back on him, ran back the way she had come, retracing her earlier footsteps, all fear gone, vanished with the need to reach the police and bring them back to rescue Cameron before it was too late.

She streaked through the darkened rooms which she had crept through with such trepidation such a short time before; their shadows held no terror for her now, banished by the greater evil that had occurred.

She reached the staircase and pounded up its length. She reached the entryway and stood there in the doorway, clinging to the frame, panting with exertion. Her hair was in her eyes. She brushed it away and saw a group of figures, two policemen and the doorman, on the far side of the heavy glass door, staring at her in amazement.

Relief flooded through her. She staggered to the door and tugged it open. "Hurry," she cried. "Hurry before it's too late. They've taken my baby. You've got to come with me before it's too late!"

The policemen exchanged glances, the kind of glances men seemed to reserve for humoring women. One of them, heavyset and red in the face, his jowls showing the need of a razor's attention, stared down at her with a patronizing air, easily resisting her repeated attempts to move him.

"And where are we goin', little lady? And who is it who's taken who?"

The doorman spoke, puzzlement written on his face. "What's going on, missus? Nobody's come by here all night."

"How would you know?" Katherine said with fury. "You've been sound asleep. Anyone could have walked in here and you'd never have known!"

The doorman stared at her with hurt eyes. "I never went to sleep. I been awake all night!"

"It's all right, Fred. Mrs. Sinclair's just upset."

All eyes turned to the figure in the door. Stone had appeared behind Katherine. She had not heard him approach.

"Stone, building superintendent," he said, moving toward the police with outstretched hand. The policemen relaxed visibly, as each of them took his hand in turn.

"What is this about a missing child?" asked the taller and thinner of the two patrolmen, one Henry Wisnowski according to the nameplate affixed to the starched front of his shirt. His comment was addressed to Stone.

"Don't ask him, ask me!" Katherine snapped truculently. "It's my daughter who's missing, and I don't know this man and I think he had something to do with it!"

That seemed to make some impression on the two policemen who stood up straighter and looked a little less friendly than they had before.

"Why don't you tell us what's happened. Start at the beginning," Wisnowski said, taking out a pen and a small notebook.

"There's no time for that!" Katherine cried in frustration. "You've got to come with me now, before they take her away!" Never had she felt so impotent, so helpless, so incapable of righting a situation gone wrong, she who was usually so cool and competent.

Some degree of her desperation must have gotten through, because the heavier of the two policemen, a Sergeant Maloney, gave his partner a look, no doubt pregnant with volumes of unspoken messages gained by years of shared experiences, and said, "Maybe it wouldn't hurt to take a look, eh?"

"Couldn't hurt," Wisnowski said with a shrug.

Katherine was so relieved, she did not even bother to hide the look of childish spite she threw at Stone. "This way," she urged, hurrying back down the stairs to the basement, with the others clattering heavily behind her, their heavy footsteps pushing back any remaining fears she might have felt.

Soon, they were all crowded into the small space at the foot of the stone stairs. She pointed to the gray planks. "There," she cried. "They took her through there!"

The officers merely stared at her with eyes that were guarded once again, their faces blank, impassive. Maloney cleared his throat and looked down, seemingly embarrassed. "Through there?" he asked, gesturing toward the cobwebbed planks.

"Yes," Katherine said impatiently. "But it didn't look like this before. There were no cobwebs and it was open, I swear it was. Come help me. We can open it, I know we can!"

"Look, lady . . ." Wisnowski began, but Maloney waved him to silence. Positioning himself before the webbed planks, he tried to grip the edges with his fingertips, but the planks were butted tight against the stonework frame. Glancing at her briefly, he gingerly wiped the webs away and then placed his shoulder against the gray wood and shoved. His face grew red and his cheeks bulged at the effort, but the old wood did not even groan beneath the force of his effort. Once more he tried to find a handhold between the spaces of the boards, but it proved impossible.

Avoiding Katherine's eyes, Maloney directed his gaze further up the stairs. "What's this thing? Where's it go?" he asked.

"I have no idea," Stone replied. Turning, Katherine saw him standing behind Wisnowksi and the doorman who had taken it upon himself to join them. "Never paid much attention to it; it's always been like that."

"Ever see it open?"

"I tell you it was open," Katherine cried in desperation. "I saw it open no more than ten minutes ago and they took my baby through there. You've got to open it!"

"Lady, this door, if that's what it is, hasn't been open in the last ten years. Why don't we go upstairs and you can take us through it from the beginning. Tell us what happened, show us."

"But . . ."

"Show us," Maloney said gently but with an underlying tone of firmness that Katherine knew she could not hope to sway. Any further arguing would only serve to alienate the man. Already he was thinking that she was no more than an hysterical woman. She would have to take him upstairs and start from the beginning, convince him that she was sane and rational and make him understand, see how it had happened. With one last glance at the hated door, she pushed past Wisnowski, Stone, and the doorman, and led the way upstairs.

She paused at the top of the basement stairs and pointed to the marble tiles, intending to show them the footprints. But they were gone, obliterated by the passage of their own footsteps.

Wisnowski whistled as they trudged up the broad staircase, admiring the thick burgundy shag underfoot, the smooth mahogany banister, polished to a high gloss by a hundred years' labor of faithful servants, and the intricate, jewellike stained-glass windows that paralleled their progress. He whistled again, stopping to study a window that featured a shepherd ministering to his flock. It was a handsome example of the art, with faceted stones serving as eyes and sparkling brilliantly, despite the late hour, backlit by the lights of the city. It was one of Katherine's favorites, but now she felt nothing but impatience for even the slightest delay.

"Nice," Wisnowski said thoughtfully, turning away from the window at last. "Must cost a bundle to live here." It was a statement, but also a tacit question.

"My husband's family owned the building. He died recently,"

Katherine replied, hating the sudden look of understanding that came into the policemen's eyes. She bit back the words that came to her lips. No need to antagonize them any further; they already thought she was crazy, now they had added emotionally distraught to their diagnosis. She would just have to make them see.

Everything was exactly as she had left it, the apartment door ajar, the accumulation of mail mounded between the door and the wall, the room dimly lit by the flickering television. The policemen moved into the room slowly, observing each detail with careful eyes. Suddenly, Katherine saw the apartment as they must, cluttered and unclean, the plates of half-eaten food forgotten beneath couches and chairs, unread papers and unopened mail littering every surface, soiled clothes hanging from doorknobs and thrown over chairs. For the first time, she became aware of the smell, sour and slightly fetid, the television droning on in the background like an accusation. She could feel their eyes upon her.

"I—I haven't been well," she heard herself stammer, seeing the condescending look in their eyes. Did her slovenly housekeeping obliterate the fact that her daughter had been kidnapped? She felt her cheeks flush with anger as well as embarrassment. "It doesn't usually look like this," she added lamely, hating herself for the apology, but wanting, needing for them, to believe her so that they would help instead of judge.

"Here's the baby's room," she said, hurrying out of the living room and into the hall. "I was watching television, there in the chair, when she was taken," she said, trying to get them to understand the way it had been.

Maloney stared at her. "If you were watching television, how did they get past you? How did they get in? Did you see them?"

"Well, no." She turned to face them. "I wasn't really watching, I was kind of asleep. I don't know how they got in, but I felt them, smelled them in the dream. That's what woke me up, the smell."

"The smell," Maloney said heavily. "You smelled them."

She was losing them. Katherine could hear the thinly veiled irony in Maloney's voice. It was too much, she could not bear their pompous, superior male attitude. They would never believe her, no matter what she said; they had already decided that she was an unstable woman whose story and behavior were questionable.

"I know you don't believe me," she said, fighting back the tears that once more threatened to escape, "but you can't deny the fact that Cameron is gone. Look, here's her room." She stood aside as she pushed the door open, feeling relieved that this room was clean, knowing instinctively that such things mattered to them. They moved past her, Maloney and Wisnowski, and entered the room. Stone paused beside her and once more she felt the strange current of energy that flowed between them. She stared into his dark eyes defiantly, knowing that once the policemen realized that Cameron really was gone, they would believe her, know that she had been telling the truth about everything. They would go back down to the basement and . . .

"Nice kid," Maloney whispered, appearing in the doorway, Wisnowski on his heels. "Look, I can see how you've been under a lot of strain lately with your husband and all. Why don't you try to get some sleep. Call the doctor in the morning and get something for your nerves, help you get past the worst of it, y'know." He took her elbow and spoke to her as though she were a small child in need of comfort.

Katherine stared at him in disbelief, wondering if he had lost his mind. What was he talking about? She thrust him aside rudely and stalked into the room. She could feel them standing behind her, feel the heat of their bodies, feel the weight of their eyes upon her as she moved slowly toward the crib.

Cameron was lying on her stomach, bunched into the far corner as was her custom. Her head was turned to the side, and a fine line of saliva, glistening in the pink glow of the lamp, stretched from the corner of her rosebud lips to the sheet. It was obvious from the circle of wetness on the fabric that she had been in that same position for some time. Her tiny fists were balled on either side of her shoulders and the soft exhalations of her breath were clearly audible in the silent room.

Katherine moved to the side of the crib, reaching out with trembling fingers to touch her daughter's cheek. Maloney cleared his throat, and she could hear their feet shuffle on the carpet. "Uh, we'll let ourselves out, Mrs., glad everything's all right. You think about what I said now, get some sleep and call your doctor in the morning."

She heard them go, heard their voices in the hall and then the click of the door, but she was not alone. She turned. Stone was there, leaning against the door frame, watching her.

"I don't know how you did it," she said, her voice trembling. "I don't know why you did it. Maybe you fooled them, but you didn't fool me, I know what happened. I want you to leave this building,

Mr. Stone, and do it quickly. Don't ever come back, and tell your friends, whoever they were, that I'll be watching."

He did not answer, made no response to her words, merely watched her with his large, dark eyes for a long, silent moment. He nodded once and straightened, his wide shoulders filling the doorway. Then he was gone.

She waited a moment and then filed through the hallway, sensing, still feeling the emanations, the vibrations of the presences that had passed between the walls, wanting them gone, wishing they had never been there.

She locked the door, filled with a strong impression of Stone still standing on the other side of the door. She leaned against it, feeling that same strange flow of energy that had connected them earlier, despite the old-fashioned massive door that separated them. She jerked back with a gasp and stared at the door, somehow knowing when he left, even though she heard nothing, and she felt a sense of loss that perplexed and annoyed her.

She touched her forehead with her fingers, felt the mass of tangled hair that slid forward over her brow, and sighed, knowing what she looked like, too dispirited to confirm it in a mirror, afraid she would look like a crazy person, which was undoubtedly what the police report would reflect.

Moving into the baby's room, she settled in the rocker and watched the small sleeping figure, watched the slow rise and fall of the tiny back, reassuring herself as she had not done since the days following Cameron's birth that the child was really alive.

How had she made such a mistake? The question was unavoidable and had to be asked. Cameron was obviously here and in her crib where she belonged. But Katherine was also equally certain that the baby had been gone. The crib had been empty; she had seen and touched the cold sheets with her own hands. She had not been mistaken. Nor had she been mistaken about the footprints or the strange scent. Both had been real.

For the first time, she allowed herself to ponder the policeman's words, as well as what he'd left unsaid, and wondered if she were crazy or had temporarily lost touch with reality due to the combined effects of grief, exhaustion, and despair. She did not think so; what had happened had been real. But even as she thought over the events of the last hour, they took on an air of strangeness that seemed peculiar even to her. The more she thought about it, the odder it all seemed. No wonder the police thought she was demented. She had been asleep, perhaps it had all been a dream that she had acted on without realizing what she was doing. Could such a thing be possible?

Whatever had happened, the baby was safe in her crib, the door was locked. Nothing could harm them now. Rocking slowly, Katherine closed her eyes and slept.

FIVE

❦

In the darkest pre-dawn hour, the baby wakened and began to cry. It was not the lusty, full-lunged effort that she usually put forth as she demanded to be fed, but a half-hearted, defeated sound, almost as though she doubted that anyone would respond. Instantly awakened by Cameron's cries, Katherine surfaced from the heavy sleep that had wrapped her in its fuzzy embrace once she lowered her guard. For a moment, she was puzzled, confused by the pale pink light that bathed the room. Then she remembered and moved quickly to the crib. Cameron was still hunched into the corner, her lightweight gown hiked up, revealing the tiny legs, slender feet, and diminutive toes. Katherine's hands halted above the crib as she stared down at the little feet scrabbling fitfully at the sheets, barely making any impression. They were so very small. Her legs looked thinner than normal. Was it possible that the baby was losing weight? What if she were sick! What if she died! The thought hammered at Katherine like a spike being driven into her brain. The mere thought of losing Cameron was agony.

Katherine snatched the baby up out of the crib and clutched her to her breast, wrapping her arms around the child as though she could form a physical barrier that would protect her from harm. Cameron squirmed restlessly within her embrace, and made small mewling noises like a sick kitten. Alarmed, Katherine sat down in the rocker and lowered her arms so that she could look at the baby. What she saw shocked her. The healthy, rosy glow that always lit Cameron's skin was gone, replaced by a wan, grayish pallor. Her cheeks, normally fat and rounded, adhered starkly to her cheek-bones, dark hollows lay beneath her eyes. And her eyes! They were washed out, leached of color, gray rather than blue and glittered feverishly, reflecting a stolid resignation more fitting an adult beaten down by years of adversity, rather than a newborn infant. Her hair was thin and had lost its sheen, lying limp, plastered by sweat against the drawn skull.

"Cameron!" The cry was wrung from Katherine and she pressed the child to her breast, enveloped by fear. What could be wrong? The baby had been fine at her last feeding. What could have happened in such a short time? As though her fear were conta-gious, Cameron's feet beat an angry tattoo against Katherine's ribs. Startled, Katherine released the child, fearing that she had squeezed her too tight. She stared down at the baby, dumbstruck, wondering if she had lost her mind. Gone was the emaciated death's head that had looked out at her with fevered eyes. Here was her child, plump, rosy, healthy, filled with life, lying in her arms kicking chubby, fat creased legs.

Was she going crazy? The thought was unavoidable, the horrible vision following so closely on the heels of the earlier experience. It had seemed so real, but here was Cameron, safe and sound and she knew that the building was all but impregnable.

She had acted badly toward Mr. Stone. He must think her a lunatic. She had fired him, told him to leave. Katherine sighed as she rubbed her forehead. She would have to see to him in the morning, make some sort of apology and ask him to stay. The mere thought of interviewing people for the job, checking refer-ences, making a decision, was too much to contemplate.

Katherine loosened the belt of her robe and raised Cameron, settling her into the crook of her arm, so that she could nurse. The baby turned her head aside, seemingly disinterested. Katherine stared down at her in surprise. That was unusual; Cameron was always interested in nursing, especially this feeding when she slept longer than at any time during the day.

Katherine could feel the heavy lines of milk that filled her breasts, aching with the need to release their pressure. She took the baby's face and guided it to her swollen nipple, prodding the soft lips apart. Cameron did not suck. Katherine stared at her in alarm. This had never happened; the baby always nursed with a gusto that never failed to delight and amuse her. She tried to calm herself, to suppress the sudden specter of some dread, fatal disease. It was normal, she told herself firmly. There was no law that said that babies had to nurse on a regular schedule. She was overreacting; she knew from her reading that new mothers often did just that. "Well, sweetie, if you don't want to nurse, that's all right," she said as she lay the baby back in her crib and straightened out her gown. "Let's get you changed," she added, knowing with certainty that a dry diaper would be needed. To her amazement, the diaper was scarcely wet at all, only the merest hint of moisture that gave off a rank, sour smell. Katherine held the diaper in her hand and frowned, then bent over the baby and felt her forehead with trembling fingers. It was cool to the touch. The baby stared up at her impassively. Katherine ran her fingers down Cameron's cheek, tracing the sweet contours, worried, despite her attempts to reassure herself. She put a fresh diaper on the baby, who lay without moving, staring at her with large, unblinking eyes. Katherine broke eye contact, averting her gaze, feeling a sickness in the pit of her stomach, an instinctive knowledge that something was wrong. She turned Cameron over on her stomach and pulled the light cotton flannel blanket up over the small hunched shoulders. She rested her fingertips in the center of the baby's back for a moment, trying desperately to convince herself all would be well.

As she left the nursery and entered the cluttered, dirty living room, she was swept by a sudden disgust. How could she ever have let things get so bad! She looked down at the grubby bathrobe that she had worn for too many days, at the wrinkled clothing beneath, and felt the weight of her hair, lank and uncombed, resting on her neck. Rod's death had hit her hard, the despair swallowing her up like a warm, black, comforting cocoon, but it was time to get on with her life, if not for her own sake, then for the sake of the baby. Just look at what had happened tonight—it was a warning signal that she had allowed her life to drift out of control.

Filled with resolve, she strode into the master bedroom, stripping off her soiled clothes, promising herself that they and all the other piled-up laundry would soon be history. She turned the shower on full blast, and stepped in. She stood there for a long time without moving, allowing the steaming water to beat down upon her head and shoulders, imagining that it was washing away the enervating fingers of despair that held her in their implacable grip for so long. Finally, feeling somehow absolved of her heavy burden, she roused. She worked shampoo into her hair and soaped her heavy breasts, enjoying the feel of the intense heat, watching the flow of milk as it mingled with the streams of shampoo foam trailing down her belly. She rinsed the last of the thick lather from her hair, scrubbed her body with a soapy loofa sponge till it tingled, then shut off the water. Wrapping herself in the folds of a heavy bath towel already heated from the warming rack, she toweled her hair briskly. Despite her resolve, the events of the night kept trying to worm their way into her consciousness, sending little niggles of fear as forerunners, but she shut them out firmly, determined to put it behind her. It was a moment of madness, nothing more.

As for Cameron, if she was really sick, she would do something about it in the morning. She was almost too tired to brush out the knots in her hair, but remembering the look of distaste on the policeman's face as he took in her disheveled appearance, she worked her way through the tangled mass before allowing herself the comfort of her bed. She pulled the covers up over her head, feeling like an embattled animal retreating to its lair, telling herself that everything would be all right in the morning.

She was wakened by the sound of crying, thin, reedy, monotone wails without spirit or hope. Instantly, the ball of fear returned to her belly, larger and heavier than before. She sat up slowly, dragging her legs out of bed and sat on the side of the mattress, afraid to answer the crying child, afraid of what she would find. But there was no way she could ignore the cries; they tugged at her like invisible strings that ran from the child to her heart. She had to go to her.

The morning sun was streaming through the window in the nursery. The window faced the lake and received the first light of the morning. Filtered by the sheer, translucent pink curtains, it filled the room with a bright, shimmering radiance reflected off the water below. The waves of light danced on the walls in ever changing patterns and seemed to entrance Cameron, who would stare in fascination for long periods of time. The crib had been aligned so that the rising rays struck the mobile that hung above the crib, a handmade affair fashioned of dangling, faceted crystals, once part of an elaborate chandelier and pewter-rimmed bits of stained glass. The resulting brilliantly colored shafts of light played across the surface of the crib, delighting the child, who waved her small arms and opened and closed her tiny fists as though she would seize them. She often let out squeals of joy and kicked her legs in excitement as she stared upward, the rainbow of colors streaming across her rapt face. Only now, the prismatic light brought no joy to the small figure who huddled into the corner of the crib, her face burrowing into the spittle-drenched sheet. The thin thread of her cries reached out to Katherine in a wave of sour, fetid air. Katherine gasped at the smell, and hurried to the crib, thinking that Cameron had spit up during the night, knowing how easy it was for babies to choke and suffocate on their own vomit. But when she reached the crib, there was no sign of vomit, nothing but the stench of sickness. The baby hung limp and unresisting in her hands, feeling lighter than usual, as though she had lost weight in the night hours. The baby continued to cry, that same strange, flat, dispirited wail that she had made during the night.

Katherine clasped her lightly and sat down in the rocker, baring her breast, knowing that Cameron would need to nurse, especially since she had missed the night feeding. But once again the baby turned her head away. A ray of light touched her face and she shrieked as though she had been burned, and buried her face in Katherine's chest. "What's the matter, sweetheart? Tell mommy, what's the matter!" Katherine's voice was shaking. What could be wrong? She carried the baby over to the window and parted the curtains so that she could see better, hoping to find some simple explanation, a cold sore on the baby's lip or, or . . . but as the clear, bright morning light poured into the room, the baby screamed louder than before as though in agony, and squinting her eyes shut, all but threw herself out of Katherine's arms. Katherine was stunned at the strength in the small form, and only when she quickly drew the curtains shut and lowered the blinds, cloaking the room in darkness, did the baby cease her tormented shrieks. Katherine sank into the rocking chair, cradling the crying child, rocking back and forth and patting Cameron reflexively, her mind searching for an answer to the baby's bizarre behavior: the lack of desire to nurse, the skeletal transition that seemed to transpose itself on her features, and now, this aversion to light. What could it mean? The baby was still crying. Katherine did not know what to do.

As she stared down at the baby's pinched features, a sound broke her concentration, a bell, a soft insistent pealing. Rousing as though from the depths of a bad dream, Katherine realized that someone was at the door. For a moment, she tried to shut the sound out, but it persisted. The doorman had not called on the intercom, which could only mean that it was one of the tenants, or perhaps Stone. Katherine rose, clutching Cameron to her chest, almost grateful to have something else to think about. She hurried to the door, composing the words of her apology to Stone, asking him to overlook her behavior and to stay. She had been so certain that it was Stone, she was struck dumb for a moment, staring blankly at the figure who stood outside her door. "Is a bad time, dear? I come back later, maybe?" Katherine stared at Mrs. Orlowski's plump figure, clad as always in a two-piece Butte knit suit that Katherine was quite certain dated from the early sixties. Her hair was a mass of unruly waves, dark brown shot through with streaks of gray. Periodic perms attempted to tame the riotous hair, but seldom worked for more than a day or two.

"What? No, no, come in, now is fine," Katherine said, moving aside and opening the door, remembering another door quietly closing as she followed the elusive odor in her hurried flight. Perhaps Mrs. Orlowski had seen something. Why else would she be here? They were not in the habit of paying social calls on one another and any maintenance requests would be directed to the super. Katherine closed the door and led Mrs. Orlowski into the living room with a rising sense of anticipation. She lifted a pile of papers off the cushions of an overstuffed couch and tried to sweep several coffee cups behind a lamp, but Mrs. Orlowski stopped her with a motion of her plump hand.

"Sit! Sit!" she commanded. "I have come to see you, not your house."

"I'm sorry it's such a mess," Katherine said, flustered in spite of herself, hating the clutter that filled the apartment. "It . . . it's not usually like this. . . ."

"Sha . . . child, sit," Mrs. Orlowski said even more firmly, grasping Katherine's wrist gently and drawing her down beside her. "Things do not matter. People matter. I have come to see how you are. And the baby. I have stayed away thinking you do not need to bother yourself with an old lady, a stranger, but today I think maybe I have been wrong. There is maybe something I can do to help. You are well?" Katherine felt the kind eyes resting upon her, the warm compassion that emanated from the older woman, and suddenly she felt like weeping. All her resolve, the barriers she had tried to erect between herself and the rest of the world were breached in an instant. She felt a trickle of hot tears flowing down her cheeks and swiped at them with the back of her hand, feeling like a small child. Mrs. Orlowski drew her forward and Katherine's shoulders stiffened; then she was smothered against Mrs. Orlowski's ample bosom and the tears began to fall as though a dam had broken inside her. She cried as she had not

allowed herself to cry before. The grief that she had held inside
poured out in a flood of emotion, racking her with an intensity she
had denied herself. It was as though if she did not grieve, she could
somehow deny the fact of Rod's death. It seemed a long time
before the tears stopped, but when it was over she felt drained,
calm, sleepy. She struggled upright, and accepted a sturdy cotton
man's handkerchief from the older woman. It gave off a fragrance
of Yardley's Old Lavender, as did the knit jacket which bore the
damp imprint of her tears. "Better, yes?" Mrs. Orlowski smiled at
her proudly as though she were a child and had brought home a
report card with top grades.

"Better, yes," Katherine agreed, blowing her nose and feeling
better than she had in a long time. "But . . ." Memory returned
with a rush.

"And the baby?" prompted Mrs. Orlowski, her bright eyes
studying Katherine closely.

"I—I don't know." Katherine's voice faltered and she looked
down at Cameron, who lay passively within the bend of her arm.
"Until last night, everything was fine, but now she won't nurse and
the light seems to bother her and, I don't know, something's wrong
and I don't know what to do."

"What a beautiful little girl," crooned the older woman, and
opening the large leather purse which always accompanied her,
she searched through the contents until she found what she was
looking for, a long strand of amber beads. Interspersed between
the beads were slender metal cylinders, red with rust and a
blue-green patina of age. "Here, sweetheart; here, love, play with
the pretty." The necklace swung back and forth above Cameron,
who followed its path with her eyes. A tiny hand rose hesitantly
and reached for the dangling necklace. The little fingers closed
round one of the metal rods and a shriek of pain filled the air.
Cameron released the necklace as though she had been burned,
and, grabbing the child's hand, Katherine was horrified to see
blisters rising, fluid filling each bit of tender flesh that had come
into contact with the trinket.

"What have you done! What have you done to my baby!"
Katherine screamed, leaping to her feet and backing away from
the motherly figure who sat looking down at the necklace with
sorrow written on her face.

"I have done nothing," Mrs. Orlowski said softly, "I only
thought to bring a smile."

"That necklace, it burned her fingers, Look! Look! There's

blisters!" Mrs. Orlowski handed the necklace to Katherine, who snatched it angrily, expecting to feel warmth against her own fingers, but strangely, it was not hot; if anything, it was slightly cool, metallic, nothing more. She drew Cameron closer, jiggled her up and down and shushed her softly, trying to comfort the screaming child. She kissed the widespread fingers, the bloated blisters already larger than the small fingers. The baby did not stop crying, drew no comfort from Katherine's ministrations. Dropping the offending necklace on the couch, she hurried into the kitchen and reached out to break off a stem of the fleshy aloe plant that grew on the sill, a handy poultice for kitchen burns. The baby's cries grew shrill and frenzied and she twisted in Katherine's arms, squeezing her eyes shut, raising her poor, burned fingers to shield her eyes from the light which streamed in through the open curtains. Katherine was frantic, torn between the need to comfort Cameron, close the curtains, and obtain a piece of the healing plant. She felt herself coming apart, tears rising hotly behind her lids, the baby's cries feeding directly into her own sense of inadequacy and confusion. Never had she felt so helpless, so out of control. She sank to the floor, cradling the screaming child against her chest, burying the small, contorted face against her own body to block out the light, weeping with despair.

"Here, here, child," Mrs. Orlowski entered the kitchen and pattered over to the window, drawing the curtains shut; the room faded into a shadowy darkness. Grunting slightly, the elderly woman lowered her short, bulky form to the floor, seated herself beside Katherine and gently pried the baby from her grasp. Murmuring in a language Katherine did not recognize, she held the baby in her plump arms and applied the end of a broken aloe stem to the swollen fingers. The agonized cries tapered off into thready whimpers as the gelatinous green flesh soothed her own. They sat that way for a long time, neither woman saying anything. Mrs. Orlowski drew Katherine's head down upon her shoulder, and strangely, Katherine felt no need to withdraw, felt safe and protected within the circle of the older woman's motherly aura, as though nothing more could go wrong as long as she did not move.

"What's happening?" she asked softly. "Am I going crazy?"

Mrs. Orlowski sighed and patted her on the shoulder. "Death is never easy, my dear; it affects us in strange ways. You have so much to bear. First, the husband and the baby, so soon, all alone. It is not easy."

"No, it's not that—I mean, well, yes, I miss Rod. It's hard being without him, it's so unfair. But it's more than that, something's happening, something strange and I don't understand it." Haltingly at first, and then faster, the words tumbling out, she related the night's events, pouring out all of her fears and half-formed questions, sharing them with the elderly woman who had been a stranger such a short time before. Mrs. Orlowski listened without interruption. When the tale was done, she was silent. Katherine turned to her and found the old woman looking off into the dimly lit kitchen, a remote look on her face. She was patting the baby on its back, slowly, repetitively, without conscious action, and Katherine could see that her thoughts were no longer in the present. It was almost as though she were looking at a stranger: lines of unrelieved grief marked the old woman's face; her eyes were pools of dark sorrow. At last, the older woman shook herself, roused from the lethargy of old memories, and turned to Katherine with a chiding, self-deprecating smile.

"Child, these old bones are not used to sitting on floors, even though they are so well-padded." Huffing and puffing comically, she allowed Katherine to help her up from the floor. She bustled back to the sofa and plumped herself down with obvious relief. "You have a doctor, yes? For the baby?" she asked once she had caught her breath.

"Well, yes, of course," Katherine replied. "Dr. Bosch, over on Broadway. But, what about last night? What about . . . I saw your door close," she blurted impulsively, wanting to know what the older woman had seen, wanting her to know that she knew . . .

Mrs. Orlowski rose to her feet, the handle of her purse draped over her wrist.

"Doctor," she said firmly as she turned toward the door. "For both of you. You are not eating right, not sleeping right, not taking care. Both of you need a doctor, a schedule. You call, make appointment. I will come back tonight. We will talk more, yes." Suddenly, Katherine was distraught at the thought of being alone. Cameron now lay limp and unprotesting in her arms, sucking quietly on her fingers with only an occasional whimper. But Katherine was afraid; it was all too much and she did not want to be by herself. As much as she had needed to be alone before, the very thought was now frightening, overwhelming. She did not want to be left with her fears. She was not strong enough to protect Cameron and herself against whatever was happening.

"No, don't go," she implored. Mrs. Orlowski turned, her dark eyes solemn, and studied her carefully. She reached out and stroked Katherine's cheek with pudgy, heavily ringed fingers, the old-fashioned heavy silver settings glittering with diamonds. "Sha, sha, *liebchen*, nothing will happen. Nothing will hurt you. Call the doctor. Take the baby to him, he will make you well. I will come back, you are not alone."

"Before dark," Katherine pleaded. "Please!"

"Before dark," Mrs. Orlowski agreed. "Remember . . . you are not alone."

SIX

Making an appointment was difficult; the doctor was booked weeks in advance and seeing him that day was impossible, as the receptionist repeated over and over, growing more exasperated as she patiently explained that the doctor was at the hospital attending a difficult delivery. There was no way of knowing if or when he would be back. She suggested that Katherine take the baby to the emergency room of the hospital if there were a serious problem.

Katherine hung up the phone feeling bereft, frightened, and more alone than she had ever felt in her life. Was it serious or was it only her imagination? True, Cameron wouldn't nurse, but surely that wasn't all that unusual; there was probably some good reason for it that she was unaware of. Colic, maybe, or some other typical baby distress. She would feel a fool if she took Cameron to the emergency room only to find out that it was something ordinary. They would think her stupid and send her home.

As an only child, Katherine had only limited experience with babies, and even when she was old enough to babysit, she'd never taken care of anyone younger than toddler age. Her parents were dead and she had fallen out of touch with her aunts and cousins. She and Rod had been their own best friends, and even though she had formed other relationships, they were not close and she had cut off all connections following Rod's death. She did not feel comfortable calling any of these people now.

She was deeply bothered by her inability to decide what to do.

Cameron had fallen into a restless slumber and Katherine carefully deposited her in her crib, making certain that the curtains and blinds were tightly drawn, drowning the room in darkness. She even turned off the Mickey light, extinguishing his bright pink smile.

She gathered a small pile of baby-care books and took them to the couch, where she began searching their pages for a clue to what was happening.

Katherine pushed a heavy wave of hair out of her eyes and looked blankly at the far wall without seeing it. The books had offered meager comfort. Cameron's disinterest in nursing could be explained by colic, gas, or simply a bad mood. Other than mentioning the fact that babies' eyes were extremely sensitive to bright lights, the books made no reference to a reaction such as Cameron had exhibited. Nor could she find any explanation for the blisters that had risen after the baby had touched the necklace.

Perhaps it was an allergy. She had never heard of anyone being allergic to metal, but she supposed it was possible. She recalled, with a shudder, a scratch test she had undergone in her teen years; it seemed that there had been several hundred possibilities, although strawberries and chocolate eventually proved to be the culprits responsible for the rashes and sneezing bouts that plagued her. At the time she had fumed and raged over the results, wondering why she could not have been allergic to liver and sauerkraut.

Although there were no real answers, she felt as though she had done what little she could, and told herself that when Cameron wakened, all would be well. She looked around the living room, taking note of the large dust balls curling in the corners, the cluttered and unkempt look of the room and felt a flicker of anger, directed at herself. How could she have let things disintegrate to this point?

Warm red light filled the room, glancing off the shining wood, brought back to its customary sheen with energetic applications of broom and oiled dust mop. The mounds of unread papers had been neatly tied and stacked outside the kitchen door for the super to collect. The dirty plates, glasses, and silverware were washed, dried, and tucked away in their proper niches. She herself was weary but filled with a sense of accomplishment as she stared at the restored rooms, feeling at peace with herself for the first time in weeks.

Another shower, the water hot as she could stand it, washed
even the weariness out of her bones, and she dressed in clean
jeans, a comfortable red and green cotton flannel shirt, terry cloth
socks, and a favorite pair of loafers. Her auburn hair hung around
her face, smelling clean and sweet. She brushed through the thick
tangles with resolution, suddenly anxious for Cameron to waken,
to prove her fears groundless. Everything would be all right, she
told herself. It just had to be.

The last glimmer of crimson had faded from the western skies
and still Cameron had not wakened. Katherine could not stifle the
cold flicker of fear that lanced through her belly. Nor could she
stop herself from hurrying to the nursery and opening the door,
suddenly terrified of what she would find.

The sour smell struck her like a physical blow as the door
swung open on the darkened room. It was like entering the lair of
a sick animal. Katherine flung herself at the crib, her fingers
gripping the top rail like a survivor of a sinking ship. The baby's
eyes were open, staring listlessly at the intricate slats. Her mouth
hung lax and a thin line of saliva fed a damp pool that her chapped
cheek was pressed into. She had not moved from the position she
had been placed in hours earlier.

Katherine snatched the baby from the crib and pressed her to her
chest, overcome with fear, no longer able to convince herself, to
believe that everything would be all right. She felt as though
nothing would ever be all right ever again.

By the time Mrs. Orlowski returned, bearing a large porcelain
tureen wreathed in steam and the rich aroma of chicken soup,
Katherine had retreated to the comfort of Rod's big armchair.
Cameron was cradled against her breast, lying limp and unresisting, seemingly without the energy needed to cry.

She had cried for a time, earlier, as the shadows began to
lengthen at the living room windows, but it was a thready, reedy,
monotonic cry without hope or rage. Even that had stopped after
a time, as though the baby did not have the strength to continue.

Katherine was filled with a quiet certainty that Cameron was
going to die. She held the small, silent body, her hands pressed
against the tiny back, feeling the flickering beat of the baby's
pulse, needing the constant reassurance that the too-small heart
was still beating, fearing the moment when it would cease.

She could barely stir herself, making her legs move, cross the
open expanse to the door and open it to admit the motherly figure
she'd been so loath to part from such a short time before. Now, she

was reluctant to speak, to show her the child, for it seemed that if she remained silent, did not voice her fears, share the sight of the too-still infant, it might somehow not be true. It was as though speaking the dire words, voicing her fears, would make it all real.

But she did not have the energy to resist the knock at the door, or the bell. Mrs. Orlowski would persevere, knowing that she was inside. For all her kindliness, she was too forceful a presence to ignore.

She stared at Mrs. Orlowski, unable to return the warm smile, unable to do anything more than stare at her with huge eyes. The smile faded from the old woman's face and she searched Katherine's eyes with her own. What she read there caused her to hurry into the apartment, cross to the dining room table, and deposit the steaming tureen. Without a word, she held out her arms and Katherine handed over the motionless bundle.

Mrs. Orlowski settled herself on the couch, her thick legs encased in their heavy nylons and laced-up sensible shoes crossed at the ankles, barely reaching the floor. She drew the edge of the blanket back from the small face and her eyes met those of the small, solemn creature who stared up at her.

"You have fed her, yes?"

"She wouldn't nurse," Katherine said dully. "She's going to die, isn't she?"

"Sha," said Mrs. Orlowski, never taking her eyes off the small creature nestled in the blankets. "Give me a bottle."

Katherine took a small nursing bottle from the freezer. It was filled with excess milk, which she had carefully saved, thinking it might come in handy. A few seconds in the microwave brought it to the proper temperature. She handed the bottle to Mrs. Orlowski, who was murmuring nonsense in her foreign tongue to Cameron, whose eyes never left the old woman's face.

Continuing her soft murmur, she maneuvered the nipple inside the baby's lips. For a moment, it seemed that the child would suck; her lips formed around the soft rubber form and she mouthed it tentatively, but then she turned her head aside, away from the bottle, rejecting it.

They urged her to take it in soft, pleading voices, but the baby became fretful and began to cry. In desperation, Katherine took a spoon from the kitchen drawer and poured a tiny amount of milk into its bowl. She pressed the tip of the spoon against Cameron's lower lip in an attempt to dribble some of the milk into her mouth. If she could only get her to take just a little . . . but no sooner had the edge of the spoon touched the tiny rosebud lip, than the baby began to shriek. Katherine jerked back, spilling the small amount of bluish white milk contained in the spoon. The baby's cries became more frenzied, almost hysterical, and as Mrs. Orlowski hurriedly raised the child and placed her over her shoulder, Katherine saw an angry red weal forming on the baby's lower lip!

She looked down at the spoon, and noticed that it was one of the older silver-plated pieces that she and Rod had acquired in their Saturday searches of flea markets and the old dusty shops that lined Clark street. Examining it more closely, she saw that the silver-plating on the tip and the undersurface of the bowl was completely worn away, worn down to the base metal.

It took a long time before they were able to quiet the baby, and even then it seemed that she ceased her cries more from exhaustion than from any degree of comfort. The women stared at each other, the fear naked in their eyes.

Mrs. Orlowski was the first to put their unspoken fear into words. "You must call the doctor."

Katherine told of her earlier efforts.

"Then we must go to hospital, take the baby. We must go now."

A feeling of dread came over Katherine, and it seemed that her nostrils were filled with the smell of alcohol and iodine. She shuddered at the thought of the hospital, which had so recently absorbed all of her nights and days.

"We will go now!" Mrs. Orlowski said forcefully, perhaps mistaking Katherine's reluctance for refusal. Katherine merely nodded. She allowed herself to be bundled into a jacket, Cameron wrapped in a thick, fluffy quilt, and urged out the door, all within minutes of the decision.

A cab was summoned by the doorman, who leaped to obey Mrs. Orlowski's terse command. Almost before Katherine could comprehend what was happening, they were on their way down Sheridan, the bright lights arching over the busy drive, filling the interior of the cab with flashes of white light that banished the shadows of the night.

It was the first time that Katherine had been out since she had returned home with her child and without a husband. Now, making the journey in reverse, she had a hard time keeping herself from picturing the next trip. Would she still have a daughter?

Dr. Bosch practiced at Edgewater Hospital, a genteelly fraying hospital on Chicago's north side. A relic of the forties, its lower levels were still covered in the pink stucco that had been ultrachic at the time of its construction but now gave it the appearance of an elderly dowager dressed in a too-youthful, out-of-fashion style. Friends had urged Katherine to choose a doctor with privileges at the most prestigious and modern Wesley Memorial in the heart of downtown, but Katherine had felt comfortable with Dr. Bosch, who reminded her of the doctor she had grown up with at home. Now she wondered if she had made the right decision.

The cab pulled up under the covered arch outside the emergency room and Katherine hurried inside, barely noticing that Mrs. Orlowski remained behind to pay the driver out of her own pocket.

Inside, everything was brightly lit, too bright. Squinting against the glaring fluorescent lights, Katherine quickly covered Cameron's face with the comforter before she could become distressed. Wheelchairs and stretchers lined the sides of the wall to the left. To the right was a cluster of mismatched, uncomfortable-looking chairs; directly ahead was a glass window labeled ADMITTING, in English, Spanish, Arabic, and an Asian script. Katherine hurried to the window and waited for the young woman seated behind the desk to raise her eyes. When she did so, her manner was polite but noncommittal as though she disapproved of the people she came in contact with. The thick glass which separated her from those who sought assistance furthered the impression.

Katherine gave the required information impatiently, answering the girl's queries in short, sharp replies which gained her nothing but a look of hostility.

"Next of kin, someone not at this same address," said the girl.

"Look, none of this is really important," Katherine cried. "I'll tell you everything you need to know, later. Can't we see a doctor now!"

"Is it an emergency?" the girl asked with total disinterest, tapping at a key of her computer.

"Would I be here if it weren't?" Katherine replied, knowing that speaking to the girl in that tone would not help, knowing that she needed to win her cooperation, but unable to bear the stupid, tedious questions, wanting to shake her hard, break through the shell of indifference. "I . . . I'm sorry," she said, biting back the sharp words that teetered on the tip of her tongue. "I'm worried! Couldn't we please see a doctor right away?" She hated herself for the pleading tone in her voice.

"Next of kin, someone not at this same address," the girl

repeated, and bowing her head to hide the tears that pricked behind her eyes, Katherine gave the information.

The wait was no more than a half an hour, but it seemed like an eternity. Finally she was summoned by a kindly looking nurse. She and Mrs. Orlowski rose quickly and followed the woman through a pair of swinging doors and into a curtained cubicle.

She explained the problem, hearing her words as though from a distance, and realizing how lame they sounded. "I guess it doesn't sound like much, but I'm afraid . . ." Her voice tapered off; she could think of nothing more to say.

"Probably nothing," the nurse was saying as she took the small bundle out of Katherine's arms. "Your first?" Katherine nodded. The nurse smiled as she lay the blanketed bundle down on the raised gurney. "Everything always seems scary when it's your first," she said in a reassuring tone. "Now, let's see what we've got here." She unwrapped the comforter with adept fingers. As soon as the bright white lights reached inside the blankets, Cameron began to cry, a thin, frightened wail of pain. "Now, now, little one, it's all right," cooed the nurse. The cries did not stop.

When at last she turned back to face them, the nurse's eyes were averted. "I'll get the doctor," she said in cool tones, the friendliness gone from her voice.

She returned within seconds with a tall, thin, ascetic-looking blond man close on her heels. He nodded brusquely to the two waiting woman and immediately turned his attention to the crying child.

Straightening, he thrust his hands in his pocket and fixed the women with a cold, appraising stare. "What happened here?" he asked in a hard-edged voice.

"She won't eat," Katherine said, taken aback by his tone, "and the light seems to hurt her eyes and . . ."

"I'm not talking about that. I'm asking you how she got these burns."

"They're not burns. I—I mean, I know they look like burns but, they're not. She grabbed a necklace and the blisters appeared immediately and then later I tried to feed her some milk with a spoon and that's where the blister on her lip came from. . . ." Her voice trailed away as she became aware of the way the doctor was looking at her. Contempt and anger burned in his eyes.

"A necklace, a spoon?" he said sarcastically. "When's the last time you fed this child?"

Katherine gaped at him. "You think I . . . are you saying you think I hurt her?" Her voice rose in disbelief. She felt her fingers clench into tight fists, and her voice shook as she glared back at the physician.

He did not reply except to curl his lip derisively. His eyes moved away as though he could not bear to look at her a moment longer. "Admit her," he barked at the nurse. "Get an IV going, let's get some fluids into her, stat."

"Wait a minute," Katherine protested. "You're going to keep her? Can't I take her home? Can't you give me something to make her eat? What's the matter with her? Talk to me, please!"

The doctor turned back to face her, his eyes fastening on her with undisguised anger. His words were tight, and carefully chosen. "We'll keep her overnight and run a few tests, get some fluids into her. Go home, there's nothing you can do. You can see her in the morning."

"Go home? But I want to stay with her!"

"That's not possible," the doctor said in clipped tones. "Your own doctor will see you in the morning. "Good night, Mrs. Sinclair."

Already, the nurse had gathered Cameron up in her arms and stood there holding her defensively, as though daring Katherine to argue or attempt to take her away. She opened her mouth to speak and took a step forward, staggered by the realization that they should she had harmed her own child. She wanted to talk to them, convince them that it was not so. Surely they could not believe that she would hurt her own baby! But before she could say anything, Mrs. Orlowski seized her by the shoulder and pulled her back. She turned to the older woman. "They think . . ."

"Yes, yes," Mrs. Orlowski said quietly, as she drew Katherine out of the cubicle. "Come away, child, it does not matter what they think. Let them care for the little one. That is all that matters, yes?"

"Of course," Katherine said in confusion, her mind sick with the unspoken implication. "But . . ."

Mrs. Orlowski hurried her out of the hospital before she could say any more. The cold, sharp night air was redolent with the aroma of burning leaves. The sound of traffic from Lake Shore Drive filled her ears with sibilance, a sound not unlike the hissing break of the dark combers that crashed upon the beach beyond the narrow strip of greensward that separated the boundary of the ancient lake from the edge of the city.

They walked for a time in silence, Mrs. Orlowski taking two steps to Katherine's one, the rapid pace fueled by her anger. Their path took them along the grassy lip of the parkway, perhaps not the wisest or safest choice in a city that could be dangerous even in broad daylight, but Katherine was too angry, too disturbed to think rationally. Mrs. Orlowski trotted alongside, her large satchel-like purse swinging at her side.

At length, Katherine stopped at a bench and hurled herself down, fists still jammed in her pockets, an angry scowl creasing her forehead.

"How dare they think that I would do anything to hurt her! She's my daughter!"

Mrs. Orlowski was unable to speak. Unaccustomed to such physical exertion, she could do no more than gasp and press her hand to her chest, attempting to regain her breath. Some of her hair had straggled down over her forehead and her glasses had slid halfway down the length of her nose. Katherine did not even notice her distress.

Katherine glared out over the dark water and surged forward as though to rise. Quickly, Mrs. Orlowski's hand shot out and gripped her arm, restraining her. Only then did Katherine become aware of the discomfort suffered by her companion, and was instantly stricken with remorse.

"Please, *mädchen*, one guilt at a time," the older woman said with a spark of humor. "Will you take on the burden of the whole world? I am an old woman who has enjoyed her meals too much for too many years. Now I pay the price. Was it you who forced me to eat those schnecken, those bowls of dumplings? No, so hush, allow me my misery."

Katherine was almost tempted to smile, but she was too angry. Over and over she played back the nurse's words, her abrupt change of attitude, the way she had looked at her as though she were a monster. And the doctor. He too had all but accused her of burning Cameron, or purposely depriving her of food. They would not even allow her to stay! What would they have done if she had insisted? In spite of the knowledge that she had done nothing wrong, she trembled.

Mrs. Orlowski patted her on the arm as though discerning her thoughts.

"What am I going to do?" Katherine asked, despair weighing down her words.

"Go home, get a good night's sleep," the older woman answered promptly. "You are tired. You have not been taking care of yourself. How can you take care of the little one if you yourself are tired?"

"I can take care of her fine!" Katherine protested, sensitive to any hint of criticism. "Everything was all right until last night!" Anger, combined with worry and the need to find someone else to blame other than herself, fashioned her thoughts. "I know you saw something!" she blurted. "I saw your door close. Tell me what you saw!"

"Nothing! I saw nothing! I am an old woman. I do not sleep well. Often I am up at night!"

"But I saw your door close! You must have seen something," Katherine insisted angrily, pushing the old woman for an explanation. "Do you know who it was? Why won't you tell me?"

Mrs. Orlowski was wringing her hands; Katherine had never seen anyone do that before. It was somehow unnerving, and at any other time, she would have felt compassion, but now there was no room in her heart for kind thoughts or sympathy for anyone else's distress.

"It was nothing!" cried the old woman. "I heard the stairs, they make sounds when people come down. I think, Who can it be, so late at night? I do not want to open the door, to act like a nosy old lady, but I wonder all the same. Then when I open the door, I see nothing, but the smell . . ."

"Yes! The smell!" Katherine seized on the old woman's words. "If you smelled it too, that means . . . What was it? What did it remind you of?"

"Mushrooms," Mrs. Orlowski replied slowly. "It smelled like mushrooms and dirt after the rain."

". . . dirt, after a rain," repeated Katherine as she leaned back against the rails of the bench, lapsing into silence, lost in thought.

A cold, driving wind was slicing in off the lake, carrying with it a hint of the winter that was soon to come, but Katherine did not seem to notice. Nor did she notice her companion's obvious discomfort until the older woman tugged tentatively on her sleeve. "Please, we can go now?" she asked softly. "I think perhaps it is not safe here, and the night air, it is not so good for old bones."

Only then did Katherine rouse from her deep silence. "Yes," she said without looking at the old woman. "It's time to go home."

"What are you going to do?" Mrs. Orlowski asked fearfully. "You will not do anything foolish?"

Katherine turned to look at her, her eyes clear and focused now, filled with steely determination. Mrs. Orlowski felt a shiver of apprehension.

"I know something happened in my apartment. Someone was there. I didn't see them, but I know they were there and when they left, the baby was gone. No one believed me. Not this new superintendent whom I've never seen before, not the doorman, nor the police. They all thought I was crazy or, at the very least, acting like an emotionally disturbed woman who needed to be humored. Then, the baby reappeared, even though I know she was gone. The crib was empty. I saw it, touched it.

"Now, you appear on my doorstep, wanting to be my friend. Why? Why now? You've never wanted to be my friend before. And I know you saw something even though you pretend that you didn't.

"And then there's Cameron, who won't nurse and can't tolerate light. She used to lie in her crib in the morning and try to catch the sunbeams; now even normal daylight makes her cry.

"And what about the blisters? I don't believe you just happened to bring that necklace, just wanted to make her smile. I think you know something, something you're not telling me.

"My husband is dead, my daughter may be dying, and something very strange is going on. I don't know what it is, but I'm going to do my best to find out. You can't make it better with chicken soup, Mrs. Orlowski, nor with vows of friendship. It's going to take more than that. Am I going to do something foolish? I don't know. I just know I'm going to do whatever is necessary to save my daughter's life."

SEVEN

❦

Walking away from the old woman, leaving her standing there on the park path in the dark was hard. Mrs. Orlowski was right, it was undoubtedly a very unsafe place to be. Gangs of youths often roamed the parkway looking for easy prey, and what could be easier or more inviting than an old woman with a large purse? But her anger drove her forward, refused to allow her to look back to see if Mrs. Orlowski was following.

She waited for a break in the traffic and then sprinted across Lake Shore Drive, drawing the crisp, leaf-smoked air deep into her lungs, feeling life and anger return in equal parts. It had been wrong shutting herself up in the apartment; isolation and grief had drained her of energy and the ability to think. The cold air seemed to shock her back to life.

She hailed a cab slowly cruising the Drive and gave him the address, knowing that she would have to ask the doorman for the fare. She sat hunched over, leaning forward, as though her posture could make the cab arrive more swiftly.

She was uncertain how to proceed, but she knew one thing: she would not allow the opinions of others to sway her from doing whatever she thought necessary.

She instructed the doorman to pay the cabfare, without apology or explanation. Let him think whatever he wanted. She watched as he passed through the heavy glass doors and approached the waiting cabby. Unobserved by the doorman, whose back was

51

turned to her, she moved swiftly to the basement door rather than the main staircase that would take her up to her apartment.

She took a deep breath, yanked the door open, stepped through, and closed it firmly behind her before she could change her mind. Whatever the explanation was for the strange events that had occurred, somehow she knew that the answer lay in the basement.

Oddly enough, she seemed to have lost her lifelong terror of basements. The dark rooms that lay between her and her goal now seemed merely a time-consuming inconvenience rather than the heart-pounding journey it had been only the night before.

She hurried through the echoing rooms, ignoring the shadows that closed in around her, barely hearing the soft breath of the giant furnace, all of her concentration focused on the man Stone and what she would say to him. She was uncertain whether he was involved in whatever was happening. She remembered his eyes and the way he had looked at her, the feel of his hands, remembered the current of electricity that had arced between them. She shuddered, pushing the memory away from her.

If he was involved, she would force him to tell her, and she would not allow him to touch her or hold her with his eyes. The memory of how she had felt, the confusing stir of emotions, caused her a momentary hesitation, a weakness in her knees. How could she have felt that way with Rod barely dead and Cameron so sick? She felt angered and betrayed by her own body. She was determined that it, whatever *it* had been, would not happen again.

Her steps slowed. The furnace room was directly ahead of her now, the room brightly illuminated by the glow of the furnace compared to the solid darkness that surrounded her. She should have felt relieved by the light, by the nearness of one who could explain, give her answers, but instead, she felt a sickness in her stomach, a fluttering nervousness, a reluctance to proceed any further.

She stood there in the darkness at the outermost boundary of the light and was suddenly overcome by all the uncertainties that she had succeeded in ignoring until that moment. What if Stone was nothing more than what he said he was, a building superintendent? What if he truly knew nothing about Cameron and the old door? What if everything was merely the product of her imagination?

Then the image of Cameron came to her. Cameron lying thin and listless in her crib, the look of death imprinted on her features. Cameron screaming with pain in the sunlight, the blisters, the hideous blisters rising on her tiny fingers and lip. The memory of her daughter carried her forward without conscious thought. It did not matter if she made a fool of herself, it did not matter what others thought of her, if she could save her daughter's life.

She crossed the room without noticing the tools or the machinery or even the immense furnace, focused on the small flight of stairs in the far corner of the room, the steps that descended to Stone's apartment and to the mysterious doorway.

She paused at the top of the steps, one foot extended, frozen in place, every nerve ending tingling. The door, the old cobwebbed door that no one believed she had seen open, was pulled away from the wall! It was a mere crack, no more than two inches; but it was there and once again it was open. She had not been wrong!

Waves of excitement and fear coursed through her. She crept down the stairs, conscious of even the tiniest sound, the infinitesimal crunch of grit beneath her shoes, and flinched, praying she would not be heard, although by what or whom, she could not have said.

She stood on the bottom step, her eyes fastened to the strip of darkness between the door and the wall. The opposite wall, barely four feet from the door, the wall that abutted the encroaching lake was beaded with moisture. That alone would make the door difficult to open and close as the wood swelled with increased humidity.

She wondered briefly if she should knock on Stone's door and show him the opening. She did not want to go in there alone. Stone would have a phone, they could call the police. It would be good to see the policemen forced to accept the fact that she had been telling the truth.

But what if she were heard? She could not afford to make a sound, any sound that would alert whoever was hiding in the space beyond the door. Moving as quietly as possible, she slipped past the dark opening and positioned herself in front of Stone's door. The thought that whoever had entered her apartment, whoever had taken Cameron, might still be hiding on the other side of the mysterious door gave her a moment's pause.

Who would live in such a place willingly? Desperate people, people without homes, without jobs, without hope. To such people, kidnapping a newborn child from a rich widow made helpless by grief would represent the means to escape from their dire circumstances. Something, perhaps the swiftness of Katherine's pursuit, had caused them to abandon their mission, to return the baby, but in that brief interim they had done something which had caused her to sicken. The memory of Cameron, lying listless and pale beneath the doctor's grim, accusing eyes, helped Katherine make the terrifying decision. If they were still there, she would find them.

A remnant of sanity fought its way past her rage, urging her to call the police, to go for help, not to enter that dark, frightening place alone. She brushed the thought aside instantly, refusing to consider the whisper of wisdom. They had gotten past her once before, although she could still not understand how it had happened; she would not allow it to happen again. Her daughter's life was at stake, fear and personal safety were of little consequence.

She feared that the door would squeak, make some sound that would reveal her entrance, but to her surprise, it moved effortlessly beneath her touch, swinging wide to allow her to pass through. The door was soft and cool beneath her fingers, coated with the satiny patina that wood acquires with great age.

She slipped over the sill and pulled the door shut behind her. It closed tight for a moment, leaving her in total darkness; then, as she was trying to decide what to do next, it sprang open with a soft popping sound, exposing the same two-inch gap that had led to her discovery. The wood, swollen by humidity, could not create a tight seal. They, the kidnappers, had tried to hide their tracks, but had been betrayed by nature.

Katherine forced herself to wait for the pounding of her heart to subside and to allow her eyes to adjust to the darkness, relieved only by the tiny slit of light at the door. She had not known what to expect, thinking to find another space for the storage of coal, or a deep, hidden cistern, certainly not a large space, for there were ample coal bins on the floor above, and with the lake so near, what need would there have been for a cistern? But as her eyes adjusted to the dim light, she was able to see that she was standing in a narrow corridor carved from the substratum on which the building stood. It appeared to be a tightly compressed aggregate of stony soil, mid-sized rocks, and huge boulders. Katherine knew that following the great fire of 1871, the city had been extended by pushing most of the rubble from the fire into the lake and backfilling it with soil. The Sinclairs' home had been built on this landfill.

The ground was level underfoot, not concrete but smooth, hard-packed soil. Katherine was no expert in such matters, but it seemed to her to have the feel of a trail that was traveled often.

Whatever this place was, was it possible that it connected somehow with the outside or maybe even another building? That had to be the answer!

Katherine knew that several buildings on the near north side of the city had such connecting passages. One magnificent boulder mansion which had stood at the corner of Banks and State until it was demolished for a hotel parking facility had a tunnel that traversed the entire block, ending in the subbasement of another mansion. Local legend had it that the passage had been constructed so that a man and his mistress might meet without the knowledge of their respective mates. Katherine had never quite believed the story, but now it did not seem quite so unlikely. She hurried forward, still with caution, but now more determined than ever to discover who else had discovered the tunnel and what they had done to cause her daughter such harm.

A dark opening appeared in the wall to her left. It was round in shape, its uppermost point level with her chin, the bottom sill a foot or more above the trail. She could not see anything beyond the entrance, for the space beyond the opening lay in total darkness. The edges of the doorway, if that's what it was, were smooth, deftly carved out of the surrounding stone without a flaw or any roughness to be found beneath her questing fingertips. There was no sense of any human presence lurking in the darkness, so she turned her attention back to the path before her.

The smell was stronger now. She had been struck by it as soon as she had opened the secret door, a combination of perpetually damp earth and something else, mushrooms perhaps. The scent was everywhere, not unpleasant but reminding her forcefully of being underground, away from the light of day. For a moment, her fears returned and she was struck by a jolt of panic that nearly overwhelmed her. She forced back the desire to flee, to take herself out of this place and back into the light. She fought to control her fears, and after a moment, was able to continue.

She had gone so far that the light from the doorway cast no more than a faint opaqueness, a paling of the darkness rather than true light. But now she thought that she sensed a growing brightness ahead and the murmur of low voices. Heart pounding in her chest, she crept forward.

Several more dark openings appeared on either side, but these gave no hint of occupation, and she passed them by with barely a glance. Directly ahead, on the right, another circular opening appeared and this one emitted a pale, dim glow of ruddy light, not the clear bright light of electricity, but more like that of firelight, although there was no flickering or play of shadows on the wall opposite the circular doorway.

She slipped quietly down the passage, pressed flat against the wall, feeling ahead for each footstep, unwilling to reveal her presence by a careless step or rattled rock. The opening was near; her heart was hammering so loud that she could feel it in her eardrums. There was a sickness in her belly and a sour taste in her mouth. She was frightened by what she would discover, but excited as well. Soon, she would know what had happened to Cameron.

She tried to imagine the response of those she was about to confront. They would not take kindly to the discovery of their lair. It was warm and safe, protecting them from the brutal elements and more dangerous denizens of the city. For a moment, she felt pity for them, for the circumstances that would have brought them to this state, living in secrecy underground. But she hardened her thoughts and steeled herself for the confrontation. Many people were homeless but they did not resort to kidnapping, and even now, Cameron lay dangerously ill in the hospital, the direct result of some street illness they had passed on to her.

Armed with her anger, Katherine discovered within herself a courage she did not know she possessed. Moving abruptly, she placed herself directly in front of the lighted doorway, ready to confront whomever was inside. Despite all of her thoughts on the matter, Katherine was completely unprepared for what she saw.

The baby lay still and unmoving within the confines of the hospital crib. A gaily patterned mobile swung unnoticed in the air above her. The room was darkened, as it had been quickly learned that what the mother had said was true—any light at all caused the child to scream as though in pain.

The admitting doctor had followed the infant out of the emergency room after his preliminary workup. This was a departure from normal procedure. Ordinarily, after a patient had been admitted and seen by the emergency room doctor, they were transferred to the appropriate floor. There, their charts were annotated with the name of their own personal physician who would assume responsibility for their care. Occasionally, if their affliction was unusual or interesting in some way, they were included in the daily rounds conducted by teaching physicians and their attendant resident students.

Ordinarily, once Cameron had been seen, Dr. Anderson's responsibility to her would have ended. As a senior resident, his busy schedule, long hours spent in the chaotic emergency room, back to back with long hours in study, seldom allowed him more than a passing thought as to the fate of patients he had admitted. But this one was different.

Dr. Bosch had not yet seen the child. His answering service had been unable to do more than pass along a message, for he was involved in a difficult delivery at another hospital. It could be many hours before he was able to break away. Anderson was convinced that they did not have the luxury of those hours. From all indications, the baby would be dead by then.

He had been wrong to accuse the mother of abuse, even obliquely. He had tried to contact her to find out more about what had happened to the child in the hours before her admittance, and to advise her to return, but there had been no answer to his calls. He had summoned the resident pediatrician, a young man named Scarborough, waking him as he slept in an easy chair in the doctors' lounge and filled him in on the details of the baby's condition as they hurried toward her room.

"So what are you saying, that the mother burned the kid?" Scarborough asked, combing his unruly thatch of dark hair with his fingers and blinking the sleep out of his eyes. "Wouldn't be the first time, won't be the last, either."

In the short number of years that they had been working with the public they had already seen numerous horrifying instances of child abuse that their sheltered Midwestern, upper-middle-class backgrounds had not prepared them for. To protect themselves, to keep from breaking, they, like most others in their profession, tried to grow a shell of cool detachment, to distance themselves from the pain and the heartbreak that they could not solve with medicine or bandages, sick, warped lives that would never be well. But they were still young and all too human, and occasionally their wall of protection was breached.

"No, that's not it," Anderson said, striding along the corridor, forcing Scarborough to match his long steps or fall behind. "That's what I thought at first, practically accused her of it, wouldn't listen when she denied it."

"They all deny it," Scarborough said, "except the nuts who tell you that they did it for the kids' own good, you know, to drive the devil out of 'em."

"Yeah, well. I don't think that's what's happened here. She, the mother, said that the kid was fine and then all of a sudden it couldn't tolerate light and wouldn't nurse and the touch of metal raised blisters."

Scarborough made a rude, disbelieving sound.

"Light does bother the kid, she can't bear it, starts screaming. I touched her with my stethoscope, nothing happened. Couple of instruments. All stainless steel. Nothing happened. Then I touched her, lightly, with that Roman coin I carry on my key ring. Dave—" Anderson stopped abruptly and Scarborough nearly ran into him. "Dave, I've never seen anything like it. I touched her on the back of the hand, lightly, like a feather, and she screamed and this blister appeared out of nowhere like I had burned her!"

Scarborough stared at him, brows lowering. "What do you mean it burned her? That's not possible. I never heard of anyone being allergic to metal, and even if they were . . . that quick a reaction? Not bloody likely!"

"I'm telling you it happened just like that," Anderson said, remembering how he had reacted when the mother had first related that same story to him in the emergency room.

"But it's more than that, there's something funny going on."

"What do you mean . . . funny?"

"Don't know exactly. I ran a CBC and its thin, red blood cell count is way low; only a six. The white cell count is lower still, but the kidneys are enlarged and tender to the touch. I found elevated plasma, urea nitrogen, and creatinine levels."

"Sounds like prerenal failure," Scarborough said with a frown, staring at Anderson, sensing there was more.

"Maybe," Anderson said hesitantly. "She's definitely dehydrated and it's likely that there's an electrolyte imbalance, but Dave, it's more than that, her blood . . . it doesn't match type."

"What do you mean it doesn't match type?" Scarborough stared at his friend, perplexed, wondering if Anderson was getting enough sleep, imagining things. It happened to all young residents at some point, although usually in their earlier years, thinking they had discovered some new disease, some never-before-seen virus, imagining themselves heroes. "Look, Lou, there are only four basic blood types, the kid's got to belong to one of them."

"No, Dave, she doesn't. I've never seen anything like it."

At first, Scarborough thought that Anderson was pulling his leg, playing another variety of the many jokes residents played upon one another, a shagging of sorts, but also a means of keeping their sanity in the final exhaustive and demanding years of their schooling. But as Anderson finished reciting the number of tests and readings he had done, Scarborough became convinced that this was no prank. He stepped up his pace toward Cameron's room, almost running over the green and ivory linoleum tiles of the corridor. Now he, not Anderson, was leading the way.

The room was dark and silent. Scarborough paused for a moment after the door closed, with Anderson poised behind him. The dark blue curtain was drawn around the crib to shield it from the light. The heavy drapes were drawn and the room was completely silent. Scarborough had entered many such silent rooms in the last several years and, always, there was a sense of presence. No matter how deep the patient's slumber, how long the coma, one always knew that a living being was in the room. There was no sense, no such feeling in this dark, oppressive room, and Scarborough worried that the child had died; that he had come too late.

Anderson brushed past him and drew the curtain aside. Scarborough moved to stand beside him and looked into the crib, fearing what he would see.

EIGHT

Katherine stood in the doorway, stunned, senses reeling, unable to move, to think, to act. She had been so convinced that the people who had entered her apartment and stolen Cameron had been homeless drifters that she had never considered any other option. What she was seeing now changed everything.

The chamber that lay beyond the circular doorway had never served as a coal bin nor any other place of storage. It was unique, unlike anything Katherine had ever seen, as was the person, the *thing* slumbering on the far side of the room.

The *thing* lay outstretched on a low couch, head turned toward the doorway, one hand outstretched, dangling over the edge. Katherine shuddered, fought down the desire to flee. The creature appeared to be sleeping soundly; she studied it, wondering what it was and how it had come to be here.

The lower half of its torso was wrapped in a blanket made of a smooth gray pelt, but the upper half of its body was clearly visible. The head, covered with a coarse, shaggy thatch of whitish-blond hair was deformed; the space between the hairline and brows was very short, barely an inch. The skull sloped back at an extreme angle from brows to hairline. The brows themselves were thick and heavily matted across the prominent bony ridge. The eyes were sunken in shadows. The cheekbones were high, pressed up directly under the eyes, and here too, the contours of the bone were grossly exaggerated. The flesh beneath the cheekbones seemed to fall away without support until it reached the chin, which was heavy, aggressive even in slumber. The nose was large and broad, the nostrils flared and spread wide as though the nose had been smashed flat and never repaired. The mouth was wide and protruding, the lips thick and slightly agape, revealing very large strong teeth. Adding to the horror was the fact that the creature's skin was dead white, without even the slightest hint of color. It was a primitive face, brutish, one of naked aggression, a visage out of nightmares, a face that would inspire fear and revulsion among all who viewed it.

The upper torso was massive, broad across the shoulders and chest and heavily muscled. The arm that hung over the edge of the couch appeared to be far longer than a normal human arm, and the hand and fingers were curiously shaped. The space between thumb and the first finger was abnormally wide. The fingers themselves were thick and the nails flat and yellowish, the color of old ivory.

The creature—Katherine could not bring herself to think of it as a man—wore no clothing on its upper body, despite the fact that it was chilly and uncomfortably damp. Its flesh, all that was exposed to view, except the small space between hairline and lower lip, was covered with a dense mat of fine white-blond hair.

It seemed to be human even though it bore a strong resemblance to a gorilla. The features, although coarse and rough, were those of a human, not an animal. And the way it was living—no animal had created those surroundings. Despite her fear that the creature might awaken and discover her, Katherine allowed her eyes to travel around the room, absorbing everything she saw.

The chamber was circular, carved out of the surrounding rock and faced with a smooth white substance similar to plaster or a gritty stucco stubbed with tiny specks of something like mica that picked up the light in the room and seemed to glow, almost shimmer, from within. The light itself was coming from what appeared to be a chunk of rock about a foot in length and four inches wide, oblong in shape with a long groove carved along one edge. Light flowed from the rock, a steady, soft emission no brighter than a 60-watt light bulb, but softer and less obtrusive than ordinary incandescent light. There was no indication of the source of the power; the rock was nearly translucent, the light emerging from the very heart of it, filling the room with a soft, warm glow.

The light-rock was perched on a low shelf, on a level with the sleeping figure. The shelf had either been affixed to the wall or had been carved out of the wall itself during the room's construction.

There were several other pieces in the room, and even though their shapes were somewhat unusual, Katherine could easily discern their purpose. This was clearly a living area, and from the look of it, one that had been occupied for a lengthy period of time.

There were four pieces that were obviously chairs, although their seats were much lower than Katherine would have found comfortable. All were made of stone, and Katherine marveled at their construction. In her teen years she had attempted to whittle and carve things from wood as her male cousins did and she knew how difficult a medium wood could be; she could not even imagine the skills necessary for working with stone.

Nor were they simple pieces; all of the chairs exhibited some form of ornamentation. The largest of the four had graceful arches spanning the legs which had open, intricate fretwork that reminded her of the elaborate gingerbread on the Victorian houses of her youth. The design was echoed atop the high back and along the wide arms as well. The seat and back were cushioned with the same type of gray pelt that covered the sleeping figure.

Several of the chairs were drawn up before a long pedestal-type table; it too was lower than standard height. Its surface was a single large slab of limestone that had been polished to a high gleam revealing the complexity of fossilized life contained within. Its length was supported by a single pillar the base of which was nested in a long, slender, four-pronged foot.

Eating utensils were placed on a corner of the table. There were a number of plates and bowls, somewhat oversized and all fashioned from different types of stone. Katherine, not very knowledgeable about geology, was nevertheless able to recognize several of the more common types of rock. There was a large platter that she thought was some form of agate. Black, and interspersed with small snowbursts of white, it too had been polished to a high gleam and was a very handsome piece. Had it been displayed in one of the expensive boutiques that dotted the near north side of the city, it would undoubtedly have commanded a healthy price. There were four plates, each made from different types of rock, and two cups or tumblers, each of which was so large it would have taken two of Katherine's hands to hold comfortably. There was a small cluster of utensils, all fashioned from stone as well, the handles, tines, and bowls delicately turned, a miracle of design and workmanship. Their creator was clearly a master of his trade.

There were a number of hooks set into the wall nearest the

entryway, and from them hung a variety of pelts; some were gray, like the coverlet and the cushions, others were brown. From where she stood, Katherine could see a sleeve and it appeared that there was some specific construction to the pelts. She could not be certain but it seemed likely that they were clothes. A single pair of large boots, beautifully made of a heavy dark leather, stood neatly just inside the entry. They were quite big, a man's size 13 at the very least, and wide in the foot, exceptionally wide.

Katherine's mind was a jumble of conflicting thoughts. The creature on the couch was . . . was what? She could not tell whether it was animal or human or some monstrous combination. But no animal could have created such masterpieces of design, exhibited such perfection of craftsmanship. What was this thing and what was it doing here? Had it been responsible for stealing Cameron? If so, no amount of artistry could prevent her from exposing it to the authorities and finding out what it had done to Cameron to make her so sick.

Perhaps, just maybe, the pathetic creature before her was a freak, horribly disfigured like the Elephant Man, someone who had chosen to hide himself underground, away from the hurtful glances and comments of the rest of the world. It appeared that his talent, his mastery of stone, was as great as his disfigurement. It was unlikely that such a person would be able to face the cruelty of the world and preferred to live his life in isolation away from others.

Her thoughts were interrupted by a sound, one that was so familiar it took a moment for it to break through her concentration. Belatedly, she recognized what it was, and she realized that she had been hearing it for some time, but because of its familiarity, had excluded it from her thoughts. Now, the sound electrified her. A jolt of adrenalin coursed through her body, and she could literally feel the hair on her arms and the back of her neck prickle. It was the sound of a child, a baby, chuckling, gurgling, the wet, guttural sound a baby makes in response to some pleasant stimuli.

Her feet seemed to move by themselves. Without any instruction from her brain, they took her down the corridor toward the sound, drawing her along like some powerful magnet she was helpless to resist.

The corridor turned sharply to the right, and no sooner had she slipped around the corner than she was bombarded by light. After the dark corridor, the light seemed unbearably bright, but soon she was able to see that the long passage that stretched away in the distance before her was lit by a succession of the glowing rocks, round in shape and nestled in niches carved in the walls. A number of circular doorways opened on either side of the passage. Most, as she crept stealthily past, were dark and empty. Others were apparently lived in but thankfully their owners were absent.

What was this place and how could it have existed without her knowledge? How could she have lived here above what appeared to be an entire colony of people and not know of their existence? It was incomprehensible. Perhaps they were all deformed. Or maybe albinos, she thought, grasping at straws, living below the earth away from the light. Her mind was reeling from the implications as she crept toward the lighted circular doorway from which she heard the sound of voices, the sound of a baby at play.

She looked behind her, worried at the distance she had traveled, trying to calculate the distance to the basement door, suddenly afraid. These people would not welcome discovery. Even if they were merely street people, homeless families seeking protection from the approaching winter, they would undoubtedly fight to keep their precious shelters.

But if they were something else, deformed monstrosities like the sleeping figure she had seen, outcasts of society, it was possible—no, probable—that they would do anything to prevent discovery. She would have to be very careful.

An inner voice told her to go back, to creep away unseen and turn the matter over to the police. She had actually paused in midstep, aware of her danger and ready to retreat, when the baby chuckled again. It was the sound of delight, naive amusement that tugged at her, pulling her toward the lighted doorway, a sound that was impossible to resist. It was a sound that Cameron made often, joy over the ripples of reflected prismatic sunlight dancing on her wall and ceiling. The laughter created by puffed cheeks and funny faces, rubbed noses, gently tickled ribs. It was a sound no mother could ignore.

Katherine flattened herself against the wall and inched the last few paces, careful to make no sound. She need not have bothered; the occupants of the room would not have noticed her unless she had thrown a stone at them, so involved were they in their own drama.

There were three of them, a man, seated sideways to her, his features clearly visible in the warm glow of the light-rock. He was identical to the sleeping figure, deformed in the same manner, his features heavy and somehow primitive, his body covered with a layer of hair. But apelike as his features were, his eyes surprised her; they were bright with intelligence.

The second figure, seated with its back to the door, was clearly female, for its physique was smaller and more finely boned. There was only a faint sprinkling of pale hair on the backs of her arms and down the crest of the spine. She wore a graceful fold of gray fur, fastened at the right shoulder with a bright blue stone. Her hair was white-blond and hung past her waist in a thick, intricate braid, the pattern not unlike one that Katherine had often admired in a famous Etruscan mosaic. But even though the creature was definitely feminine, there was no doubt that it too was as deformed as the males; there was far too much dissimilarity between it and a normal female human physique.

The woman held an infant on her lap; Katherine could see nothing of it but chubby legs and fat little feet waving in the air. The male was bending over the infant, dangling a shiny stone that twinkled with light over the baby, who crowed with laughter. The sound grabbed at Katherine's heart. Strangely, the woman did not seem to be involved in the game between the man and the child; her arms lay loose in her lap and her head was tipped forward in an attitude of what seemed like intense sorrow or grief.

Katherine became more attentive to the interplay between the two adults. The man lifted his face to the woman and spoke to her in a soft, sibilant language that Katherine could not identify. His eyes were fastened on her face and he seemed to be speaking earnestly, imploring her to do something. The woman's posture slumped even further, her head dipped lower, and it seemed to Katherine that she might well be crying quietly. Despite her concerns and fears, Katherine, so recently immersed in her own grief, felt herself drawn to the woman.

The male's voice faltered, broke off. He sighed heavily, a sound of sadness and despair as well as resignation. His chin fell to his chest and he seemed lost in thought for a moment. Hesitantly, he reached for the child and lifted it up to the woman, held it out to her, gestured with it, and even without knowledge of the words, Katherine knew that he was urging her to take it, to hold it in her arms. He repeated the words, jiggling the child, who chortled in delight.

The sound was so like those Cameron made that Katherine closed her eyes against the pain. When she opened them, they were blurred with tears and she saw the woman reach for the child slowly, reluctantly, and lift the baby to her shoulder. It was only

then, when Katherine blinked away the tears, that she saw the
child's face. She clung to the rock, for her knees had gone weak
beneath her, but she could not suppress the gasp that slipped from
her lips. It was Cameron! The child in the woman's arms was
Katherine's child—fat rosy cheeks, silvery blond curls, a dimple in
her right cheek, blue, blue eyes. There was no doubt whatsoever
that the baby in the woman's arms was Cameron!

She was so shaken, so stunned by the impossibility of what she
was seeing that it took a minute for her to realize that her presence
had been discovered. There was a movement, and she lifted her
eyes to meet those of the woman, who had twisted around to face
her. The woman's eyes were wide with shock, her mouth open.
The man had leaped to his feet, and in his eyes, which even in
Katherine's own sense of shock she noted were a pale, clear gray,
she read conflicting emotions, fear and rage foremost.

Katherine was stricken, unable to think what to do. She took a
step into the room, her hand lifted toward Cameron, who stuffed
several fingers into her mouth and began to suck noisily. The man
seemed jarred to action by Katherine's movement, and he leaped
to the far wall with two long steps and seized a gnarly club, made
from what appeared to be a heavy twisted root, and brandished it
at Katherine. He resembled nothing so much as a figure in a
museum diorama, a figure directly out of some prehistoric era. He
grunted at Katherine and waved the club above his head in a
threatening manner as he took a step toward her. His fear, if it had
ever truly existed, had been replaced by rage.

Katherine dared not take her eyes off him, for she knew that if
he could circle around behind her, he would kill her in an instant.
Already he was sidestepping toward the circular doorway; two
long steps such as he had taken to seize the club would certainly
bring him to the entryway. Katherine did not doubt that his speed
was greater than her own; she would never be able to make it to
the basement door before he caught her. She wanted to scream, she
wanted to cry, she wanted to run, to be safely away from this
place, to erase all knowledge of what she had seen, and most of all,
she wanted her child. She was afraid of this terrifying creature
with the club. All of her instincts screamed at her to run, to run as
fast as she could, but how could she leave without Cameron?

As though he had read her thoughts, the man roared, a
surprisingly deep, animalistic sound, unlike any made by humans,
and rushed toward her, eyes glinting madly, drawn back in a snarl,

exposing two long canines, and broad, overly large square teeth set
in a jutting jaw.

Katherine was so frightened that she stumbled backward. Only
an outthrust hand kept her from falling to the ground. Even then,
it might have been her undoing had not the woman flung out her
arm and called out to the male, who looked back at her with an
anguished, distraught look. The woman rose and placed herself in
front of the man. She flung a look back at Katherine, a look that
even without words conveyed meaning. The look told her clearly
that she was to take the brief opportunity to run, to escape; it told
her that the woman was not her enemy but that she could not hold
the man for long. All of this and more was conveyed, shared in the
single, agonized look.

Katherine gazed back, and in her eyes was longing and grief and
a silent prayer that the woman protect the child she was leaving
behind. She rose to her feet and ran along the darkened corridor,
past the dimly lit chamber with the sleeping figure who was now
rising groggily from its bed and stumbling toward the doorway.
Katherine raced past, seeing the sleep-filled eyes go wide with
shock. A voice, unknown words, called out to her. She ran.

Heavy footsteps beat the ground behind her; a crack of light
appeared in the darkness, an opening into another world. Breath-
less, her throat dry and raspy, she hurled herself at the door and
plunged through, fell hard onto the rough concrete, feeling her
knees bruise and bloody with the impact. She struggled to her feet,
reaching for the stairs, grabbing the rough stonework in her hands,
pulled herself up, propelled herself up the stairs, falling upward
more than climbing, and staggered, ran into the darkened room
beyond, feeling the darkness close around her like the embrace of
an old friend, hiding her, sheltering her from the horror she had
found.

NINE

❦

Katherine raced through the darkened rooms of the basement listening for footsteps behind her, expecting the club to come whistling out of the dark, wondering if she would hear it before it struck her down. Reaching the main room, the room nearest the stairs to the lobby, she dared to risk a backward glance and was surprised to see that there was no one behind her. Her steps faltered, but thinking that it was a trick, suspecting that the creature with the club was paralleling her in the darker shadows that ringed the area, she did not slow down. She took the stairs two and three at a time, her legs and lungs protesting, aching and burning as though she were scaling a mountain.

She threw herself through the door and slammed it shut behind her, twisting the small, brass knob that shot the lock. It would not stop such a creature for long, but it was better than doing nothing.

"Call the police!" she screamed, pressing her palms against the door and bracing her feet on the black and white marble tiles, the full weight of her body reinforcing the small lock.

"Call the police!" she cried in despair, turning her head to see if the doorman was doing as she bid. The man was standing as though frozen, half out of his chair behind the console, staring at her as though she were crazy. Standing no more than six feet away was the couple from 2B, Murdock, corporate lawyers, the pair of them. He was dressed in a tuxedo, his wife in a black velvet sheath and stiletto heals, a chinchilla stole, and diamonds at throat, wrist, and ears. The Murdocks stopped for a brief moment and then averted their eyes as they would while walking through a crowd of panhandlers. It was as though she did not exist.

Katherine burned with embarrassment and rage. She could feel the trickles of sweat dripping down her face, knew that her hair was wild and that her clothes were torn and dirty. Worse, she had never liked the Murdocks, had always thought them to be uptight, self-satisfied yuppie prigs. Now she literally burned with hatred and the injustice of being confronted by them of all people. But it didn't matter; none of it mattered, there was far more at stake than appearances and personal likes. "Call the police," she said through gritted teeth. "Hurry!"

The Murdocks did not even bother to ask her what the trouble was; the inappropriateness of her appearance and behavior made it possible for them to ignore her completely. She hated them in that moment as she had never hated anyone. Even in her panic, she could not help but wonder what they would do or think if they were confronted by the horrors she had discovered.

The doorman was torn between his regular duties and his obligation to his employer. Katherine could see him hesitate, tipping his hat to the Murdocks and glancing back at Katherine with worried eyes as though hoping that she had disappeared or composed herself. The Murdocks had evidently commanded him to whistle down a cab, but the doorman had come to a decision; crazy or not, Katherine was still his employer. He raised a finger and smiled ingratiatingly at the Murdocks, no doubt begging them to wait a moment, then turned to his phone and quickly tapped out 911. He spoke hurriedly into the receiver and then hung up. He stared at Katherine, clearly uncertain what to do next. She glared back, pressing her shoulder against the door, feeling the futility of such an action. The doorman turned, and with a ghastly parody of a smile, edged around the console and out the front door. She could expect no help from him.

There had been no sound from the other side of the basement door and her muscles were beginning to tremble with fatigue. Remembering the look of disdain the Murdocks had cast upon her, the look of apprehension in the doorman's eyes, she forced herself to think over what she had discovered. No. She was right and they were wrong, as they would soon learn. As everyone would learn as soon as the police came. They would go down with guns and lights and find those things and take Cameron away from them. But if Cameron had been kidnapped, taken away by those monstrosities, then who . . . what baby did *she* have? What child lay in the hospital and how could any two babies look so much alike?

Her mind was reeling by the time the police arrived. The number of questions without answers just seemed to grow no matter how hard she tried to put things together. She could not understand what was happening; she only knew what she had seen. Soon, others would know as well.

They were not the same two policemen who had come before, and for that she was grateful. Disheveled as she was, she was bathed and better dressed than the last time she had called for assistance. The police who had come before had already judged her, and she suspected that no matter what she said or did, their thoughts could not help but be colored by their unflattering opinion of her.

The two officers, one black, one white, were ushered into the foyer by the doorman. Katherine sagged against the door, muscles tense and aching with anxiety. Never had she been so relieved to see someone. She raked her fingers through her hair and smiled tentatively, hoping that she did not appear too disheveled.

The young black officer, whose name tag identified him as Wendell Collins, drew a notebook and pen from his pocket. "Yes ma'am," he said. "What appears to be the trouble?" Though he wore a pencil mustache, perhaps to make himself look older, Katherine realized that he couldn't be more than twenty-two, and she wondered if someone so young could handle the situation.

She chose her words carefully, fully aware that it would be all too easy for them to label her a nut case and then there would be no one to help her at all. "There's a door in the basement. It's old, hard to open. But I was down there just now and found it ajar. It seems to go under the building. I found rooms and people living down there, strange people, and two of them have stolen my baby."

The patrolmen stared at her. Collins had ceased writing and was observing her with a curious lack of expression on his face.

"Ma'am? Could you be more specific?" The question came from Callahan, who appeared to be even younger than his partner, slim and blond and looking as though a razor had never touched his smooth cheeks.

"Look, I know it sounds odd," Katherine said with a sigh, "but it's true, every word. There *are* strange people living down there. They have my baby and one of them chased me with a club. If you'll just go down there with me, you'll see that I'm telling the truth. I've got to get my baby back. Please, please help me!" She hated the pleading note in her voice, hated to be begging these two men, barely out of their teens, to help her, hated that she was so desperate and had no other alternatives.

The two men exchanged a glance. Katherine knew what they meant. They too had decided that she was merely another hysterical woman: too much time on her hands, too much money, too many drugs or alcohol, whatever—the look said it all. They did not believe her and they would not help.

"Look, I know what you think!" she said, stepping forward and gripping Collins by the wrist. She stared directly into his eyes, hoping that by making eye contact, she could force him to recognize that she was sane and make him listen to her. "There are strange people living beneath this building. They have my child. I'm begging you, go down there with me and see for yourself."

Collins stared into her eyes, still young enough and untouched by the layers of protective cynicism that came with the job, to be touched by the passion of her words. He blinked, breaking the connection. "C'mon, Ernie, we can spare the lady a few minutes to check it out. Lots of street people looking for a warm place to bed down. Maybe they've set up housekeeping in her basement."

Katherine could see that Callahan was less willing to humor her, but he did not argue, merely unclipped a long, heavy flashlight from his belt and reached for the door.

Katherine could scarcely believe that she had succeeded. Her mind whirled with conflicting emotions—elation that they had agreed to accompany her and fear of what lay ahead. She felt as though her nerves were leaping, twitching beneath the surface of her skin. The feeling was so strong that she had to look down at her hand and arm to convince herself that it was not so, that her distress was not visible.

There was no one on the stairs. The two officers went first. Collins motioned for her to stay behind, but she whispered, "You won't find them if I don't show you where they are." There was a moment of whispered conversation between the two young men and Collins gestured for her to follow. "You go back as soon as we reach this door," he said firmly. She nodded her agreement, knowing that she would do nothing of the kind. Callahan was staring at her coldly and she could feel his growing animosity. To him, she was nothing more than just another crazy lady.

The basement had the feeling of emptiness, there was no sense of others lurking in the shadows. Once again she traveled through the dark rooms, the silent observer in her mind marveling at her new-found courage, but after all that had happened, mere shadows were no longer capable of frightening her.

Then they were there, at the stairs to Stone's apartment. She motioned to them and pointed to the stairwell. The two policemen glided forward so swiftly, so silently, that she could not help but be impressed. They crept forward, flashlights held horizontally above their shoulder, gripped at the base where, if necessary, they could be used as weapons. The furnace humming softly in the background ignited with a sudden whoosh, breaking the tension that had built up in the small room, and startled them. Collins leaped back and Callahan gave a small, nervous laugh. Katherine could feel her heart pounding against her ribs. Collins and Callahan advanced to the edge of the steps and peered over the edge for a moment or two; then they withdrew, and all the tension seemed to drain out of their bodies. They straightened and looked at each other, then turned toward her. Collins avoided her eyes. Without being told, Katherine knew that something was very wrong.

"What is it, what's the matter?" she asked, pushing past them, stepping down into the stairwell. Her voice died in her throat. On the right was Stone's door, quite normal in every respect. Opposite, the wood door was once again fitted flush with the cement wall, heavily draped with cobwebs and grime, looking as though it had been there, untouched, for centuries. Had Katherine not opened it and passed through herself, she would not have believed that it was possible.

"Is this the door, ma'am?" Collins asked in a polite and impersonal tone. Suddenly Katherine was angry, furious. Without answering, she turned and ran up the steps, crossed to the workbench, and pulled a short crowbar off its peg. She took the steps two at a time, and before the policemen could stop her, dragged the tool across the thick panels, ripping the cobwebs away. "I don't know how they do it," she said between clenched teeth, "but I'm no dummy and I'm not going to be put off this easily. It'll take more than a few cobwebs to get rid of me." She fitted the crowbar into the tiny space between wood and stone, and bracing the bar against the cement, began to lever it back and forth, driving the wedge deeper and deeper. The old wood resisted her efforts. Hasty steps approached her.

"Here now, lady, you can't do that!" Callahan tried to take the crowbar away from her. Katherine turned on him in a fury. "Don't tell me what I can do and can't. This is *my* building. I own it. If I want to tear it down one stone at a time, or dynamite it into rubble, I'll do it. And I'll do whatever's necessary to get my daughter back. Now, she's in there, behind this door with strange people, people that don't even look human. And if you think I'm going to let a few cobwebs or two wimpy policemen keep me from getting her back, you're wrong. So back off!"

She did not even realize that she was holding the crowbar like a club, brandishing it as though she was about to strike, until the flickering eye motions of the two young officers brought her back to her senses. She lowered the crowbar, rested it on the ground and leaned on it, her hair falling over her eyes like a heavy curtain. She raised a shaking hand to her forehead and pulled her hair back, tucking it behind her ear. "Look, I'm sorry, I was out of line, but you've got to believe me. This door was open not twenty minutes ago, and I was in there. There are people in there and they have my daughter. I don't know how they did this cobweb stuff, but I tell you, I'm not crazy and I know what I saw. I'm going in there with or without you. Frankly, I'm scared to death of those people, and one of them did chase me with a club, but getting my daughter back is all that matters to me. Now, will you help me or not?"

Collins cleared his throat. "You know, Ernie, they have these spray cans now that make phony cobwebs," he said to his partner. "Saw it at a Halloween party; didn't look as good as these, but hell"—he shrugged—"maybe this is a new brand." His partner glared at him, unconvinced, and obviously angry that he was siding with Katherine. Clearly aware of his partner's displeasure, Collins continued in a conciliatory tone, but Callahan interrupted. "If there are people in there, then how did they spray all these cobwebs all over the door and the stone? Let's call it in," he said, starting back up the steps. "If there are people in there, people with clubs, plus a kidnapping, then . . ."

Katherine wanted to scream at him, to hit him with the crowbar, drag him back down the steps and make him help her. A seething wave of rage swept over her. She felt crazed, out of control, and at that moment she hated the young man whose only crime was that he doubted her and was exhibiting common sense, a fact she realized even as she was powerless to accept it. She opened her mouth to speak, but before she could say anything, the sound of whistling—cheery, happy whistling—filled the room, and a shadow fell over them. A figure started down the steps and then halted above them. The whistling stopped abruptly. Katherine looked up and saw a man silhouetted darkly against the warm brightness of the room. Just from the casual, loose-jointed way he held himself, she knew it was Stone.

"Something wrong, Mrs. Sinclair? Something I can help you with?"

The words were ordinary enough, the tone polite, but a shiver ran through Katherine, and she felt nervous and unsure of herself, a feeling she had not experienced since junior high. "Mr. Stone," she said coolly. She turned to Collins to give herself time to gain control of the confusing rush of emotions that had seized her. "Mr. Stone is the building superintendent," she said with a calmness she did not feel.

The three men nodded at each other, and even though the two officers retained the noncommittal form of professionalism expected of all policemen, she could tell that they were much more comfortable with Stone than they were with her. The same good-old-boy fraternity that never failed to infuriate her, the exclusive club whose only requirement for membership was that you were not a woman. The same club whose credo was that all women were emotional, fluttery, unreliable creatures, and that all men were solid and dependable. She closed her eyes for a second, trying to release the anger. Now, more than ever, she would need to stay calm.

"What seems to be the problem?" Stone asked with just the right amount of puzzlement in his voice. Callahan repeated her allegations. She watched the three of them with a dispassionate eye. Collins stood beside her, glancing at her from time to time, and she sensed a feeling of protectiveness and concern about him. She found herself wondering—no, it was more than that—betting that he and his mother were very close. He had been brought up to respect women. Which was more than she could say for his partner, whose every word dripped with barely veiled sarcasm as he finished the chronicle of Katherine's story, twisting her words to make them sound even more bizarre. There was a leaden feeling in her stomach as she waited for Stone to respond, to add the final touch, some word, some shared male joke, accompanied by a clap on the back, a wink, a laugh, and then they would be gone and nothing would have been accomplished except the destruction of her credibility with her only source of help, the police.

"Well, you know, Mrs. Sinclair has been troubled by this door for a while now," Stone said, his voice warm and concerned, seemingly worried about her welfare. "Don't have a clue what's behind it . . . never seen it open; it's always been like this, so far as I can remember. But if it'll make her feel better, why don't we open it up and take a look?"

Katherine could only stare at him in amazement, wondering if she had misjudged him. He had actually offered to help! She let him take the crowbar, and then moved aside, conscious of the warmth and scent of his body as he smiled his lopsided smile and edged into place in front of the door. He fit the crowbar into the crack, and setting his feet solidly, began to exert pressure. The ancient wood groaned, shrieked as though in pain, the agonized protest ringing in their ears in the narrow enclosure. Katherine realized that she was holding her breath. She leaned forward as a length of wood broke off. Stone drove the crowbar deeper into the opening, forcing the wood, slamming the gleaming blue-black length of metal into the crevice repeatedly, now arching it back and forth until finally, with a crack as sharp and as stunning as a thunderbolt, the bond was broken and the door sagged on hidden hinges, open at last.

TEN

❧

The hospital room was now bathed in a soft light, dim enough not to cause the child any further discomfort but bright enough to allow the doctors and technicians to work. The low wattage lamp stood outside the heavy curtain and only a diffuse glow lighted the small space where the child lay. She had been removed from the metal crib on Scarborough's orders, now that he was convinced of the truth of Anderson's claims. He would take no chances of the child being blistered by the metal rails of the crib. She had been placed in one of the plexiglass-and-plastic chambers used for premature babies. There was no metal here that could burn her skin, and more importantly, they could monitor a number of the baby's vital functions. The high-tech chamber was an invaluable tool in difficult cases, saving lives that would otherwise be lost.

But even the marvels of modern-day medicine might not save this one, Scarborough thought as he scanned the most recent statistics gained from the incubator and the battery of technicians who had responded to his worried summons. He was seeing it, but even so, he was having a hard time believing what he was reading. It just couldn't be true.

In a four-month-old child one might expect the red blood cell count to range anywhere from 3.1 to 4.5 million; her hemoglobin should range from 9.5 to 13.5 and hematocrit anywhere from 29 to 41. Those were the norms. But this child . . . her red cell count was 2.0, the hemoglobin was 6, and her hematocrit was 14. Her white count was a frightening low of 2.0. With those numbers, she

76

should be dead. There was also evidence that her fluid and electrolyte balances were seriously disturbed. His initial diagnosis of prerenal failure seemed correct; the child exhibited all the classic signs—extreme lassitude, fatigue, coarse muscular twitches, anorexia, vomiting, and malnutrition. It seemed impossible that she had lived this long without treatment.

But more than just the numbers and the symptoms, it was the matter of the child herself, the way that her features seemed to undergo actual physical changes periodically, rearranging themselves, shifting before his eyes, revealing an oddly shaped, thin, shrunken face. The brow was heavily pronounced, the forehead sloping back at a sharp angle, the cheekbones prominent under the wan skin which was drawn tight against the large skull. The eyes were huge, a pale silvery blue, and the wide mouth hung open in a listless cry. She looked like a misshapen gnome, similar to the children dying of famine in Ethiopia and Somalia. Then, just as quickly, in the blink of an eye, the features blurred and once again Scarborough found himself looking down at the rosy-cheeked, plump, blue-eyed infant with the rosebud mouth, whom Anderson had admitted. What was he to think? What was he to do? Which of the two visions was he to treat?

Had he not watched the child intently, personally observed the rapid, flickering changes transform the infant, not once but several times, he knew that he would not have believed it to be true. He had not believed Anderson, when the information was first relayed, thinking only that Anderson needed some sleep. Scarborough sat back and ran his fingers through his thick hair, his mind flicking through the vast accumulation of knowledge that he had acquired over the past ten years, trying to think of something, anything, that would account for the shape changing. He could think of nothing.

His first thought had been that of a pituitary disorder, similar to dwarfism or gigantism. But those disorders took place over a long period of time. Renal failure was potentially reversible if diagnosed and treated early, but progressed swiftly in infants if balance was not restored. If left untreated, there was the risk of bacterial infection from the use of IV's due to the compromised immune system. With her white count so low, she would be unable to fight off even the slightest illness. There was also extreme danger of congestive heart failure.

There was little or no urine output, and palpitation of the bladder did not give him reason to believe that it was obstructed.

Catheterization would be a matter of course, but not in the case of an infant this young.

In the absence of Dr. Bosch, who had not as yet answered his page, Scarborough, considering the critical state of the child, had taken it upon himself to order up and begin administering glucose and essential amino acids.

Patients, especially infants exhibiting advanced renal azotemia, often deteriorated in an unpredictable manner. It was absolutely necessary to maintain a normal fluid balance and blood volume as well as eliminating the intake of sodium and potassium. Immediate dialysis was also desirable but that procedure could not be initiated without the mother's approval, and so far they had been unable to locate her. He sighed, knowing that he had done all he could for the moment. Soon a nephrologist and a hematologist and a score of other specialists would swarm onto the scene. Bosch would take charge; at best Scarborough would be left hanging on the fringes of the scene. He knew that he had done all within his power, but still, he couldn't help wondering how and why the child's features had undergone the extreme physical changes he had witnessed.

Scarborough leaned back in his chair, feeling the deep ache of exhaustion in his shoulders and neck. He rubbed his tired eyes and forehead, trying to force his sleep-deprived brain to function. Then, it came to him with a lancet of electricity that snapped him upright and drove all thought of sleep from his mind. Suddenly he remembered what it was that the child reminded him of: prehistoric man, Neanderthal man! That sloping frontal bone, the prominent brow ridge, the recessive chin—that was exactly what the child looked like during the astonishing transformations!

Scarborough laughed then, and rapped himself on the forehead. That was what happened when you tried to get by on two hours of sleep a night; you started imagining impossible things. He chuckled wryly. There had to be some other explanation. He didn't know what it was, but sooner or later they would find it. He only hoped the child lived that long.

There was a commotion at the door, the heavy tread of footsteps, the scent of cigar smoke. Dr. Bosch, the baby's own doctor, had arrived. Scarborough rose hurriedly from his chair and pushed through the curtain to meet him. The two men eyed each other and nodded without speaking. The older man moved to the quietly humming incubator and looked down at the small, motionless figure within. He clasped his hands behind his back, the ever-present cigar, now extinguished, clenched between his big white teeth. He rocked back and forth on mammoth size 13 feet encased in expensive hand-stitched English leather brogues that made his feet seem even larger.

Dr. Bosch lifted the curved lid of the incubator and ran his hand lightly over the back of the motionless child. The huge, thick fingers, seemingly more appropriate for a butcher than a physician, were absorbing knowledge through his touch, transferring information in some mysterious manner from patient to doctor. It would be easy to write off the older man, ridicule him as a caricature as many of the younger interns did, but it would also be a mistake. The thick thatch of silvery white hair, the bushy brows, the lumpy potato nose, the thick lips clamped around the dead cigar, and the immense barrel-chested laborer's body was the costume that concealed a brilliant analytical mind as well as a truly compassionate heart.

Many doctors, exhausted by the demands of their profession, and, even worse, the demands of their patients who expected them to be everything from father confessor to divine healer, all in ten minutes time and for bargain-basement prices, learned to guard their emotions and protect the unceasing demands on time and soul. Benjamin Bosch was the exception. He had absolutely no patience with those who indulged themselves in whatever disease or psychosis was fashionable that month. He seemed to know at a glance who was truly sick and who was not.

Scarborough had seen him dismiss a wealthy society matron who was determined to find some clinically sanctioned reason why her child needed to spend time in a warm climate, preferably the Bahamas during the month of February. It would have been a harmless white lie, which would have satisfied the school system, and earned him the mother's gratitude and a fat fee. But there was nothing wrong with the child, other than an overindulgence in sweets and starches, a fact which he bluntly pointed out to the tightly corsetted irate mother.

Yet Scarborough had seen those same thick fingers soothe the tormented cries of a crack baby, racked with the agony of withdrawal from the addiction bequeathed by its vanished mother, the tiny limbs jerking and twitching in the grip of a million frazzled nerve endings. Those same fingers had caressed and soothed the small, damaged bit of humanity until its cries turned to whimpers and then deep, hiccuping sighs before it drifted into the all too temporary respite of sleep.

Anderson appeared then with a sheaf of papers in his hand and gave them to Bosch, who moved outside the curtain to study them. "You the admitting doctor?" he growled around his cigar. Anderson nodded. "You saw this blister form?" Anderson nodded nervously.

"You have to believe me, sir, I barely touched her. . . ."

Bosch waved him to silence and continued reading. "Scarborough, isn't it?" he asked, jabbing a thick finger at the pediatrician. Scarborough nodded. "What do you make of this?" Bright blue eyes regarded him intently. Scarborough gulped inwardly, not wanting to look or sound stupid in front of this man.

"It doesn't make a lot of sense, the red and white count, the whole CBC for that matter; none of the numbers are right and a few things are missing entirely." He recited the litany of symptoms, concluding, "I figure renal azotemia, I've started fluids." He turned the query back on the older man. "You delivered her, didn't you? Was there anything unusual at birth?" Turning the question back on the questioner was a trick favored by teaching physicians and it drew a brief appreciative quirk of the lips from the senior physician.

"Nothing unusual about the birth except it was a bit early," Bosch rumbled. "The mother was under a lot of stress, husband died of a heart attack couple days earlier. Too bad really, good folks, liked each other a lot, wanted a baby for a long time." He blinked, looked around the room, then turned to the two young doctors standing before him. "Where's Katherine? Where's the mother?"

Anderson squirmed like a child caught outright performing some misdeed. "Uh, I sent her home."

Dr. Bosch's heavy eyebrows shot up, bristling like angry caterpillars. "Sent her home?"

"Uh, I thought . . . it seemed . . . well, look, there were these huge blisters, right? And this stupid story. What was I supposed to think? It seemed obvious that she'd burned the kid and then got worried that she'd gone too far. We see it all the time!" he added somewhat desperately, hoping to justify his actions.

"I know you do." Bosch raised a hand to appease Anderson. "I might have thought the same thing had I not known the mother. Not Katherine, never in a million years."

"I've got a call in to Wilson in Hematology and Michaels, the nephrologist at Mt. Sinai; maybe they can give us some answers,"

Scarborough said, earning a look of gratitude from Anderson. "In the meantime, we can try to balance the electrolytes and get some glucose in her. She doesn't seem to tolerate formula. I've tried a couple of different things; everything comes right back up. Corroborates the mother's story."

Bosch merely nodded. "The temp is subnormal," he mused, scanning the papers he held.

"Yes, ninety-five. At that temperature we should be seeing some evidence of hypothermia, shutdowns, systems starting to fail aside from the renal system, but that's not happening—heart, lungs, brain scan, everything seems all right."

Scarborough hesitated, wondering if he should mention the altering of the infant's features, and exchanged a look with Anderson, who was obviously thinking the same thing. He hesitated a moment longer, trying to think of a way to tell Bosch what he had seen without the older man thinking he had gone completely insane. Then the opportunity passed as Bosch nodded, then shook his massive head. "I don't know if she'd live through a flush, dialysis, she's so small. We need to get hold of the mother, find out if she could have been exposed to any toxic substances, maybe something that got into her formula."

"I've tried to reach her," Anderson said. "There's been no answer. I'll try again." He seemed eager to leave.

The two remaining doctors regarded each other. "If it's renal failure," Scarborough asked, "then how do you explain the CBC, the light and food intolerance, and the blisters?"

"I don't have any answers," the older man answered slowly, rocking back on his heels. "All you can do in a case like this is deal with what little you do know, what we can do something about, and work from there. Can't do anything about this blood anomaly; we'll have to wait for Wilson and hope he can give us some answers. You've done the right thing ordering up the fluids; keep a careful watch on those." Scarborough felt a flush of pride at Bosch's words; his praise was doled out in small doses. "But there are a number of things we can do. Try to raise her temperature and balance her electrolytes. Give her some B12, try to get her hemoglobin stabilized. If that doesn't work, we'll try some whole blood. That's a start."

Scarborough frowned. "Do you think it's enough?"

"No, son, it's not enough, but it's all I can think to do at the moment, until we get some more answers."

For a moment, just for a brief moment, Scarborough thought

Rose Estes

about telling the older man about the shape-changing and the striking similarities between the baby and prehistoric man, but remembering how Anderson had acquitted himself under Bosch's disapproval, he quickly banished the thought from his mind. Besides, it just didn't make sense. What could a four-month-old human child possibly have in common with a being that had vanished from the earth more than four million years ago?

ELEVEN

The cracking splinter of the wood was loud in the small, confined area. But when it was done, the silence seemed to weigh even heavier on Katherine's trembling nerves. She became aware of her heart pounding in her chest and there was a nasty, bitter taste in her mouth. Her hands were clenched tightly together as though she were praying, and perhaps she was.

There was a brief moment of awkward shuffling as they sorted themselves out. Collins stepped through the dark opening, leading the way with flashlight at shoulder height, its bright beam illuminating the dank corridor. Callahan followed his partner, with Stone behind him and Katherine bringing up the rear.

"Smells funny, kinda like mushrooms," Callahan commented. His voice echoed eerily in the darkness and made them all uncomfortable, as though the sound of voices was somehow wrong in this place. No one answered, and Callahan did not speak again.

Everything was as it had been before—the dust, the cobwebs, the hard-packed dirt floor. Katherine wished that they would increase their pace instead of creeping along so slowly. The thought of Cameron being so close, in the arms of strangers, was almost more than she could bear. The room where the sleeping man lay was just ahead of them; she could see the outline of the doorway in the bright white beam of the flashlight. Grasping Collins's sleeve, she pointed to it silently. He nodded his understanding. They advanced slowly.

Raising his palm to indicate that they should remain where they were, Collins flattened himself against the wall and inched his way toward the rounded opening, flashlight in one hand, gun in the other. Pressed close to the wall at one side of the entry, he shouted inside, "You in there, this is the police. Do what we say and no one will get hurt. Toss out your weapons and come out now!" There was no answer, and he called out again, and then again. A sick feeling began to gather in Katherine's stomach. Instinctively, she knew that something was wrong, knew in that moment that there would be no answer.

The silence grew more and more oppressive each time Collins spoke, and when it finally became apparent that thee would be no reply, he shined his light into the room, then swung away from the wall and stepped into the doorway, crouching low, gun pointed into the room. Katherine could see the reflection of the beam as it probed the dark perimeters. Even before the young patrolman stepped back into the corridor, his gun hanging loose at his side, she knew what he was going to say.

"You say someone was living in this room?" His voice was polite, neutral. It was not what she had expected to her. A cold finger of fear sent a shiver up her spine. She pushed her way forward. Collins shined his light into the room so that she could see.

Everything was gone; the furniture, the clothing, the stone dishes, and even the lights that had been mounted on the walls. There was only a bare room, with one crumbling brick wall. A small mound of earth and rubble extended halfway into the room like the morraine at the foot of a glacier. The rays of light picked out a few lumps of coal coated with a heavy layer of dust; they appeared to have been there for some time.

Katherine put a shaky hand to her forehead. Could she have been mistaken? Was it possible that she had passed this empty room without noticing it? That the room she had seen lay still further down the corridor? She did not think so, but the only other explanation was impossible to contemplate.

Someone cleared their throat. "It's possible I made a mistake," she said, trying to keep her voice steady. "Maybe it's the next room." She pushed past them, lowering her eyes so that she would not have to see the looks she knew they would exchange, the looks men always shared, equal amounts of benign indulgence and tolerant exasperation, as though to say, "Women, what can you do!"

They made no move to stop her, merely fell in step behind her, lighting the way with their flashlights. It was clear that they had already decided that there was no danger, no intruders, no kidnapping; otherwise they would not have allowed her to lead the way. But they would see. She would show them. They would have to believe her once they saw the room and its furnishings.

Only there was no such room. Anywhere. The next doorway, which appeared on the left, not the right, was thickly draped with cobwebs, gray and dingy with age. Dried, brittle fragments of long-dead insects crumbled and rained to the floor when Collins tried to poke his way through. The next room, also on the left, was equally empty, with only a single wooden crate with the words GREEN RIVER written on its side, barely visible through the heavy layer of grime.

Collins turned toward Katherine, and his mouth opened to speak. His face was devoid of expression, but his eyes betrayed him; they were filled with pity. But Katherine did not want to hear his words, the words that would put a halt to their quest. Before he could speak, Katherine pushed past the cluster of men in the doorway and began to run down the corridor calling Cameron's name, barely able to see her way. Collins called after her, and she heard the gritty press of his footsteps as he hurried to catch up with her. The beam of his light bounced up and down erratically as he ran; had the floor not been so level, she would surely have fallen. And then out of the gloom, a wall appeared before her. The passage ended, just ended in a solid stone wall that had not been there before. It was at the juncture where the corridor had turned to the right, the corridor where she had last seen her daughter.

She stared in at the wall in utter disbelief and then, despite her resolve, she lost what little remained of her composure. She knew that she needed to remain calm so that Collins and Callahan would believe her, but all of her fears just seemed to rise up and overwhelm that small voice of reason. She reached out with a shaking hand to touch the wall, to feel it, to see if it was solid, real, not trusting her eyes. But it was as solid as brick and mortar could be.

"Nooo!" The cry was wrung out of the depths of her body and her hand turned to a fist and she began pounding on the wall, beating against it, feeling the edges of the brickwork cut into her flesh, yet not caring, knowing that somehow, *they* had erected the wall, put it up to stop her in the short time she had been gone. That was why they had not bothered to pursue her; they had used the time to wipe out all traces of their existence. But she knew what she had seen. She knew that they had been there and were still there, beyond the wall. Waiting.

Collins and Callahan were on either side of her, speaking soft, gentle, persuasive words, trying to calm her, trying to pull her away from the wall. But she wrenched free of their grasp, determined to find a way to break through the wall. They had just built it; there had to be a weak point, a chink somewhere. She could feel them there on the other side of the wall, feel their tension, feel them waiting, listening. She knew with every fiber of her being that they were there. Her fingers, dug, pried, ripped at the brick, ignoring the pain. The mortar that bound the bricks together was wet; she could feel the moisture under her nails. No, it was blood, her blood, but it did not matter, nothing mattered except finding a way through the wall.

Hands. Hands on her arms, hands gripping her own, soft, insistent voices in her ears. She shoved them away, reached out and ripped a flashlight out of an unsuspecting, incautious grip, began to bash it against the wall. Breaking glass, wildly radiating light coursing across the ceiling and walls. Curses. The flashlight was taken from her, and then she herself was gripped from behind by strong arms that pinned her arms against her sides, lifted her and turned her away from the wall, back in the direction they had come.

She screamed and tried to break free but it was impossible. She cursed and cried and tried to tell them what she knew, that *They* were there, there on the other side of the wall if only they would believe her. The overwhelming futility of her actions, the hopelessness, the sense of failure and loss, rose up in her, compressing her heart with pain.

Cameron. Cameron. It was all too much to bear; she felt the hot tears begin to seep from under her lids. She had lost control, they would never believe her again. Who would help her now? She sagged in the arms that held her and gave way to her tears, the sobs tearing through her body, wrenching her with their intensity. She felt a rough, bearded cheek pressed against her own, felt herself rocked gently back and forth, enfolded in arms that were protective rather than restrictive. A soft voice whispered in her ear, "Shhh, shhh, shhh, I know, I know." Slowly the tears stopped. She straightened, turned, freed herself from the strange embrace but was unable to raise her eyes, unable to face the embarrassed looks and averted eyes that she knew she would see.

Then, as though sensing her fears, a hand clasped her shoulder and squeezed it gently, reassuringly. She was aware of a presence behind her. There was another gentle squeeze on her shoulder, no more, nothing was said, but in that instant, Katherine suddenly felt that she was no longer alone. It was not the hand or the touch of a stranger, but of someone who cared. She did not need to look behind her to know that it was neither of the two young policemen; she knew that it was Stone.

They retraced their footsteps, returning the way they had come, filed up the steps into the basement, blinking against the sudden light and then, avoiding each other's eyes, they trailed silently through the darkened storage rooms until they emerged in the marble-tiled foyer.

There were words then, a good many words, words about misunderstanding and misinterpretation, words about grief and worry. Words. Words. Words. Too many words and none of them meaning anything. It was difficult to make the young officers leave, even more difficult than it had been to persuade them to stay in the first place.

Even though she knew that they wanted nothing more than to leave, to share the shaking of heads and amused jokes at her expense, they had to perform their duty. It would not do to leave a crazy woman on the loose, a crazy woman who might cause problems for them later. They queried her endlessly about friends and relatives she might ask to spend the night, and urged her to call her doctor. All this and more was endured before they finally took their leave. Even then, they only did so when Stone stepped in and assured them that he, a virtual stranger, would look after her, as though she were not competent enough to look after herself. *Hide the sharp knives and glass objects,* she thought bitterly as she watched the three men move toward the outer doors, shaking hands all around, nodding and smiling indulgently.

A burn of anger coursed through her as she watched them, the warm camaraderie that was so exclusively male—no women need apply—and then the anger faded, leaving total and complete exhaustion in its wake. Suddenly, she wanted nothing more than to be in her own bed with the covers drawn up over her head, safely hidden from whatever it was that was happening to her life. She turned away from the men and started climbing the stairs, not even glancing at Mrs. Orlowski's apartment as she passed, not wanting to see or talk to anyone.

Stone caught up to her at the second-floor landing and walked beside her without speaking. She turned to look at him when they reached the door to her apartment. "I'm not crazy, you know. They were there. It was just like I said it was."

Stone met her gaze for the briefest of moments; his eyes were a curious mixture of gray and green with flecks of silver. She had never seen eyes like that before. Then he dropped his gaze and seemed almost shy, yet there was still that sense of connection, a warmth between them that she had felt before.

"You've been in there, haven't you? You know I'm telling the truth. Why won't you tell me? The police are gone now. They won't be back; they think I'm a lunatic!"

Stone dug his heel into the deep pile of the carpet, his hands jammed into the pockets of his jeans. Katherine noticed that they hung from his hips far too loosely. She wondered if he was eating enough. *Listen to me,* she thought, *talking to someone I'm sure is holding back vital information, and I'm worried about whether or not he's eating enough!* Her anger at herself caused her to snap at him. "I'm not going to give up. You know that, don't you? They've got my child and I won't stop until I get her back. You can tell them that for me!"

She felt a childish sense of satisfaction in slamming the door in his face, but then, just as the door was closing, he raised his head and looked at her, and in that fraction of a moment as their eyes met, she read sadness and longing and unspoken sorrow. She raised her hand, started to reach forward, and then the door passed between them and closed, breaking the connection. She brought her hand up to her forehead, and closed her eyes, swaying for a moment with the opposing emotions warring within her. She wanted nothing more than to open the door, to feel the quiet strength of his arms around her, comforting her as they had done in the darkness of the black corridor. But how could she do such a thing? The man was a stranger. A janitor. Possibly even involved in the taking of her daughter. He was no friend; he was the enemy.

She forced herself to move away from the door, and as she did so, waves of exhaustion enveloped her. Her eyes wanted to close; it was hard to keep them open. She stumbled down the hallway to her room, her legs feeling as though they were made of stone, her feet numb. She tumbled across the bed, dragging the comforter over her body. Oblivion rose up to seize her, but just before it dragged her down into its depths, she remembered his words, those curious words he had spoken, whispered in her ear in the darkness: *I know . . .* he had said. *I know.*

Her dreams were a jumble of nightmare images, a collage of horror complete with sounds and smells. Once more she stood frozen in the doorway and watched her daughter being held by a strange woman. Once again she met the enormous, eerie eyes filled with hatred and rage. Once more she fled down endless dark corridors pursued by massive figures bearing clubs. Walls rose up before her, inexplicable walls that stretched in all directions, impossible to get around. Through it all, there was the sound of a child, a baby—cooing, chortling—normal happy sounds at odds with the horror she was dreaming. And the smell, it was there: mushrooms, damp forest loam, the smell of darkness. She wanted to waken, to stop the nightmare from unfolding, but she was unable to break free of the bonds that held her. Toward dawn the images faded and she drifted into a deep, unbroken sleep.

Her eyes opened. Light on the ceiling, playing over the dresser and mirror. Late morning, far later than she usually slept. It hit her immediately. The smell. They had been here while she slept! Katherine scrambled from the bed, heart pounding, looking around wildly. Cameron! She ran down the hall and threw open the door to the nursery, hoping against hope, praying that she would find the baby in her crib. Why else would they have returned? What more could they want? But the crib was empty. The sheets were still rumpled and soiled and there was a faint sour smell of sickness in the air.

She turned away suddenly dispirited, almost too enervated to stumble down the hall. She clung to the doorway of the bathroom for a moment, then entered, stripping off her clothing as she went, leaving a trail across the small white octagonal porcelain tiles. She rested her forehead against the coolness of the wall tiles as she turned the water on, hot, hot as she could take it.

Later, wrapped in one of the oversize Turkish towel bath sheets, she padded back to her room to dress. While showering she had paused to wonder whether she was being foolish, wondering whether she was in any personal danger. They had been in her apartment twice now. How they entered, she could not guess. They had been there in the night while she slept. Why? They had her child. What more could they want?

She found the answer the moment she returned to her room. How she had missed it before was hard to imagine, but tangled in the blankets was a small bundle that she knew had not been there when she went to sleep.

It was quite small, a long slender roll of some strange fur, tied with a strip of softly tanned creamy leather. She sat down on the edge of the bed and touched it gingerly, rested her fingers on it lightly. It was soft, nothing more. She got no sense of danger from it. She picked the bundle up; it was lighter than it appeared, the whole thing weighing less than a pound. The strip of leather was tied in a simple knot, which came undone with a single pull and the roll fell open on her lap. Carefully she spread it apart.

The fur was a baby's coverlet; that was all it could be from the size. The fur was extremely short and fine, a muted silvery gray color and soft as down to the touch. Katherine could not identify it; it was like no fur she had ever seen. Nor was it a single large pelt but hundreds of tiny squares joined together with tiny, all but invisible, stitches. Why? Were the small pieces the soft underbelly of some unknown creature or, impossible as it seemed, were the tiny pelts the size of the creature itself? If that were so, the animal could have been no larger than a mouse! Who would go to the trouble of skinning and tanning a mouse? Immediately, the vision of the woman with the braid came into her mind. Nonsense! This could not be a mouse fur, at least she did not think so.

Intrigued, she examined the coverlet more closely. The underside of the fur was lined with a single length of silky fabric that shimmered softly in the morning light, a pale ivory—no, more ecru in color—rich and lustrous and even softer than silk. It was joined to the fur at the edges, the edge of the fabric turned under and the two joined with the same fine stitchwork. The fabric was bordered by an elaborate bit of embroidery in pale blues, greens, and yellows. The pattern was vaguely reminiscent of early Greek or Minoan pottery designs. Again, the memory of the woman's elaborate braid flashed into her mind's eye.

Well, whoever had done the work was a master seamstress. Raised by a mother for whom the art of sewing, knitting, crocheting, quilting, and a full lexicon of embroidery skills were a matter of course, Katherine could appreciate what she was seeing. Nor could it have been an easy matter to piece all the skins, to join them so flawlessly and persuade the seams to lie flat. In the hands of anyone less than a skilled professional, the coverlet would have been a lumpy, irregular mess instead of the work of art and love that it was.

Lying in the last fold of the coverlet were two more items. One was a rattle. It was unlike any Katherine had ever seen, but it could not be mistaken for anything else. It was fashioned in a circle, just big enough for a baby to hold comfortably. But it was made out of what appeared to be polished bone! Threaded onto the circlet were smooth stones of varying colors. Summoning up her rusty geology, Katherine was able to identify golden amber, sky-blue turquoise, sea-green aventurine, scarlet carnelian, violet amethyst, moss agate, and inky obsidian, before her limited knowledge gave out. This too was a work of art, the smoothly turned beads clacking gently against one another as the circlet was turned. The beads caught the warm light that streamed in the windows, and held her riveted. She could easily imagine how a baby would enjoy such an object.

The third item was lying facedown and had been left for last because the coverlet and the rattle had drawn her attention with their startling workmanship and beauty. Yet as soon as Katherine lifted the object, she knew that it was by far the most important of the three. It was almost more than she could bear. She closed her eyes and let out a deep sigh. A rush of emotion swept over her and she felt like weeping . . . or laughing, she didn't know which. This, the object that she held in her hand, was the proof that she had been searching for. The proof that she was right, that someone, the people in the dark corridors below the building, had stolen her child.

It was a small cloth doll. She opened her eyes and looked down at it, examining it more closely. Compared to the beauty and workmanship of the other two items, it was almost crude. Clearly, it had been fashioned by other, less skilled hands. But that was not the point. The point was that the doll, although humanlike, was, like the creatures below, not human.

The head was overly large, the brow prominent, the forehead recessive. The nose was large and flattened with widespread nostrils. The cheeks were broad and flat and the chin almost nonexistent. The arms were longer than human arms, hanging nearly to the knees, and the body was thick and short. The doll was made of fabric, a different fabric than that used to line the coverlet—rougher, more durable, almost like cotton duck cloth. But it wasn't. Although she could not have said why, Katherine knew that it was not cotton.

It was clearly a girl doll, and the hair, attached to the head and drawn into a single long braid that hung down the back, was made of hundreds of strands of silky embroidery thread, pale yellow in color. The thread-hair had been anchored to the head by half a dozen large, tight stitches. Adequate, but impatiently done. No, the maker of this doll had not made either the blanket or the rattle.

The features were drawn on the surface of the material and these too were equally revealing, for the eyes were huge and silvery gray in color, much larger than human eyes and exactly like those she had seen on the creatures below. The brows, nose, and mouth were merely sketched in with a few brief marks, but they were more than enough to enable her to recall the features as they had been in life—heavy, brutish, primitive—frightening and definitely not human.

She turned the small doll over in her hands realizing belatedly the most important fact of all. These were gifts of love, the impassioned gifts of a grieving mother. Tears welled up in her eyes without warning and her heart began to ache, mirroring the pain in her breasts. Without a child to nurse, to relieve the pressure, the pain was always with her, a constant, physical reminder of what she had lost.

With the pain, came the thought of the other child, the one lying in the hospital. The child who looked like Cameron but was not. The child for whom these gifts of love had been intended. She knew then, as she regarded them through the blur of tears, stroked the soft fur, fitted her fingers through the circle of the rattle, that she had never been in any danger from whoever had entered her apartment and left them for her to find. No, it was not a case of whoever. She knew who had left them. The woman. The one with the braid. The woman who had held Cameron in her arms. That was who had left them.

Katherine wished that she could work up a rage, a feeling of hatred for the woman, for it would be easier if she could hate her. But it was not possible; she could not forget the slumped shoulders, the head bowed down with the weight of grief and loss. She knew that feeling. They were sisters, she and that woman, joined by their pain.

Whatever it was that was happening, Katherine could not believe that the woman had had any part in it; no mother would inflict such pain upon another. Somehow she knew that the woman had come here without the knowledge of the two men, slipped away in the dead of night to bring these small tokens of her love, and perhaps in a way, to reassure Katherine . . . a message from one aching heart to another.

For the first time, Katherine stopped to consider what the other woman would be feeling. Pain, sorrow, loss, the same terrible void that was tearing Katherine apart. She had a child but it was not her own. How could she help but worry about her own baby.

And what about the baby? Katherine had scarcely given it a moment's thought after seeing Cameron. The face of the child came back to her, the face she had seen for a few brief seconds at a time as Cameron's face blurred and the other face looked out at her with eyes devoid of hope. She could almost feel the tiny weight resting in her arms, smell the sourness of her faint breath, hear the weak cries as the child writhed in the light of day.

Two babies; one sickly, the other healthy. Somehow, the men had learned of Cameron's existence and they switched the babies, most likely without the mother's knowledge or acquiescence, perhaps thinking that Katherine would never notice the difference. She could not even begin to imagine how they had altered the baby's appearance; she could think of no way that such a thing could be done. It was like magic or a spell, but such things were not real.

But that was not the point. If they wanted Cameron so desperately, enough to kidnap her, surely she would be safe. But could she say the same for the child in the hospital?

Suddenly, a new, more terrifying scenario sprang to mind. What if that was not the case at all? What if they had counted on her discovering not only the difference but their existence as well? What if they were holding Cameron hostage, forcing Katherine to help them heal their own child!

All the pieces seemed to fall into place then. Who or what they were no longer mattered. Whether they were merely homeless derelicts or a colony of misshapen mutants, it would be impossible for them to walk into a hospital and seek medical assistance. They would have neither insurance nor funds, and their mere presence would most likely cause a riot. Cameron was being held as a hostage for the life of their child, and if it died, she would never see Cameron again.

TWELVE

It had been a small village; never in all the years of its existence had there ever been more than a hundred people. In Helga Orlowski's childhood, the streets, hewn from the flanks of the mountain on which the village nested, had bustled with activity. Long trains of muscular mules, laden with bundles of wood to keep the cold at bay, plodded up the steep slopes from the forests below.

But as she grew older, it was clear that the population was shrinking. Young men left with the pack trains, guided them up over the mountain passes and never returned, choosing instead to go out into the world to seek their fortunes. The young girls grew up and went down the mountain and entered into domestic service in the grand chalets. They too shed their ties with the old village life and returned only briefly to show off their machine-made clothing, stylish, insubstantial high-buttoned shoes, and ridiculous hats, to those they had left behind.

But Helga had never wanted to leave, for the mountain provided everything she wanted. Her parents had already been well past the usual child-bearing years when she was conceived. She had been much loved, and deserting them in their old age and infirmity was unthinkable.

It was not a difficult decision, for the busy towns of Below, as they were commonly called, had little attraction for Helga. She preferred the cold, clear vistas of snow-capped mountains, the pocket-sized grassy glades where icy springs bubbled and tiny strawberries filled the senses with the sharp sweet rush of taste and fragrance. The shaggy goats, with bells hung from their necks on stout leather collars, clearly identifiable by sound alone, provided thick, rich, creamy milk and cheese as well as wool for spinning. She even loved the sound of the wind howling around the eaves of the house, plucking at the heavy shutters, flinging ice and snow against them in the age-old battle between man and his environment. She loved the long winter nights curled in front of the roaring fire, toasting nuts and apples and thick crusts of bread dripping with cheese.

And in the year following the first great war she had also learned to love a young Polish soldier, one of the multitude who were sacrificed to the Cause. He had been found lying in a small wood at the edge of a huge bomb crater. At first the old men who had gone there in search of wood had thought him dead, for his uniform was in tatters, his skin blue from exposure, and his wounds terrible to behold. Only the bitter cold had saved him, staunching the flow of blood with a bandage of ice.

By the time he recovered, one leg was permanently shorter than the other and his left arm drawn up with bands of scar tissue, but it was of little concern, for the war was entering its final days and the front had long since passed them by. Crippled as he was, he was beautiful in Helga's eyes, who found much to love in his gentle nature and his delight in her mountain home. They were married in the spring.

Together they explored the mountain, and Helga shared her knowledge, naming flowers and trees and rocks and teaching him the labyrinthine paths that crisscrossed the slopes. Together, they had explored the dark, primitive mine shafts that men had sunk into the sides of the vast mountain, attempting to pry its riches free.

Gunter was intrigued by the dark, silent cavities, echoing with whispers of the past and drips of distant water, but Helga had been afraid. It seemed to her that someone or something stood just out of sight, holding their breath, waiting for them to take just one more step. After a time, she had refused to enter the tunnels. Gunter had teased her but he had not insisted, saving his exploring for moments of his own. The old men had warned him that the diggings were unsafe, but he merely nodded politely and continued on. Helga knew that she could not stop him, and prayed for his safety while doing her best to hide her fears.

All of those fears were forgotten in the excitement of her

pregnancy, and to please her, Gunter gave up his exploring. When the child was born, a healthy boy, strong and loud of voice from the very first moment, Helga had felt that her life and her happiness had been made complete. What more could any woman want?

All had been well until the child's third month. Helga had wakened later than usual, wondering what was wrong. Then it came to her. The child never let her sleep this late; usually he was awake at first light, crowing loudly, demanding to be fed. This morning there was nothing but silence. She turned to the cradle that stood beside the bed and tickled the baby beneath the down-filled comforter, waiting for the chuckle of sleepy delight. There was only a thready whine. Even now, after all the years, she could still remember the icy trickle that ran down her spine at the sound. She had snatched the baby up out of the cradle and looked into his face. It was his face, his beloved features that she saw, but the eyes, the eyes were the eyes of a stranger.

The child had burned with a fever that could not be quenched for three days and four nights. In that time Helga had barely left his side. She had watched helplessly as the fat red cheeks and plump belly withered and hollowed, and his skin turned a pasty bluish-white. He would not nurse, no matter what she did, and all the while the eyes had watched her with a haunted, defeated air. She watched in disbelief as the child's features changed. The forehead grew larger, more prominent, the brow jutting out over the fevered eyes. The nose had flattened and the chin receded. The women of the village had turned away then, crossing themselves. She had cried, she had prayed, she had bargained with her God, but in the end, despite everything, the child had died.

The women had tried to comfort her, tried to tell her it was God's will and that she was young and would have many more children, but nothing they said assuaged her grief. For a time she was inconsolable and the words of those who sought to comfort her brought nothing but pain to her heart. She took to wandering the mountain to be free of their voices and their pitying eyes. Among the towering pines, the high, windswept tors and bright blue vistas, slowly she healed. But one day as she sat on a rock watching the clouds perform their magic, she thought she heard the sound of a child's laughter, a young child, a baby. The sound was so like the one her own precious child had often made that she half-rose, anxious to be on her way, unwilling to share the spot with some happy family. But there was no one to be seen. She was on an isolated stretch of the mountain where no one, not even the goat herders, traveled. Curious, she turned and began to look for the source of the sound. Still, there was nothing, only the adit of an old mine all but hidden behind an ancient trailing of earth and rocks. Surely no one would be in there.

She had almost convinced herself that she had been mistaken, that she had heard only the wind, when the sound came again. This time it was easier to identify the source, for she was looking directly at it. The laughter had come from the old mine.

Cautiously, she crept to the opening, and brushing aside a curtain of trailing vines, she slipped inside, making every effort to keep to the side so that her shadow would not blot out the few rays of sun that filtered in through the mouth of the mine.

She could not have said what it was that made her so cautious, other than the fact that everyone she knew avoided the mines. Whoever it was, was most likely a stranger.

Moving slowly, silently, she advanced until she saw the soft glow of a light flickering on the earthen walls. She had reached a juncture in the tunnel. The light was coming from the left. As well as voices. She could hear the murmur of voices, male as well as female, although she could not hear the words. It seemed to be in a different dialect. There was also the sound of children playing, and there, there it was again, the sound of a baby cooing in delight!

There was nothing to shield her, nothing to hide her from sight, but the need to see who it was in that tunnel, the need to see the child, was far greater than any sense of caution. Without hesitation, she stepped out into the juncture of shafts and there before her was the most astounding sight, so astonishing that even after the passage of fifty odd years she could remember every single detail, for the scene was engraved in her memory and on her heart so sharply that mere years could never dull it.

It was a family, seated on stones around a stone lantern. Perhaps it was an outing of some sort, for there were plates of food placed on a pale blue blanket. But even though her mind absorbed those facts, it was the people themselves who drew her attention. There were two adults, a male and a female, an adolescent female, and on the blanket lay a baby, her baby. Dumbstruck, she could do no more than stare at the child. Then the infant turned his head and looked at her, even as his fat fingers grabbed at the toes waving so tantalizingly in the air above his fat tummy. He gurgled happily and the sound released her from the bonds of shock. She cried out his name and took a step forward, hands outstretched.

Equally stunned by her sudden appearance, the adults scrambled to their feet. The girl-child began to scream, a sound of utter terror. The woman snatched the baby from the blanket, and before Helga could move, the woman whirled and vanished into the gloom behind the lantern, dragging the girl-child with her. The male made no attempt to flee. He turned toward Helga with a look of steely resolve and lifted a club which she had not noticed before, thumping it into the palm of his hand as he advanced toward her. There was no doubt in Helga's mind that he meant to kill her; she could read it in his eyes. But she would not die in this place. She had to get back to the village and tell Gunter!

It was clear that she would not be able to outrun the man; he was only a few paces from her and would be on her in an instant if she turned her back on him. Her hand brushed the wall and her fingers settled on a stone, a stone as large as a fist which came loose as though it had been waiting there for her. Tending goats, one learned to be accurate with stones; it was necessary to drive off the wolves and wild dogs who came for the newborns. She threw the stone in a single, swift motion and struck the male in the center of his forehead. She did not wait to see what happened, but ran as fast as her feet would carry her. Ran all the way back to the village.

She entered the village screaming, almost hysterical, and soon a large crowd had gathered around her. Her words spilled from her lips like the torrents released in the spring when the ice caps began to melt. She tried to tell them what she had seen. At first the women were outraged, the men shaking their fists and pressing her for directions. But as soon as she began to describe the people in greater detail, the huge silvery eyes, the strangely shaped heads, the overly long arms, the women grew silent and turned away from her, drawing the younger children away, making the sign of the cross in the air above them, then covering their ears with the palms of their hands as though fearing that her words would cause them harm.

The men too fell silent and one after another turned away, averting their eyes, although whether from shame or fear she could not have said. She clung to the arm of the stonemason, a large, muscular man who had been a friend of her family all her life. A man who was afraid of no one and nothing. But not even he would meet her eyes.

Finally, only the priest was left. She fell to her knees in front of him, grasping the hem of his cassock in her hands. Tears poured down her face as she implored him to help. Even now they might still be in time if they hurried.

"The child is gone forever," the priest had replied. "He is dead and buried."

"No! No! I just saw him! He's alive!" she argued.

"The child is dead, he is lost to you," the priest said firmly yet gently, and there was pity in his eyes.

It was the same everywhere. No one would listen. No one would help her. For the first time in her life, every door was barred to her, friends and relatives alike. No one would talk to her.

Only Gunter, and it was clear that he was doing so only to humor her; clearly he thought that she had lost her mind out of grief. Helga did not care what the reason was, so long as he listened and went back with her to the mines. Once there, he would see the signs and they would follow the shaft and find their son.

Despite her exhaustion, she all but ran back to the cave, dragging Gunter along without regard for his leg. They could rest after the child was found. The cave was just as she had said it was; they entered, pausing only to light two lanterns, then plunged into the darkness with Helga leading the way. They came to the intersection and Helga turned left and found herself standing in an empty corridor. She had not expected to find the man still lying on the ground, but surely there would be some sign revealing their presence; tracks, blood, a bit of spilled food, something. Anything. But there was nothing. Nothing at all to support her claims. She would not accept the fact that they were gone, would not allow herself to believe that the child she had so miraculously found was lost to her again. She insisted that they search further, and they did, penetrating deeper and deeper into the inky depths until it was Gunter who became afraid and insisted that they leave. She would not listen and hurried on, sliding now, slipping down a steep incline that ended in a black pool of water. There was no way around it and the dying flames of her lantern showed her that this was where the shaft ended. Even then she did not give up, but retraced her steps over and over in the days that followed, searching for another corridor. She never found one. Nor did the right-hand tunnel provide any answers, ending abruptly in a rock fall a short distance from the intersection.

The priest tried to reason with her, reminding her over and over of the child they had buried. Her friends and relatives talked loudly and cheerily, ignoring the issue completely, changing the subject whenever she tried to bring it up. Only her mother, now very, very old and confined to bed and rocker, listened to her. Late one night as the tears came again as they so often did, her mother called to her.

THIRTEEN

The phone rang as Katherine left the apartment, but she did not stop to answer it; such things had little meaning for her. Cameron was all that mattered; she had no interest in anything else.

Mrs. Orlowski was waiting in the foyer, sitting on one of the gilt chairs that stood against the wall. She rose to her feet as Katherine descended the staircase. Katherine was shocked at her appearance; the woman seemed to have aged greatly, dark, bruised-looking circles sagged beneath her eyes, and the lines alongside her nose were more deeply engraved in her flesh. She stood clutching her huge purse, clearly uncertain of her welcome. "We will talk now, yes?"

Katherine was anxious to get to the hospital, but she was concerned about the older woman and wondered once again if she knew something, had some bit of information that would help. She nodded brusquely. Together, without speaking, they left the building, crossed the street, and walked a block to a coffee shop located in one of the nearby condominiums. Neither of them spoke until their cups of coffee and hot tea arrived.

Mrs. Orlowski stirred several heaping teaspoons of sugar into her tea, an air of distraction on her face.

"You had something to tell me," Katherine prompted. The older woman nodded and then began to speak in a low tone. "I could not be sure, you see. I did not know . . . it has been so long. I did not want to speak, to say. So many people would think I was crazy. You understand, yes?" For the first time, she raised her eyes and met Katherine's gaze. The pain was clearly visible, the anguish apparent.

Katherine nodded. After all that she had been through in the last few days she most certainly understood what the older woman was saying. "How do you know about them?" she asked. The older woman stirred her tea, the spoon clinking against the sides of the cup. She seemed to come to a decision. "I would like to tell you a story," she said, her accent becoming more pronounced, her voice taking on the singsong rhythm of a storyteller.

"I was born long, long time ago in the mountains between Germany and Poland. Sometimes we belong to Germany, other times Poland. We live high, high up on the mountain, far from people below. When I was little, I think there are so many people in our village, but now I know that this is not so. It was simple life. The men, they take people over the mountains, through the passes, and they go Below to cut wood. The women, we tend the goats and sheep, spin and weave the wool, and mind the babies and the families.

"I am happy in my village. My mother and father, they are already old when I was born. I am only child. The young men, many leave, they guide people over the mountains and they do not come back. The young women, they go to the grand manors Below. They come back only to show off their fancy store-bought clothes and their babies. I do not wish to go, and I cannot. I must stay and care for my parents.

"And then the war comes. The first Big War. Mostly, we stay out of it; high on our mountain we are safe. Down Below they are not so lucky. One day the men, they go Below to cut wood. There are big holes in the ground. Bomb holes. Many people have been killed. They find one young man who is not dead, and him they bring back to the village. Gunter is his name. He is hurt bad; his leg it is mangled and at first we think that we cannot save it. But the cold, it was his friend, it stop the bleeding. When he heals, one leg is shorter than the other, and one arm, it cannot move as good as before. But still, he is alive.

"Gunter and I, we spent much time together that winter as he heals, and in the spring, we marry. He cannot go back to war and so he stays with us. Everyone is happy.

"For a time, everything is good. Gunter and I, we get along good, spend much time walking on the mountain, making Gunter's leg stronger. Gunter is from big city, has never spent time in the outdoors before. He grows strong and healthy. Soon, he leads the way and we explore many places that I have not gone before. I think that I know my mountain, but Gunter, he finds places I have not been.

"On mountain there are many caves; some are made by animals, but others they are made by men long, long time ago. I tell him they are not safe, but Gunter is like most men and will not listen to women when mind is set. He go into holes and want me to come too. I do not want to go. I do not like the dark and I am fearing that it is falling down on us. Gunter he just laughs at me.

"Then I am pregnant, and to please me, Gunter does not go in tunnels anymore." Here Helga's narrative tapered off and she regarded her cup of tea without really seeing it.

"Did he change his mind later?" Katherine prompted impatiently, wondering where the story was leading.

"No, he does not break his word," Helga said slowly. "The child is born. It is a boy. Martin, we name him, after my father. He is big, strong, big voice, healthy. All is good. Then, one morning, he does not cry, does not wake me with his noise, does not say 'pick me up, feed me,' as he say every morning. At first I do not know what is wrong. Then I see sun on the wall and know it is late. I think maybe Martin he is growing up, let his poor mother sleep longer. Then I get up and go to cradle."

Helga's voice had dropped to a whisper, forcing Katherine to bend over the table toward her to hear what she was saying.

"I see my baby, Martin. He is just lying there looking at me. His eyes, they are so big, bigger than before, and there is a look in them that I do not see ever. It is like he is very sad, like he knows something too terrible to say. His eyes, they are not brown like before, but they have silver in them, like little streaks."

Katherine's heart gave a little leap. Silver flecks—she had seen those same streaks in Cameron's eyes—silvery streaks that had not been there before!

Helga continued without noticing Katherine's startled movement. "Always before, he was pink and red on the cheeks, and everywhere he looks fat and healthy. Now, there is no more red cheeks and the pink it goes away. The fat it melts away. Soon, he is thin and pale and I think this baby will die. The men they go to Below for a doctor, but he says there is nothing he can do, that the baby will die.

"We sit with our little one day and night, we do not sleep. He will not nurse. He will not take honey from my finger and always he gets thinner and his skin I think it gets gray. The light hurts his eyes and he cries if there is even a candle shining on him. We sit in the dark and hold our child. He dies on the morning of the fourth day. I never forget that moment. His eyes, they are all silver now, they look at me, watch my face. So sad, so sad those eyes. It is like he begs me to help him but he has no strength and no words to say. I never forget. That is why, when I see this baby, your baby, I think, I must help if I can. But I do not know how."

"The blisters—" Katherine began. "Did your baby . . ."

"Ya, it was the same. I wrap a necklace, a cross blessed by the priest, around his wrist, and the blisters came up right away."

Katherine thought that the tale was done, but Helga continued. "We bury my Martin, my beautiful little boy in the churchyard, and all the women they tell me that soon we will have another. That he was taken home by God and that it was God's will. They think to make me feel better, but I do not feel better, and every day the pain it is worse. Soon I cannot sit indoors and pretend that everything is all right. I must be outdoors or I think I will go crazy. I only can bear the pain if I am walking. I do not want to hear voices saying stupid words. They do not feel my hurt, how can they think to make it go away with their words?

"One day I am high on the mountain in a place I have never been. I am sitting on a rock seeing the clouds and thinking about my Martin. Then I hear his voice. He is laughing like he do when I tickle him or blow on his belly. At first I think I am maybe crazy like everyone whispers, then I listen good and I hear the sound again. I do not dream it, I really hear it. It is a baby. It is Martin. I get up and I look around me very careful, very quiet. I see nothing at first. Then I see dark hole covered by bushes. I go listen. The sound, it is coming from the dark place. I do not want to go, I am afraid, but the sound, the laugh, it will not let me go. It is stronger than my fear. I go into the hole. It is a tunnel I see, made by the old ones. I walk quiet, very quiet so I can get close to the sound. My mind, it asks me, *Helga, how can this be, the baby is dead?* but my heart it does not listen, it hears only the sound of the child.

"The tunnel, it is older than others, dirt comes down on my head every step, but I do not stop. It is hard to see but I keep going. I come to a place where tunnel goes to left and to right. The sound of the baby, it comes from left. Now I hear other voices, words I cannot understand. I think, someone has stolen my baby, and I walk faster. I see a light. It is strange light, silver and gold and soft, not like fire or electricity which I see one time when I go Below.

I creep up, oh so quiet, and then I see this light, and what I see in the light I never forget."

Katherine wanted to shake the older woman, who chose that moment to stop and stir her tea. Her eyes were averted as though she was not seeing the coffee shop at all, but the inside of a dark tunnel.

"There were four of them," she said abruptly. "One was man, big, many muscles, with very big round silver eyes. There was small girl with thin arms and body, and long, long white hair. And there was a woman and she holds my Martin in her arms. We look at each other, the two of us, and I start to walk to her, holding my arms up like maybe she will give me the baby. Sometimes still I dream about this. The woman, she is not my enemy—this I know and I am not afraid. She looks at me and gives me the child. I feel his weight in my arms and then I wake up. Those dreams are very hard. I still feel very bad even after so long."

"But she did not give you the baby," Katherine said.

"No, she did not give me the baby. The little girl, she scream, and the man, he picks up a club and start to come after me. I know he will kill me. My hand, it finds a rock in the wall and I pull it loose and throw it at the man. We girls, we learn to throw rocks to keep the baby goats safe from eagles and foxes and wolves. I hit the man in the head and he falls down. There is blood everywhere and the little girl she is still screaming. I run as fast as I can. I go to my village and tell everyone what I see. I try to make them go back up the mountain with me, but they do not want to go.

"The men, they think I am crazy, I can see it in their eyes. The women, they try to take me home. The priest, he tells me that I should pray and that God will ease my pain. But I cry and cry and beg them to come with me. But they will not go.

"Only Gunter will go and I think it is only to calm me, but I do not care so long as he comes. Gunter, he has gun. If they are there in the tunnel, I think we will get the baby back. It is nearly dark when we get there. Right away, I know something is wrong. The smell of dirt is in the air. I run down the tunnel ahead of Gunter. He calls to me to stop but I am too afraid to listen.

"I come to the place where the tunnel branches, and on the right, the tunnel is collapsed, blocked from top to bottom with dirt and big stones. I go left. I come to the place where I see the people. They are gone, there is nothing there, no light, no blood, no nothing to show that I tell the truth. I cannot stop, I keep running, calling Martin's name. Finally, I come to end of tunnel, a black pool of water. On the other side, there is a wall of rock. There is nowhere else to go, nowhere else to look."

Helga continued to stare down at the table, her eyes bleak and empty. The cups of tea and coffee had grown cold, untouched by either woman throughout the long story. The waitress, annoyed that they were taking so long to vacate a table that could be used by others who would leave better tips, approached with their check, only to be put off by a grim glance from Katherine and the sight of tears glittering in the older woman's eyes. Katherine turned back to Helga. Her story told, she seemed depleted, physically smaller.

"And you never saw them again?" Katherine asked softly.

The older woman did not answer, merely shook her head. "But always I think that they are there, somewhere close. I feel them here." She touched her heavy breast. "I know that the child, my Martin, is there even though I cannot see him. I go back sometimes to that tunnel and I leave things, food, toys, clothes I make. Sometimes they are gone, sometimes not. I do not know who takes them, maybe only animals."

"And your husband . . . Gunter?"

"He never believe me. He think like all the others that I lose my mind when the baby die. It was not good between us after that. He want to have more children, but I, I cannot forget the other. Then, my father, he died, and then Gunter, he leave. We cry, the two of us, but we know it can never be all right again. You. You understand what I say, how I feel?"

Katherine nodded, taking the older woman's hands in her own, trying to imagine what it would be like to have Rod here to share this nightmare. But what if he too refused to believe her? What would she have done? "What happened then?" she asked. "Did you ever seen them again?"

"No. I never see them. I walk mountains for many years. People in village avoid me. I am the crazy woman," she said bitterly. "Only the old women, my mother, they believe me, but they say that my child is changeling. You know about this?"

"Changelings?" Katherine's brow furrowed at the word, trying to dredge up the memory it evoked. "Aren't they something that fairies bring, charmed babies, something like that?"

"Trolls," Helga said bitterly, spitting the word out of her mouth like a bad taste. "Not fairies. They bring sick babies and change for healthy babies. Magic makes them look the same. I do not believe the old women and tell them to leave me alone. Then no one speaks to me and I am alone. One day mountain shake. Ground shifts, moves under the feet, rocks fall. Many houses in village, the church, they are destroyed. Some people die. After that, the feeling here is gone." Once again she touched her breast. "I know my child is dead. There is nothing to keep me on mountain anymore. My mother is gone now. I leave the mountain forever."

"But you married again," Katherine prompted.

"Ya. I marry two times more, but there are no more children. I think something dies inside me. And never I tell anyone this story until now."

"I believe you," Katherine said, and taking a sip of her cold coffee, she related the events that had occurred the previous evening. The two women looked at each other, realizing the importance of their shared knowledge. "Do you think that they are the same creatures?" Katherine asked.

"The smell, it is the same. The way you tell me, it is the same as what I see that time on the mountain."

"What are they? Why are they taking our children? Surely you don't believe this nonsense about changelings—that's a fairy tale!"

"At first I do not believe," Helga said, sipping and then grimacing at the taste of her overly sweet, cold tea, "but now I think maybe yes, it is true." She held up a heavily ringed pudgy hand to silence Katherine. "No. Listen. I spend much time thinking, thinking about this. This is what I think. Sometimes babies are born with things worse—harelips, cleft palates, club feet, big heads. People in small villages long ago, they do not have learning, doctors. What are they to think? Sometimes they think such babies are punishment from God. Sometimes they think it is the evil eye, witchcraft. But sometimes, to make themselves feel better, to take blame from them, they say babies are changelings. This lets them think that healthy babies are stolen by fairies, trolls, whoever, and replaced with horrid changelings. You see, this takes guilt away, makes them not to blâme."

"Yes, I can see how that might be," Katherine acknowledged. "It would be a lot easier than thinking you had produced a malformed child, but the difference is that this is only a fairy tale. Surely those women did not really believe those stories."

"In heads, maybe not. But maybe the stories, the fairy tales, start because babies are stolen. Who is to say which come first?"

"So, these things. They are the same both in Europe and now

here. How could that be? How could such creatures cross an ocean?"

"I do not know. I do not see them, but what you say . . . they are the same. And the smell, it does not change."

"What am I going to do?" Katherine asked. "What about the baby in the hospital? Do you think if she lives that they will give Cameron back?"

"I am only old woman. I do not know the answers to these questions. I only tell you what happen to me. I will help if I can, but how can I help you when I could not save my own child?"

"I must go to the hospital," Katherine said. "But they will have questions. What will I tell them?"

"Just what you say already. The baby is fine and then she is sick. You are the mother, you do not hurt the baby, you have nothing to hide."

"Don't I?" Katherine said, shaking her head.

"We do not tell them that," Helga replied firmly. "Come. I go with you. I think it is better not to be alone."

"Yes, it is. Thank you for telling me your story. I'm sorry if I made you feel bad, but I thought . . ."

"You thought maybe I keep something from you. That maybe I steal baby. I know what you think, is all right."

The young intern's eyes were filled with exhaustion; his thinning blond hair lay limp and streaked with perspiration on his high forehead, but he hurried toward them with outstretched hands the moment they stepped out of the elevator on the pediatric ward. "I've been calling you," he said in an aggrieved tone.

"Sorry, I wasn't answering the phone," Katherine said, taken aback by the change in his attitude. Yesterday he had thought her on a par with child molesters and practically commanded her to leave; today he was welcoming her with open arms. "The baby . . ." Her voice faltered, unable to voice the question.

His face grew grim. He looked down at the floor, his eyes hooded. "Her condition is stable but serious. We've raised her temperature and gotten some fluids into her, but there are some abnormalities that we'd like to ask you about." Katherine drew back.

"No, no, I didn't mean that the way it sounded." He raised a hand and drew it back across his hair. "I've been up all night. I'm tired. I didn't mean to suggest that you have anything to do with these problems. We'd just like to talk with you, see if you can help us out with some information, help us understand what it is that's going on here. And I'd like to apologize for the way I acted last night. You have to understand, we see so many children with burns, bruises, injuries . . ."

Katherine waved his words aside. "There's no need to apologize, I understand. I couldn't believe it myself when it happened. Could we talk later? Can I see her now?"

"Oh, sorry!" Anderson seemed younger and younger with every apology. "Of course, we'll talk later."

It took a moment for her eyes to adjust to the darkness of the room. A dim light was burning in a corner, and a dark curtain encircled the crib. Katherine pushed it aside and entered the small space. The crib was gone and in its place stood a cold, sleek, modern-looking stand which supported a fully enclosed box. The base was a maze of dials and softly glowing red and green lights. There was a steady whoosh in and out, in and out, as though someone were pumping a bellows. The hood of the box was made of clear, rounded plastic, and Katherine stepped up to the side and looked down into the interior. The baby was lying on her stomach. There were a multitude of tubes and wires connected to her tiny body, so many for such a tiny scrap of a thing. Katherine ached at the sight of her.

At first she thought that the child was sleeping, but then, as her eyes adjusted to the pale filter of light, she realized that she was awake. An eyelid twitched, the eye gleamed. Katherine wanted to raise the lid of the machine—it seemed such a horrid, cold device—and hold the child. But she stopped herself. The machine, those tubes, they might be the only thing keeping the baby alive. But it took the heart out of her seeing the child like this.

Already there were changes in just the short amount of time that she had been gone. The skin seemed thinner, more translucent, as though if she looked closely it would be possible to see the bones beneath. It also seemed as though the structure of the skull was changing. The forehead seemed to bulge a little more than it had, the fine blond brows pushing out further over the sunken eyes. The tiny fist moved, the fingers fluttered and then hesitantly moved upward, slowly, as though it took all her strength to make even that small gesture. Three little fingers crept between the dry lips, and the eye closed as the baby sucked on its finger, drawing what little comfort she could from her own small body.

Tears came to Katherine's eyes and she swallowed hard against the lump that had formed in her throat. Was it possible that they could save her? Surely with all their knowledge they would be able to keep one little baby alive. She willed herself to believe that it was so.

Anderson and Helga were waiting for her in the corridor. Helga's eyes held questions. Katherine could do no more than shake her head, the tears burning behind her lids, ready to fall. Anderson guided her to a chair.

"I, I brought a toy, her favorite rattle," she said with a shaking voice. "Could I give it to her?"

"I don't think it's a good idea to introduce anything foreign at the moment; it's a controlled environment," Anderson said. "But Dr. Bosch is the man to ask, he's in charge now. I'm just here because, well, because I wanted to know, to see . . ."

"To see if she would make it," Katherine finished the sentence for him bleakly. Anderson blushed.

"He knows you're here. He wanted to know the minute you arrived," Anderson said, and soon, all too soon, they were surrounded by Dr. Bosch and a bewildering number of associates with specialties Katherine had never heard of and barely understood the meaning of, and all of them were seeking answers.

The interrogation, for that was the only word that could describe how it felt, seemed to go on for hours. In fact, it lasted barely forty-five minutes. The two women had been bombarded with questions, few of which they could answer.

FOURTEEN

The light had faded from the windows outside the curtain. All day Katherine had sat beside the incubator, listening to the soft humming, the muted bleeps of sound that indicated respiration, heartbeat, and a dozen other bodily functions of the small creature huddled beneath the lucent dome.

She felt so helpless and useless. There was nothing that she could do to help the dying child. The doctors had tried to encourage her with the soft, comforting words that health-care practitioners liked to use, words and phrases that upon analysis really said nothing at all that one could hang any hope upon. She supposed they learned to talk like that in order to avoid malpractice claims.

Throughout the course of the day they had drawn numerous vials of blood, too many for the small child to spare, Katherine thought, but Dr. Bosch swore that it was necessary to help them in their search for the source of the problem.

Katherine wanted to scream at them, to shake them, to make them see the *child*, rather than the "problem" or the "case" as they tended to refer to her. She supposed that such terminology helped them distance themselves against the possibility that the "case" might be "lost." *Case* and *lost* were much easier words to deal with than the alternatives, "baby" and "die."

It seemed to Katherine that the child would surely die. Already, in the time that she had been here, the baby seemed weaker, her breathing more labored. Late in the afternoon the doctors had conferred, a solid wall of white coats, and a tank of oxygen had been wheeled into the room, and yet another set of tubes had been connected to the infant. Katherine unconsciously matched her breathing to the baby's and grew apprehensive each time a breath came more slowly, labored raggedly with a bubbling, fluid sound that was painful to hear.

Helga had wanted to stay, had insisted that she would do so, but it was clear that the old woman was not feeling well. She touched her hand to her chest often and her color was a pasty white. Katherine had overcome her objections by promising to call if there were any changes in the baby's condition. Helga had not wanted to leave her alone, but strangely, Katherine felt stronger, more in control, than she had before. Perhaps knowing that the child was not really Cameron enabled her to be strong. She did not want anything to happen to this baby or to any other child, but still, the knowledge that it was not Cameron in that incubator, was not her child who might yet die, made all the difference.

The child seemed to know that she was there. From time to time when Katherine stood over the arched plastic hood, the baby's eyes turned in her direction, and the fingers with their impossibly tiny nails twitched on the sheet. Katherine wondered at the fact that no one mentioned anything about the baby's appearance. Surely it had to be obvious to someone besides her that the child's brow was jutting so prominently out over the eyes. Didn't they think that was strange? And what about the eyes which were becoming more and more silver, crowding out the dark blue pigment. The irises were nearly totally silver now. She had pointed this out to the young resident Scarborough, who had patiently explained to her that infants' eyes were often blue at birth and then changed as they grew older. Obviously, Cameron's eyes were taking on their permanent color, which would be gray.

"They're not gray, they're silver, can't you see that!" she had cried, gripping the young man's upper arm tightly. He had smiled patiently, and filled with despair at his inability or unwillingness to see, she had turned away.

She sat in the dimly lit enclosure and wondered what it would take to make them believe. Then, with the baby's breathing harsh in her ears, her eyes drooped and she slept.

"Well, what do you make of it?" Benjamin Bosch asked the younger, smaller man, Robert Wilson, a renowned hematologist who had been poring over the data contained in the manila file.

"You're certain that all of this is correct?" Wilson asked, tapping his folded tortoise-shell framed glasses against the palm of his hand, a gesture Bosch knew well, having worked with the man before. It was a move he used to give himself time to think.

The older physician snorted his displeasure and lit his cigar, which by this late hour was half its original length as well as soggy and unappetizing to anyone but Bosch. The thick blue aromatic smoke swirled around his head, wreathing his overly large features in a dense cloud. "Of course I'm sure. You think I'd waste the time of an important man like yourself with inaccurate figures?" He did not bother to hide the sarcasm in his voice.

Wilson looked at him with exasperation. "Must you smoke that foul thing?" he asked in an aggrieved tone.

"I must," said Bosch as he grinned around the short smoking stub. "Quit stalling. What have we got here?"

"What we've got here is an impossibility," Wilson said petulantly. "The figures just cannot be true, the child could not be alive with blood like this. The red count alone . . ."

"I assure you that she is alive, although for how much longer I cannot say."

"You delivered her, you say." Bosch nodded. "And there was nothing wrong with her blood at birth?"

"Entirely normal, A-positive, just like her mother."

"Interesting. I'd like to do the postmortem."

"I'd like for there to be no postmortem," Bosch shot back angrily. "I'd like for the child to live. Come on, man, help me out here, you're the expert. What's going on? What can I do to save this one?"

Jolted by the older man's tone, Wilson turned back to the papers in his hand. "I don't know what's happening," he said in a distant voice. "According to these figures, there's no reason for this child to even be alive. None of it makes sense. Her blood simply does not match any known blood type. Other than a complete transfusion, I don't know what you could possibly do to save her. If the extreme anemia doesn't kill her, then anything could hit her. With this low a white blood count, her immune system is practically nonexistent. Pneumonia will undoubtedly set in and then some secondary infection will finish her off."

"A transfusion? Would it help her?"

"Who's to say? It might, but you'll have to find out the underlying cause of these deficiencies or it will only serve as a temporary respite, a stopgap measure."

"But it'll buy us some time and that's what we need," muttered Bosch, his big square teeth clamped around the cigar.

"You need a miracle, is what you need," replied Wilson.

"You'll monitor the procedure?" Bosch asked.

Wilson nodded brusquely. "First thing in the morning."

Katherine got little sleep during the night, her eyes popping open with every change in the baby's breathing, every unexpected beep from the monitors. The nurses slipped in and out on a regular basis, checking the output of urine, changing the hanging bags of fluid, copying down numbers from the monitors. They were silent and even comforting in their professional, no-nonsense uniforms, seeming capable and possessed of some supernatural ability or presence. They seemed more competent than she who had been unable to save her husband and now, the ailing child. She felt helpless and almost inadequate in comparison. Although she had never wanted to be a nurse, in that moment she envied them their ability.

Shortly after the hospital began to awaken, the corridor filled with the metallic clank of trays and crockery. Dr. Bosch arrived and told her of his decision to give the baby a transfusion.

"Is it necessary?"

"We think it's mandatory," the physician said, taking her two hands in his and drawing her over to a couch on the other side of the curtains. "She is severely, critically anemic and her immune system is underdeveloped."

"And this will fix her, make her better?"

"I can't promise you that, Katherine, but I don't think she has much chance if we don't transfuse her. We're attacking the problem of her renal failure aggressively, but if it doesn't stabilize, we'll have no alternative but to try dialysis. I don't like it in one so little, but it may be necessary."

Tears flooded Katherine's eyes, and she looked down to hide them. The man had huge hands, competent, capable-looking hands spotted with age and covered with a fine sprinkling of reddish-brown hair. His hands reassured her; they were good hands and she trusted him. She nodded her acceptance.

Only after he had gone to make the arrangements did Katherine stop to think about what he had said. Something was wrong with the baby's blood. *If she were a normal human child.* But what if her blood was just what it was supposed to be? What if, as she suspected, the child was something other than a normal human baby? What effect would it have on her if they gave her a complete transfusion? Switching the blood might be a death sentence.

She had done a lot of thinking during the night. She no longer believed that Cameron was being held hostage, for it was hard to believe that the creatures had thought she would seek them out and find them. They had taken every precaution to remain hidden. There was no way they could have expected her to trail them to their hiding place and discover her own child.

But, during the night, she had come to believe that her only hope of getting Cameron back was to heal this child, return it to health and, somehow, strike a bargain, trading it for her own child. If she allowed the doctors to transfuse the baby, would she be helping it or harming it? That was the question.

She tried to decide what to do. Dr. Bosch seemed so certain that it was necessary, believed that without the transfusion the child would die. But the more Katherine thought about it, the more her instincts told her it was the wrong thing to do. Before she could talk herself out of it, she hurried out to the nurses' station and caught up with Dr. Bosch, who was speaking into a phone. He patted her on the shoulder. "We'll be ready up here in about twenty minutes," he said into the mouthpiece. Katherine shook her head No. The physician frowned at her. "Just a minute." He covered the mouthpiece with one huge hand and looked at her questioningly.

"I, I've changed my mind," Katherine said all in a rush. "I don't want to do this, not yet. Can't we wait just a little while, and see what happens?"

"I'll call you back," Dr. Bosch said as he slammed the phone down, grabbed Katherine by the elbow, and steered her to the nearest chair. He looked down at her expectantly, one bushy white eyebrow crooked, waiting for her to speak, to explain herself.

"I, I just don't think it's a good idea. I mean, just because her blood isn't just like everyone else's, doesn't mean it's bad. What if it's right for her? We could be doing more harm than good by giving her this transfusion."

Dr. Bosch sighed and ran a hand over his face; she could hear the rasp of whisker stubble. He sat down beside her, the chair dwarfed by his bulk, all but disappearing under the flow of his crisply starched white coat. "Katherine, I know you graduated from the University of Wisconsin. I assume you took basic biology. How much do you remember about the different types of blood?"

"Not much," Katherine admitted, trying to recall information that she had never had occasion to use. I know there's A and B and O and Rh negative and that's about all."

"Yes, well, there's a little bit more to it than that. Do you remember what the main components of blood are?"

"White cells, red cells, hemoglobin . . ." Katherine's voice faltered, grew less certain.

"Katherine, there are four main blood types A, B, AB, and O, which can be either positive or negative. Every man, woman, and child on the face of the earth fits one of those four blood types. The problem here is that Cameron's blood fits no known blood type. Her red blood cell count is critically low, and her white cell count is also low. Her blood is contaminated with high levels of urea nitrogen and creatinine. According to everything we know, she shouldn't even be alive!"

"But changing her blood isn't going to fix whatever's wrong," Katherine insisted. "It would be like getting a permanent and changing the color of your hair because you were going bald. Even if you give her a transfusion, you won't fix whatever is wrong, whatever is causing her blood to be so different, to be sick. Isn't that true?"

"It's possible. But it also might buy us the time to find out what's wrong and deal with the renal failure."

"It might also kill her. Maybe she's different. Maybe she'll be the first to have a new blood type. I'll bet that whoever discovered the different blood types, didn't identify all of them on the same day. What if this is the right blood for her? If you change it, put a new blood in her, wouldn't it be the same as poisoning her system?"

"Not necessarily," the physician replied. "It's routine to give total transfusions on Rh negative babies at birth, and in some instances 'washing the blood,' cleansing it of impurities with dialysis, has almost become routine."

"Cameron's not routine. I think we should wait and see, try to find out what else might be wrong. She's losing weight. Isn't there something you can do about that?"

Dr. Bosch hesitated, regarding her with a shrewd eye. "We're giving her glucose with appropriate additives, but she refuses all formulas. Have you tried to nurse her?"

Katherine was taken aback. "No one suggested that I do so. Can she be removed from the incubator? All those tubes and the needles . . ."

"I'll make you a deal, Katherine. You hold her, try to get her to nurse. Talk to her. She needs to know you're there. I'll have a nurse show you how to hold her. It's important for her not to become depressed. We can lose them when that happens. Once they give up, nothing you do can save them.

"I'm not making any promises. I want you to sign, to give us permission to go ahead with the transfusion and the dialysis. I respect your opinions, Katherine, but I can't have my hands tied here. If she starts to fail . . . well, I want to be able to act."

Katherine nodded slowly, and reluctantly scribbled her name at the bottom of the page of paper he thrust toward her. She knew that she had merely bought herself a few hours' time. As much as she hoped that they would be able to find out what was wrong with the child, in her heart, she feared that they would not.

Helga had spent another sleepless night, turning over the events of that distant time brought back to her so forcefully by the events of the present. The pain was so real, so intense, it was as though Martin had been lost all over again. Only now it was worse because this time she had known what was happening from the first minute she had smelled the scent of mushrooms and earth that she would always associate with Martin's loss.

She had not been completely truthful with Katherine, although her omission had been out of concern rather than any wish to deceive. Over the years, as she had grown older, the need for sleep had decreased. Now, at the end of her seventh decade, she found that three hours sleep per night was the most she could hope for, coupled with a light nap in midafternoon. Trying for more sleep was merely a waste of time, tossing and turning, and watching the ceiling and the clock. Instead, she filled the long, silent hours with reading and writing letters and watching strange television programs which were only to be found on obscure channels in the middle of the night. Often, she sat by her window and watched the lake, and the traffic on the outer drive. It had a soothing pattern that frequently eased her mind.

She had heard the footsteps that night, as they pounded down the stairs from the upper floors. She had become an expert in identifying who belonged to which pair of footsteps and secretly prided herself on her unusual ability. Mrs. Murdock had quick, tappy, impatient steps; irritable, sharp sounds. Mr. Murdock walked heavily, his steps always quick to descend and slow to rise. No small wonder, if he had to go home to her each night! Carol

Blankenship at the other end of her floor had prissy, hurried little steps, and up until recently, Katherine had always had solid, quick, skipping-type steps. All the others were as identifiable to Helga as birdsongs to an ornithologist.

She did not consider herself a nosy person, but being alone as she was, she tended to keep track of those who came and went, and she was sensitive to the patterns of her fellow tenants.

The steps she heard that night belonged to no one who lived in the building. More curious than alarmed, although the rapid descent should have alerted her to the fact that something was wrong, she moved to the door. Since the tiny peephole was more of a nuisance than an aid, the way it distorted features, she cracked the door a sliver so that she could peek out.

What she saw was far more than she had bargained for. There were two of them, both males. They were fighting or rather struggling on the steps as one attempted to turn back while the other prevented him from doing so. It was not this that shocked her so, bur rather the look of them. They were not human.

It was only as they reached the landing and passed directly in front of her door that she realized exactly what they were. It was the smell that brought it all back to her, the smell of forest mushrooms buried deep in the thick, rich, earthy loam. Although she was not aware of it, it was possible that she gasped, made some small noise, for the two males stopped abruptly in front of her door and stared directly at her.

She had always thought that the expression—of one's blood running cold—was an absurd figure of speech, a physical impossibility, until that moment. Her blood felt as though it had frozen in her veins, and she was paralyzed, unable to move. It was as though she had turned into a statue. She could feel the blood draining from her head, and her pulse pounding in her temples as she locked eyes with the terrible, frightening creatures who stood no more than three feet away. There was a very solid door between them which she could slam and lock before they reached her, but she felt as though she were standing there naked, exposed, helpless to protect herself.

Afterwards she wondered what would have happened had they not been interrupted. But thankfully, all three of them heard the sound of a door opening above them and then hurried footsteps running down the steps, taking them two and three at a time. The two males shot her a final glance from their silver eyes and then reached to the end of the landing and quickly descended the next flight of stairs.

Even after they were gone, she could feel the weight of their eerie eyes, feel the implicit threat. She raised her hand; it came up shakily and rested against the door. Before she could move, Katherine, disheveled and distraught, appeared on the landing and she too glanced at the door. Helga knew that something had happened, knew that she should announce her presence, for Katherine had undoubtedly noticed that the door was ajar. But at that moment, nothing was possible. Helga was gripped in such a powerful conflux of emotions that neither speech nor action was possible. It was all she could do to close the door, set the seldom-used locks with trembling fingers, and then totter to her armchair, where she spent the rest of the night racked by the pain of her memories.

By morning, she had brought her shaken nerves and emotions under control and had busied herself in the kitchen, cooking, a familiar and comforting action which always brought her pleasure. There was something about feeding people, especially in times of trouble, that provided her with a feeling of deep satisfaction.

While her mind fretted and worried over the appearance of the creatures in the hall, her hands moved with an intelligence of their own, creating the dish that was capable of soothing even the most disturbed beast. In lesser hands, chicken soup is the stuff of cliché and comedy; in Helga's competent hands, it was elevated to the status of nectar of the gods. She used only plump, meaty chicken breasts, the skin left on, which she placed in a heavy enameled iron cauldron. Water was run until the cauldron ran clear and only then was it set upon the burner on a low flame. Here it simmered, never boiled, until the meat was tender and literally fell apart at the touch of a fork. Then, the chicken was lifted from the cauldron and placed on a platter to cool. The broth itself was strained through a cheesecloth to catch the tiny bits of sediment and fat and then returned to the cauldron. Onions, celery and tiny carrots were added as well as salt, white pepper, a bay leaf and a pinch of poultry seasoning. This was once more brought to a low simmer until the vegetables were done, and then the meat, divested of its skin and torn into tiny bite-sized pieces, was returned to the pot. Once the chicken was heated, the fire was turned off and the heavy, tight-fitting lid placed atop the pot. Only then were a handful of tiny frozen *petits pois* added and allowed to soften in the heat of the broth. Homemade dill noodles were cooked separately and these too were added, stirred into the heavy cauldron, creating a thick, fragrant mélange of tastes and aromas capable of tempting an anorexic.

She was not certain until the dish was done what it was that she intended to do, which was to visit Katherine and find out what had happened and how much she knew.

Putting on a clean outfit and arranging her hair carefully, she had climbed the steps to Katherine's apartment, not even certain that she would gain access. Although they had exchanged numerous casual comments over the years, they were certainly not close friends.

Katherine was at once suspicious, nervous, antagonistic, and distraught. It was clear that she would have preferred for Helga to go away, but the young woman had no experience with rudeness and Helga had pushed past her and entered the apartment.

The rooms were shrouded in darkness and gloom. They were littered with papers and mail and plates bearing food that was hardened and dried. Little appeared to have been eaten. Katherine's appearance was even more disturbing; there were terrible dark circles under her eyes and her skin was sallow. Even shrouded in the huge bathrobe she wore, it was obvious that she had lost a good deal of weight from a body that had always been spare and athletic. She did her best to conceal her distress, babbling on and on in a manner that she herself would have found annoying. Forcing herself to be intrusive, Helga all but demanded to see the baby, praying that all would be well.

As soon as she saw the child she knew that she had not been mistaken. She had to close her eyes and take a deep breath before she could reach out for the baby, settling its small form in the crook of her arm.

It too looked sickly and there was a sour smell emanating from the blankets. Still, one had to make allowances; the mother had been through an ordeal, she could scarcely be blamed for letting conditions slide. Helga reached into her voluminous purse and drew out a primitive, slightly gaudy necklace made of bright amber beads and metal which had oxidized over the years. No sooner had the baby's fingers closed around it than she began to shriek. A huge blister rose up on the tender flesh. A feeling of dizziness seized her. *Dear God, how could it be! Here in this place! No, it was not possible, but it was, the horrible creatures with their silver eyes, and now the child was the proof.*

Katherine had been angered, suspicious, and who could blame

her? Helga felt badly about deceiving her, holding back the truth, but what good could come of telling what she knew? Katherine had related her experience with the police. If Helga came forward and told what she had seen, what had happened to her and the loss of her own child so many years ago, would she be regarded any differently? No. Instead of one crazy woman, there would now be two crazy women. Helga had dealt with police many times in many different countries during the course of her long life, and while they had their good points, imagination was not a necessary requirement for the job.

She had hoped to help in some way, to lend Katherine strength, but things had not transpired as expected. The baby was still alive. That was good. But she was worried about Katherine. Helga, more than anyone else, could understand Katherine's refusal to give the child up. She remembered, all too well, how she had wandered the mountain searching for her child, refusing to listen to those who had tried to dissuade her. But her case had been different; she had never seen the creatures again, they had avoided her with ease. It seemed obvious that those who had stolen Katherine's child were still in the area, as proved by the appearance of the coverlet, the rattle, and the doll.

Katherine was occupied for the moment with keeping the child alive. If she succeeded, it could only mean one thing—more interaction with the creatures. And if the child died, as she feared it would, Katherine would not give up, would not lose her child to the creatures without a fight. She would go back down into the basement and she would search until she found them. Or, until they found her.

All the platitudes that she herself had rejected so many years before came flooding back to Helga as she tried to convince herself that what she was about to do was the right thing, the only thing to do. Katherine was a young woman with her whole life ahead of her. She could marry again . . . have more children, forget her ordeal, put it behind her, and get on with the rest of her life.

She, on the other hand, was an old woman and she was tired. It would not matter if she were gone, especially if she could accomplish something of value with the time she had left. She got to her feet, feeling the cold numbness in her feet and the ache in her chest, and crossed over to the heavy, dark buffet. She opened a cabinet door and unlocked a drawer. The gun was heavy in her hand. It always surprised her how very heavy it was. It was a German gun, a Mauser. She had not fired it in years, but one did not forget such things. She brought out the cleaning kit and methodically broke the gun down and began to clean it. Her mind was made up. She knew what she had to do.

FIFTEEN

Throughout the long day, Katherine sat beside the child, watching the nurses, doctors, technicians, and nameless specialists as they went about their business. They seemed so certain of what to do, each of them performing their appointed tasks with such efficiency that Katherine began to envy them. They might not be saving the child with their chores, but at the least, they had something to do. Never had she felt so helpless, so useless, sitting there in the rocking chair unable to do anything to ease or comfort the baby.

Dr. Bosch had urged her to hold the child, but there was so much activity that it never seemed to be the right moment. The child did not even cry anymore. Only once, when yet another sample of blood was being drawn, did her eyes seek out Katherine's and she whimpered as the needle pierced her fragile flesh.

A strange thing was happening. Even though Katherine knew in her heart that the child in the incubator was not her daughter and she had every reason to both resent her and the situation that had robbed her of her own baby, she found herself being drawn to the child.

It was clear that the baby was suffering, in pain, yet she bore it with a dignity and strength of character that was remarkable in one so young. As much as Katherine wanted her own child back, her heart went out to this tiny child who had in no way asked to be used as a pawn in this deadly game.

As the long day stretched interminably before them, Katherine pulled her chair as close to the incubator as possible, trying to comfort the infant with her continued presence.

The baby's eyes seemed to grow larger, more striking as the day grew to a close, becoming almost luminescent, silver rather than gray. Her hair was fine and silky, actually finer than Cameron's, and it too was a silvery shade of blond. It curled in tiny tendrils on the back of her neck and above her ears. Cameron's hair had been unrelentingly straight.

But other, more significant changes were occurring as well. Even though Katherine was no longer repelled by the prominent brow and sloping forehead, which was so distinctive a feature on the adults, she realized that the child's very bone structure seemed to be changing from one hour to the next. She found it hard to believe that no one else seemed to notice the dramatic changes. Perhaps it was because none of them were on duty for longer than eight hours and seldom came in more than twice on their shift.

There was also the matter of the rippling images. Unless Katherine stared directly at the child, she seemed at first glance to look exactly like Cameron. At least that had been the case initially. Now, the image never held for more than ten minutes at a time, and if she watched continually, the image seemed to waver, almost to ripple around the edges, allowing the true image of the child to show through. Now, the image of Cameron seemed to be fading, seldom lasting more than five minutes and breaking down even more swiftly under intense scrutiny. If this was what had happened to Helga and all the other mothers who had been given changelings, she could understand how the myth had come to be. Increasingly, she wondered how long this had been going on, and even more importantly, who these "people" were.

As the day dragged to a close, Katherine's feelings went through a number of changes. She no longer admired the technicians and the horde of young interns who poked and prodded the baby. As darkness arrived, she had come to resent them, each of them bringing some new method of pain and torture. She wondered how much the tests and examinations were being performed on the baby's behalf and how much to merely satisfy curiosity, like a freak in a circus sideshow. Although she said nothing, her resentment grew.

Finally, the midday shift came to an end and the night shift arrived, along with yet another technician bearing a tray with the shiny needles and syringes intended to suck even more blood from the tiny scrap of being.

Surprising even herself, Katherine stood up as the young woman advanced on the incubator. "No," she said, the sound of her voice strange and unrecognizable to her ears. "No, she's had enough."

The technician stared at her, uncomprehending. "But, Dr. Wilson, he . . ."

"Sorry, you'll just have to tell him it's not going to happen. They've drawn lots of samples today. Dr. Wilson will just have to satisfy himself with those."

"But . . ."

"No buts about it," Katherine said firmly, feeling amazingly good about her stand. She placed her hands on the technician's shoulders, thin and hunched, and clothed in a slightly less than clean tunic. She steered her to the door.

"But what am I gonna tell him?" the girl whined, and Katherine noticed that she had a really terrible overbite, which coupled with her slumping posture gave her the appearance of a frightened rabbit.

"Tell him that the mother said no!" Katherine said emphatically as she propelled the technician through the door and shut it in the girl's astounded face. Then, while her determination was still strong, she dragged a dresser over and placed it in front of the door. Her thinking was unclear. There had been no clear-cut decision, no well thought out intention to defy the staff; it just happened. The day had been difficult for her, she could not imagine how the child had stood it. She moved to the phone and dialed the nurses' station at the far end of the corridor. "This is Mrs. Sinclair," she said smoothly, then gave a small laugh. "I'm afraid I've acted rather badly. I refused to let one of the technicians draw some blood."

From the tone of the voice at the other end of the line, Katherine could tell that the technician had already made her complaint. "I know it was wrong of me, but, well, to tell the truth, Cameron's just gotten to sleep and I didn't have the heart to waken her. She's had very little sleep today. Surely this can wait till morning."

It took a great deal of apologizing and promises to cooperate in the morning before Katherine was able to appease the voice and wring out a reluctant promise that no one would disturb them till morning.

As she hung up the phone, Katherine knew that she had no

intention of cooperating in the morning or at any other time. She feared that the child might not even make it through the night. Katherine had had little experience with children but much experience with animals. She recognized the look she had been seeing in the child's eyes. It was the look of death. She had seen it many times; in calves who broke bones, in foals who developed pneumonia, and in kittens with distemper, all of whom approached death with wide-eyed, unresisting acceptance.

It was not that the child refused to fight, she was a plucky little thing, but she seemed overwhelmed by her pain and suffering. Katherine also wondered how much she was affected by the separation from her mother. Knowing her own grief, Katherine could only guess at how much the child felt.

There was also the very real physical pain of the unrelieved ache in her breasts. With no child to nurse, the pressure was insistent, her breasts heavy and swollen with the excess. She had tried to relieve the pressure by expressing milk in the tiny bathroom. But there had been almost constant traffic in and out of the room and she felt as though she were performing in public. Nursing was a very private affair, a serious time of bonding between mother and child and it felt completely wrong to be wasting the precious fluid. It felt so very wrong that she had been unable to continue. Now, the pain was all but unbearable.

She moved to the side of the incubator and looked down at the baby. She was awake. The small fingers clutched weakly at the tightly drawn sheet. The large silvery eyes stared into hers, and the little cupid's bow that was the upper lip sucked on the lower lip, drawing no sustenance and little comfort from the act. The child fairly bristled with tubes and needles and circles of adhesive that connected various monitors to her frail form. Katherine could hardly bear to look at them.

Then, moving without any preconceived plan, she raised the lid of the incubator and began separating the baby from the cold, mechanical devices. An inner voice cautioned her that the various drips and monitors were all that anchored the child to life. But another voice answered defiantly that it was not life but merely a prolonging of the agony. If the child was going to die, she would die in the arms of a mother, someone who cared, and not in the embrace of an unfeeling machine.

The baby hung limp in her arms. Katherine needed no elaborate machine to tell her that the small body weighed less than it had before being admitted. The eyes contained the only bit of strength left to the child; they seemed to burn with an intelligence, an awareness that was far beyond her young age. In that moment, with the eyes clinging to her as to life itself, Katherine felt a bond begin to form between the two of them. It was tentative, fragile, but real.

And why not? Katherine wondered as she cradled the silvery blond head and settled herself in the rocker. *The two of us have both been used, or rather, discarded. My child was taken and this one put in her place. They—whoever they are—knew that she would die. The two of us have been sorely used; we are joined by our loss and our pain.*

Her breasts, sensitive and tender to the touch of fabric against her skin, ached as she drew the child toward her, cradling it against her chest. She winced as she reached down toward the package on the floor and drew it onto her lap. The soft fur coverlet came free of the envelope with a whisper. Katherine placed it against the child's naked back. The eyes widened with a flash of recognition, and a tiny fist waved in the air. Katherine tucked a corner of the coverlet into the small fingers, which seized it tightly and brought it up to lie alongside the tiny translucent ear. It was obviously a familiar action, and one that brought the child pleasure. Her eyes blinked shut and a long sigh escaped her lips.

Katherine was astounded at the child's reaction to the blanket. She lowered the baby to the crook of her arm and wrapped the blanket around her. It was just the right size. She raised the rattle and the doll, and the baby reached up to close her fingers around the smooth curve of the rattle, then clutched it tightly to her chest. Katherine suspected that she did not have the strength to hold her arm aloft for more than a few seconds.

The baby drew such obvious comfort from the fur covering and the rattle that Katherine felt a sense of guilt at not having given them to her earlier, even though "foreign objects" had most definitely been forbidden.

She began to rock the child back and forth. The steady motion seemed to please her; she made a little humming sound and fastened her eyes on Katherine. "You and I, we're all we've got," Katherine said, whispering down into the pale, pinched face. "We've got to stick together. Don't die. Don't give up, fight back. Please don't die and leave me here all alone."

It was ridiculous. She knew it even as the words poured out of her, but the need was so great, she felt better for having spoken.

Nor could she escape observing the curious intelligence that shone out of the child's silvery eyes. They were not the eyes of a child, but of an old soul. And in them there was an understanding. As they stared into each other's eyes, Katherine slowly, tremulously, unbuttoned her blouse.

SIXTEEN

Helga was ready. There was nothing left to do but go. She looked around her apartment for what she imagined to be the very last time. She wondered what would become of her possessions gathered over the decades during times of poverty as well as plenty. Jacob, her last husband, had never been able to understand why she was so stubborn and insisted on clinging to bits of furniture and odds and ends more befitting a charwoman than the wife of a very wealthy man. But how did one explain the memories contained in the scrubbed surface of the little oak kitchen table? She had stenciled the bright enamel flowers and twining leaves in each of the four corners, now chipped and fading with age. Often, it had been the single bright note in the dreary and frightening war years.

Then there were her heavy cast-iron pots and pans. How many hot, comforting meals had simmered in them on simple wood-burning stoves? They could never be replaced with the overpriced lightweight sets of cold stainless steel one saw in stores today. Those newer pots and pans might well be more efficient and have no aggravating hot spots, but they also lacked soul.

Helga shook her head at her thoughts. Here she was, old enough to be a grandmother many times over, old enough to know better, thinking about pots that had no soul. She smiled at the convoluted paths her mind traveled. The smile faded. Such things would have to look after themselves; she had more important matters to attend to. She picked up her handbag, draped the handle over her arm, and resolutely walked to the door, shutting it firmly behind her.

Her first problem was in getting past the doorman. She had hoped that since it was so early, barely daylight, he would be asleep in his chair as he so often was. Unfortunately, he was wide-awake on this occasion, and beamed at her as she crossed the marble foyer, no doubt anticipating one of her special pastry treats.

She did not fail him. Employing her thickest accent, her most droll, grandmotherly persona, she fussed over the man, asking after his wife and children while laying out in front of his console a large thermos filled with steaming-hot Dutch chocolate-flavored coffee, decaffeinated of course, and a plate filled with large schnecken, still hot from the oven. The pastries filled the small entranceway with the irresistible aroma of yeasty dough, Ceylon cinnamon, and caramelized sugar.

She knew from past experience that the doorman would spend a few minutes protesting her generosity and grumbling about his expanding waistline before eating every last crumb. She assured him that his portly figure was one of heroic, classic proportions rather than fat, and left him concentrating on the pleasures of his palate.

She worried briefly that the dose of Seconal might do him some harm, but reassured herself that his considerable girth would safely absorb the sleeping powder. Nor was it a strong enough dose so that afterward he would suspect anything unusual about his unplanned nap. He was so intent upon devouring his treats that she was able to slip through the door to the basement unobserved.

Although she had been in the basement many times before, visiting her friend, Mr. Kramer, the sheer size of the place always took her by surprise. To her mind, basements were tiny, damp, confined quarters, not this great echoing expanse with columns that stretched away in the distance. She followed the dim trail of light bulbs back into the furthermost reaches until she came to the steps that led to Stone's apartment as well as the mysterious wooden door.

She allowed her eyes to rest on the cobwebbed doorway briefly. She thought it odd that it was still covered with a thick layer of cobwebs despite the traffic that had recently come and gone. They were very industrious spiders.

Stone's door was as familiar as an old friend; Helga knew it well. Kramer, Stone's predecessor, who had died so suddenly under such strange circumstances, had been as good a friend as she'd ever had. He was a comfortable man, a man who had no need to dominate conversation or space. They had spent many a pleasant hour in each other's company, frequently without words, content simply to be together. She missed him.

Helga fought back the blur of tears that threatened to spill down her cheeks, chastising herself for being a foolish old woman. If indeed there was something wrong, something that had played a role in Kramer's death, she would soon know. She lifted her hand and knocked.

Surprisingly, she had caught Stone asleep. What with the duties of the building and his suspected complicity in the baby's disappearance, she had thought that he would be awake. Kramer had been an early riser.

Stone was clearly surprised to see her. His chestnut-brown hair was rumpled and stood up in peaks and whorls around his head. His beard, although more crinkly in texture, was mashed to one side, and his eyes were still foggy with sleep. He was dressed in an odd conglomeration of long white underwear, knee-high wool socks, and an old, threadbare flannel shirt. The look was both boyish and very endearing. She could almost picture him with a ragged teddy bear tucked under his arm, and she had to remind herself that he was the enemy.

"Is something wrong?" He peered at her blearily.

To her astonishment, she found that she was flustered. Now that the moment was here, the moment on which her plans rested, she began to stammer and she could feel her face growing flushed.

"Something is wrong, *ja*," she agreed, her accent becoming broader as it always did under stress. "Katherine called. Mrs. Sinclair. The baby . . . she want you to come to hospital right away."

"She wants me to come to the hospital?" Stone was clearly surprised. His eyes opened wide, all traces of sleep vanishing as he focused on her. She felt the weight of his eyes on her—such strange eyes. How had she never noticed before what a peculiar shade they were, gray-green with specks of silver in them. A tiny alarm, a pinprick of worry, something she needed to remember, went off in her mind and then it was gone, too quick to grasp. "The baby, is it . . ."

"Dead? . . . No, no. I do not think so, she do not say. She just say, please to ask you to come to her, quick. She need you."

Helga watched Stone carefully, wondering if he would accept her word or would call the hospital and speak to Katherine directly. Even to her, the story seemed farfetched. There was no plausible reason why Katherine would want Stone to come to the hospital, but it was all that she had been able to think of. Somehow, she had to get him to leave the building. It was the only way she could do what had to be done.

"I answer phone and I tell her that I come get you right away," she embellished. "Now, I think maybe I hurry too much." She touched a hand to her chest. "You let me sit down for a minute to rest." It aggravated her to portray herself as a helpless, fluttery old woman, but it was necessary.

Stone was clearly uncomfortable at the suggestion, but there was no way that he could refuse her. He stood aside and motioned her in.

Little or nothing had changed with Stone's occupancy of the apartment. She looked around with interest as she settled into the deep cushions of the down-filled couch, a relic of the building's more elegant days. There were numerous chairs, none matching, lining the walls of the apartment, and multiple layers of overlapping carpets on the floors, the patterns and textures dissimilar but creating a colorful montage much like a stained-glass window. Scores of pictures hung on every available bit of wall space, their frames exhibiting every style from gilt baroque to geometric modern.

Kramer had been a true "collector," as he called it, unable to allow anything of possible use or value to be thrown away. He had scrupulously separated the building's garbage, composting organic material which he then spaded into the small but beautiful flower and vegetable garden he had created at the rear of the building. Newspapers and paper goods were flattened, stacked, bundled and tied, and then sold to paper dealers. Aluminum and glass were resold, and everything else that could be reclaimed for possible repair and use was carefully retrieved.

Toasters, electric fry pans, clocks, outdated or unappreciated goods disposed of by the building's wealthy residents, were judiciously recycled, sold if possible, but often given away to those in greater need.

The apartment was like a pack rat's warren, every available space filled with items that had been rejuvenated, waiting for new homes, or those still in need of attention. It was a complicated, fascinating hodgepodge with something of interest no matter where one looked. While she was not surprised to see Kramer's treasures still in place—after all, how could Stone had disposed of them short of renting a moving van?—she was surprised to see nothing new, nothing to indicate that someone else was now occupying the apartment.

Stone was dressed and ready to leave in no time at all. She pressed her hand against her bosom and fanned herself with her other hand, smiling ruefully. "You go," she said. "I let myself out when I catch my breath."

"But . . ." Stone was hesitant, clearly uneasy with the idea.

"Go, go," she said, shooing him away. "I promise not to steal nothing."

His eyes were troubled, regarding her thoughtfully. But, as she had known, there was little he could do. What was he going to do, heave her up out of the chair and push her through the door? It was unlikely. In the end, he bowed to the inevitable and left her in the apartment, cautioning her to lock the door when she left.

Helga waited until she was certain that he was gone, then left the apartment, locking it as instructed. She crept up the stairs and peeped over the edge to make sure that he was nowhere in sight, feeling foolish and much too large and old for such games. Stone was nowhere to be seen, but there, in plain view, just where Katherine had said it was, was the crowbar. While very heavy, it had a satisfying heft in her hands.

The webbed door slowly gave way under her determined attack, the newly nailed planks groaning and squealing loudly as she pried them away from the frame. It was hard and awkward work. She had led an active and athletic life as a young woman, but those days were long behind her and the sudden tightening in her chest was a strong warning that she was exceeding her physical limits.

There had been other such warnings in recent years, odd flutterings and a roughness in the rhythm that one took for granted over the course of a lifetime. Helga was a stubborn woman, and other than lowering her arms and worrying the wood at waist-level, she did not give in to her discomfort. She had a job to do, then she could rest.

She stood back and looked at what remained of the door, smiling with pleasure at her handiwork. The door was all but demolished. It would take more than a few planks and nails to repair it this time! Shouldering her crowbar, purse slung over the crook of her arm, she entered the corridor, the bright beam of her flashlight cleaving the darkness.

Having listened to Katherine's story, avidly absorbing all the details, Helga knew what to expect and marched straight to the first doorway on the right, the one where Katherine had seen the sleeping figure. It was exactly as Katherine had reported, seemingly no more than an empty room once used for the storage of coal, and long abandoned. Certainly not the site of recent habitation. Or so someone had wanted them to believe.

Helga directed the beam around the perimeter of the room. There were the obvious chunks of dusty coal, too obvious. She half expected to find fingerprints on them, but didn't. There were two piles of brittle, yellowed newspapers dating back to the 1920's and several rungs from the back of a chair. Undiscouraged, Helga widened her search, walking back and forth over the entire floor. Nothing. Still determined, she moved away from the center of the room, shining her beam toward the back wall, paying close attention to the junction where floor met wall. And that was where she found the evidence she had been seeking. It was a small, intricately worked bit of stone, somewhat reminiscent of the ivory balls that had been so popular around the turn of the century. It was a circular ball of stone filigree, delicate and impossibly fragile, almost lacelike. In the center of the hollow carving was yet another carved ball, and in its center, still another ball no larger than a cherry pit. It too was carved, only this ball was solid, not hollow. She shined the beam directly on the object, attempting to see what the carving was.

So intense was her concentration that she failed to hear the first of the sounds. Aggravated by her capricious vision, which could not seem to decide whether an object needed to be extremely close or at arm's length before it could be seen clearly, she ignored the faint grinding sound.

It was difficult to juggle everything at once. Sighing over the infirmities and inconveniences of age, she divested herself of her heavy purse, and the even heavier crowbar, thus freeing her hands to deal with the delicate carving. Much better! Unencumbered, she focused the beam down on the ball and then touched the button that raised the beam to a greater intensity. It was a face! She squinted, trying to bring the blurred image into focus. The sound was louder now, a rumbling sort of growly noise that distracted her. She lifted her eyes from the ball, annoyed rather than alarmed, for she had caught an image of a nose, lips, and the smooth roundness of a cheek before her concentration was broken.

Helga blinked at the darkness, her retinas still retaining the bright white fall of light, the darkness crowding in around the edges, unable to see anything. Thus is was that when the hand

appeared out of the wall—knobby, dirt-stained fingers fully
extended—she caught only the briefest glimpse before the ball
was snatched out of her grasp.

It was the very worst luck that caused her to swing the flashlight
up as she stumbled backward in surprise and sudden fear. The
spread of light caught the hand and arm in its beam. Helga stood
like a statue, too stunned to move, and then, realizing that the
evidence as well as the hand that had stolen it, was retreating back
into the wall from which it had emerged, she stepped forward with
an angry cry and struck the clenched fist hard on its prominent
knuckles. There was no sound, but the fingers shot open, dropping
the ball to the ground. Ignoring her stiff and protesting knees
encased in their tubes of sturdy nylon, she bent and scooped up the
crowbar and brought it down hard on the outstretched arm.

Not even she could have known what was to follow, for caught
up in the moment, she had failed to think the matter through. Had
she done so, she might have imagined a secret hole the size of the
arm, but she would have been wrong.

No sooner had the crowbar landed on the fleshy inner arm than
a great welt rose up. She landed a second, harder blow, this one to
the wrist, and the same stigmata appeared on the pale flesh. Only
then did Helga's mind accept what her eyes saw—the figure of a
body, the shape of a face pressed against the wall, stretching it,
molding it against the alien form as though it were warm, pliable
dough rather than solid stone, and by then, it was far too late.

SEVENTEEN

Katherine wakened slowly, vaguely aware of the change in tempo in the halls outside the room. She looked down at the child sleeping on her chest and smiled, more content than she had been in days.

The child had nursed. Too weak to oppose her, it could do little to resist as she lowered her swollen breast to the small lips. The warm milk, bluish-white and thinner than man-made formulas, dropped into the tiny mouth, coated the tongue, and slipped down the little throat.

She settled the child comfortably in the crook of her arm, wrapping it up in the fur coverlet with one edge protruding so that the fragile fingers could grasp it. The other hand clasped the rattle firmly. With those familiar assurances, the child allowed Katherine to continue. She did not actively nurse, but neither did she offer any resistance.

There had been numerous tappings on the door, some hesitant and uncertain, others more imperious and demanding. Katherine ignored them all, concentrating only on the child. After the first nursing, the baby had drifted off to sleep. Her temperature had fallen. The sheen of perspiration, which had filmed her skin as soon as the temperature was raised inside the incubator, dried. At first Katherine was alarmed, but the baby seemed to breathe easier and a faint rosy blush colored her wan cheeks. Perhaps it was normal for these people to have a lower temperature. Was it possible that they had done the baby more harm than good by artificially raising her temperature?

Shortly before dawn, the child awakened, its silvery eyes glittering in the dim light. Katherine watched with tender amazement as the pupils grew larger and larger, admitting what light there was in order to see.

"My little kitten," Katherine murmured softly, stroking the strange contours of the downy cheek with the tip of a finger. "You see in the dark, don't you?" The baby blinked as though in answer and Katherine began to rock back and forth, talking to the child. Sweet, nonsensical words, they held little import in and by themselves, but together with the sound and emanations of caring and love they were the cement that bonded mother and child together.

The baby nursed again, just before morning. This time, it was of her own volition, the tentative, whisper-soft touch of lips and tongue releasing the sweet ache of the milk. Katherine could have wept, so great was her joy. The baby would survive, she felt certain. It seemed to have gained the will to live. And she had brought about that miracle, she was responsible for the small but important victory. Even more importantly, she felt that now it might be possible that Cameron would be returned. If she was correct in her supposition that her child was being held as a hostage for this child, then . . . Her thoughts were rudely interrupted by a heavy pounding on the door. Her name was being called. The voice sounded familiar.

Hating to disturb the child, but knowing that she would undoubtedly waken if the pounding continued, Katherine placed the baby in the incubator and moved to the door. She was surprised at how heavy the dresser was; it slid away from the door reluctantly, its steel-clad feet catching on the edge of every tile. She threw the door open angrily, fierce words poised on her lips, anticipating yet another round of technicians, their trays balanced on the flats of their palms, demanding entrance. The words died on her lips, unspoken. She stared at Stone, seeing him, but unable to understand the reason for his presence. He was dressed in an odd conglomeration of clothing, what appeared to be several layers of old flannel shirts tucked halfheartedly into a pair of faded and torn blue jeans. He wore high-top leather hiking boots, the leather supple with age and well oiled, the laces tied only halfway up. The multitude of shirts was topped by a thick camouflage jacket which had been buttoned incorrectly so that one end of the collar tickled his ear and the other dipped down at a crazy angle. His beard was unkempt and his hair uncombed. Either he had dressed in the dark or there was some terrible emergency. His odd-colored eyes glittered brightly, seeming more silver than gray in the dim light.

"What's the matter!" she cried in alarm as she imagined all sorts of disasters befalling the building.

Stone had started to speak at the same moment, his words a jumble, lost in the torrent of her own. Finally he held up his hand to silence her. "What's wrong? I came as quickly as I could."

Katherine stared at him, unable to comprehend what it was that he was saying. "What? What are you talking about?"

"Mrs. Orlowski. She said that you called, wanted me to come as quickly as possible!" Stone stared at her as though wondering if she had forgotten.

Katherine looked at him, perplexed, her hands wanting to reach out and straighten his disarray. "I never called Mrs. Orlowski. Nothing is wrong. In fact, I think things are better."

"Better? You mean the baby's improved?" Stone took a step forward, no longer looking at her, his eyes focused on the dim interior.

"Well, yes," Katherine said hesitantly, more than a little bewildered at the man's interest in the child. He took another step forward, which brought him immediately in front of Katherine. She would either have to step aside or come into direct contact with his body. She could feel the heat of him; he was that close. She looked into his silvery eyes which were on a level with her own. She felt as though she was being drawn into the dark vortex of his pupils which were open wide in the darkness of the room. Something tickled at her memory, some thought demanding to be acknowledged, but the physical presence of the man blotted out all other thoughts. She shut her eyes and sighed, stepping aside, allowing him to pass. There was no doubt that she was attracted to this strange man, but now, at this time and in this place, it was entirely wrong. His presence seemed to disorient her, confuse her every time he was near. She sensed him enter the room. The air felt empty with him gone from her side. It was strangely discomforting. Her mind was whirling with confusion.

He was standing beside the incubator, looking down at the sleeping child. His fingertips caressed the child's back. The baby wriggled under his touch, stretched and then brought her fingers up to her mouth and began to suck, more from habit than from hunger. One edge of the coverlet was draped over the baby's cheek and ear. The dark fur outlined the sweep of the high cheekbone and was clutched wetly in the sucking fingers. Looking down at her, Katherine felt the warmth of happiness. This was a different child from the one that had been brought to the hospital. This child was still thin, too thin. She still bore the scald marks of the burns she had sustained, but she was a child who had regained the will to live. This baby would not die.

But Stone appeared more alarmed than pleased; perhaps he did not realize how near death the baby had been. He stared at the array of medical equipment that surrounded the incubator. "They're not going to use these things on her, are they?" He drew back, all but flinching at the sight of the IV's with their needles dangling, the tubes still bearing traces of the baby's blood.

"It's all right, I disconnected everything," Katherine said, moving to his side, wondering at his apparent distress. "She's much better now."

"You mustn't let them do these things to her! Those needles—!" He was trembling visibly. Katherine reached out and touched his arm, thinking to say something light that would jolly him out of his mood. Many people were afraid of needles. But beneath the heavy jacket and layers of shirts, his arm was rigid, the muscles tight and hard. The words went out of her mind and she could think of nothing to say.

He turned to her with stricken eyes. "She's going to die. That's why you called me. You know, don't you?" He brought his other hand up and clutched her arm hard, much harder than her own grip.

She tried to understand his distress. "Die? She's not going to die. You're not listening to me. I said she was going to be all right. She nursed twice during the night. Look at her, does she look like a baby who's going to die?"

Stone stared deep into her eyes, searching out the truth, continuing to grip her arms in a painful hold. "She's going to be all right?" He seemed like a man laboring under great strain. He could not be reacting more strongly had the child been his own. The thought popped into Katherine's head out of nowhere. For the first time, she looked at Stone with critical, nonemotional detachment. She took note of the strange eyes, the high cheekbones, and thought about his sudden, unexplained, convenient appearance.

Belatedly, some of her words seemed to filter through his distress. "You nursed her?" he asked.

She nodded. "Twice." Some of the tension seemed to ease out

of his body. His shoulders slumped, his head fell forward, and he exhaled heavily.

Katherine wanted to question him about the child. She was now certain that he knew more than he was saying, but he was so disturbed, it didn't seem right to press him. An irreverent inner voice argued that this was precisely the moment to press her advantage, learn what she could while his defenses were down. She wavered, but before she could make up her mind, Stone roused himself. His head came up, and he looked at her, his eyes clear and focused. "You didn't call." It was a statement, not a question. She shook her head. His jaw tightened and he turned toward the door. She put out a hand to stop him.

"Wait a minute. You're saying that Helga, Mrs. Orlowski, told you that I called and asked you to come here?"

Stone seemed anxious to be gone. "Yes. She came downstairs to my apartment. Woke me up. Said it was an emergency and that you wanted me to come right away. I thought . . ." The words trailed off and hung in the air between them, weighted with ominous implications.

"But why would she do that?" Katherine asked. "Is she here too?" She looked around him, half-expecting to see the familiar bulky figure outlined in the light of the door.

"No, she's not here. She said she was too tired from all the stairs. I left her in my apartment and she . . ." Sudden silence was followed by an explosion of angry words. Stone plunged past her.

"Wait a minute! Do you think . . . ! No! She's an old woman. Surely she wouldn't try to go in there alone!"

Stone turned angry eyes toward her. "That's exactly what I think she's done!"

"But they could kill her if she finds them!" Katherine snatched her jacket up off the chair where she had thrown it so many hours ago and thrust her way through the heavy circle of curtains. Stone grabbed her by the wrist and pulled her back. "You stay here with the baby. I'll go after her."

"No, the baby's asleep. She'll be fine. I'm going with you. Helga's my friend. She's doing this because of me. Don't you see, I've got to go!"

They stared at each other. Stone's eyes were filled with worry and indecision. Katherine was determined. The thought of Helga down there alone . . . "Look," she said patiently. "You can stop pretending. I saw them. I know they're there. You know they're there. We can't let them hurt Helga. Maybe if we tell them that the baby is going to be all right, it would help."

Stone was clearly caught on the horns of a dilemma and didn't know what to do. He jammed his hands into his pockets, stared down at the floor, and fidgeted with uncertainty. He looked up. "If you know about . . ." he began. The door thumped open, slammed against the wall with a loud crash. Light poured in from the corridor, illuminating the room. The horde of technicians Katherine had been dreading charged into the room spearheaded by two angry-eyed nurses. Awakened from a sound sleep, the baby began to shriek as the curtains were swept aside allowing the light to stream in assaulting her sensitive eyes.

"Wait! Don't do that!" Katherine turned toward them, trying to bar them from the room, pulling the curtains back, shrouding the inner space with darkness. But the damage had already been done. The baby continued to scream. Katherine snatched her up out of the incubator and held her protectively, glaring at the intruders. "No more tests! No more needles! No more blood!" she said firmly. "Get out of here, all of you!"

There were several exchanges of tight-lipped grim words concerning hospital procedure and the need to follow the doctor's orders, but Katherine held her ground, refusing to allow them to enter or touch the baby. She demanded that Dr. Bosch be called, and seeing that she was unlikely to change her mind, the team of nurses and technicians withdrew. It was only then, as she attempted to calm the hysterical child, that she realized that Stone was nowhere to be seen.

Dr. Bosch was somewhere between the western suburbs where he lived, and the hospital. A sleepy Scarborough was routed from his bed in the doctors' lounge and entered the room, raking his fingers through his hair and blinking the last of his interrupted sleep from his eyes.

It was difficult convincing him to do as she wanted. "No more blood drawn. No transfusions. No needles. No temperature adjustments," she demanded. "Or I'll take her home."

"She'll die," Scarborough said, clearly angry over her mandates.

"Look at her," Katherine said, turning aside so that he could see the child more clearly. Her cheeks were stained with tears, her eyelids swollen and red, but she was holding her head erect and had a tight hold on her coverlet. "She's not going to die, if you do as I say." She outlined her terms, and reluctantly Scarborough agreed.

It was hard calming herself enough to settle in the rocker when every muscle wanted to leap up out of the chair and run down the hall in pursuit of Stone. But the child had to be taken care of first. She nursed eagerly, bringing her small hands up to help guide the breast to her mouth. She made little sounds of contentment and hummed deep in her throat, almost like a cat's purr. It was a wonderful sound. Her eyes met Katherine's, the silvery gleam almost like starlight. Katherine smiled down at the child, feeling her heart swell with emotion and love. What courage and strength were contained in that tiny body!

The child fell into a deep sleep after she nursed, and Katherine placed her in the incubator, wrapping the fur blanket around the small body, draping it over her cheek as she seemed to prefer. Rattle and doll were placed within easy reach.

Scarborough had done what she asked. Two small sterile nursing bottles, the kind generally filled with distilled water, were waiting just inside the door atop the dresser. Even though the baby had nursed several times, there was still more than enough milk to fill both bottles. Katherine screwed the tops on tightly, deeply relieved to have freed herself of the pain of her swollen, milk-gorged breasts. Now, the child could be fed with the milk that had seemed to sustain her, and Katherine could leave the hospital to search for Helga and Stone.

"I'll be back," she cautioned Scarborough, who stood waiting at the nurses' station as she handed him the two bottles filled with still-warm milk. "Don't let anyone touch her unless it's to feed, change, or comfort her. And the blanket and toys stay."

A thin blond nurse, her hair tightly permed in rows of horizontal crimped waves, stared at Katherine with obvious disapproval, her lips compressed in a thin line. Katherine spoke to her as much as to the resident. "If you do what I say, she'll be all right."

"We'll be the judges of that!" snapped the nurse. Katherine stared into her eyes, small, hard, pale blue orbs lacking soul. "I'm going to take her home," she said, turning to Scarborough, ignoring the nurse completely.

Scarborough caught up with her halfway back to the room. He took hold of her arm. "There are always some like that," he said quietly. She turned to face him. "They like the power. But most are nurses because they have a need to mother, to heal, to love. Cameron needs to stay here. Even if you deny treatment, this is where she needs to be. She's not ready to go home yet." They stared at each other. Katherine wavered. As much as she disliked the nurse, she trusted Scarborough and Dr. Bosch.

"Something happened last night, didn't it? Why don't you tell me so we have a better idea of what's going on here."

"I can't." Katherine shook her head. "I don't really know anything yet, I just have some ideas that I have to check out. But I know I'm right about the transfusion. It would kill her. And the temperature, ninety-eight point six is too hot for her; she needs to be cooler. Give me a little bit of time and I think I can find some answers."

Scarborough stared at her. He nodded. "Don't worry, no one will hurt her. I'll watch out for her until you get back. But come back quickly."

Katherine smiled and squeezed his arm. "As fast as I can," she whispered. "As fast as I can."

EIGHTEEN

Katherine leaped from the cab and sprinted up the steps of the building. The doorman half rose from his seat as she raced past him. He gaped at her, his mouth open. Before he could say anything, she hurtled past him and was through the inner door and plummeting down the steps to the basement. No doubt everyone in the building now thought she was insane. It scarcely mattered. She wondered how long ago Stone had arrived. For the hundredth time since leaving the hospital, she wondered if she would be able to follow him. But Helga was first and foremost in her mind. She whispered a prayer that the old woman was all right. What could have made her decide to do such a foolish, dangerous thing? She thought back over their conversation, but could think of nothing that had been said that might have caused her to take such an action. If what Helga suspected was true, then these people could and would be dangerous.

She raced through the darkness of the outer storage areas, her mind awhirl, barely noticing the black shadows and hidden places that she had found so terrifying only days before. Three days that had been a lifetime ago, when she still had a child, Helga had been a seldom seen, little-known tenant, and Stone had not existed.

She came to the furnace room and stopped, catching her breath as she approached the steps with trepidation. She had thought that Stone might have stopped at his apartment, but one glance at the shattered door opposite convinced her otherwise. There was no way that one could ignore that yawning hole; the few ravaged planks that still clung to the door frame were an ominous invitation to the darkness that lay beyond. She hesitated. It was very dark. It would be suicidal to enter without some form of light . . . and a weapon.

The workbench provided the weapon, a three-foot length of pipe, rusted at one end but solid and reassuring in her hands. The bottom shelf of the bench held a heavy, boxy, wide-beam light, the kind most often carried on boats. Its yellowish beam was not as strong as she would have liked, but it did not flicker or fade. She hoped it would last, as she did not want to waste any more time searching for a better light. She felt the passage of every minute and prayed that she was not already too late. Just as she was about to turn away, another tool caught her eye. It was small, no longer than the length of her hand. It had a short, rounded wooden handle. Attached to the handle was a broad, curved, sickle-shaped piece of metal with a pointed end. The inner curve appeared to be quite sharp. Memory pricked at her. She thought that maybe it was either a carpet- or linoleum-cutting knife. Without thinking, she snatched it up and stuffed it into her pocket.

She could feel the difference as soon as she stepped foot inside the shattered door. It was obvious, in some intangible way, that others had passed this way before her. The aura, the feeling of the place, was different. The odor of mushrooms and damp, dark earth was still the most powerful, pervasive smell, filling her nostrils and coating her senses. But the air had been disturbed by the passage of others. Katherine could pick up the faint thread of lavender, Helga's scent, a sharper, cleaner smell that cut through the earthy aroma that permeated the area. She sniffed the dark air, sensing another smell. Was it Stone's warm, musky scent, or did she merely imagine it, wanting it to be there?

Physically, the place was as it had been before; nothing appeared to have changed. The broad beam of the boat light illuminated a wider area than the policeman's bright, narrow beam. She hugged the wall, dragging her fingers along the rough surface, letting it anchor her. She felt safer clinging to the wall; it was when she moved into the open with the darkness pressing in around her on all sides that she felt frightened.

The doorway loomed on her right. She scanned the floor, hoping for a sign of footprints, scuff marks, anything to serve as a guide, telling her where the others had gone. There was nothing; the ground had been trod by two sets of policemen as well as Katherine herself and Stone, yet revealed no signs to one as inexperienced as she. A Girl Scout badge in outdoor lore attained in childhood was of little use in these circumstances.

She shined the beam around the room, somehow loath to enter. Boxes. Lumps of dust-covered coal. Stacks of newspapers and streamers of cobwebs swathing the corners and draped from the ceilings. Her light swept the walls, more as a perfunctory gesture than in the expectation of finding anything. She caught something out of the corner of her eye just as she was turning to leave. The beam swung back. There. There it was. Curious. She entered the room for a closer look, doing her best to stay clear of the dusty webs.

The walls were brick, covered with a brittle layer of white-washed plaster, so old that it was cracking and chipping away in large sections. Only this spot was different. She shined her light on it and moved in close to examine it. It was an inverted dimple in the brickwork. She stared at it, perplexed, wondering how it had been made. The sides of the depression were smooth, very smooth, slicker than the surrounding brickwork. It was like a small inverted cone. Like someone had pressed a paper snow cone into wet clay and then allowed it to harden before removing the form. But why would anyone do that? And what difference did it make? Helga and Stone could scarcely have vanished through a depression no wider than three inches in diameter.

The floor showed some indication of disturbance beneath the inversion, vague scuff marks, nothing more. She did not remember clearly, but thought that one or more of the policemen had entered the room.

She sniffed the air, hoping for a further hint of Helga's lavender, but was unable to find it. The smell of the dusty, musty place heavy with the overall scent of mushrooms, seemed to clog her nostrils, overwhelming whatever or whoever else might have been there.

She left the room and turned to her right, determined to find Stone and Helga. They had to be here somewhere! As before, the corridor ended in the blank brick wall. But this time she was not to be so easily discouraged. Taking the linoleum cutter from her pocket, she placed the boat light and the iron pipe on the ground and slowly, quietly, began to work.

The tool was perfectly suited to the job. The hooked point dug into the mortar and pried it loose as though it were putty. Some areas were more difficult than others, but it was not impossible.

The thought crossed her mind that despite the aged, weathered appearance of the bricks, the mortar felt as though it had barely set. Her uncles had often repaired sections of the massive fieldstone foundations of their homes and barns. She and her cousins had dared each other to dart in and steal handfuls of the gray glop which they would then mold and shape until it grew too stiff to work, leaving their hands rough and parched.

She lowered her head toward a chunk of mortar and inhaled the long forgotten scent of those distant summers. The gray, crumbling stuff gave off a smell of moisture, and the chalky, somewhat sour smell of lime, which old mortar no longer possessed. These bricks had been recently laid. She had not been wrong.

Even though the mortar yielded to her tool, the work did not progress as quickly as she would have liked. She wanted nothing more than to pick up the iron pipe and bash her way through the wall, but the need for caution and quiet was paramount. The kidnappers would vanish, throwing up even more obstacles in her path if they learned of her approach. As much as she wanted to find Helga and Stone, she also wanted to find the mother of the baby and tell her that the child appeared to be gaining in strength. Perhaps she could reason with the woman—were they not both mothers? Maybe she would be able to see Cameron, hold her, even bring her back.

The thought of the woman and Cameron was instantly replaced by the memory of the male. Despite her resolve, her mouth went dry and her knees felt weak at the thought of him. He had been terrifying, more frightening than any monster or horror film she had ever seen. She had no doubt that he would have killed her, bashed her skull with his club, had he caught her. And yet here she was doing her best to find them, him, again.

The hole was widening, growing larger. There was no hint of light on the other side, only more darkness and the strong earthy smell which she had come to associate with their presence. They were close now, she knew it. Hidden at the back of her mind, carefully suppressed, was the fear that they might already have gone, taken Cameron and left the building for safer quarters, but now she knew that they were still here. As frightened as she was, part of her rejoiced.

When the hole was large enough for her to fit through, she picked up the flashlight and directed the beam into the darkness. Everything was just as she remembered it, round doorways opening on either side of a long corridor that stretched away into the distance. Holding the pipe in front of her like a lance,

Katherine stepped through the opening. She thought about replac-
ing some of the bricks but then decided against it; she could not
hope to make it look as it had before.

She turned the light down to its lowest setting, a pale, wan
beam, and pointed it at the ground. She moved as she had before,
close to the wall where she felt safest. A doorway appeared on her
left; it was the room where she had seen Cameron. It too was
shrouded in darkness, but she could not resist slipping inside and
looking. Just to be somewhere that her daughter had been was a
necessity, a deep need, as though by breathing the same air,
moving through the same space Cameron had occupied, imbued
her with a greater degree of strength.

She had more than half expected the room to be empty, stripped
of all its possessions and made to look as though no one had ever
been there. But that was not the case. The room was definitely still
in use. She had seen little before, aside from Cameron and the man
and the woman with the braid. This time, there was no one to
distract her.

It was an astonishing room, filled with furniture and ornamentation that could easily have been part of a museum collection. All
of the furniture—tables, chairs, lounges, lamps—were made of
stone, worked in ways that Katherine had never seen before. Every
single piece was a work of art. Rather than appearing cold and
hard and lifeless as marble and other stone normally did, every
line was fluid and graceful; you could feel the soul and the heart
of the stone as though it were somehow alive.

Nor were the designs typical. Ordinary bits of furniture were not
merely functional but excuses for flights of fancy. A piece that
looked like a Roman chaise was made of a deep marbleized red
stone—carnelian, she thought. It glowed in the soft beam of her
light, rich and fiery in color and smooth and glossy, its curves
graceful and flowing. It looked as though it had been formed,
sculpted, while still in a molten state. She could not understand
how anyone could carve stone into such shapes. Could stone be
melted and molded? And the cost! Perhaps it was not real, but it
looked very real. She thought that carnelian was a moderately
expensive stone. The chaise did not appear to have any seams or
joints that she could see; it looked as though it had been made
from a single piece of stone. Surely the cost would have been
astronomical!

A number of pillows were tastefully arranged against the arm of the chaise and these were just as startling. Several of them were made out of the same soft gray fur skins as the baby's coverlet, but others were woven of a strange fabric that she could not identify. It was similar if not identical to the material that lined the underside of the baby's coverlet. The only thing she could liken it to was silk, which seemed crude and rough in comparison. Like the fur skins, they too were all in muted tones of gray and ivory. Along their edges was a continuous wide band of embroidery, a neat satin stitch, more expertly executed than anything Katherine had ever achieved. But it was the pattern that caught her attention. Just as the woman's braid had reminded her of a portrait of an Etruscan woman, the pattern on the pillows was Roman or Greek in origin.

She swung the beam around the room, illuminating it so that she might gain an overview. She knew that she should not stay, knew that she should be trying to find Helga and Stone, but Cameron had been here and it was hard to make herself leave.

Most of the furniture appeared to have been made from the red stone, and all of it was as beautiful and of the same fine degree of craftsmanship as the chaise. The pieces seemed to have been custom-made as well, for several of the chairs were smaller than usual. Katherine tried to sit in one and felt like Goldilocks trying to fit into Baby Bear's chair; she was just too big. But other chairs were huge. She shuddered with the memory of the man with the club. The larger pieces had undoubtedly been made to accommodate his larger frame.

The walls were hewn from the earth and plastered with a type of stucco which had been drawn into graceful swirls while still wet. They were a pale terra-cotta in color, serving as a subtle backdrop for the furniture and the room itself. The swirling stucco reminded her of the motion of water; it was beautiful as well as calming.

The floors were stone, polished to a high gloss. Woven carpets were scattered about, some larger than others. Most of them were patterned in an intricate, multicolored design that looked vaguely like paisley.

As her beam explored the room she began to realize just how large it was, at least 20 by 30 feet, and it looked as though there were another room beyond. She took a step forward, and then, totally unexpected, like a sudden clap of thunder breaking above one's head on a cloudless summer afternoon, a hand clasped her shoulder.

She whirled around swiftly, her heart pounding wildly, a high-pitched ringing noise in her ears. The beam of the flashlight careened from floor to furniture to ceiling as she turned. With shaking hands she raised the light.

NINETEEN

Helga was dreaming. She was dreaming that she was a little girl again. She was high in the mountains. It was dark out, so it must be night, but she could not see any stars; that was odd. She was riding on Papa's shoulders, or perhaps he was carrying her as he had often done when she was very small. She could not remember just how it was that she had gotten so small, or even how it was that Papa was here and young and strong himself. But it was a dream; such things happened in dreams.

It was all very confusing and it hurt to think. Also, there was a lot of pain. Her head and her chest hurt, and why did her arm ache so awfully? It brought tears to her eyes. She wondered where her mother was. Mother always kissed away the hurts and made them better. She wanted her mother, smoothing the hair back from her forehead and telling her that everything would be all right.

Suddenly, Helga was desperately frightened. She didn't know why. Something was wrong and she didn't understand what she was supposed to do. A great wave of nausea and pain rose up in her, and before she could tell Papa to stop, to put her down, she turned her head to the side and retched. It hurt. Her throat and her chest were burning and her arm would not work, would not rise to wipe the sickness from her chin. Hot tears fell from her eyes and ran down her cheeks. She wanted to tell Papa that she was sorry, but the words wouldn't come. Her tongue felt too large and oddly wooden and strange noises emerged when she tried to speak. What was wrong?

151

Strong hands lay her down on the ground. She felt something soft being wrapped around her. A hand cradled her head and gently wiped the sickness from her chin. Soft fingers stroked her forehead and then caressed her eyelids and cheeks, slowly calming her, easing her anxiety.

Her breathing came easier now, but her heart still pulsed and leaped in her chest, fluttering against her ribs like a wild bird caught in a trap. Papa took her hand, holding it tight to let her know he was there. But it was such a big hand—Papa's hands were small and delicate, not so big or strong. But it was a dream. It *was* a dream, wasn't it? Why was everything so dark? Why couldn't she see the stars or Papa's face? She became afraid again. Somebody was whimpering. She could hear someone crying and she realized that it was she who was making those noises.

Papa cradled her to his chest and stroked her head, smoothing back the hair from her forhead. It wasn't Mama but she wasn't alone, and when the pain grew larger and larger inside her, spreading in hot lapping waves, he held her close and whispered soft, strange words in her ear. And then as the pain engulfed her and the darkness cleared, she raised her hand to greet them, for at last she could see the stars.

The beam of the boat light illuminated the woman's face, throwing her features into strong relief, causing them to appear even more foreign and strange than they already were. The two women stared at each other and Katherine realized that after the first terrible shock, she had lost her fear. The woman made no move, hostile or otherwise, merely stood quietly as though waiting for Katherine to speak, to indicate by tone or word what the mood of their meeting would be.

The two women gazed intently at each other, studying each other closely. The women was shorter than Katherine, no more than five feet tall and slender. Her hair was the same white-blond that Katherine remembered; fine in texture but quite thick. It grew low on her forehead, and a tightly drawn twisting braid followed the hairline, keeping all but a few tendrils away from the woman's face. Other braids gathered her hair from the side and back, and all converged just below her left ear in a single thick plait which hung down over her shoulder to the middle of her chest.

Her forehead was long and broad and sloped back sharply from the eyebrows, throwing the brows into sharp prominence. They too were pale blond, nearly white, so light as to appear nonexis-

tent. Her lashes were equally pale and served to make the eyes all
the more startling. Pale blue in color with flecks of silver, they
were like the baby's in that the pupils were huge and the iris but
a small ring around the dark centers. The cheekbones were sharply
drawn, high, placed immediately beneath the cheeks, the cheeks
falling away into hollows alongside the small and slender nose.
The mouth was wide, extremely wide, the lips nicely shaped and
somewhat full. The chin was small and pointed but lacking the
aggressive thrust that had been so noticeable on the male.
Altogether it was a very unusual face, shorter and wider than
normal.

Katherine tried to place the facial structure, but it was unlike
anything she had ever seen before. Still, the woman was not
deformed or even ugly, just different. That pale hair, those icy blue
eyes; there had to be some Slavic blood there. Many middle
Europeans exhibited the same slightly tilted eyes and high
cheekbones. But still, why would a family of Slavs be living in
secrecy beneath Katherine's building? From the look of the
woman and her possessions, they were certainly not poor. It made
no sense at all.

The woman was dressed in a short flowing ecru tunic made
from the same strange silk-like fabric that covered some of the
pillows and lined the baby's coverlet. Soft knee-high leather boots
completed the outfit. Most noticeable, however, was her jewelry.
At her ears there hung simple hoops of pure gold and from them
were suspended faceted diamonds that glittered brightly in the
subdued light. A pendant suspended from a gold filigree chain
hung at her throat; it too was a diamond, blue-white in color,
shaped in the form of a heart and framed in the same gold filigree
as the chain, which was delicate yet strong and beautiful. She wore
numerous bracelets on her slender arms, all of them gold, some
patterned, some plain, in varying widths. There was also a bracelet
that matched the necklace. Small hearts of diamonds, each of them
framed in gold, were attached to two strands of the woven filigree
so that they could move freely, sliding back and forth, clicking
softly with her every move. On the middle finger of her right hand,
she wore a single wide band of gold. The woman was wearing a
fortune in gold and gems. Who was she and why was she here?
None of it made any sense!

Moving slowly, so as not to offer any hint of threat or
aggression that might frighten the other woman, Katherine set the
light aside, placing it atop a small stone table shaped in the form

of large, overlapping lotus leaves supported by legs craved to resemble twining vines.

The light was not a problem to the woman; her eyes began to adjust as soon as the light moved away from her, the pupils expanding visibly. It seemed certain that she was able to move freely in the darkness. How else had she been able to traverse the dark corridors and the roomful of furniture?

The woman moved to a low couch and sat down, looking up at Katherine, waiting. Katherine hesitated only a moment before joining her. She brought the light with her but placed it on the floor, facing away from them, its beam directed at the wall, where it cast a faint, diffuse glow. Although she did not fear the woman, there was no way of knowing when or if the man would appear, so she lay the iron pipe on the floor at her feet. The woman eyed it uneasily.

"I am Crystal." Her voice was soft and low-pitched, but strong and proud in a way that told Katherine that the woman was not afraid of her. Though she spoke English, it was apparently not her native tongue. The strong accent was like nothing Katherine had ever heard.

"I am Katherine," she replied, although she suspected that the woman already knew her name as well as other information about her. Katherine was taller than Crystal by a full head, but the woman's bearing was so regal that she gave the appearance of being much taller.

"You have my daughter," Katherine said, doing her best not to allow her emotions to surface, knowing if she demanded the child's return or accused the woman of wrongdoing, she would jeopardize her chances of getting Cameron back.

The woman nodded her head stiffly. In her eyes, Katherine could read fear, the desperate need for knowledge as well as the absolute terror of hearing the words that would put an end to all hope. It was a feeling that Katherine had come to know well during the last dreadful hours of Rod's life.

Having experienced it herself, Katherine could understand the terrible pain and fear that the woman had lived with, not knowing whether her child lived or died, dependent upon the actions of others for the baby's very existence. She spoke quickly to alleviate the woman's fears. "The baby is all right. I think she will live."

Crystal's head sagged, fell nearly to her chest, like a puppet whose master had dropped the strings, leaving her limp, without the strength to act on her own.

Alarmed, Katherine took the woman by the shoulders, feeling the small, fragile bones beneath her hands, the odd coolness of her skin. "Don't worry, everything will be all right."

The woman swayed and then straightened, opening her eyes and staring at Katherine. "How can you say this? How can you be so kind after we . . ."

It seemed odd even to Katherine. Here she was comforting a woman who had been responsible for stealing her child, a woman whose husband had tried to kill her. What was she doing and why? "I—I don't know," she said in a stricken voice. "Cameron, how is she?"

"The baby is good. She is strong and eats often, although I think she does not like my milk so much."

"Where . . . ?" Katherine asked, looking around and wondering if Cameron could be near without her knowing it.

"She is not here. They take her away to the Gathering."

"Who? Why did they take her!" Katherine half rose as though to go in search. Crystal seized her hand and drew her down firmly. "No, you must not think of going. You do not find them. It is not safe. The baby is fine, she is cared for with much love. Please, you will tell me now about Amber."

Amber, it was a good name, it suited her. Katherine sat down slowly, still wanting to try to find Cameron but realizing that the woman was right. She could not go rushing about in the dark corridors by herself. She had to win the woman's help.

"Amber is better now. In the beginning, I did not know what was wrong. I still don't know, really. But there were some things that were obvious; the light hurt her eyes and her skin blistered . . ." The woman's eyes closed and she groaned softly, feeling her baby's pain. "When she wouldn't nurse, I got scared," Katherine said, rushing her words, trying to reassure the woman. "We took her to the hospital." The woman's head came up with a jerk and she pressed her hands against her chest. "The hospital? No! They will do bad things to her!"

"I stopped them," Katherine said, taking Crystal's hands in her own. "She nursed last night. Twice. She is sleeping easier and I think she will be all right. They will not do anything to harm her, no needles, no transfusions, no bright lights, no tests, nothing without my approval. But I cannot help her, they cannot help her, unless we know what is wrong with her. Can you tell me? Is that why you brought her to me, so that I could help her?"

Crystal looked at Katherine, trying to make up her mind what to say. The struggle was obvious. "Please tell me the truth," Katherine pleaded. "You want your child back alive and well. And I want my daughter. We are mothers, not enemies. We can help each other. But I cannot help you unless I know what's happening. Please tell me—I have the right to know!"

Crystal looked up, met her eyes. Her chin firmed. "She is poisoned. She cannot be well again. She will die, that is why they sent her away, change her for a healthy baby. But I do not agree. Always before, my babies they die inside me. Sometimes they live a little while, but then they die. But Amber, she lives. I think she will be healthy, that they will let her stay. But then the sickness comes. I try to hide it from them, but they know. They always know. They say Amber must be changed and they try to take her from me. Jasper, he try to help me and I know that he has pain like I do. But we cannot stop them.

"Everyone is angry; there is much danger for us if we do not do what they say. Finally, the Guardian, he has an answer. He say there is a baby close. A strong, healthy baby the same size as Amber. The mother, she is sad and has much pain of the heart. Maybe she will not notice the change, only sickness, and will help Amber. The others, they say no, there is too much danger for us. We must change Amber with another baby, one that belongs to people who do not care or woman with the drugs in her mind and body. But I will not agree, will not let them have Amber. People who do not care, people with the drugs, they will not help Amber and she will die. This I know.

"Jasper, he does not want to agree with them, but he say where will we go if we do not let them change Amber. There is nowhere to go if we are alone. Changing baby with you is the only way, the only chance that Amber will live. The Guardian say that you are a good person, that you will help. But I worry. I do not know you. How can I say?

"I make them promise to take me with them when they change the babies. They say no; again there is much angry words. Jasper tells me we must do as they say. They are too many. I am afraid I cannot be alone. I know that if I say no, they will take Amber from me or turn us out to be alone. What can I do? The Guardian tells me not to be afraid.

"We come in the night. I come too. They change the babies and take your Cameron away. I stay, just for a little while. It is so hard to leave. I hold Amber in my arms for the last time, kiss her, and tell her not to be afraid. The others are gone. Then I hear a noise.

It is you! You come into the room and see the baby is gone. I am
behind the door, you do not see me. I am very afraid. But you go.
I know that I must go too. But it is so hard. I kiss Amber and put
her back in bed; then I follow you. I am more afraid to be alone
in the light. My eyes, they are crying, and the light, it is so bright.
Jasper, he is waiting beneath the stairs and we wait until you come
back before we come here to the new baby.

"I do not wish to make you cry. I do not wish to bring you pain.
I wish only to have my own baby, that she will live and be strong.
But I cannot do these things. I am not allowed."

She was crying openly now, the words broken by her tears and
the depth of her sorrow. Katherine gathered the small woman into
her arms and held her against her chest, patting her back to
comfort her as she tried to understand the woman's story. None of
it made any sense.

From what she said, it sounded like there were a lot of people
involved, and from what she had seen, it did not seem unlikely.
Was it possible that there was some sort of hidden society living
down here?

And who was this Guardian who knew so much about her, who
had been directly responsible for Cameron's kidnapping? And
who was it who held so much power and control that they could
tell Crystal and Jasper, whom she could only assume was Crystal's
husband, what to do with their lives and their only child? None of
it made any sense at all.

But all of those questions could wait. What mattered now was
calming Crystal, reassuring her about Amber and finding out how
she might go about getting Cameron back. It had seemed far
simpler when she thought she was only dealing with two or three
people at most. Now, it appeared that there were many more.

"Crystal, what did you mean when you said that Amber had
been poisoned? Who poisoned her? What kind of poison? I will
have to tell the doctors so they can know what to do."

Crystal pushed herself upright and wiped her tears away with
the back of her hand. "The poison will not go away; it is in the
blood and the—the—what you call the liver. It holds the poison.
We do not do this, no one would do this; it comes from the water.
The water is poisoned. It kills all of our babies."

"What water? This water here? I drink this water, so does
everyone in Chicago; it doesn't kill our babies!"

"We are different, you and I. Our bodies are not the same."

Katherine was about to disagree, but looking at Crystal's

features, she thought that possibly the woman knew what she was talking about. "But how can . . ."

Crystal held up her hand abruptly and turned her head toward the corridor. Katherine heard nothing, but Crystal turned back to face her, her eyes huge and filled with fear. "They are coming! It is too soon, but they are here!"

Katherine rose to her feet, her heart leaping. Cameron! She started toward the door, but Crystal grasped her by the wrist and pulled her back sharply. "No!" she said forcefully. "They kill you if they see you!" In one swift motion she seized the lantern, and pressed the button that extinguished the light, plunging them into total darkness. "Come!" she hissed. "They cannot find you here!"

"But, but what about Cameron . . . !"

Crystal did not answer, nor did she release her hold on Katherine's wrist, moving swiftly in the darkness and pulling her behind in an awkward stumble. Katherine barely had time or thought to grab the iron pipe up off the floor. Unable to see in the all-enveloping darkness, she had taken no more than a few steps before she crashed into something that teetered and then fell. There was the sound of a large object careening to the floor.

"Crystal! *Wo bist du?*" The man's voice was sudden, unexpected, and alarmingly close. Katherine had doubted at first that Crystal had really heard anything, but the harsh voice was convincing proof. A flare of fear spurted up in her abdomen. Crystal had stopped when the man called out. Now, she began to run, and this time, Katherine made every attempt to follow the pressures on her wrist that indicated the direction they were to go.

There was a startled comment, a loud whisper rather than spoken words. "Crystal, *nein, nicht die mutter! Kommen sie hier!*"

Crystal did not stop. The man kept after them, calling to the woman, begging her to stop. Then, suddenly, there were other voices. The man tried to talk to them; there were sounds of some confusion and then angered cries. Crystal increased her pace. There was a sudden sense of space narrowing. The pipe clattered against a wall, the metal ringing out loudly. There was a sharp intake of breath from Crystal and loud, angry cries behind them.

Their pace increased, Crystal dragging her along at a rapid rate. She thought that they had passed through one of the peculiar rounded doorways. Yes, the feeling was different here, the floor rougher underfoot and there was a slight current of cool air. Behind them, the voices grew louder, more argumentative. There was a sharp expletive and then the sound of footsteps, many footsteps, following them. Voices called out demanding that they halt. The words were not in English, but their meaning was clear.

Crystal began to run even faster, and Katherine, frightened by the angry sounds behind them, did her best to keep up. They turned sharply left, then right, then straight for a time. It was hard running in the dark, trusting yourself so completely to another. There was a sharp pain in her side, and her mouth and throat were as dry as flannel. She could not remember ever having been so thirsty. Where were they going?

Finally, after what seemed like hours, Crystal pulled her into a small enclosure. They waited there in the darkness, but there were no sounds of pursuit. Somehow, they had lost their followers. When Crystal was satisfied that no one was behind them, she switched a light on. Katherine was taken by surprise; she did not realize that the woman had taken the lantern. Crystal pressed the glass face directly against a wall so that there was no more than a pale glow to illuminate the space. Even so, her eyes contracted in pain and she covered them with her hand. Faint as it was, the light was shockingly brilliant after the total darkness.

When Katherine's eyes had adjusted, she lowered her hands and looked around her. They were in some sort of concrete cubicle that was filled with massive bundles of multicolored wires and cables. They lined the walls in thick rows like massive mechanical worms hibernating for the winter. "What is this place?"

"It is just a place," Crystal said, leaning back wearily. "You will be safe now."

"But who were those people? What happened back there? Why . . . ?"

"No more questions." Crystal waved her hand in the air between them. Looking at her, Katherine saw the bleakness, the hopeless fear, that filled her eyes.

"Will you be all right? They won't hurt you, will they? We didn't do anything but talk!"

Crystal looked at her strangely. Katherine faltered; her words died on her lips. Nothing made sense here. She was talking about things she knew nothing about. These people obviously lived by rules other than her own. Crystal had helped her and now, it was clear, there would be trouble. "What's going to happen? Will I see you again?"

Crystal looked down at the ground; a look of desolation swept over her features. Her eyes filled. Looking up, she grabbed Katherine's hands with her own, her fingers as small as a child's.

"Amber, she is so . . ." The words were filled with anguish. Tears ran unnoticed down her cheeks. "Do not let them hurt her, the doctors. No metal. The blood is sick, but our blood, it is not like yours. You will make them make her well!" she said fiercely, squeezing Katherine's fingers in a painful grip. "I do not ask you to do this for nothing. I will pay!"

"Yes, of course! But Cameron . . . !"

"I do what I can. I try to bring her back. You must trust me. But do not come again; it is not safe. They will kill you if they find you here. You understand."

Katherine understood nothing. She did not understand why she was agreeing with everything the woman was saying when she was receiving nothing in return, not even the assurance that she would ever see Cameron again, much less get her back. It was very confusing. She felt like a fool, but Crystal was so adamant, and the danger had seemed very, very real. What was she to do? She could hardly disagree or threaten the woman, nor could she bring the police; they would never believe her again. She would not even attempt to tell them about the people who lived beneath the building in total darkness with possessions fit for a king.

She opened her mouth to speak, but before she could utter a word, there were angry shouts and the pounding of footsteps, coming toward them. Crystal snapped off the light, grabbed Katherine by the arm, and pulled her forward. There was a sharp click and a rush of warm, fetid air. Crystal shoved her hard; Katherine stumbled forward, and when she found her footing, the flashlight was there at her feet and Crystal was gone.

There was a loud, clacking noise above her, coming straight toward her, almost overwhelming in the volume of the sound. It seemed as if some huge, unstoppable object was rushing unseen in the darkness and she was directly in its path. Then, just when the level of sound was so great that her whole body trembled under the assault, it passed her by, still unseen, and then was gone, vanishing rapidly into the distance.

She sagged against a clammy concrete wall, fear pounding through her body like a pulse. It was several minutes before she could gather her shattered nerves enough to turn on the light and think about finding her way to safety.

She was in a narrow concrete-walled corridor. On the low ceiling above her there was an aluminum conduit and a light bulb. She followed the metal tube and found another bulb and then another and another. Warm, rank air, filled with the stench of rotting garbage and urine, washed against her face. She knew that smell: every Chicagoan knew that stink. It was the smell of subways. She hurried forward now, anxious to know where she was. The corridor ended in a heavy, institutional-looking green metal door. She twisted the spring lock and let herself out.

"You! Lady! Whatchoo doin' in there?" An immense black woman dressed in the navy blue uniform of the RTA advanced on her with a belligerent scowl.

"I—I, uh, I was looking for a rest room," Katherine answered, knowing that the woman would not believe her. The woman scanned her slowly, taking in the incongruous sight of the disheveled woman standing there clutching a boat light and a three-foot length of rusty iron pipe.

"Uh-huh. Well, get your skinny white ass outa here and go look for a rest room somewhere else. You hear!"

Katherine nodded and scuttled toward the exit, daylight filling the grimy window panes with a dull, gray light. She could still feel the woman's sarcastic gaze burning between her shoulder blades as she pushed through the swinging doors. Much to her amazement, she found herself standing directly beneath the Thorndale Street elevated tracks, a mere six blocks from home.

"Yo! Mama! You wanna buy a dog? Nice, pritty dog?" A tall, emaciated black man with the yellowed corneas and hollowed cheeks of a crack smoker, slouched toward her, a small, white Bichon Frise tucked under his arm, a crimson bow encircling a perky topknot at the peak of its forehead. The dog had undoubtedly been stolen from its apartment or back yard, livestock on the hoof for this modern-day rustler, to be peddled for whatever the market would bear, a tiny fraction of its true value. If it could not be sold as a pet, it would most likely wind up in a stockpot of one of the many Vietnamese, Korean, or Cambodian restaurants that now filled the neighborhood.

Suddenly, looking at the small, frightened puppy, Katherine was filled with a great anger. Unable to influence any of the strange circumstances that had robbed her of her husband and her child, faced with dangers so unbelievable that no one and nothing could help, this more familiar evil—one that she could actually meet face to face—was an event to be welcomed. The lantern fell from her grasp and bounced onto the sidewalk unnoticed. She advanced on the man with the iron pipe clutched in both hands like a bat. "Give me the dog," she snarled.

The man looked at her in astonishment. "Yo, sweet mama, no

need for vi-o-lence." He tried to laugh as he backed away from her. The dog whimpered. Its large eyes filled with confusion and fear, the tiny pink tongue lolling out the side of its mouth, panting hard. The man, the dog. They were all too typical sights; it was hard to walk down the street without someone trying to sell you something, snatch your purse, or beg spare change. It was the price of living in the city and one learned to deal with it, but somehow, this time it was different. Maybe it was the look of terror in the puppy's eyes, ripped from its loving, secure home and roughly handled by uncaring hands. Whatever it was that had triggered this reaction, it was the proverbial last straw for Katherine.

"Three hunnert dollars," the man said, backing up further as a few passersby gave them brief sidelong glances and then hurried on. *Never stop. Never. That was the rule of the city. Never become involved.* The man looked around him for support, but those that might have been his associates, dressed in oddments of mismatched clothing suddenly became busy elsewhere, their eyes averted.

"Two hunnert! That's fair, you cain't say that ain't fair!"

Katherine raised the pipe higher, ready to strike, already anticipating the solid smack of the pipe against his skinny arm.

"Fifty! You cain't do no better'n that!" Unwilling to take his eyes off the crazed white woman advancing on him with an iron pipe, the man failed to see where he was going and fell off the edge of the curb where it met the alley. He fell hard, still clutching the tiny dog in his arms. Then she was standing over him and, scrambling awkwardly to his knees, he scuttled off on all fours, looking over his shoulder to see if she was following.

Had it not been so awful, it might have been comical. Suddenly, her anger as well as her resolve deserted her. Katherine dropped the pipe from nerveless fingers. It struck the gritty sidewalk and rolled away with a brittle clatter before coming to rest in the gutter. She sank to the ground at the edge of the curb, her knees trembling, no longer able to support her. She buried her head in her hands and began to weep.

The puppy, whimpering uncertainly, took a few steps in one direction and then another before crawling between her legs under the umbrella of her arms and began to lick the hot tears from her face.

TWENTY

Dr. Bosch glowered at the report he held in his hand. He had read it numerous times, but additional readings did not change the words or the meaning. It was a report from Wilson, the hematologist he had asked to consult on the Sinclair case. It didn't make sense, nothing about the damned case made any sense.

Benjamin Bosch had been the Sinclair family physician from the earliest days of his practice. He was intimately familiar with the Sinclairs from the grumpy and dour great-grandfather who had established the family's wealth, down through the various descendants to the final Sinclairs, Rod and now Cameron. He had nursed them through a variety of ailments, some minor and others more serious. He had tended to their births and been present at their burials.

His was one of the last true family practices. His patients were loyal to him and it was not uncommon for him to become deeply involved in their lives, serving as far more than a physician. He had often been a trusted confidant, a witness to wills, and a friend to be depended upon in times of trouble.

He had known Rod Sinclair since his birth, having delivered him without complications at this same Edgewater Beach Hospital where his daughter was now a patient. Rod's death had been a personal blow. The two men had been close friends for many years, enjoying chess, skeet shooting at the lakefront, and lengthy hours of conversation over smoky single-malt Scotch whisky long before it became the in drink of yuppies.

The heart attack had occurred with no advance warning. It was far too late to do anything by the time he had arrived at the hospital. Rod had been a good man, honest, forthright, and intelligent with a truly unique sense of humor. His loss was especially bitter.

As a physician, especially one who had been practicing as long as he had, Benjamin Bosch had learned early to erect a professional barrier between himself and death. It was not that one did not feel, or care, but rather a form of acceptance that enabled one to continue on.

But occasionally there were those cases where the barrier fell and could not be raised. Rod's death had been such an instance, and in some complicated manner, Bosch knew that if he did not allow himself to experience the pain of the loss, he would somehow be denying the depth of their friendship. It was at times such as these that being a physician was so very hard, a healer who was unable to heal, unable to do anything but watch and grieve.

Perhaps that was why he was so determined to save this child; he owed it to the father who had been his friend. But it was difficult; nothing made sense, nothing at all.

He had been present when Katherine went into premature labor. They had attempted to stop the contractions but had been unable to do so. Katherine had received the very best care, and the birth, although traumatic, was uneventful. The child was small, as would be expected, and had been placed in an incubator immediately.

Edgewater's natal care unit was adequate, but this baby was special and she had received the very best of care that Benjamin Bosch had been able to provide. As a senior staff member, as well as a legendary personality, his mere presence elicited crack performances from personnel anxious to earn one of his rare smiles and even more anxious to avoid his towering rages.

He was aware of his reputation, although he seldom gave it much thought. This time, however, he put it to work for him, letting the staff of the unit know that this baby was personally important to him and that he would welcome their support. Cameron had been tended with scrupulous care and, due in part to their conscientous performance, she had left the hospital weeks earlier than anticipated. Now, despite all those earlier efforts, it seemed likely that the child would die.

If the report was to be believed, and Wilson was world-respected in his field, Cameron's blood which conformed to no known blood type, was contaminated with a number of heavy metals. How could it have happened and would the contamination explain the peculiar composition of the blood itself?

Aside from the numbers, the report included an analysis of the situation, suggesting other tests that needed to be performed to judge the degree of damage suffered by the liver and other organs. Wilson also advocated a program of treatment that included "washing" the blood to cleanse it of impurities. Still, his final conclusion was not encouraging. Based upon the degree of contamination, death was the inevitable conclusion.

Benjamin Bosch clamped his teeth down on the end of his unlit cigar and frowned. A young nurse, passing at the time, thought the frown was directed at her and scurried away as quickly as she could, wondering what on earth she had done to earn his disfavor.

He could not, would not, allow this child to die if there was anything at all he could do about it. Aside from the fact that Cameron was his patient, he owed it to Rod. Furthermore, he thought that if the child died, Katherine might well suffer a complete breakdown.

But beyond the report and his allegiance to the parents, there were things about this case that troubled him deeply. Things that he did not feel comfortable discussing with his colleagues. Stuffing the report into the pocket of his lab coat, he entered the baby's room, ejecting a nurse with a single sideways jerk of his head.

He stood above the incubator and stared down at the child. The baby was awake and alert. The two regarded each other with solemn expressions. The baby was free of all tubes and monitoring devices other than the one taped to her chest which recorded her heartbeat. As he knew from examining the child and from studying the readouts at the nurses' station, the baby's heart beat 40 times a minute. The norm was 62, yet Cameron did not show any of the typical signs of low blood pressure or cardiac distress. How could that be? She was pale, very pale, but she did not exhibit any of the signs one would see in an infant who was suffering from a cardiac disorder. The sclera were clear and white, not yellowed or tinged with blue as one would expect to see with severe anemia or renal failure.

But what troubled Benjamin Bosch the most was the look of the child herself. The Sinclair family were, for the most part, all of a similar physical type. Their heads were long and square, large heads to fit large bodies. The women occasionally had oval faces, but most often their jaws were squared as well. Jaw lines were prominent and well-defined.

Katherine was tall and well-formed, a good-looking woman in all respects. Her head was a long, perfect oval with a delicate, almost pointed chin. Bosch could see no way in which Katherine and Rod could have produced a child with a skull such as the one he was looking at now. He had delivered the child; she had been tiny but perfect in every respect. Her head, just like Katherine's, had been a perfect oval, allowing for the typical swelling and temporary puffiness that accompanied birth. He could think of no way that the skull could have gone through the changes necessary to present its current appearance.

He picked the baby up out of the incubator, feeling the silvery gray eyes locked upon his own. The tiny fingers were stuffed inside the baby's mouth and the change of position did not stop her from sucking on them as he wedged his bulk into the rocking chair and settled her into his lap. In her other hand she clutched a circle of stones, an odd toy, but one she seemed unwilling to relinquish.

"Who are you, little one? What are you and where did you come from?" he murmured. Seeing a bottle sitting on the tabletop alongside the chair, he tested it for temperature and then guided it into the baby's mouth. She withdrew her wet fingers and clutched the bottle, sucking from it greedily, but still, her eyes never left his face, regarding him with a look that held far more awareness and intelligence than he was accustomed to seeing in a child this young.

While she was occupied with the bottle, he stroked her head with his free hand, feeling the structure of the bone beneath the thin layer of flesh. There was no doubt that the occipital ridges were far more prominent than the norm. The skull itself sloped sharply back from the brows and the cheekbones were broad and flat. The jaw structure was also definitely aligned in a far different manner than he had ever seen.

He picked up the tiny arm that held the stone toy, taking note of the unusually elongated ulna and, despite their small size, the broad, spatulate fingertips. The space between thumb and first finger was also very wide.

There were other atypical skeletal differences as well. While the number of vertebrae was correct, the neck appeared shorter than usual and the spine had an obvious curve. The pelvic girdle was exceedingly wide and the legs short and slightly bowed. While the upper thigh bone was the appropriate length, the lower leg bone appeared shorter than normal. Even the tiny feet were odd in that the ball of the foot was extremely wide and the toes slightly curled, almost prehensile in appearance.

"I think you're a little throwback, that's what I think," the doctor rumbled. It seemed to him that the baby smiled at him around the nipple, but it was probably just gas or a reaction to his voice. But once he had spoken the words, which had been uttered in jest, heard them aloud, they stuck in his mind, causing him to think about what he had said. Unbidden, a picture of Neanderthal man came to mind, the picture one most often saw in textbooks, the foreshortened skull, the broad forehead and high cheekbones, the broad nose and receding jawline. No, it couldn't be, it just wasn't possible! He stared at the baby in stunned disbelief. Or was it?

Katherine patted the dog in an absent-minded manner, then wiped the last of her tears from her face. The gutter was strewn with an accumulation of gum wrappers, squashed soft drink and beer cans, and other city detritus. Ebb lines of filth from the last rain nibbled at her shoes; she could feel a layer of grit beneath her on the sidewalk. Tucking the puppy beneath her arm, she tried to rise and found that her legs were weak and trembly. She staggered and nearly fell.

A woman clad in a long, tailored dark wool coat and smart black leather pumps polished to a high gloss emerged from the swinging doors of the station. She glanced down at Katherine and Katherine could read the disdain in the woman's eyes. Clearly, she thought Katherine was drunk. The woman transferred her leather briefcase to the opposite side of her body and strode away, her heels clicking sharply on the sidewalk. Katherine felt a wave of anger and helpless despair flood over her.

She felt like shouting after the woman, cursing her and her easy assumptions. For the first time in her life she felt a sudden kinship with the homeless street people whom she had so often hurried past, averting her gaze as though to meet those despairing, imploring eyes might in some way contaminate her or force her to take some action.

She was in no condition to go anywhere; she doubted that she could walk the short distance home and the day was already drawing to a close, the sky dark and lowering. A cold wind swept in off the lake, chilling her. And what was she to do with the puppy?

Just across the alley, warm light bathed the sidewalk, streaming out between the flaking iron grid that guarded the windows. Some of the icy terror that had chilled her seemed to melt at the sight of that warm light. It was a familiar place, the site of many a happy memory; the Thorndale Deli, one of Rod's favorite places which he had introduced her to early in their courtship.

The deli was owned by two brothers or perhaps two brothers-in-law; Katherine was uncertain of the relationship. But precise relationships scarcely mattered, for the place was swarming with relatives in a vast extended sort of family. Anyone who was fortunate enough to become a favorite customer, and there were many, instantly became part of that family, regardless of religion or lineage. Katherine stumbled along on shaking legs, reaching for the door with her last bit of strength.

Neither of the two owners was present behind the counter as Katherine entered the store. She breathed the spicy fragrance of salami, pastrami, corned beef, smoked fish, and herring, feeling safe and grounded in the all-encompassing aromas.

"Hey, no dogs in here! Lady! You gotta . . . Hey, Miz Sinclair? You all right?" It was Mike, a tall, strapping, broad-chested fellow—a son-in-law, she thought—blond and blue-eyed and never without a large silver cross dangling from his neck and worn like a social comment which she'd never had the nerve to inquire about. He hurried to the door and took her by the elbow, carefully guiding her to the small, dimly lit room behind the storefront where he seated her in an enormous high-backed wooden chair. "You all right? You gonna faint? One o' them *schvartzes* hurt you, maybe? You want I should call the cops?"

She held up a hand to silence his stream of questions. "No, no, I'm all right. I—I just felt sick there for a minute."

"You sure? You look real pale. White, y'know? Here, you wait a sec!" He returned in an instant, pressing an icy cold bottle of Dr. Brown's Celery tonic into her hand. She had never liked the stuff, but could not summon the strength to tell him so. She took a drink, urged on by his evident concern. Much to her surprise, the strange-tasting brew slaked her terrible thirst and eased the knot of pain that gripped her chest. She finished the entire bottle in several long swallows and managed a shaky smile.

"That's better. What'd I tell you! Fix you up in no time." Mike beamed at her, pleased that he had done the right thing. "Didn't know you had a dog. Cute little thing."

The puppy seemed to sense that it was being talked about and whined, wriggling in Katherine's grasp, trying to reach the outstretched fingers that smelled so very enticing.

"Not mine," Katherine managed. "Took him away from one of those men who stand outside the el station. It's probably stolen. Could you take it, try to find out who it belongs to?"

"Well, sure . . . I guess," Mike said more slowly. "But you shouldn't oughta mess with those guys, Miz Sinclair. They're bad business. You could get hurt." A look of sudden comprehension flowed over his face. "Hey, they didn't hurt you, did they?" He half rose as though ready to go out and bash a few heads on her behalf.

"No. No, he didn't touch me. I'm all right, it's just . . ."

"I understand." Mike patted the back of her hand. "It was rough you losin' Mr. Sinclair like that. He was a nice man. Here, listen. Lemme get you a cab, take you home. You still don't look so hot."

She nodded gratefully and rested her head against the tall back of the chair in the semidarkness as he left to make the call. She had fallen into a half doze when he returned. A large earthenware bowl of steaming soup was placed on the desk before her. A plate mounded high with creamy potato salad and a mountainous pastrami sandwich accompanied it.

"Oh, thank you, Mike, but I'm not hungry. I couldn't possibly—"

He raised a hand to silence her. "Just try a nibble or two," he said. "Can't hurt." He slid a paper plate with a generous serving of chopped liver on the floor for the puppy, who had none of Katherine's reservations, and then returned to the store before she could voice further protests.

Much to her amazement, she found that she was ravenous. She could not even remember the last thing she had eaten. The matzo ball soup, which she normally found overly filling, was a mere overture to the rest of the meal, the hot, rich broth warming her and banishing the chill that had been with her for so long. Every last scrap had been consumed by the time Mike come back to tell her that the cab had arrived. She half suspected that he had waited until she was finished eating before he even summoned the taxi.

The puppy was asleep next to its well-licked plate when Mike escorted her out the door and handed her into the cab, giving her a heavy paper bag as the door closed. "Can't hurt," he said with a lopsided grin and a jaunty two-fingered salute as the door thunked shut.

The doorman would not meet her eyes when the cab delivered her to her door, paying the driver without comment as she instructed him to. She did not have the energy or the desire to explain her comings and goings or her disheveled appearance. If people chose to think that she was going crazy, that was all right with her.

"Have you seen Mrs. Orlowski or Mr. Stone?" she asked just before the inner door closed. The doorman replied that Mr. Stone had arrived many hours earlier, shortly before she herself had come in, but had not been seen since. "If you see him, tell him I'd like to talk to him," she directed, allowing the door to close behind her.

The stairs seemed endless. She was exhausted before she had even reached the first landing. They had discussed installing an elevator, but the layout of the building did not lend itself to the addition. It would have necessitated removing large portions of the stairs and banisters which no one was willing to sacrifice. Any other plan would have meant that the elevator would have had to pass through apartments, which was clearly not desirable. So they walked. The issue was raised at every tenant meeting and the same conclusion reached. Rod teased them all that it was good for their hearts. Since he and Katherine had the furthest to climb, it was hard to argue.

She stopped on the first landing, her heart hammering in her chest, and rang Mrs. Orlowski's doorbell. There was no answer. She knocked and tried to see in through the tiny magnifying lens of the peephole. Faint light could be seen coming from one of the front windows, nothing more. She thought that she could hear music, but there was no answer to her repeated knocks. Too exhausted to continue, she dragged herself up the remaining flights of stairs, unlocked the door, and shut it behind her. Never had she been so glad to be home.

She placed a call to the hospital and found that Amber's condition remained unchanged. There was also a message from Dr. Bosch asking her to contact him as soon as possible. No doubt to argue about her restrictions. She didn't have the strength to fight with him right now; that too would have to wait.

She dialed Helga's number, but there was no answer despite the fact that she allowed it to ring twelve times. Stone's phone remained unanswered as well.

There was nothing more she could do. She was filthy and needed a shower. She sat down on the edge of the bed to take off her shoes, then crumpled sideways, dragging the edge of the blanket across her, telling herself that she would rest for just a minute. Within seconds, she had fallen into a deep, unmoving sleep.

TWENTY-ONE

When Katherine awakened, she could not, for a time, remember where she was or how she had gotten there. She was on her side, cramped and stiff from lying in one position for too long. She was staring at a corner of the room she did not ordinarily see upon waking. It had been dark when she lay down; now the room was filled with a cold, harsh, brittle light. She turned her head to one side and saw that she was in her own bedroom. The brown paper sack, its sides nearly transparent with grease and redolent with spices, sat on the satin comforter where she had placed it the night before.

It was snowing. She could see the huge, soft white flakes drifting lazily down past her window. Winter had arrived. She shivered and sat up, feeling her body ache and protest from a hundred different normally unused muscles. Memory came back in a rush as she brushed the tangled fall of auburn hair back from her forehead. No wonder she felt so bad. When was the last time she had run so hard or so far? When was the last time she had been in a fight? Not since she was a child on the farm, tussling and skirmishing with her cousins. A very long time ago.

She was stiff and achy. And dirty. But the scent emanating from the greasy sack drew her like a magnet. Her stomach rumbled loudly, reminding her that she had been filling it on a less than regular basis. It wouldn't hurt to look. She unrolled the top of the sack and was instantly assailed by a strong, heady, foreign aroma. None of the food inside the sack was familiar to her, but it scarcely mattered. She ripped the sack apart, heedless of the damage she was doing to the expensive and delicate fabric of the comforter, and devoured everything that the thoughtful Mike had provided. It was fish of some sort, white and firm-fleshed and lightly smoked, enclosed in a huge, freshly baked Kaiser roll which had been slathered with a thick layer of cream cheese and topped with a thick slice of muenster cheese and sliced onion. It was not a sandwich she would have ever thought of ordering, nor had she ever eaten anything like it in her life. It was delicious, unforgettable. There was also a container of coleslaw and a slice of rich, heavy cheese cake, now room temperature and dented around the edges, all of which she consumed and then licked her fingers wishing there were more.

Sated, sticky, and feeling the need of a hot shower before she could get on with the matters at hand, contacting the hospital, Helga and Stone, she tottered off toward the bathroom, her mind once again beset by myriad worries. She gathered up an armload of fresh clothing and entered the bathroom, filled with the need for haste. She begrudged herself the amount of time she had spent sleeping. She should have slept at the hospital; what if the baby had needed her?

The shower was quickly accomplished, and her teeth strongly brushed, ridding her mouth of the pervasive taste of fish, her filthy clothes tossed into the hamper in the corner. She slipped into a pair of brown corduroy slacks, some warm, woolly brown argyle socks, and her loafers. A tan chamois-cloth shirt and a russet-brown cable-knit sweater completed her outfit. She yanked a comb through her hair, gritting her teeth against the snarls, tying it back at the nape of her neck with a crimson ribbon that reminded her of the puppy. It would not hold the natural curl of her hair for long, but it would do for now.

She hurried out of the bathroom, taking the door that led to the hall rather than her bedroom, intending to make several brief calls before hurrying off to the hospital. Her mind was flooded with the numerous details she needed to deal with, assigning them priorities. First, she had to call the hospital, find out how the baby was, make sure that they hadn't gone against her orders and scheduled further tests. Then she had to call Helga, find out what she had been up to, then Stone to tell him what had occurred. Was it possible that he really knew nothing? She wanted to believe that it was so, but it was growing increasingly more difficult. She found herself thinking about his eyes, the peculiar glints of silver that lanced the gray, the silver that was so like the silver in Amber's eyes. Was it possible that Stone was one of them too? The thought came to her unbidden and shot through her like a bolt of electricity. Immediately her mind shied away from the horrific thought, not wanting to believe that it was true. Perhaps it would be best to see him rather than call him. A cab, she thought hurriedly, driving the disturbing thought from her mind, she had better phone down and tell the doorman to get a cab. Then . . . She took two steps and stopped as though she had run into a plexiglass wall, her harried thoughts dissipating into fragments and drifting away.

There had been times when she had seen things so foreign, so strange, so startling, that her mind had refused to function, had been unable to understand what it was that she was seeing, like looking at an Escher drawing. Such events were not common-place, perhaps happening on no more than two or three occasions in a lifetime. This was one of those times. Directly in front of her, mounded on the carpet of the hall, was a pile of what appeared to be an accumulation of precious metals and gemstones. Her eyes saw, but her mind could not comprehend.

She walked slowly, approached the pile, then looked around to see if anyone was there, someone who could explain. Perhaps it was a joke. But there was no one there.

She crouched down and stared at the strange pile, taking in details, her mind making assumptions, assigning names, assess-ments, clicking away, functioning almost as a separate entity.

It was a small treasure trove, the kind pirates buried and men killed for, right here on the carpet of her hallway in her apartment in the city of Chicago. It was a totally incongruous sight, but she had not a single doubt in her mind that it was real.

Most of the items were contained in a box—no, a small chest. The domed lid was thrown back, resting on the carpet, all but buried by the glittering contents. An effort had clearly been made to display the pieces that rested atop the profusion of precious objects. It was a strange and incongruous mixture of styles and periods and heritages.

Katherine lifted a bronze necklet that she thought to be Celtic, tracing the deep carving and admiring the irregular but highly polished chunk of amber that was set into the rectangle at the bottom of the circlet. The piece had been designed so that the stone would rest upon the breastbone of the wearer. Two clean flat swoops of gleaming bronze swept upwards on both sides to embrace the neck. There were also two carved rectangles set with amber stones that dangled from fragile wire hoops, and a matching bracelet, heavier than one could wear comfortably, that were an obvious match. It was a complete set of prehistoric, ceremonial Celtic jewelry.

She set the pieces aside, wondering who had worn them last, laying each of them reverently on the thick pile of the carpet before reaching for the next piece. She could not fix the style, Mediterranean in origin, but other than that, it was beyond her small degree of knowledge. It was a bracelet of dolphins, made of solid gold. Each of the gracefully arched creatures nosed neatly into the tail of the dolphin in front of it. Their tiny faces wore deftly incised smiles and appeared mischievous, displaying an abundance of exuberance, a joy of life. The tiny chips of aquamarine eyes sparkled brightly just as their designer had intended so many centuries before. They were hinged in some invisible manner so that the bracelet encircled the wrist in a smooth, continuous, flowing motion. She couldn't resist slipping it on; it invited one's touch and glowed softly against her skin as though it had been designed especially for her.

The next item, placed at the very center of the mound, was a tiara or crown, delicate, crumbling in places with age. It appeared to be made of crudely smelted silver and was set with a variety of precious and semiprecious stones. On the whole, it was far less artfully done than the two previous pieces, and she suspected that it was far, far older. She felt uncomfortable handling it, worried that it might break under the pressure of her fingers. She lifted it gingerly and placed it on a shelf of the phone table where it would be safe.

A small pewter box, tarnished and pitted with age, drew her attention. She plucked it out of the glittering mound. It was simple yet sturdy and opened and shut like a small book. Tiny hinges at the back squealed in protest but opened as she pried the tiny pin out of the corresponding holes. The contents were mirrored in the box that contained it. It was a tiny Bible written in Latin, the pages yellow-brown with age and crumbling to the touch. The covers of the book were brittle leather that adhered to her fingers and broke away in chunks. She returned it to its box and shut it quickly, remembering belatedly how the very air could be the enemy of such delicate acid-based papers.

The next two objects were wrapped around each other as though they had been part of each other for too long to separate. The first item was a long silver chain, simple, almost austere in design, with a large round ring at one end. At the bottom of the chain was a large silver cross with the letters INRI pressed deeply into the metal. The chain was of a length that could easily have been worn at one's waist, and when she unwrapped the rest of it and held the second object in her hand, she knew instantly, in some inexplicable manner, that the wearer of the cross had been a priest, perhaps a Jesuit priest, one of the first explorers of the New World.

The object enfolded by the chain was an Indian artifact, puzzling as to its purpose, but once again, she sensed that it had some religious significance. It was a carved stick, perhaps a foot in length with carved figures of people and animals and trees, merging and flowing into one another, the edges slightly darkened to give definition to each of the carvings.

It fit neatly in the palm of her hand, her fingers wrapped around it as though they had received some unspoken message conveyed by the wood which had been polished to a high gloss by the touch of many, many hands. The top of the stick and the bottom were both tightly wrapped with narrow strips of leather, which despite their obvious age were still supple. She suspected that they had been soaked in tallow or grease, for they were waxy to the touch. Tiny stones sculpted in the shape of animals, brightly colored feathers, red and blue glass beads, small shells, and bits of quartz crystal were attached to the ends of the leather strips at varying lengths so that one or the other was always in motion, clicking softly against the stick or one another. It was a beautiful piece, but wrapped as it was with the chain and the cross, she felt that it had been obtained with violence.

An elaborate gilt fleur-de-lis, set with a huge, square-cut emerald, caught her eye and she drew it out, discovering that it was the very end of a short sword. The rounded hilt was outlined with a line of smaller emeralds and diamonds, as was the scabbard that encased the sword. On closer examination, she saw that sword and scabbard were both silver and had merely been covered with a wash of gold, but still, it was a valuable piece.

To the side of the sword, she found a metal helmet with a high, peaked crown and a long, reinforced bit of metal that came down over the face to protect the nose. The helmet fitted snugly over the head and extended far down over the nape of the neck offering the wearer the greatest amount of protection possible. The inside was covered with leather and some form of padding underneath.

There were numerous other pieces, all smaller: bracelets, necklaces, earrings, chalices, and rings as well as a variety of gold coins from Spain, Portugal, and France. The jewelry, disparate as it was, coming from a dozen different lands and cultures, all had one thing in common: it was all beautifully worked and all were made of precious metals and stones. It was a king's ransom.

The last piece, the one that filled the remainder of the chest, was definitely Spanish in origin; a long chain forged of heavy links of gold, to be worn as ornamentation or used, one link at a time, in primitive lands for barter. She had seen one like it in a book on the treasure retrieved from the sunken Spanish ship, the *Atocha*.

Crystal had said that she would pay for the child's care. She had certainly kept her word.

Katherine was perplexed, stunned. What was she to do? How could she leave the apartment with this pile of treasure sitting in the middle of her floor! It was unthinkable. The whole situation was unthinkable. Where had it come from and what was she supposed to do about it? She had no doubt at all that Crystal was responsible for the treasure.

She thought back to the jewelry that Crystal had worn, to the delicate golden bowl she had poised atop a table. At the time she had spared these articles little thought, never completely believing that they were genuine, but now . . . Could she be mistaken? Maybe none of it was real, only clever copies. She picked up the tiara and the Celtic necklet and knew instantly that they were real. She was no jeweler, no artisan, no historian, but there was a feel of great age and authenticity to the pieces that could never be replicated. No, she had no doubt that the pieces were just what they appeared to be.

Insurance would cover the baby's care; none of this was necessary. But she also knew that money was not the issue; it was a bribe, a silent supplication, asking for her help as well as her silence. Did Crystal really think that this was necessary? Katherine would have done everything within her power to keep the child alive without receiving anything in return. But how could Crystal be expected to know that?

On a sudden impulse, Katherine reached into the pile and took two handfuls of small objects—rings, earrings, bracelets, brooches—and shoved them deep into her commodious pockets. They would be useful when she spoke to Stone. She would demand to know the truth about the children.

Abruptly, she rose to her feet. How could she have allowed herself to become distracted when there was so much to do? Her thoughts returned to the children, the one whose life depended in part on the survival of the other. The treasure, as magnificent as it was, was a hindrance that had kept her from focusing on what was really important.

Grabbing the edge of the chest, she tried to drag it across the carpet to the hall closet. She could not budge it. The chest was built of wood, the sides and bottom neatly dovetailed into one another. They creaked alarmingly as she pulled on the side nearest the closet and she was afraid that if she pulled any harder, she might cause the chest to break apart. It was covered with a faded but intricate design of paint and faceted studs, German or Scandinavian in origin, certainly at least a century old, more than likely even older.

She tried to push the chest, and that failed as well. Finally, growing exasperated and wondering how Crystal had ever managed to carry the damn thing so far, she tossed one of Rod's oversized trench coats over the chest and its contents. It was about as convincing as trying to deposit Monopoly money at the bank, but what else was she to do?

She slammed the door behind her, checking to make certain that all of the locks were fully engaged before she left, taking the stairs two and three at a time, anxious to be on her way. Helga and Stone would just have to wait; she had to get to the hospital and find out how the baby was doing.

She glanced at Helga's door as she hurried across the first-floor landing, thought about stopping, but continued on. She would call from the hospital.

There were a number of people standing in the foyer; she could hear their voices even before she started down the last flight of steps. At first, she thought that they were tenants, but then as she started down the steps she could tell that they were strangers, their voices unfamiliar.

A sick feeling washed over her. Something was wrong. Her footsteps slowed; it was almost impossible for her to force herself to continue. She didn't want to know what had happened.

She knew as soon as she saw Stone's stricken eyes looking up at her as she descended. She could not feel the stair treads; it was as though her feet were disconnected at he ankles, no longer attached to the rest of her body.

Their eyes locked as he met her at the foot of the stairs. He grasped her hands tightly. It was almost enough to keep her from looking to the side, to keep her from seeing the two men who guided the sheet-draped wheeled platform through the entry door.

TWENTY-TWO

"I blame myself," Stone said in the coffee shop, cradling the cup of steaming coffee in his hands. "If I had only gotten there sooner . . ."

"I don't understand," Katherine said dully. "You say that when you got to the building, you couldn't find her?"

"She'd had forty-five minutes, an hour, to break into the—the area. I got my flashlight and went after her, but she was nowhere to be found. I—I thought that she had given up and gone back to her apartment when she found no more than we did."

"So you went up to her apartment and rang the bell."

"I rang and I knocked. I could hear the radio playing so I knew she was there. But she wouldn't answer."

"Didn't you think that was strange?"

Stone clenched his hands together. "I thought, well, I thought maybe she was taking a bath, all those cobwebs . . . the dirt . . . I thought maybe she couldn't hear me or maybe didn't want to see me for fear I'd be angry.

"But this morning, when she still didn't answer . . . when I heard the music still playing, I knew something was wrong. I got out my passkeys and let myself in and found her there, sitting in her chair by the window. I called the paramedics, but it was too late. They said she died sometime yesterday, that it was more than likely her heart. She wasn't young and her weight . . ."

"Do you really think that she broke through that door, investigated the area, and then neatly put the tools away before climbing the stairs and letting herself into her apartment to die? All without anyone seeing her? Without you passing her in the basement or on the stairs?"

"How else could it have happened?" Stone asked, raising despairing eyes to meet Katherine's. She searched his eyes for any hit of dissembling, wondering if that was how it really happened. She wanted to believe Stone, wanted to believe that he was telling the truth, but it was hard.

Should she confront him? Tell him what she knew about Crystal and the vast underground complex that spread far beyond their own building, show him the jewelry? She needed to, she wanted to, wanted to watch his silver-gray eyes and read them for the truth, but there was still the baby to consider.

Her grief was like a hard lump in her throat. She felt the salty prick of tears building behind her eyelids and raised a hand to press against her eyes. This was not the time or the place to mourn for Helga; that would come later when she could be alone with her sorrow. So immersed was she in her own moment of grief that she was unaware that the sleeve of her sweater had pulled back revealing the slender circlet of gold dolphins that encircled her wrist. Had she not been so preoccupied, she would have seen Stone stare at her wrist, riveted by the shock of seeing the ancient bracelet.

"Get'cha anything else?" It was the same rude waitress who had served Katherine and Helga two days earlier. The waitress was wondering if this woman, who could so obviously afford to buy a full breakfast and leave a healthy tip besides, was going to make a habit of coming here, ordering little, and bumming people out with all these tears. And why her station? There were three other waitresses in the place. Why did the woman always pick on her? It wasn't fair!

Katherine and Stone left the coffee shop and stood outside, shivering in the brisk wind that whipped directly in off the lake. The snow had stopped but the sky was filled with a feeling of heaviness, the dark clouds hanging low and full-bellied over the buildings, carrying a promise of more snow before the day was done. Both of them appeared nervous, uncertain of what to do or say next.

"I have to get to the hospital, see how the baby's doing," Katherine said.

"I could come with you, if you'd like," Stone said, torn by the

need to be in several places and not knowing what the right thing
was to do.

Katherine looked at him, pondering his offer. His eyes were
ringed with red, the corneas streaked. The skin beneath his eyes
was broken by myriad fine lines and she could see wisps of gray
in his wind-rumpled hair. For the first time, she realized that he
was not as young as she had first thought. His boyish, Mel Gibson
looks and the beard concealed much of his true nature. He
shivered as she stared at him, hands jammed deep into the pockets
of his army fatigue jacket, which was not at all adequate against
the assault of the lake wind. For that matter, neither was her own
sweater, but she did not want to return to the building.

"Thanks, I'd like that," and with a rush of surprise, she realized
that she would indeed like him there with her so that she did not
have to stand up to the doctors alone. "But it's all right. I'm sure
there are things you need to tend to. Don't worry about me, I'll be
all right."

"Maybe I'll stop by later, if it's all right."

She nodded her acceptance and then, hugging herself against
the cruel wind, flagged down a cruising taxi, looking for fares at
this slow time of the morning. She welcomed the warm, stuffy,
cigarette smell that filled the cab's interior, and gave the Middle
Eastern driver the name of the hospital. He nodded and pulled a
sharp U turn in the middle of the busy boulevard. Stone was still
staring after her as the taxi bore her in the opposite direction. It
was as though there was something more he wished he had said or
done. It was a look that she would recall often throughout the
coming days.

Dr. Bosch was waiting for her when she arrived, his large frame
crammed into the rocker, holding the baby in the crook of his arm,
a pensive look on his face.

He rose as she entered, relinquished the rocker to her, and
positioned the baby in her arms. It began to nurse immediately,
sucking greedily and strongly, the tiny hands holding her breast,
the huge eyes fastened on her own.

Already, in the short period of time that she had been gone,
further changes had taken place. The baby's hair had become a
shimmering silvery white, a carpet of fine curls that framed the
oddly shaped skull, unlike Cameron's hair which had been
golden-blond and completely straight except at the ends. The eyes
were totally gray now, silvery gray. Cameron's had been the
bright, clear blue of a Wisconsin summer's day. The hand and

fingers that flexed against her breast were different as well, the palm broader, the fingers shorter, more blunted. And the tiny feet that waggled upright, kicking at the air, they were different too. The feet were broader across the ball, and the toes were long and curved under as though they could be used to grasp and hold an object with ease, like extra hands.

"There are other more significant, but less noticeable changes as well." Dr. Bosch's rumbling bass broke into her thoughts. Only then did Katherine realize that she was holding the baby's foot, staring at it closely. She lowered the child's leg hastily, composing her features, staring at the physician, wondering what he knew, or had guessed.

"Why don't you tell me what's going on here, Katherine? We both know this isn't the same child you delivered, and if it is, there's something damned odd going on and I want to know what it is."

"I told you, she got sick, stopped nursing, couldn't tolerate the light . . . and those blisters. I thought it was maybe an allergy. But now she's getting much better, isn't she? Look how strong she is and she's nursing. I'd like to take her home today," Katherine said brightly, avoiding his eyes.

Dr. Bosch didn't speak for a minute, just studied her with a speculative look in his eyes. He shifted the unlit cigar to the other side of his mouth. "You never knew old Simon Sinclair, did you? Rod's grandfather? Hell of a man. Stubborn didn't half describe him. If he made up his mind, that was it. The good Lord himself couldn't have changed Simon's Sinclair's mind. Used to be an expression in the meat industry, '. . . not for God or Simon Sinclair,'" Bosch chuckled. "So, Katherine, you see, I've been up against the toughest. Had to talk that old ruffian into an operation that he didn't want; appendix the size of a sack of grapefruit and the old fool insisting that it was indigestion.

"I won that argument and I'll win this one. I've an idea that you can use a friend about now, so why don't you just tell me what's going on here? I'm not the enemy, you know. I'd like to help, if you let me. Anything you can tell me will only help this child's chances. She's not out of the woods yet."

Katherine hesitated, studying the strong features, the dark, intelligent eyes, knowing that he was right, knowing that she needed someone to talk to, someone to trust. Especially now with Helga gone. "Can it be just between the two of us? Will you give me your word not to tell anyone else what I tell you?"

He nodded brusquely. "Of course, but I won't promise not to argue with you if I think you're doing the wrong thing."

The words came pouring out, a torrent that she could not have stopped even had she wanted to, so great was the need to tell someone, to share the burden. ". . . and now Helga's dead and I can't help but think she'd be alive if she hadn't gone down there, looking for answers, trying to help me." Tears were dripping down her cheeks. She swiped at them angrily and threw the baby up over her shoulder, patting her on the back more vigorously than necessary.

Benjamin Bosch had never been known as a man at a loss for words, but words failed him now. He stared reflectively at Katherine, rubbing his huge hand over his chin, feeling the whiskers that had sprouted overnight. Anyone else who'd undergone what she had gone through, the trauma she'd experienced— the sudden death of a loved one and then a premature birth—well, he might have suspected a nervous breakdown or psychotic dementia, but Katherine Sinclair had always struck him as rock-solid, capable of surviving the unfair measure of sorrow that she had been dealt.

But this story, it was so—so preposterous! How could anyone believe such a story? But then there was the baby. It was just as Katherine had said, and it could not be denied that physiological changes were occurring at a rapid and noticeable rate. Changes that could not, should not, have been possible.

Perhaps Katherine could be suffering from some form of "suggestion." But he too was seeing the changes. Was he to believe that he too had been hypnotized? Then there was the matter of the blood work; there was no doubt that the blood was "different, primitive," to use his own analogy. If what she was saying was the truth, well, the first thing one needed to know was who these people were and what the norm was for them.

"This woman, the men, did they look like this child?"

Katherine sighed. She had not realized that she had been holding her breath, waiting for the doctor's response, wondering if he would think that she was crazy. She nodded. "The eyes, the forehead, the chin, the same high cheekbones; their ears are larger than ours, pointy on top, and all of them have these strange silvery eyes, big eyes; the pupils were very big, very black."

Bosch nodded. "That would make sense. It's like a cat; the pupils expand, enlarge to let in as much light as possible in the dark."

"But what does it mean? Who are they and why do they live like that under the ground and in the dark?"

"That's a good question and one that will have to be dealt with eventually, but right now our main concern is healing this child, making her well and exchanging her for Cameron. That was your bargain with the mother. Leave the mystery to someone else."

"Helga," Katherine said bitterly. "Helga wanted to solve the mystery and it, or they, killed her."

"You don't know that," Bosch said carefully. "I'd say that you have enough on your plate at the moment without adding guilt. The paramedics were probably right. The exertion of breaking down that door was probably too much for her. She was not a young woman and her color was poor; it's quite likely that she had a preexisting heart condition."

Katherine seized on his words gratefully. "You really think it might have happened like that, without pain? Stone said she was smiling when he found her."

The physician knew when to hold his tongue, to allow a person to fill in the blanks with comforting thoughts. Heart attacks were seldom, if ever, painless. The smile was in all likelihood a rictus of the muscles after death, but there was no need to distress Katherine further with the truth. He bowed his head, allowing her to draw her own conclusions.

"Now, Katherine, the child. The mother said that she was poisoned, that her blood was contaminated. We found evidence of this ourselves before you so effectively put an end to the tests. The question is, will you allow us to treat her? There may be something we can do to flush these poisons from her system."

"Crystal said that there was no way that it could be done," Katherine said. "She seemed very worried about metal, and I had to give her my word that I wouldn't let you do any more tests."

"I can understand about the metal. As we've seen, the child has an extreme reaction, but it appears to be limited to base metal like iron. It must be a sensitivity such as some women experience when they wear pierced earrings whose studs are not surgical steel or gold-plated. You must realize, Katherine, that Crystal is a mother, not a doctor," Bosch added quietly. "I'm a doctor. My job is to save lives. Now, why don't you stop throwing obstacles in my path and let me get on with my job?"

Katherine was torn by indecision. "But what about those people and what about Cameron?"

"I'm a doctor, Katherine, not a policeman. I'd like to know

more about them too, but right now we have to address the
problem of this child. If we can return her to health, do you think
that the mother will keep her word and give Cameron back to
you?"

Thinking of the mound of precious metals and gems on the
carpet of her apartment, and of Crystal's courage in standing up
against her own people, Katherine could only nod her head in
agreement.

"Good. Now, will you allow me to proceed without barricading
the door?"

The baby had finished nursing and was staring up at her with
big eyes as though waiting for her reply. Katherine could see now,
in the dim light, that the corneas of the baby's eyes were yellow
instead of white. "It won't hurt her, will it?"

"I don't know what has to be done yet. I won't lie to you,
Katherine, some of it might be unpleasant, but even so, temporary
discomfort is still better than death."

Katherine lowered her head and nodded her acceptance.

The doctor had left the room. Katherine cradled the child and
stroked her silvery curls, feeling them spring back gently under
her fingers. The child stuffed her fingers into her mouth and began
to suck, all the while regarding Katherine with the somber,
wide-eyed gaze that she was becoming accustomed to. This quiet,
peaceful time would soon be interrupted by numerous tests and
procedures. She was doing exactly what Crystal had begged her
not to do, made her promise would not happen.

She wanted to believe that the child was getting better, had
recovered to the point where she could be taken home, but despite
the intensity of her wishes there were signs that all was not well.
The muscles in the arms and legs were lax and flaccid. Amber
could wave her legs in the air and hold a breast, but only for short
periods of time before the limb would fall back weakly. The
corneas were a sickly yellow and the baby's gums were pale and
lacking in color.

Katherine wondered if it was because Amber's people, deprived
as they were of light, were pale. Trying one of the simple
home-health tests her mother had often used on her, she squeezed
one of the baby's fingers tightly and then released it, waiting to see
it grow pink as the blood rushed back. It was white when she
squeezed it and did not show any flush of color after the pressure
was released.

The baby did not protest any of Katherine's pokings and

proddings, which Cameron would certainly have done with lusty shrieks of anger. The brief burst of strength and enthusiasm Amber had exhibited when nursing now appeared to have been exhausted. Once more, she was the listless child she had first discovered lying in Cameron's crib. Katherine's heart ached for the baby. She wished that she could wave a magic wand and make things better.

Suddenly she was overcome with a wave of grief. Rod would have known what to do, Rod would have known how to make things better. How she missed him, missed his strong hands on her shoulders, missed being able to rest her head on his chest and feel better just for being there. Rod. Helga. Cameron. Amber. The combined grief was suddenly too much and she began to weep— huge, hot tears that slid down her cheeks and dropped onto the child she cradled against her chest.

She had reached for the child's fur-skin coverlet before the moment of grief had overcome her and now she tucked it around the baby and, mimicking the child's gesture, brought the other end up and rested her own cheek upon it. It was soothing, comforting, the tiny soft hairs whispering against her skin. She found herself doing what the baby had done, moving the coverlet back and forth so that it stroked her skin. It was hypnotic, soothing. Her tears slowed and then stopped. The ache in her heart was still there, but the worst of it had passed. She hugged the child to her, feeling a bond growing between them. The baby was no longer a stranger; she had a name, she was Amber. "Don't worry, sweetie," she whispered into the baby's ear. "We'll make you better, I promise."

Dr. Bosch did no more than walk down the corridor at his usual frenetic pace, but those he encountered would have sworn that the air was turbulent in his wake, that papers swirled and that they themselves had been buffeted by a gale-force wind.

Upon reaching his office, he threw the sodden, much chewed cigar in the general direction of the wastebasket and flung himself into the enormous leather swivel chair that over the years had shaped itself to his giant frame. The chair groaned and wheezed under the assault; the wooden joints supporting the many layers of leather and padding were like bones, a skeleton shuddering under a familiar yet too heavy burden. Bosch tipped the chair back as far as it would go, unaware of its complaints, and crossed his ankles atop his oak desk, the surface of which bore the scars of many years of similar actions.

His mind was clicking away furiously as he lit a fresh cigar and drew the pungent smoke into his mouth, savoring it for a moment, rolling it across his palate and tongue, like a connoisseur appreciating a fine wine, before blowing it out. Damn stupid, that no-smoking rule, even if he had made it himself. A man thought better with a cigar, a lit cigar, in his mouth!

A subterranean society living under the city of Chicago, living there long enough to exhibit profound physiological as well as physical changes. That prognathous jaw line, the almost simian brow, the curved spine! He shook his head, chiding himself for leaping to conclusions without the proper data, just like a first-year student!

What if they were a long-lost tribe of Indians who had sought shelter underground and never came up. After all, Illinois, Indiana, Wisconsin, Missouri, and Kentucky—not to mention New Mexico and Arizona—were honeycombed with miles and miles of interconnecting caves and tunnels. He and his wife had once been to Mammoth Cave National Park, early in their marriage. He had never forgotten the stunning sights of those caverns. The guide had told them that Indians from prehistory on had lived there. As he recalled now, there were even petrified bones of an Indian who had been crushed underneath an immense boulder and died down there in the darkness. If they had lived in Kentucky, why not here?

It was an outrageous theory, fanciful in the extreme. If one of his residents had suggested such a theory he would have cut the fellow down to size with a few well-chosen words, but dammit, something about it made him think he was right!

And what Katherine had said, or more accurately, what she'd told him the mother had said, fit. He could think of a number of problems that would occur from living underground all of the time. Upper respiratory problems right off the bat, pneumonia, pleurisy, and rheumatism. Vitamin A deficiency and arthritis—my God. He rubbed his own knuckles and winced at the thought of what living underground in a perpetual state of dampness would do to one's joints.

And poisons. He nodded, screwing his eyes up at a sudden flow of smoke that drifted upward. Think of all the industrial wastes that had been dumped into the rivers, lakes, and sewers, and directly upon the ground itself before the environment became an issue. The dumping was probably still going on for that matter, only now it was done in greater secrecy.

All those heavy metals and poisons leaching into the ground, flowing into their water, year after year, accumulating in their flesh and bones, destroying their livers and kidneys, poisoning their brains. It was a whole cornucopia of misery visited upon an unsuspecting people, helpless to defend themselves.

Well, what had the child experienced? Based on the uric acid readings and the yellowing of her corneas, he could only assume that she would require dialysis to flush her kidneys. God only knew if the damage was reversible. She was young, that was in her favor, but she was also weakened, and dialysis was not a pleasant experience.

He lifted the phone, punched out a series of numbers, and barked out several orders. That would get things started.

He leaned back into his chair, frowning heavily, a sure sign of mental activity. The baby was one matter, but he wanted to know the scope of the larger problem—no, dammit, he *needed* to know the entire picture before he could help that child. And—he suddenly grinned—by God, it was the most interesting thing that had come down the pike in many a year. More than anything, he wanted to go down there and see for himself if it were true, and, he had to admit, he desperately wanted it to be so. It was the stuff of Conan Doyle, Edgar Rice Burroughs, and Tom Swift. It would be the adventure of a lifetime.

TWENTY-THREE

It had been a long and exhausting day for Katherine as well as for the baby. They had begun dialysis to cleanse Amber's kidneys of the poisons that had accumulated there. Because of the extreme urgency, they had broken into the schedule which was set up many months in advance to accommodate the many patients whose lives depended on the process.

Seeing the child, so small, so fragile and helpless beside the vast humming machine, calming and holding her still while the technicians inserted the needles and tubes into her body, had seemed like a betrayal. She tried to tell herself that it was helping make the baby well, tried to argue away the fact that she had broken her promise to Crystal. The baby had cried and sucked her fingers fiercely, staring at Katherine with huge, unblinking eyes.

The technicians were annoyed at having to work in near-darkness, but they dared not voice their unhappiness in front of Dr. Bosch, who had remained at Katherine's side throughout the ordeal. There had been many other tests and more procedures scheduled. The doctor had tried to explain them to her, but the strange words served only to confuse her. Nothing made sense anymore; her entire world had been turned upside down and inside out. Finally, they were done and the baby was returned to her room, where she nursed and then fell into a deep sleep.

Katherine sat in the rocker, drained of energy, too exhausted to even press the doctor for reassurances.

"Katherine, there's something I want to talk to you about,"

Bosch said. The tone of his voice was somehow different and Katherine realized that he was no longer talking to her behind his title/persona of doctor. This was Benjamin Bosch, the person. He was less certain of himself. He hesitated before speaking, picking at a nubble of thread on his pant leg. He cleared his throat and then raised his eyes to meet hers.

"These people. I think it's important that we find out who they are, find out something about them; how long they've been living down there, what medical-type problems they've been having. Get a more complete picture of the baby's background."

Katherine met the suggestion with a shake of her head even before he was done speaking. "How would we do that?" she asked wearily. "Crystal's the only one likely to tell us, and how would we find her? I was lucky that time; we couldn't count on my being lucky a second time. What if I ran into those men? I think they'd kill me."

"I wasn't suggesting that you go alone," Bosch said quietly.

Katherine's head came up and she stared at him in disbelief. "You mean you want to go down there?"

"Hear me out!" Bosch said firmly, hitching his chair closer to hers. "What we'll do is, we'll go in through the elevated station. They might well be guarding the door in your basement after all the recent problems, but only Crystal knows that you know about the Thorndale Street door. I'll take medicines, try to win their confidence."

Katherine stared at him, aghast. "I don't think you understand these people. They aren't friendly. They don't like us. We're the enemy. How do you propose winning their confidence?

"These are not sane, rational people! You can't reason with them! What kind of sane people would live underground on a permanent basis and steal children? Isn't this the part of the movie where the cavalry rides in and rescues the missing baby?"

"No, this is the part of the movie where the blind, insensitive government agencies can rush in and kill a couple of the monsters so that science can study them," Bosch replied with only a small degree of sarcasm. "I'd like to change that scenario. From what you say, despite their hostility, I think that these folks are up to their ears in problems they can't control or solve. If this baby is any indication of the problems they're dealing with, I'd guess a large number of them are in need of medical attention. And there could be other babies dying besides this one. Wouldn't you like to help them?"

"But I'm afraid!" The words slipped out of her mouth before she could stop them. She was embarrassed to realize that it was true. She *was* afraid of going back down there.

"I'm afraid too, and I haven't even seen them yet," Bosch replied kindly. But Katherine had seen the light burning in his eyes, sensed his rising excitement, and realized that he saw this as an adventure, a break in his routine rather than the dangerous, potentially explosive situation that it was. Still, what he said had its merits. What if they could win the cooperation of the people? Wouldn't she stand a better chance of getting Cameron back? And what if there were more babies, sick and dying?

"All right," she said reluctantly. "When?"

"Now." Bosch all but sprang to his feet.

"Now?" Katherine said with dismay. "It's late and I'm tired."

"Yes, I'm aware of the hour. It has been a long day, but what better time? The baby's asleep and we'll both have to be back here in the morning."

She could not refute his logic, but neither could she deny her dread of those dark tunnels. She had been looking forward to going home, getting something to eat, taking a hot shower and perhaps talking with Stone before returning to the hospital.

Stone had entered her thoughts several times during the long day and she had half expected to see him appear as he said he might. It was disturbing to her that she looked forward to seeing him, drew comfort from his presence. It wasn't right. How could she be feeling this way when a part of her, the cold, rational portion of her mind, thought that Stone was involved in the situation? "All right," she said brusquely, rising to her feet and shutting Stone firmly out of her thoughts.

They were ready to go all too soon. It was clear that Bosch had been thinking about his plan for some time, for he had a bag packed and ready to go sitting just inside his office door. He hesitated for a moment, staring at a leather golf bag filled with clubs, then shook his head and started out the door.

"Shouldn't we have something to protect ourselves?" Katherine asked.

"I'm a healer, Katherine, not a killer. I'll use my fists if I have to; I'm an old street-fighter, grew up over on Stoney Island, fought my way out of many a tight spot with the odds against me."

He looked like he'd enjoy a good brawl, Katherine thought, but still, the doctor wasn't a young man and Jasper and the other man had appeared fit and quite capable of violence.

Sensing her concern, Bosch reached into his pocket and pulled out a small, compact flashlight, no more than six inches long, the handle wrapped in a black rubbery substance. The light flared out into a wide, flat circle. He switched it on and she was almost blinded by an intense white light. Her eyes blurred with sudden tears. It was several moments before she regained her vision completely.

"Sorry," Bosch said ruefully. "Didn't realize quite how powerful they are. Halogen bulbs!" He said it proudly as though he had invented and built the light himself. "If they all have this light intolerance, don't you think it will make an adequate weapon?"

"More than adequate," Katherine sniffled.

"Here, here's yours," Bosch said as he slapped an identical light into her hand.

They took Bosch's big black Mercedes, even though Katherine tried to persuade him to take a cab. "It's not the best neighborhood in the world. A car like this, it's an invitation. Like saying 'Please come take my hubcaps, please relieve me of this expensive disc player.'"

Dr. Bosch chuckled, but did not allow himself to be dissuaded. Sinking into the luxuriously padded leather seat, listening to the heavy thunk of the locks as they fell into place, Katherine felt a sense of solidity and security and was glad that he had insisted. The powerful car purred the short distance between the hospital and Thorndale Avenue in all too short a time. They found a spot to park close to the station, alongside the fruit store that always seemed to be changing hands, this week Hispanic, the next week Indian, each new owner clearly convinced that he could succeed where his predecessor had failed.

Katherine glanced in at the delicatessen as they passed. Mike was not behind the counter, but she found herself wanting to go inside, inhale the rich scents that would forever more represent a feeling of safety and welcome, and find out how the puppy had fared, if it had been returned to its home. But Bosch did not stop his headlong rush toward the station under the elevated tracks.

A train had just left; the thunderous sound still reverberated in the air, a heavy, palpable noise that assaulted the ears and body with shock waves of sound. The city would never win awards for cleanliness, but somehow, Katherine reflected as she looked around her, the el stations and subway areas always seemed just a little bit seedier than everywhere else; even the air had an unsavory aroma, as if rotting garbage lay hidden somewhere just out of sight.

There was no one on guard; the large woman in the too-small uniform was gone. Katherine was glad to see her kiosk locked for the night. Only a man wrapped in numerous layers of crumpled newspapers lay sleeping in a corner of the filthy station. A late commuter rattled down the steps from the tracks above, shot them a nervous sideways glance, and hurried away, anxious to be home, safe behind locked doors.

Katherine pointed out the door she had emerged from. It looked so ordinary, a plain institutional green metal door with the words NO ADMITTANCE printed on its face. A door like a thousand others she had seen and ignored in her lifetime, doors that had held no meaning for her. She wondered now how many of them had hidden secrets like this one; how many of them were entrances to the secret tunnels.

She wanted desperately to believe that the people who had taken Cameron were merely homeless derelicts, but she had come to accept that it was far more than that, that there was an entire society of people who lived beneath the city, inheriting its ills while stealing its children. A shiver passed through her body as she realized just how risky it was to enter their world again.

Benjamin Bosch appeared to have no such reservations; he attacked the door with vigor. The handle did not yield to his grip, but a slender scalpel inserted between door and frame and jiggled slightly, popped it open with ease. It was hot and dark inside and it took her eyes a minute to adjust to the darkness that greeted them. Bosch turned on his flashlight until he found a light switch.

The small room was just as she remembered it, filled with a complexity of tubes and pipes and dark green metal boxes all with warnings against tampering printed in large letters. She threaded her way through the maze of machinery and cables until she reached the far wall. Wedging herself behind two large whirring turbines, she saw the small green door that had released her from the nightmare of the tunnels. She stared at the small, narrow panel, the fear building inside her chest, knowing that she did not want to go back.

Katherine turned toward the doctor, thinking that she would try once more to convince the doctor of the danger that awaited them. He was right behind her, holding out a pair of glasses, strange-looking glasses, waggling them impatiently, urging her to take them. She took them gingerly, and stared at them, perplexed. They

were made of some strange gray-black substance that did not feel
like metal or rubber or plastic, but perhaps a combination of all
three materials. The eyepieces and bridge were fitted with rubbery
flanges similar to those found on diving goggles or scuba masks.
A wide elastic band stretched from one eyepiece to the other for
the purpose of holding the apparatus firmly to one's head. There
were also several dials on the upper rims similar to those used by
ophthalmologists to calibrate vision tests.

Bosch fitted his on and grinned at her, a lopsided, cocky grin
that she had never seen him wear before. It seemed easier to slip
the glasses on than to ask him what they were.

No sooner had she fitted them on, adjusting the flanges, then she
had her answer. The lighted room turned as dark as night, but
everything in it was clearly visible, brightly outlined in shades of
green, and any objects that were warm or carried heat, such as
pipes, glowed as if they were phosphorescent.

"What are these and how did you get them?" she asked, looking
up at the metal-gridded ceiling light, watching awestruck as it
turned into a huge green-gold moon shining down on her. She
looked at her hand; it too glowed slightly around the edges. Like
a child with a wondrous new toy, she laughed with sudden glee,
momentarily forgetting the seriousness of their mission. The
doctor, pleased and proud, returned her smile.

"You'd be surprised what you can buy with a good credit card.
They advertise these as the world's most intelligent eyes. They are
something called color-adjusted transmission technology and the
lenses are coated with more than nine layers of magnesium
fluoride so they work under even the worst lighting conditions.
German optics, of course." Katherine shook her head; none of
what he had said meant anything to her.

"Well, it doesn't really matter, all these details. All that matters
is that they'll work in the tunnels. Their white light transmission
is supposed to be ninety-nine point eight percent effective, which
means that with them we can see things that our eyes alone would
not be able to see."

"What are all these dials?" Katherine asked, fiddling with one
centered on the bridge, which seemed to affect distance.

"Focus on just one thing; the door will do. Then adjust the knob
here in the center so that it's the correct distance; then adjust the
other knobs to bring it into the clearest possible focus. Once that's
done, you never have to do it again. They're also supposed to be

fully waterproof, as well as shockproof and temperature-controlled. Plus they have a five-year warranty."

"Let's hope we're not down here that long," Katherine said dryly. But she had to admit that the glasses put a different slant on things. She did not feel quite so helpless, so frightened at the thought of wandering around in the dark tunnels unable to see a thing. With the night-vision glasses and the bright halogen flashlights, the odds had just improved.

The second door proved far more difficult to open than the first. It had no doorknob, no apparent lock or latch, and did not really even look like a door. Had it not been for the position as well as the hinges, she might have doubted her memory. Bosch removed his heavy tweed overcoat and hung it over one of the pipes while he studied the problem, finally concluding that the only solution was to pry the pins out of the hinges and remove the narrow panel bodily. They stepped through the opening into the warm darkness beyond and did their best to wedge the door panel back into its frame.

Freed of the heavy coat, Bosch strapped on a knapsack. Katherine wondered what surprises it might contain other than medicines.

There was no need for their flashlights as the goggles showed the way clearly. They were in a narrow corridor, wide enough for four people to walk abreast. It was a different sort of corridor than the one beneath her building. The walls and floor were neatly paved with dark red bricks, each one fitted so expertly next to its neighbor that it needed no mortar to hold it in place. They were obviously old bricks; she had seen others like them in private gardens, prized bits of the city's history. At one time most of the city's main streets had been paved with bricks just like these. Now, the few caches that occasionally came on the market commanded large prices and were avidly sought after. But here, there seemed to be no small supply of the bricks, which stretched out of sight both ahead and behind them. Some bore dark stains. Bosch pointed at them and whispered, "These bricks were exposed to a great heat, a fire. It wouldn't surprise me if they were scavenged after the Great Fire."

"But how did they get down here?" Katherine asked.

"After the fire, the city was just a pile of smoking rubble. They had to clear it off before they could rebuild, so they just loaded everything in carts and carried it down to the lake and dumped it in. This was all swampy marshland where we're standing. Your building, the hospital, the Drive, all of it was wasteland. They did the same thing in San Francisco after the great earthquake, gave both cities more ground to expand. I'd bet my last dollar that that's where these bricks came from."

"You're saying that these people have been down here for over a hundred years!" Katherine was aghast at the thought.

"Well, I guess that they could have come more recently, but look at this, this is no short-term project. This took a long time to accomplish. Look at it, see how expertly those bricks are fitted to one another; like this one here with the corner broken off. Someone went to a lot of trouble to fashion another corner to square it up."

"How do you know that they didn't accidentally break it themselves and just fit the two pieces back together?"

"Look closely, Katherine," Dr. Bosch said in a tutorial tone, just as though she were one of his students. "The smaller piece is a slightly different color; someone carved this piece to fit. And look at this." He gestured widely and she followed the wave of his hand. The ceiling was beautifully arched, curved overhead, smoothly plastered and painted to resemble a night sky, complete with cloud cover and stars which glowed strangely in the green cast of the night-vision lenses. And that was only part of it. The scene began at ground level where the walls met the brick walkway. Grass, flowers, bushes, and trees filled the giant canvas. Branches spread on either side and the tops of trees brushed the night sky above them. It was like walking down a tree-lined path on a summer's night with the stars and sky blazing above them. So realistic was the work, so convincing, Katherine could almost feel the breeze ruffling her hair and smell the scent of night-blooming flowers. It was an incredible piece of art, a vast mural that stretched off into the distance on either side as far as she could see. She pushed the glasses up onto her forehead and was immediately surrounded by the stygian darkness. Without them, she was blind, stumbling through a hole in the ground; with them, she was surrounded by beauty.

"Which way?" asked Bosch, breaking her bemusement.

Katherine hesitated for a moment and then pointed to the right. The tunnel looked exactly the same in both directions, but the right, toward the lake she thought, that's the way we had to come. They set off at a slow pace.

The man sleeping on the floor of the train station was as Katherine had suspected, a true homeless derelict. But in another lifetime, another dimension, the man had had a name, a family, and a promising future. In that other life, his name had been Charles Anthony Goodfellow III.

Goodfellow had just completed his freshman year at the University of Chicago, when the troubling symptoms first began. Initially, there were colorful dreams of a disturbing nature, which he could not always persuade himself had not truly occurred. Sometimes he thought he heard voices speaking to him from inside his head, and there were odors too.

In his junior year, the dreams were no longer confined to the night hours but played out their dramas before his eyes at all times of the day and night, sleeping or awake. It was like having a movie superimposed upon the backdrop of life which, as time progressed, appeared far less real than the visions. The colors were brighter, the textures more tactile, the scents stronger. Real life faded, became pale, a poor second to the visions. What's more, the visions made no demands upon him, did not thrust themselves upon him and insist that he fulfill responsibilities that he could barely remember. The visions were his friends, his escape, his refuge.

There were, of course, moments of lucidity, moments that allowed him to scrape the fragmenting sections of his life together. Concerned friends and family pressed him to seek medical assistance. It was then that he first heard the word schizophrenia— but that was something that happened to other people, not to him. He tried to take the medicine, but it was worse than the visions. It dried his mouth and his throat, his whole body felt parched and sere. Even worse, it emptied him of all feeling except one, anxiety. He felt like a ticking bomb waiting to explode.

Shortly after graduation, he told his family that he was taking a vacation, driving up to northern Wisconsin for a few days. Instead, he rented a room in Uptown, once a thriving upper-middle-class neighborhood near the lake which had in recent years become a battleground for desperate homeowners trying to preserve their way of life and welfare families crowded into city-subsidized housing. Goodfellow was determined to confront his demons, without medication, face them down, and win back his life. Despite his intentions, he lost the battle.

Eventually, his family found him, but by then it was too late. He could barely recognize them. As for himself, he too was barely recognizable. His hair, grown long and unkempt, straggled over his shoulders in thick greasy locks. Previously clean-shaven, his face was covered by a scraggly beard that reached his chest, and was often tucked into one of the many shirts, sweaters, and jackets he wore, one atop the other year round. But no matter how many clothes he wore, Goodfellow, or Goody as he was known on the streets, was always cold.

Goodfellow had taken his degree in Anthropology, had been quite brilliant, and thus it was that he always took up his position each night, standing guard as he saw it, in front of the utility room of the Thorndale elevated station. There were Neanderthal men living behind that door. He had seen them coming and going late at night when they thought he was asleep. He had even tried to tell the police and the train station authorities about it, but they had just laughed at him and shoved him away. No one believed him, but Goodfellow knew that it was true; he had seen them with his own eyes. There were other places where they came and went—he had searched them out, once he knew what to look for—half-forgotten or seldom used doors that descended into dark basements and narrow crawl spaces of the underbelly of the city.

They knew he watched them, but they had not attempted to harm him. But there was about them a feeling of potential violence, and one could never be too sure with Neanderthal men. That was why he watched from the train station where there was light and some degree of safety.

He saw the two, a man and a woman who were clearly not Neanderthal, go into the utility closet. He lay there for a while wondering if it were true or if it was one of the visions. But the colors were flat and harsh, not the vivid colors of the dreams. But no one other than the Neanderthal men and sometimes the workmen from the transit authority ever went into the closet. It was a mystery.

He struggled with the puzzle for a while and then got to his feet and crept to the green door. It was unlocked! He opened it inch by careful inch, wanting to look inside, yet afraid. What if they were waiting for him? Goodfellow was afraid of everyone and everything. But no one came bursting through the door, and after a time, he grew brave enough to look around the edge.

The small room was empty. Relief battled with disappointment. Maybe he had imagined everything, maybe none of it had happened. But then, why was the door open? Goody edged into the room, tiny shuffling steps, keeping the door open so that he could run if they came for him. Then he saw the coat. He touched it. The wool was dense and prickly yet soft beneath his fingers. His fingers trembled with the memory, locked somewhere deep inside him, the memory of wearing a garment such as this. He tried hard to focus, but the memory slipped away from him and was gone. But even that little bit of connection was enough. Goody picked up the heavy Harris tweed coat and put it on atop his layers of rags, wrapping its warmth around him. Already the frayed connection had been joined, the past where he had once owned a coat like this and today when it had presented itself to him. It was a gift. It was his.

A dim thought pushed its way to the surface. The man, the other man who had worn the coat, his coat. What if he came back? What if he tried to take the coat away from him! His heart beat fast at the fearful thought and he bared his yellow teeth in a grimace. No, no, he thought, soothing himself. The man would not come back. The woman would not come back either. Only the Neanderthals came and went. No one else. The coat was his.

TWENTY-FOUR

It was somewhat cool in the tunnel but just right with her sweater; a coat would have been too heavy. There was a slight breeze blowing, the air fresh, not fetid, nor, Katherine was happy to note, did it smell of mushrooms. With the brick pavement beneath their feet and the continuing mural, their expedition had a peculiar *déjà vu* sense of a stroll through the city's past at a time when streets were still paved with brick and one could see the stars without a layer of smog or reflected light obliterating the view.

She was about to speak, when Bosch seized her arm and squeezed it hard. She almost cried out, but then she heard it too: the scuffle of feet, many feet, traveling directly toward them. There was nowhere, absolutely nowhere, to hide. The thick sour taste of fear returned; she was filled with the memory of that earlier terror. The doctor exhibited none of her fear. He tilted his head to one side and listened, then dragged Katherine to the righthand side of the corridor. He crouched down, making his large body as small as possible, shooting Katherine a glance that she knew would be piercing if only she could see through his dark lenses. But she did not have to be told to emulate his actions and compressed herself into a tight ball.

There were voices as well as footsteps now, voices that resonated through the corridor. Her heart still pounded in her chest, pounded so loud that she was certain it could be heard and would give them away. But the voices, all male, gave no indication of any sense of alarm. She was able to tell now that the voices

were not in their corridor but seemed to be coming from an
oblique angle somewhere off to the right. She raised her head
slightly, cradling it on her arms and slanted her eyes to the right.
Ahead of them perhaps some twenty yards further down the
corridor was an arched opening.

As she watched, a column of men moved from the furthest
righthand point of her vision, crossed their corridor, and disappeared into an arched opening on the left. Her fright was so great
that she had held her breath, certain that they would be seen. Had
the men turned in their direction, undoubtedly that would have
been the case, but so involved were they in their conversation, not
one of them had glanced down the corridor. Katherine and Bosch
waited until the last echo was gone before they even dared to
move.

"What do you make of that?" Bosch asked in a low tone.

Katherine shrugged. "I told you they were here."

Bosch frowned, his broad forehead wrinkling into a series of
deep creases. "I didn't doubt you, Katherine. Would I be here if I
did? I'm asking what you thought about what they were saying!"

"Saying? I—I guess I was too scared to listen. I didn't hear
anything they said."

Bosch sighed deeply and shook his head as though he were
dealing with an idiot child. In that instant Katherine had a quick
insight as to what it must be to work for him and make a mistake.
It was not a good feeling.

"It was a jumble, some of it English, some European, maybe
German or Latin or an odd combination of both. They were talking
about some sort of meeting that they'd just left. They seemed
pretty upset. Angry."

"Let's go back!" Katherine clutched his arm and tugged at it.
"You've seen them, you know I'm telling the truth now. Let's go
back before they find us and kill us!"

Bosch stared at her, the dark lenses giving him an alien
appearance. He was no longer the warm, comforting family
doctor; he was as frightening as the things they were stalking. She
had no idea why he wanted to pursue this course which could only
end in their deaths. The reasons he had spouted above ground in
the safety of his office had seemed logical and valid. Here, now,
with the terrifying creatures so close, the plan seemed to border on
suicide or madness.

"You go back, Katherine. I understand what you're saying and
perhaps you're right, but I'm going on."

"Why!" Katherine whispered fiercely. "We can heal Amber without doing this. She's so much better already. What good will it do her if you get killed? No one else will believe me or know how to treat her. You've got to come back with me!"

"I have to know more, Katherine. We have a few of the pieces, but not enough. She's alive now, but for how long? I have to find out the extent of this sickness, their problems. Think what it would mean if we could heal them all, make them well and bring them out of the darkness!"

Katherine stared at him in anger, suddenly understanding his motivation. "You're not doing this for Cameron, not even for Amber. You're doing this for you! You're bored, tired of doing the same thing day in and day out. This whole thing, these people, the goggles, the flashlights, it's an adventure, a great big adventure for you, one with new toys to play with. And, if you're lucky, you get to be a hero and famous, besides. That's it, isn't it!"

Bosch was silent for a long minute and then he nodded his head in agreement. "Yes, partly. Part of what you say is true. I am bored. I've been in practice for almost forty years. I still care about my patients, still care about teaching, but it's different now. Your family is a good example of what I'm talking about. I was the Sinclairs' physician from birth to death. The family and I, we had a lifelong commitment. There were other families like them, and those lives filled my own. After my wife died, being involved in those other lives made it possible for me to feel a part of things. I was invited to christenings, brises, communions, bar mitzvahs, weddings, and delivered the children of the children I had delivered. It was a continuum, it had meaning. *I* had meaning. But now, the old, big families are gone, moved away from here and out into the suburbs. This is too far for them to travel. I get Christmas cards." His voice grew scathing. "Christmas cards. The people I see now, they have no roots here in the city, they might be gone tomorrow. I might never see them again. I don't need the money. I've kept my fees reasonable. But these people, these new patients, they don't care, most of them, about paying their bills. Why bother? The insurance or the state will take care of it. And if they don't, hell, half of 'em just move and leave no forwarding address. These are the people I care for now.

"And the students, the residents?" he snorted derisively. "They're not a whole lot better. A few of them are good, some of them actually care, want to practice real medicine, make a difference. But most of them . . . I get the feeling—no, I know—that they're only in it for the money. They'll finish out their residencies, then move into glitzy medical conglomerates and what they practice won't be medicine, just something they have to do, in between rounds of golf at the club, in order to add to their investment portfolios. Don't you see, Katherine? I can make a difference here. These people need me. Their babies need me. I can help. I can keep them from dying!"

"But how will you keep them from hurting us? What if they kill us before you even have a chance to tell them why you're here? We could write them a note, leave it where they'll find it."

"No, Katherine," he said gently. "No notes. You go back. It's not so far, you'll be safe. But I'm going on."

He got to his feet and adjusted the straps of his knapsack. Then, without another word, he began walking toward the arched opening in the corridor. Katherine watched him go, watched him walk away from her, then got to her feet uncertainly. She wanted to turn around and go back, go back to the relative safety of the brightly lit, stinking train station. She wanted to leave this tunnel of fear that could only lead to violence. But somehow, watching Bosch walk away from her, striding so boldly into the unknown, she envied him the power of his vision, and despite her fear, understood what it was that he was saying.

When she was a child, at home in Wisconsin, there had been the farms, the crops, the animals, solid things that filled one's life. They were things that needed to be worked with and cared for. When you worked the land and cared for it and the animals, there were tangible rewards such as crops, milk, meat, and the security they represented, money in the bank.

Leaving Wisconsin, marrying Rod, crossing that state border and coming to the city had been a tremendous step, like moving to a different world, one filled with aliens. Chicago was full of hustle and bustle, people rushing here and there, always in a hurry, doing this thing and that, working at careers that were a meaningless collection of words that frequently meant nothing to her.

These so-called professionals seemed to care for nothing, and nobody. There was no counterpart in their lives or careers to the land or to the animals. She could not understand how you could get the same satisfaction out of a line of figures as you could a straight furrow, laboriously cleared of rocks over a period of a hundred years. A furrow where the earth was black and rich and fragrant with the promise of life. Nor could you strike a computer keyboard and feel the same warmth that comes from the steaming brown velvet neck of a Guernsey who had just delivered a foaming, buttery, bucket of milk.

Here in this city, people were born, fell in love, married, worked, had children and died, just as they did elsewhere. But in this city, and no doubt in others as well, they had lost their connection to the things that really mattered.

Now that Rod was gone, Cameron was all that really mattered. Her child's life was already in the keeping of strangers, and one of the few chances Katherine had to get her back was walking away from her. And she was standing there, letting him take the risk alone, because she was afraid. Suddenly, she was deeply ashamed of herself. Bosch was right. Even though they had taken Cameron, these people were not the enemy; they too were victims. She would not entrust the finding of her daughter to someone else. Cameron was her daughter; it was her responsibility to get her back.

Bosch said nothing when she caught up with him, just smiled and nodded at her. They reached the intersection of the two corridors and cautiously peered around the corner. There was no one to be seen in either direction. This new corridor was wider still and had the feeling of a route that was more heavily traveled. Here, as in the corridor beneath Katherine's building, there were regularly occurring recesses in the walls at about head level. Round globes of stone were perched in each niche and she touched one excitedly, feeling the sting of tears behind her eyes, an exultation of knowing that she was right. She *had* seen the globes; she had not been mistaken or drunk, or whatever the police had tried to imply. "These are like the globes I saw before. They light up in some way," she said to Bosch.

"So, they can tolerate light after all," he rumbled reflectively.

"Well, it was a very soft, diffused kind of light. It reminded me of the kind of light a lightning bug gives off, if you know what I mean."

"Still . . . a light," he murmured.

They turned into this new corridor, walking in the direction the party of males had come from. There were many other intersections that entered the corridor, all of which added to the feeling that they were traveling along a main thoroughfare. Once or twice they heard an echo that might have been voices coming to them from these side corridors, but as Bosch pointed out, it might well have been street sounds filtering down from the city above. Frequently they heard and felt the vibrations of large vehicles

passing overhead. It was a testament to the quality of the
construction of the corridors that there was little evidence of
damage from the sheer volume of traffic that passed above their
heads on a continuous basis. She had to remind herself that no
more than twenty feet separated her from the busy and dangerous
city streets.

It was hard to know what direction to go, which tunnels to
follow. Crystal had taken many a turn in their flight, but it now
seemed likely that she had been attempting to take lesser traveled
paths in order to throw their pursuers off the track. All they could
do was continue in the direction that they thought would bring
them closest to the lake, which they had set as their goal.

As they walked, they took notice of many other panels and
doorways which they could only assume gave access to the city
above. Occasionally, there were full-sized planked doors similar to
the one Katherine had found, which were probably entrances to
other basements in other buildings. Most were securely boarded
up to prevent accidental access. But a few had barricades that
could be easily removed. These, she reasoned, were still in use.
She could not help but wonder where they led and if the occupants
of the buildings had any idea what strange wonders lay beneath
their feet.

The artwork on the walls and the arched ceiling was continuous,
occasionally showing the transition of artists, some panels being
more intricate and realistic than others. It might have been boring,
using only the flora, fauna, and the night sky as a theme, but such
was not the case. There were clear, moonlit vistas, crowded with
vast forests. Individual branches glinted in soft moonlight, leaves
were picked out in detail, a nighthawk and an owl sat alert and
wide-eyed in wait for unsuspecting prey.

Another mural, for that was what they were, broken by the
intersecting tunnels, portrayed a clear sky with a full moon rising
above what could only be a stretch of lake Michigan, the waters
reflecting the brilliant orb of the moon in their gentle waves. There
was a single, glaring omission: there was no hint of a city skyline
anywhere, just trees, a spit of smooth, clean sand extending out
into the water, rocks and boulders that were not designed as a
breakwater, and everywhere, a feeling of tranquillity.

Yet another panel portrayed a stormy sky, again, a night sky,
always a night sky. Clouds scudded across the face of the moon,
all but obliterating it with trailers of dark gossamer. What few stars
could be seen peered warily through the torn clouds and there was

a feeling of violence. One could almost hear the keening of the wind, feel its vindictive wail and know that whatever dared to defy its power would be flung headlong across the heavens.

It was like walking through an art gallery, a museum; their steps had involuntarily slowed as they gazed in awe and appreciation at the gift of the unknown artists.

The next panel, one that stretched on unbroken for some distance, was a pastoral scene, one that portrayed something other than sky as its main theme. It was a pasture, a lea on the crest of a gentle hill surrounded by a dense, impenetrable first-growth forest, of the sort that had not been seen in North America for at least a hundred years. There were still a few, precious isolated stands, belonging to those who preferred to look backward to the past instead of forward to progress. Katherine's grandfather had been one such man and it was written in his will that the trees on his land should remain untouched in perpetuity, and nothing any of his children had said had caused him to change his mind. Thus it was that she recognized the massive boles, the huge, outspread branches, the vast canopy unbroken by any of the second-growth trash trees that now littered the countryside, those who lived among the latter too ignorant or too greedy to know or care what they had lost.

The moon shone down on the grassy expanse, seemingly touching each and every blade of grass, gilding it as with a brush of silvery gold. A stag, immense and regal, its rack of horns far larger than any Katherine had ever seen, stood at the edge of the clearing. It was not afraid; it stood calm and unafraid, certain of its own might. A hawk rode the air currents above the field, silhouetted against the stars. A prairie dog stood upright on a small mound of earth in front of its burrow, alert, watchful. Tiny animals, shrews, beetles, a long garter snake, and a bevy of bobwhite huddled beneath a bush, a fox creeping through the tall grasses—all appeared in the mural, a slice of night life as it might have been in some long distant past. It was after the fox, its whiskers so real she half expected them to twitch, the eyes so bright, the texture of the moist nose so very real that she would not have been surprised if it leaped away at the sound of her approach, that she saw the first figure.

It was a measure of the artist's skill that Katherine had all but lost her fear of her surroundings. Only when she saw the first of the figures in the painting did the terror return, leaping inside her as she expected the fox to have done. The figure was a male. His

back was to her and he was walking forward, in the same direction
that she was going. Even though the grasses reached halfway up
his thighs, he strode along with a smooth and easy gait. He was
wearing little, a leather tunic that was caught at both shoulders by
what appeared to be smooth bone buttons. It was not a crude
Tarzan-type garment, but one that had been well-tailored to his
broad, muscular body. Around his waist he wore what was clearly
a leather belt from which several items dangled: a knife in a
scabbard, a net with tightly woven frets, and a sack that bulged at
the bottom as though it contained something heavy. In his right
hand, the hand closest to the outer edge of the painting, he carried
a long lance with a very sharp knapped stone point.

The shock of seeing the figure was so great that Katherine
stopped and stared at it, incapable of going on. The man was at
peace, going on about his business, no threat to her, a mere
painting. But her throat constricted with fear as she studied the
broad, powerful back, the definition of the muscles easily apparent
in the silvery fall of moonshine. This was a man who was
accustomed to killing. The knife, the lance, the net. They had been
killers back when this painting was done, they were killers still.

It took Bosch gripping her by the elbow and pulling her along
firmly before she could move on, and from that point her anxiety
grew steadily worse. The man was but the first of the figures.
There were others, many, many more. All of them, men, women,
and even children were hurrying toward something. It was
obviously a great gathering of some sort, which they approached
with joy and anticipation. All of them exhibited the same
distinctive physical characteristics that she had already noticed in
Crystal, Jasper, and the unknown male. Their brows were heavy
and pronounced, their foreheads short and sloped backward at a
sharp angle. Their noses were broad and flattened and their jaws
were aggressively outthrust. There was—despite their well-
groomed hair and clothing, the glint of gold and silver and
precious gems worn by both males and females—an air that was
definitely primitive.

It was Bosch who first noticed the second group of figures.
They were far less defined, standing concealed in shadows among
the trees at the edge of the forest. They were native Americans, or
so it seemed to Katherine. There were only men, and they hugged
the shadows cast by the immense trees. Their hair was braided
more often than not and they wore simple breechclouts and little
else. They too were armed with spears, and from the watchful

expressions and the manner in which they hung back out of sight, it was apparent that they too were fearful of the people of the meadow.

The significance of the painting was not lost on Katherine. It seemed obvious that these people, whoever they were, had been here for a very long time. They were not homeless derelicts; they were not anything that she had supposed or imagined. It was no longer possible to deceive herself.

Bosch touched her arm gently. She looked up, dazed, her mind still filled with the images and implications of the mural. Perhaps it was because of this that she did not immediately realize what she was seeing. For a moment, she failed to recognize the figures that stood before her, virtually identical to those in the mural. Only when Bosch gripped her elbow, holding it tightly to keep her from making any move, did she become focused. The figures standing before them, to either side and behind them, were not figures in a mural, they were real.

TWENTY-FIVE

Katherine's fear was so great, so overwhelming, that she could not even react. It was as though she had been frozen; she could not move, she felt nothing. She was later to realize that it was this perhaps that had saved them. Eager as he had been to find these people, Bosch was curiously silent now that their mission had met with success.

They were completely surrounded by no fewer than twenty males armed with spears, knives, and swords. It should have been ludicrous, two highly educated, modern people outfitted with high tech paraphernalia, threatened by a seemingly primitive people armed with archaic weapons. But neither Katherine nor Bosch was the slightest inclined to laughter. After the initial shock wore off, Katherine was seized briefly by an overwhelming desire to run, but even if that had been possible, she doubted her trembling legs would have been capable of tottering more than a few short steps. She was nauseous with fear and felt it entirely possible that she might throw up. Some tiny portion of her brain that still functioned focused in on the ironic humor of that scenario, as though it were a cartoon drawn by Gary Larson, captioned: "Surrounded by hostile natives, Katherine Sinclair vomited on their feet, forgoing the use of her atomic laser pistol." She felt an almost uncontrollable need to giggle. All of these conflicting thoughts and emotions filled her mind in the blink of an eye. She wondered if she were losing her mind.

"We are not enemies, we come in peace," said the doctor. It

sounded like dialogue out of a B-grade movie from the forties, and Katherine felt the giggle burst past her lips. Though Bosch knew it was an hysterical laugh and not one of amusement, he quickly silenced Katherine, pinching the flesh above her elbow so hard that her arm went all tingly down to her fingertips. She bit her lower lip hard and inhaled deeply, trying to bring her quaking nerves under control.

"I am a doctor, a healer," Bosch continued. "We know about your children, how they are sick and dying. We have come to help."

There was no direct response to Bosch's statement, yet his words seemed to cause great consternation among the men, who turned to each other and spoke in low, anxious tones. They seemed to be arguing among themselves. Finally, one man came toward them. He did not appear to be afraid of them—none of the men did—but he approached them cautiously as though suspecting them of treachery.

Perhaps because Bosch exhibited no sign of fear and the man had made no immediate gesture of violence, Katherine began to pull her fragmented nerves together. The man who was approaching them step by wary step, was quite tall, taller than Jasper or the sleeping man. He was built more slenderly than his companions and his skin was a darker hue, or so it appeared in the night-vision goggles. His forehead was not sloped, although his nostrils were flared and the bridge of his nose somewhat flattened. Nor was his jaw outthrust. It was only when Katherine looked at his hair, which was a mass of tightly kinked curls worn long and drawn into a single thick braid, that she realized what it was that was different about him: he was a black man!

She stared at him in astonishment, wondering how he came to be in this place. He was dressed in a similar manner to his companions, a long sleeveless tunic which fastened at the shoulders with polished stone buttons and fell to mid-thigh. The waist of the garment was gathered in with a soft leather belt which held a leather scabbard and a knife with a hilt made of a deer's antler. The tunic, unless she was mistaken, was made of the same silken material that lined the baby's coverlet. The fabric was plain, unadorned, but the man himself was not. He wore a number of bracelets around his wrists and one wide gold band with delicate scrollwork high on his upper arm. A tattoo in the shape of a spear point was marked on his bicep. Then, with a shock, Katherine realized that it was not a tattoo at all, but a carving, the design

incised into the flesh itself. There was one further detail that she
noted, forcing her eyes away from the mutilated flesh. It was a
fragile braid, seemingly no thicker than a half dozen hairs, but
spun from gold, not thread, and woven together into a single
supple length. It hung around his neck, and suspended from this
necklet, in the hollow of his throat, was a small leather bag, tied
shut with a strip of leather. She could not help but wonder what it
contained. The man wore loose gathered pants and tall leather
boots that came just below his knees. His companions were all
dressed in much the same manner, and all of them bore the same
carving on their upper arms. The only discernible difference
among them was that some wore a type of sandal rather than the
tall boot, and a few were unshod. All of them wore a pouch on
some portion of their body and all were adorned with various bits
of jewelry.

The man did not speak to them at all. He came close enough for
Katherine to catch the slightest scent of mushrooms and earth. He
moved slowly, taking no chances, running his fingers over their
bodies lightly, delicately, missing nothing. The flashlight in her
pocket was handled with the greatest of care, withdrawn gingerly
as though he suspected it to be of great danger, as perhaps it was.
Bosch was relieved of his as well. Katherine could feel the fear
emanating from the man as he handled these objects. It seemed to
her that the men who encircled them had to force themselves not
to take a step backward and that they held their breath collectively
until the flashlights were deposited on the ground. They had been
handled with the caution one connected with live bombs.

Once the dangerous flashlights were disposed of, the man
gestured for Bosch to remove the knapsack and directed him to
empty it on the ground, still without speaking. He poked through
the contents with the wooden butt of a spear handed to him by one
of his companions. A gesture with the spear was all that was
needed to move them back several steps.

The black man crouched down before the jumbled pile. Each
item was examined with great interest, always prodded with the
spear before it was touched. Plastic bottles filled with pills were
carefully sniffed before the tops were screwed back on. Stethoscope, thermometers, a blood pressure cuff, tongue depressors,
swabs, and syringes were regarded with suspicious eyes. The
sharp, astringent smell of alcohol filled the air and its container
quickly capped. Metal items, even those made of aluminum or
other alloys, were separated into a second pile. Everything else

was returned to the knapsack. Bosch was instructed with a single wave of the spear that he could pick it up.

"Look, I know about your problem with metal," Bosch began in a reasonable tone of voice, but almost quicker than Katherine could follow, the spear was up under his throat, the point cutting into the slightly sagging flesh. But Bosch was no coward. He did not flinch, nor did he attempt to move away from the spear. "I need those things," he said tersely. "They will help me to help your people. They will not hurt you."

The two men stared at each other, struggling for domination. The tension was palpable. The black man was slightly taller than the doctor but was unable to impose the force of his presence upon the older man despite the fact that he held the weapon and was in physical control of the situation. Staring into Bosch's goggles had to be off-putting. Katherine had wondered why the men had not reacted at the sight of them; surely they knew that this was not the norm. The answer was not long in coming. The black man's hand rose in a single swift motion, the spear point still pressed up under the doctor's throat. He seized the goggles with his free hand and ripped them off Bosch's head, lowering the hand with the spear at the same time and shoving Bosch hard in the chest. Bosch staggered back several steps, trying to keep his balance, then fell hard on the bricks. Katherine ran to him and crouched at his side, half expecting to be set upon by the man with the spear.

"I'm all right," Bosch growled, sounding more annoyed than frightened. He got to his feet and walked directly up to the black man, who was clearly taken aback by Bosch's attitude. "Look here, you can shove me around all you want," Bosch barked, jabbing a blunt finger at the man's chest, "but that's expensive and necessary equipment, and if I'm going to help you folks, you better let me take it along."

Katherine was impressed by his courage; he did not seem the least bit intimidated by the men or their spears. Unfortunately, without the aid of his night-vision goggles, he was standing some two feet to the right of the man with the spear, talking and gesturing in the wrong direction.

The rest of the party had gathered around the black man and were examining the goggles with great interest. A sudden intake of breath, a startled sound of surprise from one of the men who almost dropped the goggles after looking into them, caused Bosch to realize that he was focused in the wrong direction. This made him even angrier.

"Give me back the goddamn goggles!" he roared, holding out his hand in an imperious, demanding gesture that startled even Katherine. Any suspicion she might have had that they didn't understand was removed when the men all looked at one another as though needing confirmation to act. Finally, the black man who appeared to be in charge nodded slowly. Only then were the goggles returned by the man who happened to be unfortunate enough to be holding them at the time of Bosch's outburst. He approached the doctor with visible trepidation and, standing as far away as possible, dropped the goggles into his open palm. "Thank you," Bosch grumbled. Katherine could not resist a small grin as she noted the rapidity with which the man vanished back into the circle of his companions. Nor was there further comment as the doctor scooped up the items that had been left on the ground and placed them back in his knapsack.

"Well, let's get on with it: take us to your leader, as they say," Bosch demanded, taking a few steps down the tunnel in the direction they had been heading. The black man took the lead, while Katherine and the doctor were surrounded by a circle of the armed men whose manner was distinctly cautious as well as hostile. They were regarded with fear as well as hatred. Katherine felt that it would take very little to cause one of the men to lose control and put a spear through their ribs.

They turned sharply right at the next corridor, and even though Katherine's attention was focused on keeping her distance from their captors, she could not help but notice that the mural continued as well. Throngs of people filled the edges of the walls, all hurrying in the same direction. Many of them appeared to be carrying some form of package or bundle.

Doorways appeared now, on either side of the corridor, rounded openings such as she had seen beneath her own building. Some of these openings were lighted with a soft glow, and as they passed, voices exclaimed and figures emerged, their expressions both stunned and horrified.

Soon, they were accompanied by a large crowd of men and women, and children, too, some of whom shrieked in terror and were comforted by their parents. Mutterings could be heard, some of an excited, curious nature such as occurs when any unaccustomed event takes place. But there was also an undertone of anger and ill will that was impossible to ignore. Several times they were forced to stop, their way blocked by groups of men, all of whom were armed. Angry words were exchanged in a language

Katherine could not understand. Each time, their guards won out, clearly threatening those who had dared to approach.

There was another difference, this one as startling in its own way as the throngs that surrounded them. Lights. As in the corridor beneath her building, there were niches set in the wall at head level. Each niche contained a round stone, approximately the size of a basketball, which shed a soft glowing luminescence. These glowing stones, coupled with the soft illumination from the doorways, made it apparent that the people could tolerate some degree of light. Wearing the night-vision glasses made everything painfully bright. Katherine experimented by slipping the goggles up onto her forehead and discovered that she could see, perhaps not with the same clarity offered by the goggles, but still she could see. She slipped the glasses into her pocket, relieved to be free of their claustrophobic effect. Noticing her actions, Bosch did the same.

Their party now resembled a procession or a parade. Every doorway emptied itself of the people within, whose voices joined the noisy babble that trailed behind them. But it lacked the festive air of a parade; the ominous undertone and hostile shouts that erupted from the crowd needed no interpretation. Katherine and Bosch found themselves actually welcoming the shield provided by their captors and offered no resistance when they drew inward, crowding them into a tight knot.

They had passed perhaps a dozen or more of the lighted doorways when the first missile was thrown. It was a stone, sharp and pointed at one end, which missed them but struck one of their captors and drew blood. He hunched his shoulders and uttered what was clearly an expletive, but did nothing more. That was but the first. Soon, more and more objects were being hurled into their midst, along with curses and epithets, all in the unknown language. Katherine herself was struck between the shoulder blades, a solid thump that drove the breath from her chest. She sagged, the strength driven from her knees by the shock of the unexpected blow, and scarcely noticed that it was one of their captors who grabbed her arm and stopped her from falling. Their eyes met, and in the large pale orbs, she saw a reflection of her own perplexity that the two of them should have become allied against those who wished to do them harm. But for the luck of the draw, perhaps he himself would be hurling rocks, trying to kill her instead of being forced to protect her. She whispered thank you, and the man turned away in confusion.

They had come to another corridor, this one wider and more grand than any other they had traveled. There were pillars set at regular intervals, spirals of stone that rose from the brick floor to a point above their heads where the spirals flattened and arched upward before descending to the pillar on the opposite side. Perhaps they offered some form of support, but Katherine suspected that they were simply there for show.

The murals had come to an end, replaced by panels of portraits. Most of those pictured were men, but there were several women as well. All the figures exhibited the traits that Katherine had come to accept as the characteristics of the race. The broad, sloping brow, the flattened nose, the outthrust jaw—all of these were present. There were differences to be sure. Some had eyes that were so pale as to appear more white than silver; others had eyes that were as blue as the summer's sky. Skin tones varied from dead albino white to a ruddy pink tone. Hair differed as well. All were white-blond; there was no other color. But the styles and ornamentation were greatly varied, as was the clothing. The first portraits they encountered were the most modern in terms of apparel; some of the clothing had sleeves and high-necked collars, and the hair was worn in simple yet distinctive styles. The further they went, the differences became more and more apparent. The garments were simpler, plain tunics for the most part. The hair was worn longer and arranged in more ornate styles, sometimes braided, sometimes strung with beads and shells and brightly colored feathers. There was something else, something that plucked at Katherine's thoughts which she could not pinpoint. She wished that they could go back for a minute, back to the first of the portraits, because she had the feeling that whatever it was that stuck in her mind was important, but of course that was impossible.

The crowd was still on their heels, but they were silent now, and in a way, that was even more ominous than the earlier outcries. She did not dare to turn and look behind her, but she sensed that the size of the crowd had grown. The sound of their footsteps echoed and reverberated in the wide corridor. There was something very majestic and intimidating about the passage; perhaps created by the visages that peered down upon them, regal and commanding despite the strange conformations of their features. Katherine felt the weight of their eyes upon her as she passed beneath them, despite the fact that she knew that the eyes in many portraits appeared to follow the viewer. It was merely a technique.

But technique or no, she shivered under the weight of their disapproval.

They had come to another opening. She expected to see yet another corridor appear on either side or directly ahead, but that was not the case. They had come to the end, the place where all corridors led. It appeared that they were in some vast central auditorium, a huge atrium. Corridors appeared at regular intervals all around the periphery of the area, which was perfectly round in shape.

The floor was no longer brick, but seemed to be an immense, colorful mosaic. Little of the design could be seen because she was being hurried so swiftly across its surface and all around her was the press of feet. More and more people appeared in the mouths of the corridors and poured into the central area. She felt, rather than saw, that the floor was pitched at a slight downward angle, and their pace increased so that they were hurrying forward, assisted by the urgency of the crowd behind them.

Everything was happening too swiftly for her to take in much of her surroundings, but she had the impression that they were elaborate and intricate, on the order of the grand old theaters, some of which still existed in the Chicago area.

Her arms were gripped on either side by a pair of their guards, and she welcomed their closeness, for she feared the crowd now far more than she feared those who had actually captured them. Briefly, she wondered what would have happened if they had been found by a group of the inhabitants, then quickly put the thought out of her mind.

The floor leveled off. Directly ahead, she could see a stone platform, a series of great steps really, rising above them. A cluster of figures stood atop the highest level. They appeared to be engaged in an argument or a furious conversation.

Her view was obscured, her attention distracted from the scene when a surge from the left threw her off-balance, tearing the guard on the left away from her and enveloping him in a maelstrom of shoving and pushing bodies, a living, pulsating wave of violent rage. There was a loud outcry, guttural and animalistic, as though a pack of wild hunting dogs and found its prey. Without thinking, she dropped into a crouch and threw her arms up over her head. It was a stupid thing to have done; it could not have saved her from the mob, protected her for more than a moment. Fortunately, other minds were functioning better than her own. An arm threaded itself around her waist and scooped her up like a fish dangling above the waves. She dared to look. It was the black man, his shoulder and brow streaming with blood. He held her firmly about the waist and shoved her forward, the force of his muscular body propelling her through the angry faces, the crush of bodies, the threat of injury. Forward, forward without ceasing until her foot struck the bottom of the steps. Even then he did not stop. The voices behind them had risen to a great cacophony of hatred, mob virulence of a sort she had read about, knew from history, but never witnessed firsthand. And she was the object of their hatred. It was terrifying, numbing in its intensity. She knew, then, that nothing other than her death would satisfy them.

The black man thrust her further up the steps, and she realized that in some way the steps signified safety. A glance behind showed Bosch, his clothing torn and in great disarray, blood staining his forehead and his shirt, his goggles dangling around his neck, following close behind. Two guards still clung to him, protecting his back from the violence boiling behind them, but now she had the feeling that the guards themselves feared for their own safety. By becoming aligned with the intruders, they themselves had become suspect. Everywhere, as far as she could see, the vast area was filled with those struggling to reach them.

Never in her life had Katherine felt the target of such hatred, experienced such fear. Now she understood how those who were hunted felt. Animals. People. Prey. Now she could understand the desperate measures the hunted took to save themselves, and knew that she too would do whatever was necessary to survive. She no longer needed the urging, the guidance, of the black man; her legs were filled with a strength fueled by fear. She broke free of his grip and leapt up the steps on her own. She had been right in her assumption. The crowd had stopped at the bottom of the steps and were seething around it like a storm tide, but something, some powerful taboo, more powerful than their hatred, held them back.

She took the steps two at a time, leaping them to reach the highest point, to put as much distance as possible between herself and those who wished to kill her. Vaguely, in the back of her mind, she knew that she was not alone, that there were others on the platform steps, but nothing could have stopped her flight.

And then, there was nowhere left to go. She stood on the highest step, a broad platform of polished granite six feet in width and ten feet in length. She shared it with the figures she had seen from below. Her hair had fallen in her eyes, a heavy wave of auburn that obscured her vision. She brushed it aside, panting through her mouth, trying to find the words that would work, the words that would persuade those who stood at this highest level, protected from the crowd, to extend that protection to her.

The words died on her lips. She looked. Her eyes saw. The message was transferred along the pathway of neurons and synapses, and her brain absorbed the vision, the information that had been imparted, but there was no continuum, no flow of thoughts stemming from the input. There was nothing but stunned confusion and emptiness.

There were two figures standing before her atop the stone platform. One was a tiny old man, ancient beyond belief, his skin sere and withered, his hair pale wisps that framed his skull like angel hair. The second figure was also a man, who stared at her with helpless, saddened eyes. The second man was Stone.

TWENTY-SIX

Chaos raged around the foot of the steps. A tumultuous clamor rose to the arched ceiling and rebounded, filling the immense chamber until it resounded with hatred and violence. But it was little more than background noise to Katherine, who stared into Stone's eyes, the pain of his betrayal like a knife in her heart. It was he who broke the contact first, turning away from her as though they were strangers, and raised his hands above his head. Slowly, reluctantly, the crowd fell silent.

"Monia patria, arctus sanctum fortius, Guardia!" he said quietly. There was a moment's pause, a long hesitation as though the crowd was being instructed to do something that they clearly had no desire to obey. The hesitation continued, became uncomfortable; then the moment passed, and almost as one, the entire crowd bowed their heads and repeated the words Stone had uttered. There were undertones of defiance, even sullenness in the recitation, but they had apparently obeyed his decree.

"I am the Guardian. I am the Keeper of the Gates and in me there is wisdom and safety," he said.

The crowd responded in ragged unison. "You are the Guardian. You are the Keeper of the Gates and in you there is wisdom and safety."

There was more, all in the same vein, in English with only occasional lapses into the foreign tongue. Katherine did her best to follow what was being said, but a feeling of total lightheaded unreality had come over her. It had been difficult enough believing that Cameron had been stolen by people who lived somewhere beneath her building and another child left in her place. The police had not believed her. Helga and Stone had been her only allies and now Helga was dead and Stone appeared to be the king of this unbelievable world. Stone whom she had trusted. It was madness, all of it. None of it could possibly be real.

For a brief moment Katherine wondered if Rod's death could have driven her insane, if she could be imagining all of this and that, somewhere, Cameron and Helga were safe and well. Then her dazed eyes fell on Bosch. His clothing was torn, there were bloodstains on his forehead and chest, but he still clung to his knapsack as though it were filled with gold and gems. She knew next to nothing about insanity, but if she had in fact lost her mind, it seemed unlikely that she would have involved the family doctor in her dementia. But how could this be real? Of the two possibilities—an entire world peopled by a new and different race living undiscovered beneath the city of Chicago, or insanity—madness was far easier to accept.

The old man was speaking now, his voice a surprisingly deep bass that rolled over the restive crowd, calming them, soothing them, much like a giant hand stroking the back of an enormous wild beast. His was the voice of a born orator with power and persuasion resonating from every syllable. He did not speak in English but used the unknown language which flowed off his tongue in mellifluous waves, and while Katherine occasionally caught a word that sounded familiar, the body of his speech was meaningless. Nonetheless, the gist of it was clear. It appeared that he was urging them to be calm and to return to their homes. At first there were outcries, shouts of protest; then slowly, one at a time and then in small groups, they began to file out of the hall. It began as a trickle and then increased until all of the corridors were filled with their retreat.

They did not go willingly; they left behind them the aura of their emotion, an ominous heaviness that seemed to hang in the air. Some of the men remained, stiff and hard with anger. Katherine felt the heat of their hatred when their burning eyes touched upon her. They crowded close to the steps, and Stone and the old man waited patiently for them to speak. Katherine thought that they might descend from the platform and draw closer, but they did not do so, thus forcing the men to raise their heads and speak upward in an awkward and uncomfortable manner.

Bosch had joined Katherine, creeping up the steps slowly so as to attract as little attention as possible. But it was clear that he and Katherine had not been forgotten; the small group of defiant men drew as close to the platform as was allowed. The guards, those who had first discovered them, stood at the base of the steps, their weapons held across their chests in a position of readiness, a living barrier should it be needed.

The exchange that followed was strange, as strange as anything that had gone before. The men shouted out their vitriolic words and received little or nothing in return. Stone and the ancient had about them an air of royalty. Neither man deigned to trade words with those on the floor. Instead, they waited patiently until the men had screamed themselves out. Then, and only then, did they speak, first Stone and then the older man. Their words were brief and bore the weight of authority, the kind that one is born to and cannot be taught.

In the end, the men left. It was apparent, even to Katherine, that they had achieved little or nothing with their rantings. They had been heard, and that was all the concession they were granted. They left, one at a time, stalking away with angry eyes and stiff backs, with what little grace and dignity they could muster.

Only when the last of them had departed did Stone turn to the older man, and carefully, with immense respect and patience, assist him down the massive steps. The ancient's legs were frail and delicate. Even wrapped in fur-trimmed high leather boots, they were no larger than Katherine's own arm. His great age was apparent, and the great steps were difficult to negotiate, even for Katherine's strong legs, but he refused to acknowledge any weakness. He allowed Stone's hand to remain cupped under his elbow but did so as though he were granting a favor rather than accepting one.

Not even a single glance strayed their way, but neither Bosch nor Katherine needed to be told to follow. They did so at a respectful distance, but fright crowded Katherine and she looked around constantly, fearing the return of those who had so obviously wished to kill them. She followed as close to Stone and the old man as was possible without actually touching them. She felt no shame in acknowledging her fear; she would have been a fool not to have been afraid.

When they reached the bottom of the steps, the guards, who were clearly in awe of the old man, lowered their eyes and took a step back out of respect. The old man waved his hand in irritation and made a sibilant sound, which Katherine took to mean "Stop all of this nonsense, let's get on with it." It seemed that she was correct in her assumption, for the small party set off across the floor of the huge hall at as rapid a pace as the old man could manage. By the time they reached a corridor at the edge of the open hall, it was clear that the ancient one was tiring fast. Yet he would not allow anyone other than Stone to help him, and then only with the single hand cupped beneath his elbow.

Their progress was slow, and everyone seemed aware of the tension and danger in the air, a feeling of unseen eyes resting on them, watching their progress. It was with great relief when they turned into a smaller corridor that branched off from the main passage, and stepped over the sill of one of the rounded doorways.

Stone entered first and touched one of the round stone balls which was glowing with a faint luminescence. Instantly, it flared more brightly. The old man grimaced, his eyes squinting shut as though in pain. Stone, alert to every nuance in the older man, smoothed his hand over the surface of the stone, dimming it by half. The ancient one sighed and eased himself into a chair which was piled high with soft cushions. Stone poured a measure of amber liquid into a fragile cut-crystal goblet and handed it to the elder, who took a small sip and savored it before allowing it to slip down his throat.

Only when he was certain that the old man was comfortable, did Stone turn his attention to Katherine and Bosch, gesturing toward two chairs which the guards were swift to pull into place facing the ancient one. Katherine felt as though she had been called before the principal, or perhaps even the President, for despite his gentle demeanor, the patriarchal figure carried that sort of aura.

Stone handed Katherine and Bosch goblets of their own before settling himself on a small stool beside the old man's chair. He dismissed the guards with a single sentence, once again spoken in the unknown language. They exited the room quickly and positioned themselves in the corridor outside the door.

"Cardhu," Bosch murmured appreciatively, and for a single bewildering moment, Katherine thought that he too had begun to speak in foreign tongues.

"Yes, Doctor, I find that after a hard day, a little dram of the single malt is the cure for most of my problems."

Katherine stared at the old man with wide eyes. His words, his tone, the phrasing was the very proper wording of an East Coast Brahmin! He could not have startled her more had he suddenly grown an elephant's trunk, sprouted wings, and flown away. Bosch, on the other hand, did not seem the least bit surprised.

"I myself prefer Glennfiddich; Cardhu is a little too smoky for my tastes." The two men then entered into a somewhat lengthy discussion of the relative merits of different brands of single-malt Scotch whisky! Aside from the surroundings and the patriarch's appearance, they might easily have been two retired professionals relaxing over a brandy at a private men's club!

After a time, the old man drained the last of his drink and sat further back in his chair. His feet barely touched the floor. For all of his apparent power, he was no larger than a skinny twelve-year-old. He regarded his visitors with pale, calculating eyes.

"Please excuse my rudeness. In all the excitement, I'm afraid that I have failed to introduce myself. I am Pilar. I believe you are already familiar with my grandson."

Bosch said, "I am Benjamin Bosch and . . ."

"Please, Doctor, I know who you are and your credentials as well. I've been looking forward to meeting you for some time, although I confess that I did not expect it to be so soon or under such circumstances. But that, I'm afraid, is now a moot point. The question is, what are we to do with the pair of you? You've certainly managed to cause a stir. One that I'm not sure that I can control. As you saw, we too have our more volatile factions, those who are determined to change the order of things."

"I'm sorry if we've caused you trouble," Katherine said, daring to speak, but determined to be heard. The old man seemed so intelligent, so reasonable, and possessed so much authority, surely he would understand. Surely if she explained it correctly, he would help her get Cameron back. She launched into a brief, concise recital of how Cameron had been taken and how she had discovered the switch. She outlined what she and Bosch had done to help save the life of the baby, Amber, and begged him to help her achieve the return of her own child.

There was a long moment of silence that followed her recitation, during which the old man regarded her with his pale, near-white eyes.

"You say you actually spoke to this woman, Crystal?" he asked. Katherine nodded. Pilar turned his head and spoke briefly to Stone, who rose, stepped into the hall, and spoke softly to the black man before returning to his place at Pilar's side. He had taken pains to act at ease, not once had he met Katherine's eyes since they entered the room.

"And I meant what I said," Bosch said before Stone had even regained his seat. "I think that I can help you. If what I suspect is true, then you people are in desperate need of my services. I offer them freely and without any expectations of reward."

"We have our own healers, Doctor," Stone said. It seemed that he was about to say more but the old man put out a wrinkled, liver-blotched hand, silencing him.

"And just what is it that you suspect, Doctor?" Pilar asked.

"Katherine, here, thought that you were homeless people, down on your luck and with nowhere to go. But that's far from the truth. You've been down here a very long time, haven't you?" The old man's eyelids dipped slightly. Bosch nodded to himself. "I don't know where you came from, what your story is, but if that baby is any indication, well, your people are probably suffering from heavy-metal poisoning, arthritis, anemia, rheumatism, and chronic upper respiratory problems, to mention just a few things that occur to me."

"And what would you do to solve these problems, Doctor?"

"There's a lot I can do here, but of course some of the problems would have to be treated at the hospital."

"For argument's sake, let's say that I did persuade some of my people to accompany you. What do you suppose the reaction of your own people would be?"

Bosch was clearly uncomfortable with that question. "Well . . ." His voice lost some of its positive timbre.

"Well indeed, Doctor. Well indeed. Let me tell you what would happen. Wholesale panic first, then insatiable curiosity, attempts to exploit us, make money from the oddities that we are. But all of that is based on the belief that your government would stay out of it, which of course is a naive and unrealistic assumption. No, Doctor. I'm afraid that despite your very good and generous intentions, such a thing is not possible. To allow you to help us would be to cause our annihilation."

"What you say has a certain amount of truth in it," Bosch rumbled reflectively. "But surely there's a way. We're making good progress with Amber. Are there other such children? Surely you would not deny them the chance for life."

Before Pilar could answer, there was a stir at the door, the guards parted, and a man and a woman stepped through the doorway. The woman was carrying a child wrapped in a blanket. With a glad cry, Katherine leaped to her feet and hurried across the room.

Crystal was clearly frightened, but she exhibited as much courage as she had shown that fearful night when she and Katherine ran through the darkened tunnels. She stood tall and proud, and met the old man's eyes without flinching as she handed the baby to Katherine. The man was tall, much taller than Crystal, and extremely broad in the chest. He stood behind Crystal, his hands resting on her shoulders. Katherine was focused on the child inside the blanket, but as distracted as she was, she was aware of the fact that Crystal bore a distinctly defiant attitude.

"This is the child? This is Cameron?" Pilar asked.

Katherine unwrapped the blanket and examined each perfect pink finger and toe. She smoothed back the fall of straight blond hair, allowing it to trickle through her fingers. She rubbed the tiny upturned nose with her own and hugged her as hard as she dared. She felt such joy, she thought her heart would burst. "Oh, yes, this is my child. This is Cameron. Thank you, sir, I knew you would understand. I knew you would give her back once you understood."

Katherine knew she was babbling, knew that she should stop talking, but the words just tumbled out of her mouth unbidden. It was Pilar's expression which finally halted the flow. He was no longer the benign little old man, the kindly grandfather. His expression was stern and hard.

"You misunderstand, my dear, and for that I am truly sorry. Your grief, your personal unhappiness, was never my intention. But surely you understand, the child must remain here with us."

Katherine was never able to clearly remember all that occurred next. There was a great roaring in her ears, a pressure, darkness gathering behind her eyes ringed with a corona of crimson. Then it passed, leaving her feeling as though she had been ravaged by a hurricane of emotions.

She had a vague remembrance of heated words, tears, defiance, and even an attempt to flee with the child wrapped tightly in her arms.

Normalcy returned slowly, like a drug wearing off, leaving her feeling vulnerable and bruised emotionally as well as physically. Words were spoken and heard, meanings became clear. Stone and Bosch stood beside her, their hands on her arms. Stone's face, his beard, the gray mixed in with the reddish-brown, was oddly touching. The small lines next to his eyes. His eyes silvery gray with tiny webs of green and black. Those eyes that had first raised the unconscious trickle of suspicion at the back of her mind. Those same eyes that now mirrored concern. She yearned to rest her head on his chest, to be comforted, to feel safe. She felt herself leaning toward him, drawn to him by a heat that was like a magnet calling to her soul. She knew what it would feel like to rest her head against his chest, feel his arms around her, encircling her with safety.

Suddenly, she jerked back and stared at Stone, remembering, allowing the harsh reality of the present moment to replace her emotional needs. If all of this were true, then Stone himself had been a part of the kidnapping, had duped her as well as the police. "Helga!" The name hissed between her teeth. She stared at Stone through slitted eyes as the thought jolted her like an electric stock. Stone flinched at the name. Katherine stepped forward.

"Helga guessed the truth, didn't she? She came down here on her own and succeeded in finding your people. Or did they find her first? Only she wasn't as lucky as we were; there wasn't anyone to protect her. And I was the one who told you that she was coming down here. No wonder you were in such a hurry to get back. What part did you play in her death? You liar! You murderer!"

Stone flinched at every word, every accusation, as though he had been physically struck. But he absorbed the words, and the pain they caused him, in silence.

"You were afraid that I would learn something too. They sent you, didn't they, to keep an eye on me? What are you going to do now, kill me too? And the doctor? Is that how you so conveniently happened to replace Mr. Kramer? How could I have ever trusted you, you monster!"

"You misjudge my grandson, Mrs. Sinclair," Pilar said in quiet tones. "He has ever been the peacemaker who has tried valiantly to appease our various factions. No one was murdered. Mr. Kramer was one of us as well, as was his predecessor and the caretaker before him, a long, unbroken line. As long as the building has stood, we have been its caretakers. Mr. Kramer died of natural causes.

"Your friend, now, was a different matter. She has known of our existence for many, many years. She was wrong to have told you. It has brought nothing but trouble to all of us. You are right. She did trick my grandson into leaving, and then she broke into the upper tunnels. But we did not kill her. She was old, and when confronted by one of our people, her heart could not stand the strain and it failed her. We did what we could, but it was too late."

"How convenient." Katherine was trembling with rage. "And what do you intend to do with us?"

"The two of you present us with quite a problem, Mrs. Sinclair. It would have been so much better for all concerned had you and the doctor not found us."

"What's the problem?" asked Bosch. "You give us back the baby and let us go. Katherine has what she wants, and once the baby's returned, we have no reason to harm you or cause trouble for you. I'll continue to work with Amber and we'll work out a way to get her back to you. Stone here can stay in touch, bring her back when she's ready to leave the hospital."

"I'd like to believe that it could all be handled so easily, Doctor." The old man sighed and his shoulders sagged briefly. In that moment, as angry as she was, Katherine could see how very old he was; the skin around his eyes was parchment-thin and waxy-looking, his blotched scalp visible through the white hair. "But even if I were inclined to trust you, there are those among us who would never allow such a thing to happen. You saw some of them out there. We have suffered greatly in the past at the hands of your people and trust between our two races is not a highly developed concept."

"But why do you want my baby, especially if we can make your baby, Crystal's baby, better? She was dying and now she's almost well!"

"We appreciate what you have done. But your efforts, well-intentioned as they were, unfortunately, will be in vain. The child Amber cannot live. Without you there to guide the treatments, she will soon succumb to her illness."

Crystal took a step forward at his words, her hands balled into tight fists. The man, who could only have been Jasper, seized her arms and held her tightly, his eyes worried as he glanced up at Pilar to see what he might do. He was clearly frightened of the old man.

Pilar sighed again and looked up at Crystal from under heavily hooded lids. His exhaustion was apparent. "It is not my wish, my dear; it is just what must be for the good of all. You know that your child cannot be expected to live; you knew that from the start. Even if she did, she would be flawed, unable to bear healthy young. Now you have a child to replace her. It is the best we can do."

"No!" Two voices rang out in unison, as Crystal and Katherine spoke out against Pilar. Katherine clutched Cameron to her even more tightly, determined that she would never give up her child again.

"Let me see if I've got this straight," Bosch said, breaking into the tension that stretched between the women and Pilar. "You knew that—Crystal, is it?" Crystal nodded curtly. "You knew that Crystal's baby, Amber, was critically ill and could not be saved. So you took Katherine's baby, Cameron, and switched the two, doing something that I still don't understand so that the two kids looked like each other, temporarily. Am I right so far?"

Pilar nodded. "Stone here was in place to make sure that things went all right, maybe even set up the switch," Bosch continued. Stone stepped forward, his face flushed. Pilar held up a hand to stop him, without ever taking his eyes off the doctor.

"Things started to go wrong when Katherine met Helga and the two of them brought the baby into the hospital, which is where I come into the story. That baby was never intended to live. Everything was all right so long as she died before the spell or whatever it was wore off. Once her own features reappeared, you knew there would be trouble, coupled with the results from the blood work and the other obvious differences.

"Only other things went wrong too, things you hadn't figured on—the two mothers meeting and talking—you never planned on that. And Helga, finding you and then dying with or without your assistance. That must have caused some real trouble. And now here we are, walking in like a couple of tourists and what the hell are you going to do with us?"

Before Pilar could reply, there was a sudden commotion in the hall. Voices rose in consternation, people began to rush back and forth, and there was a sense of panic about their actions that seemed to indicate a disaster of the greatest magnitude. The black man thrust his way past the clot of people gathered in the doorway and hurried toward Pilar. Falling to one knee, he spoke rapidly, gesturing and pointing in several different directions.

Pilar rapped out a series of sharp commands that sent the man scurrying. Stone had blanched at the black man's words and he put his hand on Pilar's arm and queried him in the foreign tongue. The old man shook his head wearily as though the effort was almost too much for him to expend.

Pilar looked up at the doctor. Loud shouts and high-pitched screams could now be heard echoing from the corridors beyond the room. "Well, Doctor, it appears that the matter has been taken out of our hands. It seems that our security has been breached. We are being invaded."

TWENTY-SEVEN

Homicide detective Roberts was definitely not amused. He knew this assignment was just another way of giving him the shaft. Just like the one he'd been sent out on last week. The Mex in the fleabag hotel over on Clark Street who hung his head over the guardrail of the freight elevator, probably to barf or spit on something, and then had his height altered, drastically and permanently by the descending elevator.

I mean, what kind of foul play could that have been? Stupid spic was probably drunk like they all were all the time an' he just got what was coming to him. I mean, how could you not hear a freight elevator comin' down?

They gave that one to him and everything else that was at the bottom of the barrel, stuff no one else wanted to deal with. It was all on account of they were jealous. Just because he happened to marry the chief's ex-wife, Sheila. Was it his fault that the chief was grateful for not having to pay alimony anymore? Was it his fault that he'd made detective sooner than usual? There was lots of grumbling that maybe someone, like the chief, had pulled some strings. Was it his fault if the chief liked him? But still, they kept giving him these shit assignments.

This one, what a cockamamie story it was. Have to be some kind of lunatic to believe it. Woman calls in, all crazy. Baby kidnapped. Officers respond. Woman all nuts, tells them some crazy story about monsters in her basement. The beat guys go look, keep the civilians pacified, right. Nothing. On top of it, the kid's there in its crib all along. A loony.

Next, the same loony calls in and claims she's found some secret tunnels, more monsters living in the tunnels. Beat guys go back, go down into the basement with her. Check it out. Old rooms, boarded up since God knows when just like when Geraldo tried to find Capone's secret hideout and all he finds is some dusty old bottles. What a laugh. No monsters, surprise, surprise.

Now, some old lady punches out, same building. Autopsy says myocardial infarction, fancy words, means heart attack any way you slice it. But the docs find rock dust, tiny shit, dust, ground into her skin and her clothes. All over. And in her hand, clenched real tight inside her fist, there was this strange carved ball with a real ugly head inside it. Find out, they say. Go take a look just to be sure. Yeah, right! Next week it'll be giant salmon dragging fishermen off the piers.

Roberts met with resistance right away. The doorman did not seem the least impressed with his shield, and eyed with disdain the stain that the jelly-filled donut had made on his tie. These guys with their fancy monkey uniforms sat on their rumps in their fancy buildings all day and thought they were so hot. It burned him up. He put some steel in his voice and demanded that the monkey-suit call the loony—he checked his notes—Mrs. Sinclair.

"Mrs. Sinclair is not in at the moment," the man replied stiffly. It would be a pleasure to break his balls for him, the fat shit.

"Then get me this guy Stone!" Roberts allowed some belligerence to enter his voice and pushed his belly a little closer to the doorman, using it as a means of intimidation, entering what the hotshots called personal space these days. Personal space, my ass, just scare the crap outa them. He enjoyed the look of uncertainty, the fear that crept into the man's eyes as he retreated behind his fancy console and pushed some buttons.

"Mr. Stone also appears to be unavailable at this time." Roberts took another step toward the monkey-suit, glowering in a way that he knew from experience was quite effective. "It's the truth!" the man said hurriedly, backing up as far as he could go, stumbling over his fancy little rolling chair. "I haven't seen him since yesterday. I don't know where he is!"

The man was too frightened to be lying. Roberts always knew when they were lying. He grunted and put out his hand. "Keys. Gimme the keys." The doorman was too frightened to argue. Roberts scooped them up and walked toward the goddamn fancy glass door. It made him mad just looking at it, beveled leaded glass and for an entry door yet—probably had cut crystal mirrors in the bathrooms. These rich people gave him a pain. He glowered back at the doorman, who hurried to open the door for him, then got out of his way, fast.

The man's fear made Roberts feel good enough so that he almost didn't mind the long stairway down into the basement. Almost didn't mind. But his knees never let him forget. He'd played football in high school, over at Lane Tech across town, a good school till the niggers took it over. Frankie Laine went there, even grew up there in the neighborhood. He'd been a tackle, damn good one too, and there'd been some talk of a scholarship over to the University of Illinois, until he tore all the cartilage in his right knee. They fixed it, sort of, then he did the same thing to his other knee and it was all over.

Things had gone bad from that point on. He'd had to marry his girlfriend when she managed to get herself knocked up with their first kid, the only time they did it, the night of the senior prom. His life had been shit from that point on until she took the two whiny little girls she'd managed to spawn and divorced him, like he cared or something. Best thing she ever did for him.

She was gone, but his knees never let him forget the past. And somehow, every time they hurt, like in bad weather or going up and down stairs, he hated her all over again, blaming her for his pain. At the yearly inspections the docs always told him to lose weight, stop drinking and smoking, eat different, and all sorts of shit like that. What did they know about what it took to live his life? Had they ever had to look at a spic with his head chopped off or climb down a million steps to go look for monsters in a dark basement? If a couple a plates of pasta and some beers made him feel better, hell, he deserved it. Was it his fault he had to look at shit like that?

The door opened behind him, just as he lurched awkwardly from the last step onto the basement floor. It was his partner, Mr. Smartass—I'm so classy my shit don't stink—Steiner. What kind of name was that for a nigger? Used to be you could tell a man from his name. Steiner. In the old days that would make you a kraut or a kike. But nothing was simple anymore. He wanted to work by himself, alone. But they paired him with this educated black-ass and there was nothing he could do about it. So he ignored him most of the time. Was it his fault that Steiner solved most of their cases? Let him do the paperwork, that would teach him to be a smartass. They hardly ever talked to each other, which suited Roberts just fine.

Steiner tripped lightly down the steps and moved into the lead, shining his fancy, nonregulation high-intensity flashlight into all the shadows. Roberts flipped the switches on and off, wondering why such a high-class fancy building had such piss-poor lights in the basement. Had to be 25-watters. Cheap shit, barely lit up anything. He rattled his flashlight. Nothing. Then he remembered that he had forgotten to replace the batteries. Oh, well, a man couldn't remember everything. Let Steiner lead the way, he'd follow along behind.

They found their way to the furnace room and knocked on Stone's door. Roberts eyed the dark opening behind them with suspicion. What was that smell? Then he placed it. Dirt, plants, growing stuff. A light came into his eyes. Maybe they were growing pot down here. A perfect setup, no one would ever see the lights this far down. And if they had some kind of secret room like Geraldo found, hey, they could grow a ton of the stuff. Anyone could afford to live in a building like this, they grew that much shit.

Excited with his theory, which he determined to keep to himself, Roberts took the flashlight out of Steiner's hands without explanation or apology and stepped over the broken boards and into the earthy darkness. Steiner, accustomed to his partner's ways, and intuiting, in the strange way that some policemen develop, that Stone's apartment was empty, followed along behind. Let the obnoxious boor do some of the work for a change.

They had read the reports and found the space where Helga had stood, small scrapings visible in the thick layer of dust. There was little else of interest in the room and Roberts was about to leave, when Steiner took the light from his partner and directed it toward the wall. He was careful to handle only the flashlight itself; he never physically touched Roberts, whose intense dislike of blacks was well-documented. The beam shone on the wall, illuminating the strange indentation. It was very odd, almost as though something had been drawn inward at a time when the concrete was still wet. But how could that have been unless there was another room on the other side of this one? Whatever, it did not seem to have any bearing on the case, although, from the scrapes, it appeared that the old woman had stood in this very spot and looked at the same blip. It sent shivers up his back for some

reason, almost like he was being watched. He shook himself.
Nerves. They could get to you in strange, dark places like this.

Roberts had been sniffing the air like an old bloodhound and
jerked the flashlight out of Steiner's hand, heading out the door.
Steiner had no alternative but to follow or be left alone in the dark.
Roberts was not heading back toward the furnace room, as he
would have expected, but was following the corridor.

The beam of light shone directly upon a brick wall which
spanned the corridor from side to side, closing it completely. But
something was wrong; even Roberts sensed it. He swung the beam
back and forth over the face of the wall, casting left to right, trying
to figure out what it was that was out of place.

Steiner looked down, saw the flakes of white powder, the
crumble of mortar, and pointed them out to Roberts. Roberts
picked up a small chunk and crumbled it between his fingers. He
grunted. "This stuff is fresh, feel it." He dropped the mortar into
Steiner's hand, and Steiner, who had never done a day's work with
mortar or cement, could feel the moisture it contained. There was
a hard crust on the surface, but the dampness within could still be
felt.

Roberts made another grunting sound, one that contained
excitement, like a pig on the scent of truffles. He scanned the wall,
mere inches from it, and then he found it. The bricks that
Katherine had displaced had once again been repaired, but now the
mortar that bound the bricks together was far fresher than the
mortar around it. Roberts, who had spent four summers working
on a construction crew, zeroed in on the familiar aroma, smelling
out the difference rather than seeing it. He was more convinced
than ever that they would find pot, record amounts, stacked behind
this wall. Maybe even cocaine!

It took him no time at all to lumber back to the furnace room
and find a pickaxe. Steiner, perplexed by his partner's actions, but
knowing that he was on to something, armed himself with a
pointed sharp-edged shovel and followed Roberts back into the
strange corridor.

Four, then five strokes of the pickaxe and they were through the
wall. The flashlight was propped up against the first of the bricks
to be broken out and cast its light upon the face of the wall. Steiner
lent his lean, economic strokes to the heavy bashings of his
partner's and soon there was a hole large enough for even Roberts
to step through.

Steiner had thought that he'd heard sounds all the while they were attempting to break through the wall. But between Roberts's pounding, grunting, and heavy, moist breathing, it was impossible to be certain. Rats. That was what he thought and so was not particularly eager to be the first through the opening.

"Holy fucking Christ!" cried Roberts, and then he was moving, fast. Steiner leaped through the opening as deftly as he could and caught sight of his partner vanishing into the darkness in front of him, only his run-down heels and the creased legs of his pants in view. But now there were other sounds—voices, cries of fear! Was that a child crying? There was a man's voice, loud and vehement, and a rock came clattering out of the darkness, missing his head by inches.

Roberts stopped, his breath chuffing loudly in what could now be seen was a continuation of the corridor. He leaned forward and rested his hand against the wall, breathing heavily. There was movement in the darkness beyond him. Steiner tried to take the flashlight from Roberts, making the mistake of touching his hand. Roberts snatched his hand back, baring his teeth and all but snarling. Christ, the man was an animal! The two men glared at each other. "They're getting away," Steiner said tersely, not knowing who it was who was getting away, or why, but no one who was innocent ran like that.

"No shit," Roberts said derisively, his words coming breathlessly. "Fuck 'em, I just hope they stay gone forever. Take a look at this! And he pointed the beam of the flashlight into the room that lay beyond the rounded doorway.

TWENTY-EIGHT

Virginia Peabody, R.N., was very annoyed, and if the truth were known, just a trifle worried. It was quite unlike Dr. Bosch not to appear for morning rounds, much less to miss an appointment, actually three appointments. The hospital had called and she had been forced to smile and ask his patients if they would be seen by young Dr. Gerber or wished to reschedule. All had wished to reschedule, not that there was anything wrong with Dr. Gerber, but, well, he just wasn't Dr. Bosch.

Virginia Peabody had been with Dr. Bosch for thirty-nine years. It had been her first job straight out of nursing school, originally intended as temporary summer employment while visiting a cousin. Despite the fact that it was a cliché, she had fallen in love with her employer, with his vitality and charisma, and had never left.

She had been with him through the lean years and through the fat years, through his marriage and through the death of his wife, and never, never—not even when Marjorie was dying—had Benjamin Bosch ever done such an irresponsible thing as miss rounds or appointments. It was unthinkable! Something had to be dreadfully wrong.

She had called the police of course, but they had dismissed her concerns. They had been polite, but they had not taken her seriously. "Call back when he's been missing for twenty-four hours," said the bored voice on the other end of the phone. Twenty-four hours indeed! Why, he could be dead! Lying in a gutter with his head split open! Mugged by the trash that was overrunning the neighborhood, and they wouldn't care. She had called back twice more, demanding to speak to someone else but always got the same response.

Nurse Peabody was too distraught to remain in the office. She canceled as many of the doctor's patients as she could reach and then turned the desk over to one of the young girls who assisted Dr. Gerber. She would probably find everything in chaos when she returned, but she just couldn't sit still, not for another moment without knowing what had happened. If the police wouldn't go look for Dr. Bosch, then she would do it herself!

She locked her desk under the nose of the girl and instructed her to do nothing but answer the phone. "Touch nothing!" she ordered, knowing that the "girls" regarded her as fussy and old-fashioned and laughed at her behind her back. It was a deep and grievous hurt, but at the moment, it didn't matter. Nothing mattered but finding Doctor.

It was only when she got into her car, a 1959 Studebaker, one of the very last to roll off the line of the plant in South Bend, Indiana before they locked the doors for good, that she thought of the portable phone.

Waves of relief coursed through her tightly corseted body. Not that she needed such garments with her lean and bony frame, but Mother had always said that a decent woman did not appear in public without one, that a corset was part of every respectable woman's attire. Only floozies went uncorseted.

She sat there, stiffly erect with proper posture on the nubbly fabric seat and looked at the strange black device that she always carried in her purse, ever since the first day Doctor gave it to her. But never had she used it. It was not seemly for a woman to call a man, everyone knew that. Or, rather, they used to.

Virginia put a hand to her head, feeling the tightly lacquered waves falling out of place, and gave in to a moment of weakness and uncertainty. Nothing was the way it used to be. No one wore corsets anymore. It was harder and harder to find them, and these days she had to order them through catalogues. Everywhere she looked, girls and women of all ages were wearing terrible clothing. They thought nothing of displaying large portions of their bodies, bare, naked flesh. Not only were they uncorseted, but many of them went without brassieres and sometimes even underpants!

Cars were faster, more streamlined, and cost as much or more than a house used to cost. It was becoming more and more difficult to get parts for the Studebaker. The mechanics were rude and filthy and laughed openly at her and her car as though they were both objects of great humor!

Virginia often had the feeling that the world had passed her by, that she had missed out on everything that was important, a husband, children, a home. And the only man she had ever truly loved, devoted her entire life to, had married someone else and didn't seem to realize how she felt about him.

Her God had not seen fit to reward her with any of the things that other women obtained and lost easily without seeming to care. Mother had always said that God knew what he was doing, that there was a reason for everything. Perhaps she would learn those reasons in the next life, but for now, so long as she lived in this one, she would continue to do the best she could according to the tenets she had been raised by. To do otherwise would have been to openly admit that her life had been a waste.

Virginia Peabody was not a quitter. She had loved Benjamin Bosch for thirty-nine years and she was not about to stop now, now that he was out there in trouble somewhere. The police might not believe her, but she knew it was so, knew it in her bones. You didn't love someone for that long without gaining intuitional antennae. She knew that something was wrong.

Virginia stared at the gadget. It was black and streamlined, modern, an anathema to her, but it was a link to Doctor. She set her jaw and jiggled the latch. It flipped open with a sharp snap that startled her so badly she almost dropped it. Once revealed, she saw that the interior contained a confusing array of red and blue buttons as well as the familiar push-button telephone number pad.

Her mind was such that once she heard a number, she never forgot it, if she chose to remember. Doctor had carefully recited the number of his pager when he gave her its mate. He was never without it; he could be reached at any hour of the day or night. While she had never used it, had always used the answering service to page him, it had been a link between them. Now, she would use it to find him.

She tapped out his personal number, the rubbery pads feeling strange beneath her fingertips. She put the top of the gadget to her ear and spoke into the perforated endpiece below the numbers. "Hello, hello. Doctor, are you there?" There was nothing but silence. Something was not working correctly.

Tears came to her eyes and she sniffed them away angrily,

admonishing herself. Now was not the time for tears. She examined the gadget more closely. There was an antenna on the top in one corner that she had not noticed before. She pulled it up, extended it to its full height, and then tapped out his number again. Nothing. More buttons, more switches. She pushed them at random, waiting each time to see the result. There was writing, printing beneath the buttons, but it was so tiny, and some of it was just letters that didn't convey any meaning. Finally, she heard the familiar dial tone emanating from the gadget in her lap. Pray God! Something she had done had worked! She snatched it up and pecked out the number with shaking fingers.

Charles Goodfellow was standing on the corner of Thorndale and Broadway feeling good; better than he had felt in a long time. He was warm, dressed in a handsome garment that looked as good as it felt. It empowered him. He had found enough loose change and bills in the various pockets to feed himself. It had been a good meal.

Some, no, all of the restaurants in the area would throw him out if he were to attempt to come in the front door. But many of the cooks and cooks' helpers would fill a bowl and pass it out the back door for the proper amount of money. Whether that money ever saw its way into the cash register was questionable, but that was not his problem. His belly was filled with meat, vegetables, broth, and bread, and none of it had come from dumpsters or garbage cans. There had even been enough money for coffee with lots of real cream and several spoons of sugar. It was the way he liked it. The young Filipino had also handed him several stale buns of the sort that were slathered with caramelized sugar and dotted with nuts. He put them in one of the pockets for later.

He had also purchased a bottle, a slender bottle of the semi-dry white wine he used to drink in that other confusing life that he sometimes remembered. It was the combination of the coat, the sweet warmth of the wine, and a full stomach that made him feel so good. He stood on the corner smiling at all the passersby who, as usual, avoided eye contact with him. Normally, that would annoy him, and he would often bark at them and chase them down the street, snapping at their heels. That made him feel good too. But it had been a happy day and he was feeling complacent.

Goody put his hand in the pocket of the coat, just to make sure that the sticky buns were still there, when he felt a tingling under his fingers and heard a sharp, staccato, bleating sound. He pulled his hand out of the pocket as though a snake had tried to bite him, shocked, frightened. Was someone trying to take his coat away? Was the coat itself alive? Was it accusing him, would it hurt him? He grew frantic at the thought and began swatting the coat with the flat of his hands, keeping his fingers stiff and outstretched so he could not be bitten. He ripped at the coat, struggling to free himself from it. He was inside it. If it were alive, it could easily devour him! He stripped the coat from his body, the buttons flying off in all directions, and threw it on the ground. A crowd began to gather.

Goody prodded the coat with his toe. It did not move. It was not alive. The fear, the dreadful fear began to ebb. A shred of sanity like a current of cold air cut through the fog of his mind. A coat, a beautiful coat, Harris tweed, was lying on the ground. People were watching him. He growled at them and they quickly dispersed. He picked up the coat and smoothed it out.

The sound repeated itself, oddly muffled. Only this time, Goody recognized it for what it was, the ring of a portable phone. He slipped his arms back into the sleeves. The ringing continued. He buttoned the coat with the few remaining buttons, telling himself that he would answer if it was still ringing when he was done. He took as long as he could, but still the ringing continued.

Charles Anthony Goodfellow III, graduate of the University of Chicago, resident of cardboard boxes and train-station floors and the only guard against the advance of Neanderthal man, opened the portable phone pack, raised the antenna, switched it on as though it were a daily occurrence, and spoke into the mouthpiece.

TWENTY-NINE

When the first cries came, the knowledge that some sort of disaster was at hand, Katherine had clutched Cameron to her tightly, determined not to lose her and wondering if she could take advantage of the confusion to somehow escape.

During the loud exchange of voices, with Pilar's attention directed toward the men at the door, armed men who were arriving in ever-increasing numbers, Crystal had moved closer to Katherine, edging her way across the distance that separated them. Her husband had given her a sharp look and barked a set of commands at her. She had bowed her head submissively, but as soon as he turned away to join the others, she quickly stepped to Katherine's side.

"Amber?" she asked softly. Her eyes were shining brightly and she placed a hand tentatively on Katherine's arm.

"She's doing better, I think. Dr. Bosch is interested in whatever you can tell us that will help. Crystal, can you help us? Can you get us out of here? You heard what they were saying. I don't think they want Amber to get better."

Crystal's eyes clouded; her fright was easy to read as she glanced nervously over at the knot of men. "I think they will kill her if she does not die in your hospital. Pilar will never allow her to return."

"What? Kill her? Why? Why would they do that?"

"Because she can never be healthy. They say we cannot waste food on those who do not help the whole. They say she is no good

239

to them! But she is a good baby, a beautiful baby. She deserves to live. That is why I pay you"—she gestured to the bracelet on Katherine's arm—"just like I say I do, so that you will make her well. I do not ask you to do this for nothing."

"It wasn't necessary. Crystal, I would have done it regardless. But please, can you get us out of here? Look, they'll never let me keep her, think of how you feel faced with the possibility of never seeing Amber again."

"I think something is very bad," Crystal said, eyeing the doorway which was filled with streams of men seemingly reporting for instructions. Pilar, Stone, and Jasper were surrounded by throngs of armed males. If they were going to make their escape, now was the time to do it. There would never be a better time.

"Please, Crystal, we've got to get out of here while things are still confused, before they remember us," Katherine begged, knowing that their time was limited. Once Pilar resolved whatever crisis had occurred, he would deal with them, and Katherine was filled with a certainty that it would not be a solution to her liking. "Crystal, please!"

"Promise that you will make Amber better, that you will protect her from them and keep her, raise her as your own." Crystal's voice was flat, her eyes bright with tears as she stared into Katherine's eyes.

"Keep her?" Katherine was shocked.

Crystal nodded sharply. "I tell you, they will kill her if she does not die in the hospital," she said flatly. "Promise you will do this!" she whispered fiercely, gripping Katherine's arm with steely fingers. Katherine nodded her agreement without hesitation, so desperate was she to escape from this place and bring her daughter to safety.

"Get the man, the healer, and we will go," Crystal said, looking away from Katherine, wrapping her arms around her body as though she were shivering. Her decision made, she had withdrawn inside herself and had become cold and remote. Katherine hurried to Bosch's side, pressing Cameron to her shoulder.

Bosch was focused on the group of men, trying to understand what it was that was happening. He could make out little of it, but from the way that the men were being dispersed with sharp, crisply delivered instructions, it seemed that they were not unprepared for such a crisis, whatever it was. Pilar had said they were being invaded. An incredible thought; invaded by what or whom?

Bosch was fairly tingling with excitement; he wished that he understood more of what was being said and that he were a part of it all. Pilar had rejected his offer of help, but surely, if Bosch were given the opportunity to present his case more fully, the old man could not help but see the logic of it. There would be a way around the problems, he was certain of it.

What a mind-boggling situation! Not even he had been prepared for what they had found. And the old man, Pilar, what an incredible person! There was much that he, Bosch, could do for them and so much that he could learn in return . . . the possibilities set his mind reeling. So caught up was he in his own thoughts, that for a minute, he was unaware of the tugging on his sleeve. As it grew more insistent, he wakened from his musings and looked down into Katherine's tense face.

"We're leaving now, hurry!" She glanced over at the men with a frightened gaze.

"Leaving?" Bosch said somewhat stupidly, the words not connecting. He had no desire to leave just yet; there was still much to be discussed.

"Leaving," Katherine hissed. "Keep your voice down! Crystal is going to take us out of here, you and I and Cameron. But we've got to go now before they remember us."

"You go ahead, I'll come along later. I want to talk to Pilar again."

Katherine turned on him in a fury. "There won't be a later. Don't you get it? If we don't leave now, they'll kill us, just like they'll kill Amber if we don't get back to the hospital and take her somewhere safe. And I'll never see Cameron again!"

There was a degree of truth to what Katherine was saying. He had to admit that there was the possibility of danger, but he was certain, well, almost certain, that he could talk Pilar into seeing reason. He hesitated briefly before nodding agreement. He knew the way, he could always come back again.

The two of them glanced at the men in the doorway, and as they did so, Katherine's eyes met Stone's. Anguish, anger, grief, bewilderment, and loss were sent and acknowledged in that one brief exchange before Stone's full attention was called for and Katherine turned away, her emotions churning wildly inside her. Despite everything, she could not deny the fact that he still mattered.

Crystal led the way, and they moved unobtrusively but swiftly toward the rear of the room. Here, as in Crystal's own chambers,

there was a second room and a third beyond it. The final room
obviously served as a bedroom and its decor was in sharp contrast
to the rich setting of the outer rooms. It was nearly military in its
Spartan neatness, containing only a small, narrow bed, a single tall
chest, a desk and chair, and an assortment of clothing, neatly
folded, edges perfectly aligned. Then they were out, through a
short hallway and through another rounded doorway and into
another corridor, startling a guard who was leaning with his back
against the wall.

The man leaped to his feet and rapped out several words, his
sword drawn and ready. Crystal was ready and spoke excitedly,
pointing back in the direction they had come and waving him
forward, urging him to go.

The guard examined them with suspicious eyes but Crystal
spoke again, pointing to Bosch and Katherine and speaking
derisively. Once again she urged the guard to leave. With a single
backward glance of uncertainty, he left his post and hurried to join
the others. Crystal all but yanked Katherine's arm out of its socket
the instant the man had gone.

"Hurry!" she cried. "This is bad. I did not think. I should have
realized there would be a guard! Now they will know, they will
come after us!"

Her fear was contagious; they pounded down dark corridors
turning this way and that, always avoiding the sound of voices.
Several times Crystal attempted to open doors that seemed
accessible, but were invariably locked. Not even Bosch was able
to open them with his small arsenal of equipment.

"Guess they want to make sure no one wanders in or out
accidentally," Bosch said. His hair had fallen over his goggles and
he was breathing heavily. He was not a young man and Katherine
was worried that he might not be able to continue much longer.
Already, she was feeling the burning muscles in her legs and
thighs, and it was awkward carrying the baby and running at the
same time.

They were crossing an intersection of corridors when their luck
ran out. There was a loud, excited outcry to their left and a group
of men came into view. They were armed and demanded that they
stop.

Katherine had no intention of doing so. She turned and ran off
to the right, even though Crystal's voice rang out behind her,
telling her to stop. But she could not stop; there was a lump of fear
in her throat and a band of iciness around her heart. She clutched

Cameron tightly, knowing that if they were caught, there would be no escape.

She looked back. She was outrunning them, but only because Bosch had fallen back and was straddling the corridor. "Go, Katherine, I'll catch up," he hollered. She faltered, slowing, not wanting to leave him, knowing that they would kill him, but Crystal pulled on her arm, dragging her down the corridor, turning corners, leaving their pursuers behind them.

Katherine was crying now, tears coursing down her cheeks. She was terrified of this nightmare that her life had become; she wanted out of these terrible dark tunnels. She yearned for the daylight and the cold, sharp sting of wind whipping off the lake. A door appeared on her right, an old wooden door with inset beveled panels and a white porcelain knob. She pulled at it, yanking hard on the knob. To her amazement, it opened at the first turn. Dank, musty air funneled down the rotten steps. She could smell earth, awful, rotting, dark earth. Nothing had ever smelled so sweet. She bent down to wrench away the single wood plank that was nailed across the bottom of the door, and as she did so, a hand appeared, thrusting itself out of the wall in front of her face.

Time seemed to move in slow motion as she watched the unbelievable occurring. The concrete wall that framed the staircase bulged outward in the shape of a hand as though it were wet, a glove fitted around a hand that was somehow, inexplicably inside the concrete. It stretched, grew, extended; a wrist was now attached to the hand and then an arm. Vaguely, from the corner of her eye, she saw the edge of the corridor wall beginning to bulge. She stared horror-struck, unable to move or breathe or think. Another outward pressing formed a brow, the bridge of a nose, unmistakable features. They were able to move through stone, through the earth itself!

Crystal screamed, grabbed Katherine by the shoulder, and pulled her back just as the hand broke through the concrete and began to open and shut, reaching for her. Katherine screamed then and slammed the door, knowing that it would not stop him for long. The other hand thrust itself through the wall into the corridor and began casting about. Katherine stumbled back and began to run, blindly, aimlessly, not caring where, so long as it was as far away as she could go.

Cameron began to cry then, and Crystal clung to Katherine's waist, trying to turn her in one direction or the other. Sometimes, Katherine let herself be turned; other times for no reason other

than an instinctive feeling, she refused. The two women stopped in
a dark recess, their throats dry with fear and fatigue, clinging to
each other and the baby, trying to calm her frantic wails and their
own terror. No longer could they hope to simply slip away.
Crystal's role was now well known. What could she expect if she
returned? In the eyes of the people, she was a traitor.

Cameron's cries lessened, but did not cease no matter what they
tried. Finally, Crystal whispered, "You feed her, yes. It will stop
the crying." It was an obvious solution. With shaking fingers,
Katherine unbuttoned her blouse and nursed the child while
Crystal shielded them with her body and stood anxious guard until
the child's needs were satisfied.

They crept along the corridors from one dark spot to the next.
Empty, dimly lit apartments, the residents' hasty departure evident, storage places, doorways that led to nowhere—all of them
were used to gain shelter from the armed bands of men who sought
them.

Hours passed. Katherine was exhausted, could feel it in every
part of her body. From time to time there were loud, muffled
sounds that reverberated through the earth, felt, more than heard.
A high, piercing whistle had sounded several times, a sound that
conveyed incredible urgency and seemed to disturb Crystal
greatly, although she would not answer when Katherine asked her
what it was.

Often now, entire groups hurried past them, all heading in the
opposite direction, away from the lake, if Katherine's sense of
direction was still in working order. These were not the armed
groups of men, but whole family groups—men, women, and
children—and all of them were carrying large bundles. Their
expressions were those of fear.

Crystal was weeping openly now, but still she held her silence.
Katherine was cloaked in a blanket snatched from a deserted
apartment, and abandoning caution, they made their way through
the corridors against the flow of terrified people. Many shouted at
them, gestured for them to turn around and go back, but Crystal
led blindly onward and Katherine followed.

The crowds thinned. Now the corridors were empty save for the
occasional laggard who ran past them with wide, frightening eyes
and a glazed expression. The rumblings and shaking of the earth
became more and more frequent, some terrifyingly near and others
further away. Dirt and bits of plaster rained down on them from
above, following these explosions, and Katherine felt as though

hey were running through a mine field. It was the sound of war.

They were alone now. The corridors were empty, yet Crystal did
ot slacken her pace but hurried forward with a sense of
esperation as though she possessed some fearful knowledge that
vas too terrible to share. Then, there was a single WHUMP,
ollowed by a powerful blast of air coming from behind them.
They were struck by a great force like a physical blow, lifted from
heir feet, and thrown to the ground, gasping, trying to draw breath
ack into empty lungs. "What, what was that?" Katherine cried.

Before Crystal could reply, there were other, more distant
choes of the first explosion, further away on either side. Crystal
ose to her knees, resting on the palms of her hands, tears forming
ivulets through the dust that coated her face. Her beautiful hair
ung in disarray around her face. She could not rise, and slowly
owered herself to the ground, staring up at the ceiling with an
xpression of resignation on her face.

"They have closed the tunnels. All are gone. All the people.
They are gone."

"Gone?" Katherine asked in bewilderment. "Gone where?"

Crystal waved her hand wearily. "Gone. Gone away from here.
They said it would happen one day, but no one believed that it was
rue."

"Then, then we're safe!" Katherine said, sitting up, realizing
vhat it meant for them.

"No, we are not safe. They have opened the gates. The lake and
he river will come in. What they have not already destroyed, the
vater will kill."

"The water will come in here!" Katherine realized in a flash
vhat Crystal was saying, picturing the cold waters of the lake, the
lark, murky water of the Chicago River flooding in through these
unnels, undermining the city . . . and just incidentally drowning
hem.

"Yes," Crystal said bleakly.

"Then get up and let's get going," Katherine said, crawling
hakily to her feet.

But Crystal did not move. "It is no use. There is nowhere to go."

"That remains to be seen. Come on, Crystal, there's still Amber
o think about. We've got to get her before they do. You can't give
ip now!" Somehow, she got the other woman on her feet, and
lowly at first, then faster and faster as the fear of the waters
reyed on their minds, they sped along the tunnels, trying every
loor and access point they came to. All were firmly locked.

"What, can you do that thing, going through the stone?"
Katherine gasped.

Crystal nodded. "But you could not follow. What good would
do us?"

"Can you get us to my building?" Crystal nodded. "The bricks
they're not set solid in the mortar. If we can reach that tunnel, w
could break our way through!"

Crystal did not waste time in answering but set off at a fast tro
"We are close now," Crystal said between gritted teeth
Katherine's lungs were burning and her legs felt like lead weight
that would never rise again. She stopped for a moment and knel
resting her back against the wall, and tried to slow the pounding c
her heart. Suddenly, a thrill of fear raced through her; her finger
which rested on the floor for balance, were wet!

"Crystal!" she screamed. "The water!" Her voice echoed bac
through the tunnel and now they could hear it, a cold, dark, hissin
sound flowing in toward them from all sides. The gates had bee
opened, the water was flooding in.

They ran then, in absolute desperation, even when the water
rose to their ankles and then to their calves, cold, dark, icy wate
There was no other course, nothing else they could do but continu
on and pray that their one hope for escape still existed. Katherin
tried not to think of how close her building stood to the lake, trie
to shut out the vision of the waters lapping against the breakwate
at the foot of the property, tried to believe that it was still safe.

That hope was shattered when a great wave of water, a wall c
dark current came foaming silently out of the darkness ahead c
them. They escaped it by leaping into an abandoned apartment an
standing atop a solid block of marble, and even that lifted slightly
shifting when the water coursed past.

Katherine did not need to be told that their last thread of hop
had been severed. It was obvious from Crystal's posture. The tw
women stared at each other with bleak eyes, knowing, withou
having to look, that the water was rising swiftly.

Suddenly, the light altered in Katherine's goggles, and sh
looked up, looked toward the door and saw the outline of form:
bodies. Crystal gave a small, fearful cry. Katherine looked aroun
but there was nowhere to go, and this apartment, unlike the othe
she had been in, appeared to have only the one room. There wa
no way out.

She bared her teeth and raised her hand, fingers formed int
claws. She heard herself utter a sound like a feral growl and kne

that they would not take her, take Cameron away from her without a fight.

"It's all right, Katherine, we've come to help."

She heard the words, but for a minute, they had no meaning. Then, slowly, as she stared at the figure standing before her, she realized that it was Stone. She was filled with confusion. Stone? How had he found them? Was he not the enemy? He had betrayed her before. But here he was, offering to help. She reached out to Crystal, grabbed her hand. Crystal drew close. "What should we do? Is he telling the truth?"

There was a rapid exchange of words between Crystal and Stone. Crystal queried him sharply. She turned to Katherine. "He is a friend to you even though you do not believe him. He and his men came to open the gates. He says we must go now or it is too late. The waters will rise quickly."

Another voice spoke, one of those who had accompanied Stone. Crystal translated. "He say give Stone the baby; he is not so tired, is stronger than you. We can go faster."

"Can I trust him?" Katherine asked. Crystal shrugged. "If you trust him—" Katherine hesitated, but then another wave of water crested down the corridor and cries of fear broke out among the men. Katherine knew that she was at the end of her endurance. If a wave came and knocked her off her feet, she could lose Cameron in an instant. She had no alternative but to trust Stone. She kissed Cameron quickly on her forehead and then handed her to Stone, who took the baby without a word.

Instantly, they turned back to the corridor, pushing through the frigid waters that now reached up to Katherine's waist and Crystal's chest. Instead of turning back, away from the lake, they turned to the right, going toward the lake. The men seemed to have some definite destination in mind and walked ahead of the women in a wedge, creating a slight breakwater that made it easier for them to move.

They had just turned into another corridor when it happened. One minute everything was fine, the next minute, a huge wall of black water was racing toward them, towering above their heads. She heard Crystal cry out and felt an arm go around her waist and then the water was on them. It slammed into them with tremendous impact.

There was no softness, no give, no fluidity, just a single violent force that flung her from her feet and punched her to the ground, rolling her over and over like a small stone tumbled along the bottom of a mountain stream. She could not breathe, she could not move, she could not fight.

And then it was gone. She pushed against the floor and rose upward, bursting into the air, the goggles ripped from her head, unable to see, unable to pull air down into her starved lungs. She coughed, tried to breathe, sucked water down her throat, and gagged. She retched into the water that lapped around her chest.

Slowly, she became aware of voices, cries in the darkness. Her thoughts flew to Cameron and Crystal and Stone. What of them! Where were they! She cried out into the darkness, feeling all around her, unable to see, desperate to know what had happened.

Voices responded, calling to one another. There seemed to be fewer voices than there had been. A terrible feeling of despair came over her. "CAMERON!" she cried, screaming into the darkness, knowing, somehow knowing, that the baby was gone. She stepped forward, hands outspread, reaching, casting about blindly, trying to find Stone. She called Cameron's name over and over again. She knew she was crying, knew that she was blundering into walls, dimly felt her head crack against a wall, felt the hot blood trickling down her cold skin. None of it mattered. She kept calling the baby's name, not knowing what to do.

Then someone called her name, a hand clutched her shoulder. A voice spoke in her ear. It was meaningless; nothing mattered but finding the baby. She fought against the hand, tried to go on, but the hand held her back, seized her arm and dragged her form the spot, crying out, fighting. But it was useless.

Some time later—she no longer knew or cared—she felt a current of cold air rushing against her face. Her head throbbed dully. She saw a flash of red and then one of yellow. The lights flashed repeatedly, over and over and over. She heard the staccato squawk of transmitted words. Lights. Words. Air. She looked up dumbly and saw a hole, a ragged hole above her. It was there that the lights and words were coming from.

"Look, Al, people down there! Hey folks, stay put, we'll get you outa there in a jiff!"

Hands, ropes, cold air knifing through her chilled flesh, then a rough, scratchy blanket wrapped around her and a paper cup of hot black coffee was thrust into her shaking hands. None of it mattered. She raised her eyes and met those of Crystal. She too was swathed in a thick wool blanket which she had drawn down over her eyes in a deep cowl. There was no one else.

"You folks, just stay right there, the medics'll get to you as soon as they can," said a voice in passing, and then it too was gone.

No one tried to stop the two women as they crept out of the small plastic enclosure at the rear of the city utility truck. They picked their way through the rubble that surrounded the area and did not stop until they stood in the shelter of a brick wall, all that remained of a large building.

Slowly, Katherine raised her head and looked around her. She tried to make sense of what she saw, but none of it seemed to compute. She recognized the façade of a small house directly across the way from where they were standing. It was well known to her, for it stood next to her own building. But only the façade of the house still stood; behind it there was nothing. Her eyes cast back and forth, searching for her own vast, sprawling, fortresslike building, but not a single stone of it was to be seen. Where it had stood, water glistened, beating back and forth against the land, licking at the shattered roadway like a hungry beast.

All around her was desolation. Not a single one of the towering vapor arc lights was lit even though it was now well into night. Other than the emergency vehicles, there were no lights at all. She looked around her. As far as she could see, the entire city was dark. Occasional explosions still imploded on the ear, an appropriate backdrop for the devastation.

Crystal whimpered and pressed herself closer to Katherine. Katherine blinked and looked down dazedly at the smaller woman, feeling her terror. The two of them huddled together in the lee of the building, while all around them the city died.

THIRTY

Dazed, but knowing she must make one last effort, Katherine led Crystal up and out into the street. The trip to the hospital was like a journey into hell. Buildings rose from the water raging round their foundations like war-torn shells with flames roaring from gaping windows and roofs, feeding on broken gas mains and the contents of their ravaged interiors.

The lake, not content with its newly expanded borders, battered the broken shoreline, heaving stonework, concrete, and masses of debris at the land, seemingly determined to win back all that was possible in this time of turmoil.

Chaos reigned supreme. People huddled in the open streets, afraid to remain inside the buildings which were exploding into flames or breaking apart and burying those within as they collapsed. Water erupted as pipes ruptured under the contorted streets, shooting into the sky under tremendous pressure and firing deadly chunks of pavement into crowds of dazed survivors.

The broken streets were clogged with vehicles as people attempted to flee the area, but progress was pathetically slow. Terror-stricken drivers lost all remnants of civility and fought to save themselves and their families, gunning their vehicles over sidewalks, debris and anyone unfortunate enough to be in their way. Anarchy prevailed.

The very fabric of existence seemed to be coming apart. Torrents of rain slashed down in cold sheets while thunder and lightning crashed above. Downed power lines crackled and hissed on the ground, sending deadly currents through the water. Emergency teams representing the police, fire, electricity, gas and water departments, and the Red Cross were trickling into the area, but in the face of the overwhelming disaster, their small numbers and limited resources were all but useless.

There were several half-hearted attempts made to stop Katherine and Crystal as they made their way toward the hospital, but personnel were too harried to enforce their efforts and it was not difficult to fade into the shadows and continue on their way, mingling with the crowds.

They were not far from the hospital, though the confusion of the streets made progress of any sort difficult. But driven by their need to reach Amber before Pilar's people, the two women forged their way forward with relentless determination. The going was easier once they reached the open parkway and they ran as fast as they could, ignoring all discomfort and pain, setting aside their fears as they rushed to reach the child, praying that they would arrive in time.

The hospital glowed faintly with light shed by emergency generators. The dark waters of the lake frothed at the very feet of the building. The entrance, visible but unreachable, was barricaded with mattresses. They ran gasping around the side of the building and found a lighted open doorway where injured people were accumulating in bloodied and broken numbers. Nurses, doctors and aides were attempting to deal with the situation. Pallets crowded the floors inside and groans and agonized cries filled the air.

A nurse tried to block their way, but a shout from a doctor drew her attention. They slipped through and entered a staircase glowing an ominous red, lit only by emergency lights, one per floor. They climbed swiftly to the pediatric floor, where a too-small staff was attempting to calm a mad house of wailing children.

Katherine led the way to Amber's room. Her heart began to thump in her chest as she saw a mass of people gathered outside the door. Fearing the worst, she ran forward and thrust her way into the press of bodies, Crystal hard on her heels.

They were too late. Stone was standing behind Amber's incubator, backed by six armed men.

The tension in the room was palpable. Several nurses faced the men on the other side of the incubator, and Anderson lay on the floor between them, a long ugly bruise forming on his temple.

The nurses were obviously frightened, but held their ground between the intruders and the door. Armed as they were with knives, spears and clubs, the men could certainly have cleared a path between themselves and the door, but they seemed unwilling to resort to violence.

All of this Katherine grasped in an instant. The scene was dimly lit by the light on the side of the incubator. It threw the high cheek-bones and deep orbital fonts of the strangers into sharp prominence.

Stone's eyes met Katherine's. In them she read sorrow, a mute pleading, but she had no forgiveness in her.

"Where is my daughter?" she said, advancing to within a foot of him, ignoring the sharp blades that turned in her direction. At that moment she felt such hatred for the man before her that it would not have mattered if those behind him had attempted to use force. Her hatred made her strong. She was invincible. Their puny weapons could not stop her. Gone was her earlier fear. Her own Cameron had vanished into the night, but she could accomplish this one thing; they would not have Amber.

"Where is Cameron?" She all but hissed the words. Her eyes, blazing with rage, bore into his. He was unable to hold her gaze and lowered his eyes, shaken by her intensity. "Safe," came the answer.

"Where?" Katherine demanded, her hands balling into fists. She fought for control, she wanted to attack the man, to punch and hurt him, to pound his face with her fists. "Where is she, tell me!"

"Safe where you will not find her," said another voice. She lifted her eyes briefly and saw that it was the black man. "Already she is gone with the people. You will not have her back. Nor will you have this one. They are both ours now!"

Katherine felt Crystal tense, but what might have happened would never be known. The lights suddenly flickered on and off erratically, casting friend and enemy alike into strange, frozen shapes, then dimmed and died entirely. The room was cast into darkness. There was a moment of stunned silence and then the room erupted into a press of bodies. A change in the air told Katherine that the door had opened. But there were no lights there either, only frightened cries and the wailing of children. Bodies surged forward and back. She was thrown off-balance, but held in place by a crush of people on all sides.

She cried out. She felt her arm gripped tightly by Crystal's small hand, then the hand was torn away. "Crystal!" she screamed.

"Don't let them take the baby!" Her courage was gone, stolen by the darkness.

Suddenly strong arms wrapped themselves around her, pinning her own arms to her sides. She screamed and began to writhe and kick. A voice came in her ear, the words lost in the melee, but soothing, calming. She smelled the familiar old cotton scent of a man's skin. Stone. Confused, she felt herself thrust into a corner of the room. Stone pressed his body against hers and a small warm weight slipped into her arms. And then he was gone and despite the crush of bodies still struggling around her, she felt alone and desolate.

Perhaps there had been a signal given, some silent word. If so, she never heard it. But suddenly, the room seemed less crowded, the feeling of space apparent even in the darkness. There was a sudden humming and the lights of the machine flickered and came alive, casting their dim, eerie glow on the room.

They were gone. Stone and his escort had vanished from the room. Nurses, aides, orderlies stood frozen in the dim light like a child's game of statues, crouching in combative positions. Several lay silent on the floor. Crystal moved toward her, arms extended, tears glinting in her eyes. Katherine handed her Amber, who curled into her chest like a tiny, contented kitten. Crystal's long silvery hair had come unbound and swept across the baby, shielding her from sight.

Alone, Katherine crossed to the window and drew back the heavy curtains. Outside there was nothing but darkness, broken only by the lightning lancing from the heavens and the occasional flickering red of the emergency vehicles.

Crystal pressed against her side and slipped her hand into Katherine's. "She's out there somewhere," Katherine said, her voice choked with tears.

"But you are not alone," Crystal replied. "Together, somehow, we will find her."

EPILOGUE

CHICAGO. October 21, 1992 (AP)—Today, the city of Chicago met with disaster that cannot be compared to the Great Fire of 1871 or even the San Francisco Earthquake of 1906. It compares to nothing, except perhaps to the devastation of Hiroshima and Nagasaki—after the bombs fell.

No one cause has been ascribed to the near total destruction of the city, although authorities are searching for answers. At approximately 7:15 P.M. the city was rocked by a series of subterranean explosions which instantly plunged the entire metro area into darkness. Multiple gas explosions occurred as well, rupturing gas lines and creating firestorms that swept from block to block, engulfing everything in their path. There have been large numbers of casualties, and the death toll, while unsubstantiated, appears to range in the thousands.

All underground utilities have been lost. Power company officials were unable to even estimate when services might be restored.

In an inexplicable series of events, the vast system of old freight tunnels built beneath the city more than a hundred years ago appears to have failed at numerous points, allowing the Chicago River to pour in unchecked. Extensive flooding is reported in the Loop, where it appears that the rampaging waters have entered the deep subbasements of block after block of buildings. Some buildings are reporting that as many as twenty sublevels are flooded and water is now pouring out into the streets. The entire

downtown area is cordoned off and considered extremely dangerous.

Even Mother Nature appears to have joined in the attempt to
bring the city to its knees. Perhaps induced by the fractures in the
tunnels and the numerous gas explosions, the lake itself has rushed
in to reclaim most of the land that was filled and built upon
following the Great Fire.

Additional reports of flooding are arriving from all points of the
city. Many areas are totally under water, and rumors persist that
the multibillion-dollar Deep Tunnel project which was to protect
the city from yearly flooding, has, itself, been destroyed in large
sections.

The governor has declared the entire city a disaster area.

APPENDIX

Some 300,000 years ago, the creature classified as a human being by today's standards, first made his appearance on the continent of Africa. His development was an important moment in history and fashioned the world that was to follow. But it also had a powerful impact on the world that existed.

Prior to the development of Homo sapiens, the earth was inhabited by another race of people known as Homo erectus. This ancient group of people closely resembled today's humans with a few notable exceptions, namely low foreheads with jutting brows and an exaggerated jaw line. Their similarities to Homo sapiens were, however, far greater than their differences.

While much of our knowledge of this ancient race is merely guesswork, some facts have been clearly established. It is known that they had an intricately developed social structure, culture, and religion. They had mastered the use of fire and were highly skilled toolmakers and users. Where, then, did this race of people go and why did they vanish from the earth?

There are a number of hypotheses. Some experts say that they could not compete with the taller, stronger, and more intelligent Homo sapiens, and when confronted by the superior race, they died off in true Darwinian fashion. Others say that they interbred with and were absorbed by the new race. Neither of these theories is correct.

As Homo sapiens advanced across the face of the earth, he drove the smaller, less aggressive Homo erectus before him, taking away their primitive crop lands, laying claim to the best deposits of stone for tool- and weapon-making and driving them from their hunting grounds.

But Homo erectus did not go willingly and fought for their world and their lives. In most instances they died, overwhelmed by a superior force that they could not hope to defeat. At last, beleagured on all sides, driven from the continent of Africa, they fled, crossing the vast pre-oceanic plains that separated Africa from what would eventually be known as Europe. Evidence suggests that they found a foothold in the Ionian Islands of Greece, then migrated east, seeking safety in the mountains and deep valleys of western Europe. But Homo sapiens followed close on their heels, slaughtering them at every opportunity.

Finally, when they could fight no more, flee no further, the remnants of the older race took the only option available to them: they abandoned the world of sunlight and danger and went underground into darkness and safety.

Driven underground by the unrelenting advance of the enemy, Homo erectus found life hard in their strange new world. Many of them died before they learned to adapt. In the years that followed, they became true dwellers in darkness. Over the long centuries, their bodies changed until they became more perfectly attuned to the world around them. Their eyes became larger, the pupils greatly enlarged to use whatever meager light was available. Their bodies became shorter and more compact, yet stronger and more muscular.

Deprived of the rich world of sight, their other senses grew stronger, compensating for the loss of vision. Their ears grew larger, more batlike, as their hearing became ever more sensitive and acute, attuned to the slightest vibrations and movement within the earth itself. Even their skin, now as pale as a newborn moon, served as a sensor, reading the underworld around them, supplying them with a barrage of information as diverse as temperature and the presence of others.

And even as their bodies changed over the millennia, they became sensitive to the rhythm of the earth and learned to harvest its wealth. Their numbers grew and their culture flourished, but they never forgot that the earth above had once been theirs. Nor did they forget who had forced them into their dark exile.

As time passed, Homo erectus accepted the world below as their own, and the world above became synonymous with pain and death. Indeed, long centuries of living in darkness made it physically impossible for flesh or retina to survive exposure to sunlight for any length of time. But their hatred of mankind endured. Emerging at night, they foraged for food and materials not available to them underground.

Cunning, wary, and stealthy, they were seldom seen, and on the rare occasions when they were, their white skin, strangely shaped features, and odd, squat bodies gave rise to myths and legends that varied among the peoples and countries of the world. In Germany, they were known as trolls; in eastern Europe, vampires; in Scandinavia, as ogres. And everywhere, they were feared.

Deaths, sometimes gruesome and unexplained, such as the string of murders in seventeenth century Russia, where peasants were found with their heads twisted from their bodies, or the mysterious disemboweled corpses that terrified the French countryside in the late eighteenth century, the dismembered prostitutes in England, were attributed to their depredations, whether or not it had any basis in fact.

Yet in spite of their hatred of mankind they were always to be found on the fringes of civilization. They peered in windows and watched their ancient enemy at work and at play, hating, yet somehow needing the sound and sight of humans as though to remind them of what they had once been. Now, man walked upright in the world which had once been theirs, while they were despised, feared, and outcast. Not even the night was theirs to roam with impunity, for wherever man went, he lit up the skies with his ever-present light.

Superstitious and primitive cultures around the world gave them different names. Myths and fables surrounded them and embellished their deeds, but eventually they became known by a single name, *trolls*, the dwellers of darkness.

While fearing them, our most ancient ancestors spoke no word of disrespect and placed choice offerings at the mouths of caves. Mothers warned their children against them and kept close to their cradles for it was said that trolls stole babies and left demon changelings in their place. Actually, this was not the case; trolls would no more have taken a human child into their world than humans would choose to bring a wild wolf cub into their home. These supposed changelings were a primitive peoples' only way of explaining the existence of retarded or similarly damaged children.

The population of the world increased rapidly. Pastoral life gave way to towns and towns to cities. Science and industry blossomed.

Civilization marched across the face of the earth, pushing back the darkness with knowledge and electricity.

As mankind advanced, the trolls were forced to limit their journeys above ground. Trips to the surface became more hazardous as electricity brought people, roads, and light to even the most remote areas. Gone were the offerings and even the fearful respect as people became educated and shed superstitions and old beliefs like worn-out clothes. Now, only the most primitive of peoples still believed in trolls.

This might have been a good thing in the long run. The trolls, or Under Dwellers as they called themselves, might have shaken off their crippling obsession with the world above and devoted themselves to developing their own world, but once again the actions of their old enemy threatened their very existence. For as the earth's industry, science, technology, and population expanded and benefitted mankind, the side effects began to kill the Under Dwellers. Strip mining, pollution, chemical dumping, underground atomic testing, seismic detonation, toxic waste burial, and a multitude of other ecological horrors proved fatal to vast numbers of Under Dwellers.

Whole communities were blasted or poisoned to death, and previously pristine underground rivers became contaminated with chemicals. Those Under Dwellers who did not die in agony lived to discover that they were sterile or their offspring likely to be born with genetic defects or hideous deformities. Often, those who managed to overcome these early difficulties were sickly and weak and seldom lived to adulthood.

Frightened and confused by this new menace which threatened to destroy them completely, the Under Dwellers were soon reduced to living in small, fragmented tribes with many of their finest leaders and thinkers dead.

Chaos ruled for many years as the Under Dwellers struggled to survive. Many of the finer elements of their culture were lost in the day-to-day fight for life. Many regressed to a primitive state not seen in centuries. The more civilized among them became objects of suspicion, symbols of humanity. Soon, brutality became a way of life, and those who could not accept the new rule were put to death. For those few who could appreciate the irony, it appeared that their ancient enemy was about to win a battle that they no longer realized they were waging.

As in any holocaust, there were survivors. And so it was with the Under Dwellers. Those who were the most intelligent and the most flexible, lived. And, more importantly, they found each other. It was quickly seen that drastic measures were called for if the race were to survive. Citing revenge as their motive to mask their true purpose, the "thinker trolls," suggested to their communities that human children be taken wherever and whenever possible, to be raised as Under Dwellers and ultimately increase the numbers of their ranks.

But this was not the real reason. The "Thinkers" knew that they desperately needed this new blood, human blood, to strengthen their race, to enable them to survive whatever new horrors man devised. But this could not be stated openly, nor could they allow their brethren to consider the fact that this injection of new blood, while strengthening the race, was diluting it as well. Instead, they stressed the wonderful irony of making the old myths come true, and argued that raising humans as Under Dwellers was fitting punishment for their ancient enemy. There was initial resistance of course, but in time the idea took hold and their brethren accepted the idea as their own.

There were rules. Human children could not be taken if there was any chance of Under Dweller discovery. Thus, children who were abandoned, mistreated, or trapped in some life-threatening situation frequently found themselves taken by the Under Dwellers. Those who did not die of shock were absorbed into the Under Dweller society.

Infants were also taken; in fact, they were preferred to older children. Usually they became available in similar situations, although infants born under the influence of alcohol and/or addictive drugs were becoming more and more common. The Under Dwellers, hardened as they were by the circumstances of their own harsh lives, were shocked by the indifference and cruelty with which the humans treated their offspring. To the Under Dwellers, there was nothing more precious than a child. Occasionally, there were human babies who had caring parents, but poverty, superstition, or isolation allowed the Under Dwellers access and their greater need dictated their deeds. In those instances, they replaced the human infant with one of their own, who, weakened by one of the many human-caused contaminants, had little hope of survival.

This transfer was made possible through the use of magic. For even as the humans had developed their skills, so had the Under Dwellers. Science and technology were of no interest to them. Instead, they had retained and expanded upon their knowledge of